INTRODUCTION

If you've found this via Reddit, then I'm ҉ ... ṭhat brought
you here! If you're not a Redditor and don ...ow me to introduce myself:
I am W.P. Kimball, also known as /u/Luna_ ʍrite flash fiction and short story pieces
with a different prompt every day. Those stories range across all genres, from humor to tragedy,
sci-fi and fantasy to romance and horror. If you are looking to read some of those stories, I'd
recommend checking out my collection here: https://www.amazon.com/Prompt-Me-W-P-
Kimball-ebook/dp/B014S7TDIK/ref=sr_1_1?ie=UTF8&qid=1478744933&sr=8-
1&keywords=W.P.+Kimball.

A little bit over two years ago, I nervously submitted my very first response on Reddit's
WritingPrompts community. And only a few days later, I was inspired to write on the prompt
"The Roman Empire never collapsed and the year is 1999 AD." The story focused on a
young man who is whisked away from his military camp and learns that he is a candidate to
become the next Emperor of Rome. A few short paragraphs grew into a full novel that I am
honored to share with you now. I hope you enjoy reading about Caius's adventures as much as I
have enjoyed writing them.

And finally, some thank yous:

- /u/InfernoArchon for the amazing cover
- /u/ caffeinatedlackey, /u/No_Mas_Amigo, /u/Samgalimore, and /u/SoDark for the
  feedback on the early drafts of the story
- All the amazing people who support me on Patreon!
- Everyone who subscribes to /r/Luna_Lovewell and encourages me to write every day!

And of course, you for purchasing this book! Enjoy!

TABLE OF CONTENTS

CHAPTER 1

The shadow of Caius's plane was a speck in the vast, desolate expanse of the Pacific. Sunbeams danced off the tinted plastic canopy while the propeller droned with a soothing hum. Identical planes joined him in tight formation on either side, practically wing to wing. They were close enough that Caius could see the Emperor's soaring eagle insignia emblazoned in gold across the red fuselage and underneath, the Roman Senate's own scroll icon stamped with the letters of the Eternal City: "SPQR." About a kilometer southeast of him, another tiny speck plowed through the waves, leaving an expanding white trail that rippled across the water's surface.

"OK, I think we've got the target sighted," Min-Jae said on Caius's left. He still had three years of service till he could earn citizenship and pick his own Roman name.

"I see it too," Caius replied. "Remember that we're just scouting today. We should do what we can to avoid engagement. Let's get a bit higher."

The three pilots guided their individual planes upwards in unison. Caius was temporarily blinded by light bouncing off of the aluminum wings and through his cockpit canopy. The altimeter spun until they were high enough to avoid any potential fire from the ship.

"We are approaching the unidentified vessel," Caius dictated into the microphone. A complete mission log would be distributed to Military Intelligence as soon as they landed. "The ship appears to be about one hundred and eighty meters in length. I count a total of six heavy guns placed on three different turrets, as well as four machine gun emplacements." The planes banked through a cloud for another pass by the ship.

3

"Doesn't seem to have any markings," Caius said, tipping his plane to the side and peering carefully out of the cockpit, "either on the sides of the vessel or anywhere else. No flags either. You guys see anything identifying?" He was looking for the telltale golden triple hollyhock crest that marked the Shogun's forces, normally painted prominently on the bow. An unmarked warship would be a flagrant violation of the treaty that had maintained *some* fragile peace between Japan and Rome for the past sixty five years.

"Negative," the other two pilots responded. Below, the ship suddenly changed course, sending waves sloshing everywhere. Powerful engines churned underwater as it tried to build up speed to head south. "Looks like it's running," Caius said. "Trying to avoid identification, you think?"

"Or to prevent us from knowing its port of call," Julia reasoned. "He's heading out to sea instead of back home so that we won't know where he's based." Caius picked up the microphone again: "Log note: Analyze ship's previous course to determine probable destination."

Min-Jae's voice crackled through the radio. Caius could clearly hear his thick accent; the Koreans had had some difficulty adapting to Latin. "Maybe it's coming from one of their New World colonies on the Pacific coast. They've tried to be secretive about which routes they use to get there."

"A ship this size?" Julia remarked. "It's got to have a crew of at least six hundred. It wouldn't be able to make it this far without a resupply." All three of them circled above like vultures, observing the ship's distinctive features.

4

"There's something weird about it," Caius said as they made another pass. "Doesn't this look bigger than any of the other Japanese warships we've encountered? Besides our navy, only the Indian Empire has anything this size. At least, as far as I know."

"New design, maybe?" Julia answered. She was an airplane enthusiast like Caius, and probably didn't know a thing about naval ships. "Would explain why it's out cruising with no flags or anything. It could be a prototype."

From below, sparks exploded from the deck and a rapid burst of machine gun fire sprayed through the air. Aiming straight up was ineffective for guns designed to fight other naval vessels, but it was at least clear that the battleship was hostile and recognized them as Roman. The bright red coloring of the wings wasn't particularly subtle.

"OK, split up," Caius ordered; he'd been shot at during enough missions over Japan to know the drill. The other pilots peeled off in opposite directions, flying unpredictably to avoid tracking. They zeroed in on the vessel from different angles as it crashed through the waves in its headlong flight away from land. "There's just something not right about it," Caius said, still peering down at the target. "This behavior is too erratic. Why head back out to sea instead of the closest port, where they would at least have anti-aircraft cover?"

The three pilots silently regarded the vessel as it began to pick up speed and head south. "It's going to call for reinforcements," Julia warned. "We should expect some air power coming soon."

"I need a closer look," Caius said finally, lamenting General Lucullus's decision to send them on patrol without any surveillance equipment.

The others warned him against it. "You specifically said not to engage, remember? You're going to get yourself shot down and captured."

Caius took another look at the vessel below. He could order one of the others to buzz the ship, but he needed it done right the first time. "Nah," he said with a slightly forced laugh. "I'll be fine. Just don't follow me."

The other two pilots continued to protest, so Caius turned down his radio till it was barely a whisper. They were right: it wasn't the safest approach, but it would be fastest, and that's what they needed right now. They couldn't go back to base without making the identification. Caius pressed forward on the stick and dove his plane straight toward the churning sea. The engine whined as he plummeted faster and faster. Caius had designed the thing; he knew exactly how much stress it could handle. The slate-grey waves rushed closer and closer, capped with frothy white foam. Caius had always hated the sea: cold, empty and foreboding. There was a reason he preferred to spend his time in the air.

He managed to level out the plane, almost low enough to skim the waves that swelled up toward the fuselage. Ocean spray blanketed the canopy, but the water rushed off in rivulets as he straightened out and headed directly toward the mysterious ship. His hands were sweating as he gripped the joystick and swerved back and forth, avoiding bursts of machine gun fire. He could just barely hear Julia and Min-Jae shouting into the radio, but they continued to circle the vessel and buzz the deck, attempting to keep the enemy's focus upwards. The side of the ship loomed like a grey wall rising out of the ocean in front of him.

At the last minute Caius pulled up on the stick, and his plane roared over the side of the ship, practically close enough for the propeller to bite into the railing around the edge. Caius

6

spun upside-down, hanging from his harness as his stomach flew into his throat and his lips flapped from the strain of centrifugal force. But it was the perfect level to see the shocked faces of the sailors below, staring at him through the cockpit with their jaws hanging open. And more importantly, to see the grey and black symbols on their uniforms.

"It's Ming," Caius radioed to the other pilots.

"You sure?" they responded in unison.

"Either that, or the Japanese stole a big shipment of naval uniforms from them and decided they were fashionable." A burst of gunfire whizzed past the canopy as Caius climbed higher and higher. *Their aim is getting a bit better,* he thought as he rejoined his companions circling the ship.

"The Ming hate the Japanese about as much as they hate us," Min-Jae pointed out. "So what's he doing this far north? We haven't seen one of them come past Hainan Island in the past fifty years. Why now?"

"We can talk about this when we're back in Fukuoka. We're getting a bit low on fuel, and their reinforcements will be here soon," Julia pointed out. "And we made the ID. Have we got everything we need?"

"A Ming battleship heading to a Japanese port? That's a pretty big development. I'd say we definitely got what we needed," Caius replied, banking his plane toward home. "Let's head back and report in."

Four hours later, the landing gear wheels of Caius's plane touched down on the fresh asphalt with a squeak and a bounce. Julia and Min-Jae taxied in neatly behind him and over to the Military Intelligence hangar. The automated mechanics swiveled out of their little compartments like a hive of silvery ants and rushed to meet the planes. Not for the first time, Caius wondered how advanced their aircraft would be now if only the Empire had seen as much potential in aviation as it did in automated drones and computers. The bots began to swarm over the plane, servicing the engine and removing the flight recorders to be sent into Central Processing. But the bots were not the only ones inside the large domed building awaiting the pilots' return.

Lights suddenly clicked on as Caius snapped open the canopy of his plane. The squad's captain strode out of the briefing room door. "Airman Caius Serica," he bellowed, his voice echoing through the vast hangar. Behind him, a group of heavily armed guards filled the doorway. They wore bright crimson uniforms buttoned up to their necks while bone-white masks covered up their faces with permanent scowls. *These are Praetorians*, Caius realized. He'd never seen one in person, but he'd heard stories about them.

Lingering in the doorway among the guards stood two generals, who watched him awkwardly clamber his way out of the narrow cockpit. Caius recognized General Lucullus, the man in charge of the Fukuoka base where Caius was currently stationed. After a moment Caius recognized the other man as General Kaneshiro, the ranking commander of the entire Japanese campaign.

They must have already heard about the Ming battleship, Caius thought. *How had they gotten the information this fast? And why the guards?* His mouth went dry as he desperately tried

8

to remember whether anything had gone wrong. The generals were staring intently at Caius, studying him like he was some misshapen science experiment. Lucullus turned and whispered something unintelligible; Kaneshiro nodded, stroking his graying mustache.

Julia taxied into a hangar bay next to Caius and opened her own cockpit canopy with a snap. "What's going on?" she asked, just loud enough to be heard over the automatons servicing the plane. Caius could only shrug in response.

"Airman Serica, come with us," the captain called to him. Caius tried to read his expression to no avail.

Min-Jae and Julia leaped from their seats and stepped in front of Caius's plane like protective mother hens. "Why?" they asked, eying the Praetorians in the shadows. Everyone knew that when you left with them, you usually didn't come back. "What has he done?"

General Kaneshiro stepped forward into the center of the wide, echoing room, and addressed Julia and Min-Jae first. "Do not worry about Caius here; he will be just fine. We simply need to have a conversation with him." He had a commanding voice that could quiet a crowded room with just a whisper. Julia and Min-Jae relaxed just a bit, but they still did not step aside.

Caius jumped out of his seat and onto the concrete floor in between his companions. They were all roughly the same size: Julia was fairly tall for a woman, but that was expected for people from the Western portion of the Empire. Citizens from the Eastern provinces such as China and Korea, like Caius and Min-Jae, were usually shorter. "We've taken the liberty of packing some of your clothes," Lucullus spoke for the first time. "We also ordered you a set of formal armor." A servant rushed forward and opened the large black case in his hands to reveal brand new gold-plated armor and a stout ceremonial sword. Caius saw the puzzled expressions on the faces of his companions. *Only officers are given formal armor,* Caius thought, just as Julia and Min-Jae probably realized the same thing. *But no promotion ceremony? And why pack my things?*

"I have some personal belongings that I need," Caius responded, not moving. "Specifically, the pictures of my family. They are on the bookshelf in my bunk."

"You can send for those later," General Lucullus answered with a casual wave of his perfectly manicured hand. *'Send for them later' means I am going somewhere.*

"Sir…" Caius wasn't one to disobey an order, but this point was non-negotiable. He hadn't let those pictures out of his grasp since his parents had died, even when he was homeless and had almost no other possessions. He certainly wasn't about to abandon them now with no idea where he was heading.

General Kaneshiro understood, though. Even after two hundred years of unity, the East and West were still very different places. Lucullus was from the West, and wasn't as sentimental about these sorts of things. "Get the pictures," Kaneshiro ordered a servant waiting nearby, who promptly rushed off to the barracks.

Caius gave a crisp, thankful salute and began to strap on the formal uniform. He removed his helmet and unleashed a shock of short black hair that stuck out every which way, the result of wearing the tight aviator cap all day. He removed his flight suit, revealing wiry but defined muscles and simple white undergarments. He took the robes from the servant and slipped them

10

over his head, and then began the arduous process of putting on the formal armor. Clanging metal echoed through the hangar, mixing with the sounds of the drones taking out parts of his plane. The masked faces of the Praetorian guards, twisted into terrifying grimaces, glared at him intently. Their gloved hands rested on the carved ivory hilts of their weapons like they were watching a dangerous animal that might lash out at any moment.

"Ready, sirs," Caius said as formally as possible, barely managing to keep his hand in place as he saluted. His mind raced to and fro, unable to focus. *Why did they pack my things? Does this have something to do with the Ming ship?*

The generals turned and walked in silence through the gaping hangar door out onto the runway, followed by their deadly entourage. The Praetorians were the best of the best, highly trained in every possible way except using force in moderation. Being marched outside by a whole armed squad of them seemed like a fate reserved for the worst traitors in the Empire. Caius turned briefly and looked at his companions with a helpless expression. Taking a deep breath, he followed his superiors out and gave his plane a light pat on the wing for luck.

Caius could sense the eyes of the rest of the flight crew in the barracks peering out behind him. They were probably pushing and shoving at each other for a better view. Maybe they would take bets on whether he'd return with lashes or medals. As they passed the door to the barracks, General Lucullus turned to the captain and dismissed him with a wave of his hand. He gave Caius one last long look with a mix of dread and burning curiosity. Caius nodded to him almost invisibly as the captain slipped back into the mists.

He marched in lockstep behind the two generals through the base, surrounded by the stern Praetorians in a tight formation. The path was lined with rows of pre-fabricated buildings

11

all made of the same plastic material. Spotlights illuminated the camp through the evening mist like artificial suns and cast an eerie orange glow. No one said a word as they walked along the cracked asphalt road. It had been intended to serve only for a short while during the war, and was never replaced after the Fukuoka base became a permanent installation. All of the money and effort had gone into rebuilding the city, now the capital of Rome's newest province.

The group finally arrived at Lucullus's office: A squat, ugly square building perched on a hill overlooking the entire camp and the sparkling city beyond. For a man so obsessed with appearances, this building must have been a constant insult to the general. The Praetorians fanned out around the perimeter while Lucullus and Kaneshiro stepped inside. Caius stopped on the threshold with a salute, waiting until the generals noticed him. An enlisted man must never enter the lodgings of a superior without express permission.

Kaneshiro turned to Lucullus with a smirk. "You lost him," he said gently with his almost indistinguishable Hakata accent, pointing back at the entrance. Caius maintained his salute. Lucullus turned back having forgotten that the young soldier was even with them. "Oh, of course. Enter, young man. Please," the general said with a firm tone.

Lucullus plopped down on a plush red couch, put his boots up on the table in the center, and gestured to a chair across from him. Caius clanked awkwardly in his formal armor as he took a seat. His sword banged against the chair's polished wooden frame. General Kaneshiro remained standing in a corner, contemplating Caius through small circular glasses perched on the rim of his nose. Medals and awards of a hundred different color combinations decorated his shoulder patches and draped down his arms like an old tree covered in moss. They tinkled softly every time the general moved. Instead of the traditional golden formal armor with the Emperor's eagle crest emblazoned on the front, he wore plain steel armor stamped "SPQR," not so subtly showing that his loyalty belonged to the Senate and not the Emperor. The highest generals were indeed commissioned by the Senate and were thus *allowed* to wear the Senate's insignia, but most still chose to wear the Imperial crest out of respect and tradition. Kaneshiro only got away with it without shame from his peers because of his status as a brilliant tactician and bona fide war hero who'd fought off the Ming army almost single-handedly.

"Can I get you anything, lad? I can have the servants whip up some dinner for you if you're hungry," Lucullus said, assessing Caius with suspicion in his watery brown eyes peering over his prominent Roman nose. "Or perhaps some coffee? We've got the finest beans from Ethiopia; none of that powdered nonsense." His voice carried a hint of pride as though it spoke to his clout that he was able to get coffee beans.

Caius was tempted; it had been a long time since he'd had real coffee. But he declined politely. "No, sir. I'm fine, thank you." *No need to appear greedy in front of my superiors*, he reasoned. *A good soldier does without.*

Kaneshiro gave him an almost unnoticeable nod of approval, but said, "The boy isn't going to ask you for anything, Lucullus. He's not stupid." Kaneshiro turned to a servant waiting just outside the doorway. "Three cups and a hot pot of coffee." Caius silently thanked the old man as he suppressed his stomach's urge to rumble. The servant dashed off to the kitchens. "And bring the boy some dinner," Kaneshiro shouted after him. "He's had a long flight."

"I suppose you're wondering why you have been summoned," Lucullus said, leaning back on the plump, luxurious cushions of the couch. He examined a slightly worn sleeve cuff with extreme distaste, as though his attention had been drawn to something more distracting. The

13

general pulled at a loose string as the silence dragged on. Caius fidgeted in his seat despite his best attempts to stay still. "Well… so are we," the general continued finally. He stopped, studying Caius intently for any reaction like he suspected that Caius might know the reason.

Caius waited. Surely there was more. Lucullus sniffed, disappointed that Caius did not reveal the secret.

"We received a call this afternoon," Lucullus continued, gesturing to the video monitor on his desk "From the Emperor himself, summoning you to Europe. *Only* you," the general added with emphasis. "Any reason you can think of why the leader of the civilized world might be interested in talking to *you*?" Lucullus could barely contain his disdain as he said '*you,*' emphasizing that Caius was just a pitiful worm, one grunt in an army of millions spread across every continent in the world.

The servant suddenly bustled in with a silver tray laden with cups, cream, and sugar. Caius exhaled, thankful for the momentary interruption. A second servant brought a bubbling pot of coffee spewing aromatic steam that filled the room. He poured it into the delicate silver mugs and scampered back out of sight. Lucullus loaded cream and spooned sugar into his mug, stirring it endlessly; Kaneshiro smacked his lips as he drank his coffee black. Caius took only a dash of cream and sipped quietly. After savoring the flavor for a moment, Lucullus turned back to Caius, still awaiting an answer.

"I'm not sure, Sir." Caius responded. The generals both stared, waiting for a better explanation. "Perhaps something to do with this last mission? I don't know how someone in Rome would have found out about it already, but sighting that Ming warship all the way up here by Japan is pretty important."

14

"*Ming* ship?" Kaneshiro asked, narrowing his eyes. "Are you sure it wasn't Japanese?" Caius recounted the story for him as quickly as possible, including dive-bombing the ship to get a view of the uniforms. "Interesting. This is definitely important." He stroked his long mustache. "Perhaps they are forming an alliance. We would need some confirmation from our intelligence inside the Foreign Ministry." He rushed to the map that covered the entire western wall of the room and began tracing a finger over the route between the Ming capital in the jungles of Southeast Asia to the Shogun's capital in Kyoto.

Lucullus rolled his eyes as Kaneshiro started muttering plans to himself. "Regardless of how important your find, that's not why you were summoned." His tone indicated that he didn't think it was a particularly important find either. "The message was transmitted just after you took off, before this ship of yours was even sighted. And besides, the Emperor leaves such matters to the War Council. He rarely takes interest in the day-to-day affairs of the conflict here; he is a busy man and the Empire is threatened on many fronts. What more could the Emperor need to know, and why bring you directly to Rome?" His tone was pretty clear: Lucullus did not appreciate being left out of the loop on such mysterious messages. His role as a middleman of information between Rome and the troops here in Japan was all that he had.

"There's nothing about the mission that you neglected to tell us?" Lucullus asked, trying to hide the suspicious undertones of the question. "No other encounters with the enemy? Or maybe some previous mission where you saw something unusual?"

Caius had no response, and the generals were silent. He looked down at the silver mug, emblazoned in red with the imperial crest. *Why would the Emperor need me?*

"Do you know anyone in Rome, Caius? Is there anyone you correspond with? Anyone that you have talked to about the camp here?" Lucullus' suspicious tone grew hard, almost threatening.

"No, sir. Nobody." Caius responded firmly. *No one that I could report your incompetence to,* he wanted to blurt out.

Lucullus eyed him, trying to gauge his honesty. "Well, that's that, then," he said at last, and once more leaned back and sipped from his coffee. "Let's get the boy to the train station."

The barricaded gates rolled open with a screech of metal, and the trucks pulled out onto the highway toward downtown Fukuoka. The city lights of a million different homes were just beginning to twinkle in the distance. They drove over newly built roads and bridges through sparse forests and past acres of rice paddies.

"You must be something special, son." Kaneshiro said finally. "The Emperor has dispatched a train specifically to bring you down to Europe. Even *I* don't get that kind of treatment." The old general grinned, even though it wasn't a joke. It was common knowledge that he had fallen out of favor in Rome and the War Council, but was tolerated as the only man really fit to oversee the defenses of the Eastern provinces. If he was ever called back to Rome, it *certainly* wouldn't be on a private train. But at least the general knew exactly where he stood, and was comfortable with it. For the first time that evening, Caius smiled back; Kaneshiro had a way of making people feel at ease despite his rank.

16

"You know," he continued, "If there is anything you did not want to say in front of Lucullus, you can say it now. He can be a bit temperamental. Any reason you might be sought after by the Emperor himself?"

Caius shook his head. "Not that I can think of, Sir."

The general was satisfied by this answer. "Are you at all familiar with politics, my boy?"

Caius shook his head. "Only what I have studied in history and read in a few books," he answered.

"Rome can be … an odd place," Kaneshiro continued, struggling to put his emotions into words and waving his free hand as though he could snatch the right phrasing out of the air. "For those of us raised here in the East, it can be quite a shock. Do you know much about my career, Caius?" He knew the answer already, but was asking to be polite. Everyone knew about Kaneshiro's career.

Caius nodded in response, unsure of what to say; he could sense the pain in the general's voice. He had risen quickly through the ranks of the military after his legendary campaign last time the Ming Emperor in Exile had tried to retake Southern China. Not only was Kaneshiro victorious, he had even counterattacked and claimed Hanoi in the name of the Empire.

"I was involved in the most recent war with the Ming, and the Empire's forces were very successful." He didn't want to take credit for it himself, but Caius knew the truth. "After our victory, I too was summoned to Rome in a similar manner." Caius already knew this part too. The Emperor himself had honored Kaneshiro with the Steel Crown and assigned him as deputy War Minister. Kaneshiro was even given a title of nobility, despite having just earned his

17

citizenship. "But after only a few months, the Emperor announced that he had chosen one of his sons as heir, a young man that I had never even seen around the Palace. The new heir took an instant disliking to the War Minister, and by extension, me. As soon as he became Emperor, I was dismissed from my position." *And 'reassigned' here in disgrace*, Caius mentally finished for him. Even decades later, Kaneshiro's anguish was still visible.

"I don't know why the Emperor has summoned you, but regardless of his reasons, you will be thrust into the politics of the Empire, just as I was. Be warned that you have lost control of your own fate, for the most part. You're one of their playthings now. Anyone that you think you can trust: *forget it*. No matter who it is, they want to use you to elevate their own position. They'll forget about you as soon as they stop needing you. Just be careful, son," Kaneshiro said finally. "These Westerners have no honor. They will warp you. They will try to bring you into their game. You will be best utilized once you too have abandoned your moral principles." He got a far off look in his eye, and he grimaced, gripping the steering wheel tighter. "I've seen it happen to so many others. They went to Rome with the best of intentions, and came back corrupt, disreputable thieves." *Not too different from many Chinese officials I knew growing up*, Caius thought, but didn't share his opinion with Kaneshiro. "Don't let them change you. *Promise me* that you will maintain your honor." His voice strained, like a man on his deathbed making a witness swear to fulfill a final request.

"I promise," Caius answered, honestly wanting to make Kaneshiro proud.

The conversation eventually meandered to happier topics, and the general did not bring up the subject again. Kaneshiro turned on the radio in the car and they spent the rest of the ride discussing a new program from Gaius Hansin, who was exploring the untamed Amazon River

18

over in the New World. Kaneshiro didn't think it was realistic; there was no way that *every* animal living there could be vicious and poisonous. "Definitely overdramatized," the general declared.

The vehicle crested a hill, revealing a clear look at the sprawling metropolis of Fukuoka under them. It had been an important port even back when it was part of the Shogunate. But with the Roman annexation, it had grown larger than even Tokyo or Kyoto. They passed through the ornately carved triumphal arch that spanned the entrance to the city, at least fifteen stories high and made of pink marble. The foundation was built over the crumbling remains of the city walls, a reminder to the citizens that none could withstand Rome's power.

They soon arrived at the train station, jam-packed with commuters streaming out of the city. Through the hubbub, the guards cleared a path for Kaneshiro and Caius; no one wanted to come close to a group of Praetorians. They all made their way to the far end of the track where a sleek silver train waited guarded by a perimeter of soldiers. It looked incredibly out of place: a gleaming steel beast surrounded by the old, pre-war era station made of carved wooden beams, paper walls, and peeling paint. Caius was in awe of the train's perfectly streamlined, aerodynamic shape. He made a mental note to try to get his hands on the designs; maybe that streamlined nose could be worked into the heavy bomber designs that he'd been thinking of.

Kaneshiro stopped by the door and pressed a small button on the frame; it slid open with a soft swish. "You're a good soldier, Caius. You're going to be just fine there." He grabbed Caius' hand and shook heartily, pulling Caius in close. "Just remember what I said," he whispered. "Don't trust them, and don't let them corrupt you." Then he turned and walked away, disappearing into the crowd.

The guards ushered Caius onto the train and through the cabin. The ultra-sleek, gleaming steel and chrome outer appearance of the train contrasted with the luxurious, classical look on the inside. The train cars were beautifully decorated with plush furniture, rich wood paneling, and soothing lamps. Sitting behind an intricately carved wooden desk with legs sculpted to look like roaring lions, the train's single occupant waited in a stout velvet chair. He wore spindly gold-rimmed reading glasses that framed a slightly chubby but friendly face. His formal robes, impeccably clean and white, stuck out over his paunch. His hair was a bushy mane of grey; only his thick beard retained some flecks of black.

"Good morning, Caius," the man said with a welcoming smile. He stood from his seat and clicked off the small tablet computer that he'd been studying. Caius snapped his heels together and saluted, not sure exactly with whom he was speaking.

"No need for that, son. I'm not in the military." He extended a hand and flashed a warm smile. "I'm Marcus Geganius. Your Advocate."

The train lurched and quickly accelerated out of the station with a silent whir as Caius and Marcus sat down at the desk. The brand new downtown district flew by in a flash of concrete and glass. "My advocate," Caius repeated. "What am I being tried for?" He maintained his calm exterior, but on the inside he had turned to jelly. General Kaneshiro had promised that he was not being punished. His whole military career was going down the drain, and he didn't even know what crime he was being accused of.

Marcus looked at him, slightly puzzled at first, and then with an expression of sudden recognition. "Oh, no. Nothing like that!" he said cheerfully. "No, no. You are right that normally an advocate is a person who defends you in court. But I am talking about a different type of

20

advocate." He tapped his perfectly manicured fingers together, deliberating his words carefully. "No, I'm talking about a very special type of advocate, Caius. You have been accused of no crime. Rather, you are up for a promotion, let's say. And I will be the one to speak for your qualities," Marcus finished. Caius' mind flashed back to Kaneshiro's sudden rise to fame and precipitous fall after only a few months in Rome

"We don't even know each other, Sir." Caius said, still standing stiffly and not daring to break eye contact.

"Good military form, son. That will definitely be a big plus in your favor during the Trials. But there's no need to call me 'Sir.' In response to your comment, let's just say that I have a pretty good idea of who you are already, and we're going to get to know each other *very well* over the next few days."

Caius nodded slowly at his cryptic comments. He glanced out the window at the skyscrapers of Fukuoka, rapidly dwindling in the distance as the train entered the suburbs. The moon was beginning to rise over the bay, a dull orb obscured by the hazy fog.

"I know this is all confusing," Marcus continued. "But I really don't have that much time." His face seemed pained, wracked by indecision. Caius waited patiently, studying Marcus' face as he contemplated different ways of phrasing what he wanted to say. Eventually, Marcus exclaimed: "I'm just going to be blunt. Caius, you are a candidate to be the next Emperor of Rome. And I'm here to make sure you win."

CHAPTER 2

Marcus paused and looked at Caius, expecting some reaction. Caius had none. He sat like a statue, waiting for the punchline to the joke. There was an awkward silence. *Not a particularly funny joke,* Caius thought.

Finally, Caius spoke. "How could I ever be Emperor? That makes no sense. I'm not even European, and I know who my parents were. They were wealthy, but nowhere close to royalty." By law, only the Emperor's children could be designated as the next heir.

"And they died in a car crash when you were away at boarding school, yes?" Marcus finished with a slight grin. "Their vehicle went over the side of a bridge on a rainy night in Nanjing?"

Caius was unimpressed. "So, you've seen my personnel file."

"Those weren't your parents," Marcus said, ignoring his comment. "Well, kind of. Your mother was certainly your birth mother. But biologically, down at the genetic level, you are the son of the Emperor, and of some other woman who was selected by the Senate's Breeding Committee for her genes. You were deliberately placed in that family to raise you."

"But I'm Han," Caius said, gesturing with one hand at his black hair and slightly slanted eyes. "Just like my parents. And not like the Emperor." He'd seen him on the television enough times to know how different they looked. And yet, there were some similarities that he'd never quite been able to explain. Larger eyes that weren't *too* almond shaped. A narrow, pointy nose. Thin cheeks and lighter skin. His mother always said that his grandfather had had the same features, though.

"Yes," Marcus said, nodding, "You are *half* Han. The Senate's geneticists are careful to prevent the gene pool from becoming isolated and inbred, which became a severe problem for the Empire earlier in its history, when the nobility was more rigid. Now, they pick a wide variety of different ethnic backgrounds for the egg donors or sperm donors if the Emperor is a female. This ensures that any genetic disorders or anomalies are weeded out of the Emperor's line. And it is fitting, really: the Emperor's own genetics come to reflect the varied backgrounds of the Empire's many citizens." He gestured to Caius's features with a smile: "And, if you are chosen, you would be the first Emperor of Asian descent. This will be a huge advantage to you, as the Senate has long since sought better ways to bind the Western and Eastern parts of the Empire more closely together. It's been quite the challenge." Caius nodded; small-scale uprisings (encouraged by the Ming down in Southeast China and by the Indian Empire in more mountainous regions of the Himalayas) were quite common.

"So I'm the son of the Emperor," Caius said, not hiding the sarcastic skepticism in his voice.

"Yes!" Marcus enthused, either not noticing or caring about Caius' disbelief. "One of many!" There was another awkward silence in the train car. The countryside flew by in a blur of green.

"I *knew* my parents," Caius said finally. "I grew up with them until I was six, and visited them regularly once I entered the Academy. I've seen pictures of my mother in the hospital giving birth."

"That's true," Marcus responded. "You were created through in-vitro fertilization, a process that...."

23

"I know what it is," Caius snapped. He'd taken biology before he was forced to leave the Academy.

"Right. Well. Using the Emperor's sperm, an egg was fertilized. Well, not one. Thousands. From women all over the empire." Marcus spread his arms wide, as if conveying the size of it, from the islands off the coast of Iberia all the way to the cold waters of Japan, not to mention the colonies. "Like I said, to ensure genetic diversity. These thousands of eggs were implanted into thousands of different host mothers, carefully selected to provide stable loving families to the Emperor's children. These couples are never told who the real father is, though they know enough to recognize that it is someone important."

"And these women just let you do this to them?" Caius said. His father never would have agreed to an arrangement like that. He was a man of honor who took pride in his own ancestors' achievements. He'd raised Caius to honor them as well, and he wouldn't have done that if Caius wasn't even related to them. The Serica family was one of the more prominent names amongst the Chinese citizens of the Empire. They had been one of the very first to rebel against the Ming Emperor and recognize Roman rule. He could picture the portraits of his ancestors now, hanging as they always did in his father's study, and more recently in his bunk back in Fukuoka. Caius's throat tightened, and he fought to hold back tears as memories of his family paraded back into his thoughts, and how he'd almost had to leave their pictures behind.

"Oh yes," Marcus said after he calmly took a sip of water, still not noticing the impact that the conversation was having on Caius. "It is a great privilege! Raising the son of the Emperor? Perhaps *the future Emperor himself?* I dare say that many couples fought over the honor! It was the ultimate service that they could render for their nation."

24

"Well, at least they were happy about lying to me," Caius said shortly, still knowing that his father would never accept it willingly. It had to be a lie.

Caius looked away, out the window. The speeding train slowed almost imperceptibly as they arrived at Karatsu, the entrance to the tunnel under the Korean Straits to Busan. This feat of modern engineering had connected the Japanese provinces to the continent for the first time, much to the delight of merchants seeking closer connections to the rest of the Roman Empire. It was even longer than the one between Britain and the rest of Europe, and the one from Spain over to Africa. The train was plunged into darkness as it dipped underground. Marcus flipped on the lights, bathing the train car in a warm yellow glow. For the first time, Caius noted the intricate stained glass lampshades depicting one battle or another, and the detailed wood work of the cabinets and shelves.

"That's better, isn't it?" Marcus said softly, apparently realizing the effects of nonchalantly telling Caius that his family history was all a big lie. Caius said nothing in response, continuing to look out the window at the blackness of the tunnel, occasionally interrupted by red lights marking the interior walls.

"Caius," Marcus started, almost pleading, "I apologize if I have been insensitive. This will be a very big shift in your life, but it is necessary. I really do not have a lot of time to explain. The trials begin as soon as we arrive, and I'm not even entirely sure how long the journey will be. Luckily I was able to convince the Tribunal that traveling by train would be much safer than going by air, so I could buy some time to prepare you."

Caius turned and looked back at him, ready to explain all of the reasons that traveling by plane would actually be safer than by train. But never mind; now was not the time to argue.

25

Instead, Caius tried to project calm and confidence. "Ok, tell me," Caius said, not quite convinced but at least willing to hear the old man out.

"As I mentioned, you are a candidate to be the new Emperor. But first, you have to go through Trials. A Senate tribunal will test you in every possible way that they can think of. And I mean *every* way. They are utterly brutal."

"Test me for what? I don't get it," Caius responded. "I know that the Senate ratifies the selection of the Emperor's heir. We watched a video of the last vote in history class. The Emperor went before the Senate and gave a speech to announce which one of his children would become the heir. And then the Senate interviewed him, and then they all took a vote."

"Well, that is the public part of it, yes." Marcus had a 'oh, you actually believed that?' smirk on his face. "But you have to understand that this is a closely guarded secret. The Emperor doesn't really select the heir in the first place. He's simply told which one would pass the Senate ratification. Before they get to that point, there is a different selection process to determine which one the Emperor will nominate. His own thoughts on the matter are irrelevant."

Caius nodded, still clearly confused and doubting this story even more. How could the *Emperor's* thoughts be irrelevant to anything, and particularly for which one of his own children would succeed him?

"I know you're having a hard time with all of this. You've been exposed to years of deliberately misleading information. The secrecy of these proceedings is necessary to maintain the illusion of the unbroken dynasty of the Empire. It's all about order and continuity. So the Information Ministry deliberately created this narrative about the privacy of the Imperial family, and how they just don't like to be exposed in the public media. *That* is why you never hear anything about the children of the Emperor until a new heir is announced." Now that Caius thought about it, he realized he'd never seen photos of the Emperor's children, nor did he even know their names. "You only know one small aspect of the Senate's power in the ratification process. There are far more checks and balances behind the scenes than you realize. The entire purpose is to ensure that the Empire is helmed by a strong, capable leader. How much do you remember about the Succession Wars from your classes?"

Caius thought back to his days in school. They'd certainly learned about it, but he honestly couldn't remember many of the details so many years later. "The Empire was split into multiple pieces that fought for two hundred years," he recited slowly, trying to recall the details, "until Senator Hortensius and Felix Titus reached a peace accord naming Felix the new Emperor in exchange for allowing the Senate to question and approve his choice of heir."

"Yes, exactly!" Marcus said. "I picked my Candidate well, I see!" He beamed like a proud father. "But the trials have gotten a bit more complex since then," Marcus answered. "Over the years, the powers of the Senate grew and their questions for the heir became more and more firm and incisive. At first, the Senate Tribunal simply picked between the various children of the Emperor, but there wasn't always a good option. Hell, sometimes there was only one candidate because the Emperor only had one son. They were spoiled and petulant and stupid, leading to some honestly terrible Emperors."

He shook his head in disgust remembering the history, but did not go into more detail. Caius remembered some of the stories from history class, like Emperor Metus's ill-fated expedition to conquer sub-Saharan Africa that was never heard from again.

"Some of the more shrewd Senators realized what power they had over the Emperor in this situation, because a new heir couldn't be ratified without Senate approval. The Emperor was forced to accede to their demands, or leave the Empire without an heir and potentially leaderless. And any disputes would mean war between the Citizen Republics and the Empire. The Senators began putting candidates through a series of trials. And if the Emperor's current children weren't good enough, they'd tell him to go back and make another."

"At first, it was just a set of interviews with the candidates, out of the public eye. This would come before the formal Senate hearing, asking them what their policy positions were, or a test of strength, and so on. But after a particularly disappointing series of candidates in the 1600s, leaders in the Senate met and decided that they should not just vet candidates, but actually shape them. They needed to control their education, and their life experiences, and everything that would shape a potential heir into the man you'd want as the leader of the nation. They told the Emperor to hand over the children at a young age to begin the tests. This led to the Emperor having both a private family with children not eligible for succession, and a second set of children to be raised as the Senate saw fit. Now, the trials are a strenuous ordeal that begins at birth and are designed to test every aspect of your fitness and personality and intellect." He gestured at Caius, indicating that he was a product of this system.

"Testing me?" Caius asked. *I would have noticed if I'd been undergoing tests this whole time,* he thought. "How?"

"Your life," Marcus answered as if it were self-evident. "Your time at the Academy, your time on the streets after being forced out of school, your apprenticeship, your military career… everything has been pre-arranged. The Senate believes that these tragedies and tribulations show your real character, especially when you don't know that they're watching. And now you have passed the final review period. You're part of the very cream of the crop, and you're going to start your final set of tests."

"What are they?" Caius asked. He kept asking questions, waiting for Marcus to slip up. To make a tiny mistake that would reveal the real story here. What they *really* wanted with Caius. Not this fiction about potentially making him the Emperor.

"Honestly, they don't tell me; it's a big secret. I only have information based on past trials and what they have done to other candidates. They'll probably try a lot of it again, but that doesn't mean that there are no new tricks." He raised a hand and gestured around the room at the books and the binders lining the walls. "And that's what this is all for. I need to prepare you for the trials. And I have until the end of this train ride."

And that's all?" Caius asked, sensing something more.

Marcus gave him a suspicious look. "That's all I can tell you about now," he replied.

Caius absorbed everything. The whole story was ridiculous, but the fact remained that the Emperor had messaged General Lucullus to send him to Rome, and had sent this clearly expensive train to fetch him.

"Let's say I believe you," Caius said. "Why should I *want* to be Emperor?" Going all the way back to his time at the Academy, Caius had never been one to jump at leadership. Power, which seemed to drive others crazy, simply had no appeal. It was a burden that had been constantly thrust upon him: a mantle that he would accept only when no one else was willing. And now they were asking him to fight against other candidates for it?

Marcus furrowed his brow like he didn't understand the question. "Why *wouldn't* you want to be Emperor? To be adored and idolized by *billions* of your own citizens? To have your every whim and desire fulfilled instantly? To have the resources of the entire Empire at your grasp? To be the most powerful man on the entire planet? Every citizen *dreams* of this!"

Caius shrugged, trying to look unimpressed. *That would be nice, though.* He'd certainly had money when he was running his own little business, but never extravagant wealth. Never enough where he could stop worrying about where his next meal would come from. The pain and desperation of homelessness had been permanently branded into his soul.

"Caius, have you ever been assigned to do something in the military by your superiors that you thought was misguided? Haven't you wanted to tell them how you felt? How it could be done better?"

"I see you've met General Lucullus," Caius responded, but regretted it a moment later. That wasn't something he could say about a superior.

Marcus just laughed, though. "Exactly. When you're the Emperor, you'll get to call the shots. If you think the war with Japan should be run differently, then you just have to give the command, and it will be done."

Caius nodded. That was a pretty good reason, too. He'd seen enough disastrous invasion attempts and red-stained beaches to realize the toll of Lucullus's ineffective leadership. Only Kaneshiro had managed to keep the Shogun at bay for the past few decades, but his talent had gone unrecognized.

"Not to mention your family," Marcus added in as though it were just a mere afterthought. But it had exactly the intended effect.

Caius leaned forward quickly. "What do you mean, my family?" The words flew out of his mouth like bullets.

Marcus paused, knowing that he had captured Caius's attention and he needed to milk it as much as possible. "There was no car crash." He tapped his tablet computer and brought up a photo. A photo of Caius's mother and father looking much older than when he'd last seen them more than a decade ago, but clearly still alive. They were posing together near some enormous, white cliffs topped with green lawns. His mother's long black hair was blown across her face, and his father was laughing. "Your parents are still alive, Caius. The Senate wanted to impose hardship on the candidates, so they faked the deaths of your parents. They were brought back to Europe. When you're the Emperor, Caius, you can see them again. You can be reunited with your family."

Caius had no response. He just stared down at the photo, mesmerized. He absorbed every tiny wrinkle that had grown on his mother's face. And his father had taken to wearing a mustache now, even though it was sparse and thin! Behind his amazement, anger welled up like a bubbling geyser. How could the Senate do this? How could his *parents* have allowed the government to do this?

"Caius." He was so wrapped up in his own thoughts that he'd practically forgotten Marcus's presence. He didn't even look up as the Advocate continued speaking.

"They had to, Caius." Marcus pointed down at the photo. "I know what you're thinking. Don't be mad at your parents. If they hadn't agreed to the plan, then the Senate would have *actually* killed them without even a second thought. They did what had to be done even though it hurt both you and them, and now they're waiting to be reunited with you. They need you to win the Trials. If the wealth and the power and the prestige of the position don't appeal to you, then surely the idea of having your family back does."

Caius took in a deep breath, soaking in all of the information. His stoic face broke into a broad, handsome smile at the thought of seeing his parents again. "Ok, I'm ready. Tell me about the Trials."

CHAPTER 3

A colorful map flashed onto the screen.

"Matabele Empire in southern Africa," Caius said. Marcus nodded approvingly.

"Status?" the Advocate asked.

"Currently at peace with the Empire, but not a tributary state. They do not dispute Roman sovereignty of the islands off their western coast."

"Good," Marcus said. "Chief exports?"

"Primarily raw materials: gold, iron, diamonds."

"Current leader?"

Caius rolled his eyes up to the ceiling, searching for the answer. These African names were always so difficult to remember, and they usually only lasted a few years in office anyway. Even their borders didn't endure long enough to make it onto most maps.

"Come on, Caius," Marcus urged, checking his ticking watch. "Your time is limited during the tests. You won't be able to take this long to think of each answer. You need to know them immediately."

"I know," Caius responded. It was on the tip of his tongue. Kala-something!

"Time," Marcus said, clicking the golden button emphatically and casting a disappointed glower in Caius's direction. "Kamarouta," he spat out like it was the most obvious thing in the world. "Caius, I'm worried that you're not taking this seriously enough. I mean, Matabele is one of the larger countries; we haven't even gotten to some of the smaller New World tribes. *Those are hard to remember.*"

"Marcus," Caius protested, "You know everything about my past, so clearly you have seen my grades from the Academy. And that's one of the most rigorous schools in the entire Empire. You know that I'm smart."

"No," Marcus said harshly, "I know that you have good genetics. I know that you've been able to get by with your intelligence for so long that you've forgotten the value of hard work and studying." The advocate loomed over the desk, imposing and powerful. He was no longer the same pudgy, soft old man, but a towering conqueror.

Caius opened his mouth to protest, but Marcus silenced him. "I know your entire life, Caius. Don't ever forget that. Remember that time in your sixth year that you forgot to do your presentation on mythology in the ancient empire? And you just went up in front and gave your presentation anyway based on what you remembered? You got a 96% on that presentation, didn't you?" Caius didn't remember the grade, but he absolutely remembered the moment. He never told anyone about forgetting to do the assignment; not even his mother and father.

Marcus gave a knowing smile. "From the moment of your birth, agents of the Senate have been watching you. Cameras installed above your crib, around your home, in the homes of your friends, in your school… everywhere. The Senate has *every* moment recorded, and I have seen them all." Caius was still in disbelief about the level of surveillance under which he'd lived. He hadn't believed it until Marcus showed him some of the video. The moment of his first kiss, to be exact. With Lucia, the buck-toothed girl from the Academy who had moved back to Persia when he was thirteen. "I've designed this entire training program to get you ready for the trials in just a few days. So don't try to tell me what you know and what you don't know."

Caius nodded. He couldn't deny that Marcus did have an eerily comprehensive knowledge of his life. "All right, you win," he responded. "Let's try this again."

Marcus laughed and his serious and almost threatening veneer dissolved. "I like the attitude." He pulled up another map on the projector showing the colonies in the South Pacific, but then checked his silvery pocket watch again. "On second thought, that is enough practice for now. Shall we have some lunch?" Without waiting for a response from Caius, he pressed a small button on the side of the train compartment wall.

Immediately, servants bustled in from another car of the train carrying a platter of food and pitchers of refreshments. A sudden and unexpected wave of hunger washed over Caius, though breakfast had only been a few hours ago. The advocate's interrogation was grueling and nerve-wracking, causing him to build up quite an appetite. Caius heaped his plate with food and returned to the table. He hunched over his food and started shoveling it into his mouth, but Marcus smacked his elbows off the table.

"Manners, Caius!"

Caius winced sheepishly and sat up straight. It was hard to undo the military conditioning that had trained him to eat as quickly as possible so that they could make room in the mess. It wasn't nearly large enough to feed everyone at the massive Fukuoka base at once, so eating was done in shifts, and if you hadn't eaten your fill by the end of your time slot, then you went hungry. "Sorry," he responded to Marcus after swallowing his mouthful of food. He held up his knife and fork and slowly began cutting a piece of meat. Marcus nodded in approval.

They both looked out the window together as they passed through Turfan, the "Gateway to the West." Train tracks ran along a high ridge skirting the city and bright sunlight glinted off of modern buildings in the downtown area, all built from concrete and glass. The biggest trading firms had offices here; the city marked the intersection of the North and South tracks of the Great Continental Railroad, so almost all cargo going overland between the Eastern and Western halves of the Empire came through here. The train whistled through the Turfan station without stopping, and Caius could briefly see dozens of bystanders holding luggage step back from the tracks.

Through gaps in the buildings, the massive Legionnaire monument held its rifle menacingly over the former city walls and facing the rest of China. Caius's father had brought him here when he was six, just before he was sent off to the military academy. He hadn't wanted to leave home, so Caius's father had decided that he needed a reminder of his patriotic duties. They'd spent a week touring the battlefield around Turfan and visiting the war museum, highlighting the stalwart Roman soldiers who had taken the city at the beginning of the Great War. By the end, Caius was asking if he'd be able to skip going to the Academy and join the army at age six. His father had laughed and told him that of course the army wanted him, but that he needed an education if he was going to become an officer. "You're destined for great things," his father had told him as they surveyed the desert from the observation room at the tip of the Legionnaire's rifle, more than 150 meters up. Now that Caius was thinking about it, his father had known all about who he *really* was and wanted to make sure that his 'son' knew his patriotic

36

duties, in preparation for this day. Caius had even kept a photo of them in front of the Legionnaire all these years as a reminder of that last trip they took together. One of the photos over which Caius had been ready to defy General Lucullus back at the hangar.

"So when do I get to know your story?" Caius asked Marcus, breaking the silence and shaking the memories from his mind. "We've been traveling for three days now and I hardly know anything about you. Seems a bit unfair that you memorized my entire life story and I only know your name. Where are you from? What do you do?"

Marcus smiled. "Where I am from is a pretty easy one. I was born in Scotland. In a small fishing town on the rocky shores of the Atlantic. My parents were well-to-do, but never extravagant. When I was six, I was sent to a prestigious boarding school down in Britannia. When my parents died, I could no longer afford to attend the school, so I lived on the streets, drifting from job to job, province to province. I eventually worked my way up to an apprenticeship with a chemist in Germania. Finally, my time for military service came due and I fought against the Ubeles in Africa."

Marcus looked like he was going to continue, but Caius interrupted: "I think I recognize the story now."

"It certainly should be familiar to you. It's what all candidates go through. The moderately wealthy family, the challenging school, then some time living in poverty, then a prestigious apprenticeship, and finally a military career."

"How..." Caius started, shaking his head in disbelief. "How did they do all this? For thousands of us?"

Marcus stared at him coldly. The friendly old man had once again been replaced the stern commander. He pursed his thin lips. "They did the exact same thing to you that they did to me. They faked my parent's death when I was 14 so that they had an excuse to expel me and force me out on the street. Just like with every other candidate. They want to know that we can endure hardship, and until we're chosen as Emperor, we're just puppets to them."

He casually took a sip of water as though they were discussing the weather and not how their childhoods had been destroyed. The train turned at the switch, heading south along the Taklamakan desert and through the Tian Shan foothills. The railroad tracks followed along the ancient road that had first established a silk trade route between Rome and China, and eventually carried the Imperial Roman army into the Chinese heartlands. Caius reached for a pitcher of icy water, dripping in condensation, and filled his glass. Even the sight of so much desert was making him thirsty. But the sandy yellow dunes were somehow beautiful: desolate, arid, and untamed. Only the rows and rows of solar panels that clung to the side of the railroad track signaled that civilization existed out here.

"No, Caius. I'm afraid that everything has been orchestrated for the both of us. The sooner you accept that, the sooner you will be ready to face the Tribunal." Marcus gave a heavy sigh. "So, I guess that answers your second question, about what I do." He shuffled his fork awkwardly around the plate. "I knew this would come up eventually." Marcus picked at the chicken some more, letting out a deep sigh. "Yes, I too was a candidate once. I guess that technically makes me your half uncle, although our family isn't particularly close." He gave a short, sardonic laugh. That was a bit of an understatement. "It was years and years ago. When the current Emperor was chosen. I was one of the finalists, but I guess not quite good enough."

38

"What happened?" Caius asked.

"Well, there are some allegations of cheating among the other Candidates from my generation. But I think we just had different strengths. I was more of a bookish type, and he was definitely the better athlete. Our final trial was a wrestling match. The future of the Empire came down to who could keep whom pinned on the floor longest; can you believe that?" Marcus was speaking sharply now. "Because *that* is what really qualifies a person, right? Not how well they can lead people, or how intelligent they are.... But how much muscle they had at age 18 when the Senate needed a candidate." He was shaking his head with frustration, even decades later.

"So anyways, I lost. The Senators chose another, who is now our Emperor. It's ancient history. But we had become friends of a sort, and went back to the Palace together, along with the other twenty five survivors of my generation." The word *survivors*, thrown out so casually, rattled around Caius's mind. Marcus hardly even noticed. "He was officially adopted by the Emperor and became his heir, and I went to 'the Henhouse.' It's what we call our little cage." Caius must have looked a bit puzzled. "'We' being the other candidates. The rejects. We are all required to stay in the Palace afterwards. At first, it was so that the brothers to the heir couldn't go out and raise their own army. That would just start the Succession Wars all over. Granted, they would lose the legitimacy that comes with the Senate's recommendation, but still. It was a risk that the Emperor couldn't allow. Better than killing us, I guess."

"Would you really do that, though?" Caius asked, "Go raise an army against the Emperor? It's just not realistic in modern times."

"Is it, though? There was an uprising in Arabia only a few years ago that managed to seize the capital of the province. The military was able to stamp it out pretty quickly, but even

39

today the hills in the southern part of the peninsula are full of dissidents. And does the Emperor not have enemies, both internally and externally? Think about it, Caius. You candidates are born to be persuasive, charismatic leaders. You all receive extensive education, the best military training, and many of you candidates are adept at winning the hearts of enemies and comrades alike. What Emperor would willingly release dozens of potential rivals back out into that sea of sharks?" He gestured out the window at the Chinese countryside whizzing by. "Wouldn't the Ming Emperor love to have someone else with a claim to the Roman throne in his pocket? This applies to you in particular, Caius: you know how restive the Southern provinces of China are. It wouldn't take much to light a fire in this tinderbox. Everyone knows that the East still isn't entirely integrated into Rome's fold, and if anyone could raise China against the West, it would be you." Caius hadn't thought about that factor.

Marcus smiled mirthfully. "But you're right that people don't just raise armies like they used to. The Imperial military is organized and professional and loyal. But it's still a bit of a risk. The Emperor also keeps us around in case some disaster were to happen and the new candidates weren't ready yet. It's only happened three times before, but it is useful for having an uninterrupted lineage. We could just be called in as replacements; the brother that the Emperor never spoke of. Royal privacy has its privileges, I guess. Some people would doubt the story, of course, but it would generally be accepted by the public. The Information Ministry is terrifyingly effective."

He pushed his food to the other side of the plate. "Over the years, the reject candidates became a sort of informal group of advisors, for those questions where the Emperor couldn't really consult with the Senate or his Ministers for political reasons. They are always trying to advance their own careers, but us? We have nowhere to advance to, so thus no ulterior motive. The Emperor often calls upon me, and sends me information about many different decisions he is considering."

"So you get the responsibilities of the Emperor without any of the actual benefits?" Caius asked.

Marcus forced a smile. "In some ways, I suppose that is true. We leftover candidates still get to enjoy a lot of the benefits of the palace, but we live in secret, hidden even from most servants." He let out a heavy sigh, showing his age. "It's not a particularly satisfying life."

"Doesn't sound so bad," Caius remarked offhandedly.

Marcus looked at him with an undecipherable expression. "To you right now, no. Probably not. And I hope that you never have to learn. It's a lonely life. My only friends are my half-brothers, and after twenty six years cooped up with them, I just want to get some fresh air. Is that really so much to ask? Maybe a day at the beach on my own, not thrown under a hood and shadowed by Praetorians? It's like being a servant, except we're not bred to accept that lonely lifestyle, and we're not so drugged up that we think we're happy with it."

"And this is what will happen to me, right?" Caius's hands gripped the edge of the table. "If I lose, that is. I get to live in some little cage in the imperial palace for the rest of my life? Never able to go back out into public?"

Marcus looked down at his tablet and fidgeted. "Hard to hear the last two and a half decades of your life summed up in one sentence like that. 'A little cage in the imperial palace' indeed. Sure, there's some upsides: you get all the same luxuries as the Emperor, and don't have

41

to deal with the constant press and crowds." He stroked his beard and stared off into the distance out the window. "You know, this is the first time I've traveled outside of Italy since the trials? First time I've been able to leave the palace without a hood on my face and a thick layer of makeup to hide my appearance?" He bit his lower lip, still not looking Caius in the eye. "Yes," he answered finally. "That would be your fate. Never to return to your military camp, your business, your apprenticeship, or your family. Forever cut off from the rest of the world and living in a zoo with only one visitor: the Emperor that beat you."

The silence returned. Each of them picked at their food as the train rattled through the desert. The sun beat down off of the wavy sand dunes, but the train's air conditioning kept the cabin perfectly comfortable. A few scraggly shrubs zipped by in a blur of brown. The road next to the train tracks was desolately empty, a black line traced through the desert.

"Then how did you end up as one of the advocates?" Caius asked finally.

"Oh, I volunteered. Oh yes." He rubbed his beard and the jolly smile returned. "So did a number of other surviving candidates, just like me; you'll probably see some of us at the trials. Practically every other prominent citizen of the Empire who knows about the trials also volunteered. To be an advocate for the next Emperor is a great gift, and very prestigious. But to be a *successful* advocate forever earns you the thanks of the most powerful man in the world."

"So, you only volunteered because you expect favors from me in the future?"

Marcus shrugged and pushed his half-eaten plate of food away. A servant scurried by out of nowhere, taking the discarded dish and vanishing before Caius could even figure out where he'd come from. "Well, no," Marcus said after a moment, "that wasn't *really* why. I mean, not the only reason. I've been through this before. I had an advocate myself. And I've watched

everything that the current Emperor has gone through. I helped him out with it behind the scenes.

Now I know how terrifying the process can be, and everything that you might go through. I

thought that I would be able to help you, like a mentor." He took a sip of steaming black tea. "I

won't lie, though. I would hope that, if you did become future emperor, I would be able to play

some role in the administration. To leave the palace. To have my own life. With an assumed

identity, of course."

Caius nodded. Seemed like a fair exchange.

"And how were you assigned to me?" Caius answered.

"Oh, I chose you," Marcus responded as if it were plainly obvious. Caius's eyes widened

slightly, as though he hadn't even considered the possibility of it being random. "The Advocate

always chooses his or her candidate. I've reviewed the files of *every* other applicant. It took

months of reading and watching the highlight tapes of your lives. Every one of the remaining

candidates, down to just thirty from the original thousands, is brilliant and accomplished. But

none of them had that certain something that makes them stand out, except for you. You are the

perfect mix of brilliance, morality, and integrity that the Senators are looking for. I have no

doubts. You *will* be the Emperor." He grinned and gestured back at the binder still sitting on the

edge of the table from the earlier lesson. "If you can learn the names of world leaders, that is."

Caius laughed with him and set down his fork. The plate was cleared before he'd even

finished wiping his mouth. The rest of the food disappeared with a small tinkle of silverware and

a blur of the servant's maroon uniforms, replaced by a basket of snacks and a pitcher of ice water.

Marcus again pulled out his pocket watch, and picked up the little tablet computer. "Shall we get started learning current events? You're well versed on Japan, but we have a lot of other hot spots to cover. Primarily Rome."

CHAPTER 4

Clanging steel echoed through the train car as Caius struggled to hold the heavy sword against the onslaught of his three opponents. Their blades inched closer and closer to his neck, sharpened edges shining under the bright electric lights. Close enough to see the Praetorian Eagle stamped into the base of the sword blade. These were not the dull, wooden practice swords that they'd all used at the Academy.

Caius grunted and pushed them back with a mighty shove, turning their numbers into a disadvantage as they stumbled over each other. He struggled to catch his breath before they could regain their balance. A blade flew wildly through the air at him, narrowly missing his neck. This was no game; a misstep here would kill him just as sure as a mistake on the battlefield. His sword quivered in his hand as he blocked the second lunge. His opponent bared his teeth, eyes emotionless and calculating behind the Praetorian mask. But sweat poured from his brow and Caius could tell he was trying to cover up his gasping breaths. The train car was steaming hot despite the flurry of snowflakes falling on the massive pines outside.

"Good!" Marcus called from the sidelines. "Press the advantage! Drive him back! Fight like your future depends on it, because *it will*. Back when I was a candidate, the physical challenges were tremendously important. If *I* had been a better swordsman, I might be sitting on the throne right now!"

Caius twisted the guard's sword to the side and slid under his defenses, planting a kick squarely in his stomach that was met with a satisfying "oomph." The guard doubled over, and

45

Caius knocked him out of the ring with a shove. It felt so good to stretch his legs after all of those stuffy lessons sitting at Marcus's desk. One more word about the different Imperial corporations and what industries they oversaw and he might explode. Caius turned back to the ring. Two opponents left.

The match continued for another ten minutes. By the time Caius forced the third guard out of the circle, his white practice shirt was drenched in sweat and his hands were numbed from holding the hilt against the furious attacks of his opponents. But he came through it without a scratch.

Marcus clapped him on the back proudly. Over the past week and a half on the train, the two had studied, drilled, and practiced together non-stop.

"Good work, Caius. It's not every man that can take on three Praetorian guards single-handedly. Hopefully it will be sufficient if you have to fight the other candidates as well."

From across the room, one of the guards shot him a slight dirty look, a bit offended at being beaten by just one young soldier. "Your services are no longer needed," Marcus said curtly and shooed them away with the wave of a hand. They nodded silently and began to bundle up their gear. But Caius stopped them and thanked them for the match, shaking their hands and admiring their strategies. They each grinned and returned the compliment, leaving the train car satisfied with the job they had done.

Caius turned back to find that familiar smirk on Marcus's face. The one that he had whenever Caius had passed one of his little unannounced tests.

"You were rude to them on purpose," Caius deduced.

"Aye," Marcus said. "I wanted to see whether you would correct me in front of them, thereby showing disrespect to me, or whether you would stay silent and thus give insult to them." He scratched his greying beard appreciatively. "But you did neither. You simply pretended that I hadn't done anything, and honored them on your own. Curious, but in retrospect, exactly what you should have done." He displayed an affectionate, almost fatherly expression that had grown more and more common this past week. "Maybe this is why I wasn't chosen in my round of Trials," he remarked with a wry laugh.

"Come on, old man. Give me a moment to shower and change, and then let's get some dinner." Caius wiped the sweat from his brow and entered the changing room. The train was fully equipped with every facility necessary to prepare Caius for the trials, including a gym. Marcus took a seat and waited, admiring the thick alpine forest outside being slowly draped in white. Branches and rocks were shrouded in a pale outline of snow. Only the choppy, icy river in the valley below remained visible, like spilled ink across clean paper.

Caius stepped out of the locker room, wearing his normal military uniform. He clapped a hand on Marcus's shoulder and they gazed out at the mountains barely visible through the snow flurries. "We've been through practically every possible climate in the past 10 days, but this one has to be my favorite. Reminds me a bit of the forests of Scotland," Marcus said, gesturing at the blanket of powder over the landscape. "Where I grew up." He had a faraway look in his eyes and a quaver of sadness in his voice.

After a short pause, Marcus hauled himself to his feet and they walked to the dining car together.

"So, realistically," Caius said after the servants brought them heaping plates of food. He sliced into a thick, steaming steak and feigned disinterest. "What are my chances?"

Marcus chewed his salad silently, eyes wandering across the ceiling. "There really isn't any way for me to know," he finally answered. "I have seen the files of the other candidates, but that really can only tell me so much, especially without knowing what tests you all will go through. But know that I would not have picked you if I didn't think you had the best chance out of all of them."

"But we know what the tests are," Caius responded, pointing at the thick binder that Marcus always carried with him. "We've been preparing for the trials the entire trip." He ticked them off on his fingers one by one. "Academic tests, strategy tests, sword fighting..."

"Oh, we know some of them," Marcus interrupted. He took a bite of salad, enjoying making Caius wait. "These are just guidelines, as far as I know. Based on my own experiences and the accounts of others. And based on my assessment of the Senators putting this competition together. We could arrive and find something completely different. Maybe they'll add some extra tests. Or decide they don't need others. Who knows? The point is to make sure that the candidates aren't just trained to look good at these," he tapped the cover of the binder, "but can pass any test that the Tribunal throws at them. It's like going into battle: you can prepare as much as you want, but all those plans can just go out the window at a moment's notice."

Caius nodded understandingly; he'd been in a number of those situations while he was stationed in Japan. Half a world away from where they were now, he remembered. And it seemed like forever ago.

"Well, are there any tests that I haven't been through yet? Anything else I can do to prepare?"

Marcus flipped open the binder and ran a pudgy wrinkled finger down the table of contents, lips moving as he read along. "Well, I'd like to brush up on economics with you a bit, but no: we have gone over everything at least once. And good thing, too." He gestured out the window at the mountains, "We're right in the middle of Europe. There isn't too much further to go until we hit one ocean or another. So we have to be arriving soon."

They went back to eating their meal, watching the front of the train slide around the steep curves of the mountainside like a silvery snake, dipping in and out of tunnels and sprinting across high bridges. Marcus quizzed Caius again, going over everything that they had done over the past ten days on the train. Caius didn't miss a single question. Marcus signaled to a servant to bring out the dessert; a reward for a job well done. Just as the thick pastry was being sliced, a chime rang out through the train. "Arriving at destination," the automated driver announced in a pleasant, calm tone. "Prepare to disembark."

Marcus and Caius locked eyes momentarily; Marcus seemed the more nervous of the two. "Quick, into your formal uniform," he said with a note of panic. The cake lay forgotten on the table. Caius briefly noticed the servants lurking in the shadows, ready to pick up the remains. Marcus looked Caius up and down one last time. "Good thing you just showered. Maybe comb your hair again."

"Relax, Marcus. You're not the one being judged here." He ran a hand over his hair; it was fine. They hurried out of the dining car and back into the sleeping car where Caius had left his formal uniform, freshly polished and gleaming under the light of the soft lamps. He hoisted it up and began strapping it on over the clean white robes as the train began to slow. Through the windows, he could see lights shining from a small village, roofs buried under a fresh white blanket of snow; only the slender bell tower from the local church managed to poke through it. Behind the village, the granite valley walls loomed in the darkness like enormous stone waves preparing to crash down.

The station lights, dull orange globes through the thick of the snow, became visible just as Caius was finishing strapping on his gilded helmet. "Correphius," was emblazoned on a red sign next to the station. *Never heard of it*, Caius thought. And for good reason; there only looked to be thirty or so buildings in the whole village. For some reason, Caius had expected the trials to take place in a grand city, not some middle-of-nowhere hamlet tucked away in a mountain canyon. Maybe in a giant arena like the ancient gladiators used to do. The train pulled to a stop, and the series of red blurs became recognizable: more Praetorian guards rushing out of the station house to greet the train. One took up his post right under Caius's window. Marcus knocked gently on the rich wooden door, adjusting his own robes and donning a heavy jacket. Caius's boots squeaked against the wooden floors as he strutted through the train halls to the exit; there was something about wearing his formal armor that made him feel invincible.

Caius stepped out into the swirling snow, followed shortly by Marcus. The soldiers lining the walkway snapped their boots together and saluted until Caius entered the train station door. Inside, nothing. A polished wooden floor, an empty counter, and a turned-off ticket vending machine. The only thing out of place was one lone man waiting on a plain wooden bench. His bald head shone under the bright lights of the station, and his friendly brown eyes lit up as they entered the room. His rich purple robes, emblazoned with the golden image of a scroll, the symbol of the Senate, billowed as he stood to meet the pair.

"Marcus! So good to see you again," he called out. "I trust the trip was uneventful?"

"Oh, yes." Marcus replied. "Plenty of time to relax and catch up on my reading." The two shook hands formally, then embraced in a friendly hug.

The man in the Senate robes grinned; he clearly knew that Caius had been intensely training. One of those secrets that everyone seems to know about, Caius deduced.

"Caius," Marcus said, putting a hand around Caius's shoulders and thrusting him forward. "This is Quintus Aorius, the Senatorial Sergeant at Arms. He is responsible for arranging the trials…"

"And thus one of the few people who knows of the existence of the previous round of candidates," Quintus butted in with a friendly elbow to the ribs for Marcus, who just laughed.

"Pleasure to meet you, sir." Caius responded with a formal bow, then extended his hand for a shake.

"Oh, no need to try and impress me," Quintus laughed as he pumped Caius's hand. "I'm not one of the judges, and the Trials haven't officially started. But it is a pleasure to meet you at last, Caius. I have watched your progress with great interest over the past few years as we began to narrow the pool." Caius wasn't quite sure how to respond, so he stayed silent. "I trust that Marcus has explained everything to you and what you're here for…"

"Yes, sir," he responded formally, still standing at attention. Marcus had repeatedly warned him to always be on his guard and no matter what, assume that anything unexpected is another test. Out of the corner of his eyes, he noted a slight smirk on Marcus's face, proud that Caius was remembering his training. As they spoke, the train station was washed in light from an approaching truck; it pulled up next to the station and parked with its engine idling. Two more rumbled in behind it. Caius waited on the train platform wishing he could have a peak under the hood to find out why they were so loud. Probably not very well designed; Caius could do better. He'd been building airplane engines for almost a decade now; cars weren't *that* different.

"Our chariot has arrived," Quintus said with a smile. Servants dragged a number of bags off of the train and hustled through the snow, seemingly unaware of everyone else at the station. Marcus supervised them load the luggage into the truck with great care; he was quite particular about his belongings. They all climbed into the cab: Caius in the front, Marcus and Quintus in the back. The driver turned and nodded to Caius, making sure that all of the passengers were buckled in tightly. "It's going to be bumpy," he warned them in the gravelly voice of a heavy smoker. Tobacco use was a growing fad throughout the Empire, a part of the obsession with all things from the New World after its discovery. Caius and his friends had all smoked at the Academy, but it became too expensive of a habit once he was kicked onto the streets.

The truck left the station and passed through the remainder of the small town in the blink of an eye. Fields and pastures were blanketed in white; only the occasional tree popped through.

Flakes continued to fall, plastering the truck's windshield. With a rattle, the convoy passed over an ancient stone bridge spanning a narrow canyon; Caius briefly caught a glimpse of the slate-gray water below as it rushed between rocks and the massive column supporting the bridge arches.

In the seats behind him, Marcus was shivering and rubbing his shoulders dramatically, asking the driver to turn up the heat. The soldier didn't respond, but tweaked the dial just slightly. Marcus glared at him through the head rest. "You always were so sensitive," Quintus laughed, rolling down the window just enough to cover Marcus's bushy mane in snowflakes. Caius smiled, happy to see his mentor have some good company who didn't need every single imperial secret explained. Marcus's life seemed so lonely that it was a relief to know that he at least had one friend.

The truck entered a nondescript tunnel entrance surrounded by trees and carved straight through the side of the mountain. If it didn't have a road leading straight up to it, nobody would ever have even noticed it. The truck twisted and turned up the dark, rough-hewn road into the bowels of the mountain. The motor whined as the incline grew progressively steeper. If he had wanted to, Caius could have rolled down the window and placed a hand on the rock wall of the narrow tunnel. He unconsciously gripped the armrest tight, and Marcus began to complain of being car-sick; in response, Caius thought that he heard the driver speed up just a tiny bit more just for laughs. The tunnel had no lights or markings, and it was only the driver's skill and knowledge of the route that prevented them from driving straight into a wall around every corner.

After an eternity the truck emerged back into the snowy night, on a narrow road about a third of a way up the cliff face. The valley below seemed awash with moonlight in contrast to the tunnel, and Caius had to blink a few times to adjust. He could just barely see the twinkling lamps of the village below, and a plume of steam and a flash of silver at the end of the valley was all that remained of their train. Caius felt a strange pang in his heart upon seeing it vanish down the tracks: although he had only been aboard for 10 days, that train felt more like home than anywhere he'd lived since he had to leave his parents'. He twisted around and looked back at Marcus, turning green in the backseat, and gave him a reassuring smile.

"We've arrived," the driver announced after a few minutes. The truck slowed to a stop on a small outcropping of rough rock high above the village. Buried behind a thicket of pine trees and was an enormous, gaping doorway carved straight into the side of the mountain. Caius had to lean forward to see the top of the doors through the windshield; they must have been at least fifteen meters high, and probably eight meters wide. The doors themselves were simple and unadorned, but the granite slabs on other side had been carved to form two ancient Legionnaires standing at attention. The arch at the entrance was supported by a thick capstone that seemed almost the size of this truck, carved with the Senate's ancient initialism: SPQR. But it was so weathered and faded that it was hardly recognizable. Or maybe that was just the driving snow.

Caius stepped out of the truck to get a better view. The wind howled around his shoulders and bit into his neck, and ice began to accumulate on the brittle, cold metal of his armor. The doors were ominous and dark, etched with the scene of some battle from days before even guns were invented. Caius trudged forward through the snow, each step yielding a slight crunch, and placed one gloved hand on the thick band connecting the door to some internal hinge. The aged

54

bronze was coated in a thin layer of ice that crept into the shallow lines of the image. He recognized the battle scene now, showing the Second Uprising in which the Senate took back control from the Emperor. It made sense; that was the war in which the Senate had won the right to approve the Emperor's heir. The Senators would want to memorialize that forever. Caius traced a finger over the delicate detail of a soldier's crested helmet, marveling at the intricacy of the work. It must have taken a lifetime for a metalworker to create.

Marcus and Quintus climbed out of the truck behind him, wrapping themselves in their thick fur coats. Marcus was also eyeing the door, eyes squinting and jaw set. It was an expression Caius had never seen from his advocate. Apprehension? Maybe anger? Then it vanished just as quickly.

"Impressive, isn't it?" Marcus said, practically shouting over the wind coming down the mountain. Caius had no response; he just craned his neck upward. Marcus laid a hand on his shoulder. "I know the feeling. I probably had that same look on my face when they first brought me in for my trials."

"So they brought you here as well?"

"Oh yes," Marcus laughed. "The Senate certainly loves its traditions. For them, anything that can remain the same *should* remain the same. Although I didn't have the luxury of a truck. We had to climb up that damn road with our belongings strapped to our back."

55

Quintus laughed, overhearing the conversation as he too approached the door. "We only sent the trucks because of the storm. You got lucky that Senator Oventia was feeling generous and didn't make you walk up anyway. Or perhaps she was just in a hurry."

Quintus raised his sword in a fist and pounded on the thick metal door with the hilt; the *booms* echoed through the vibrating metal. No one said a word, and even the wind quieted down waiting for a response. Only the snow continued as normal, drifting through the air like tiny feathers.

With a deep groan and the cringe-inducing sound of scraping metal, the double doors swung open wide and a blast of light bathed over them. It didn't come from a normal electric lamp, but an old fashioned fire-lit lantern bigger than a bathtub. Flames flickered wildly in the wind, casting erratic shadows of the tall figure of a man standing in the doorway. "You must be the last candidate," he said over the wind to Caius without a hint of doubt. "We have been waiting for your arrival." He raised a handheld lantern to Caius's face and studied him intensely. Caius straightened up and saluted crisply, immune to the snow and cold. "Well, come in! Come in!" the man said. "Damn is it freezing out here! It wouldn't do for one of our candidates to catch pneumonia just as the Trials begin!" He ushered the three of them inside.

A line of servants carrying bags slipped in the door behind them and hurried silently down the hallway. Marcus heard the engines of the truck rev and it pulled away, headed back down the mountain toward civilization. The motors of the door whirred and they slammed back into place. The man sealed the doors' lock with an echoing clang, and the whistling of the wind halted immediately. The interior of the mountain was completely quiet. Caius had never heard such silence.

Inside, a long stone corridor stretched into the belly of the mountain. More enormous lanterns hung low, lighting the hallways. The chains supporting the lanterns soared up to a ceiling above so high that Caius just had to assume it was there; the light didn't reach that far. Just at the edge of the shadows, Caius could see finely-wrought steel beams that seemed to grow directly out of the stone and soar upwards into the darkness. The bare stone walls were entirely undecorated, but a thick carpet lined the center of the hallway, intricately patterned and detailed. Upon closer inspection, Caius realized that the pattern was actually a list of names wrapped around each other in swirls. "All former candidates," the man with the lantern said, noticing Caius studying it. The hallway stretched far ahead, full of centuries of names of those who had failed.

Quintus cleared his throat, bringing Caius's attention back to his companions. *Damn it,* Caius chided himself. *What if this man is one of the judges, and here I am staring at the furnishings?* He ground his molars together and resolved to be more attentive.

"Marcus, Caius: this is Antoninus Ethiopius," Quintus continued, gesturing at the tall man carrying the lamp. In the light, Caius could clearly tell that he was not from around here. He was tall, at least 2 meters, with skin dark like fresh coffee, and hair black with tight, thick curls. He bowed to Caius and extended a muscular hand. "Pleased to meet you." Caius bowed back and shook his hand.

"Antoninus is the caretaker of this facility," Quintus explained. "He makes sure that everything here is stocked with supplies and that we have all of the tools necessary for the trials."

Marcus shivered, even though the hallway itself was nice and warm. "God, I would go crazy up here. A few weeks was enough to last me a lifetime."

Antoninus replied with a serene smile: "It's quite peaceful, once you get used to it." He had a distinctive deep, booming voice that seemed to warm the hallway.

"I'm sure it's nice when it's above freezing," Marcus retorted. They finally reached the end of the hallway, which opened up into a grand, enormous round room, bigger even than the outdoor amphitheater in Fukuoka. The scale of this facility was simply amazing, even more so because it was carved through solid rock. It must have taken decades to complete! Natural columns, sculpted from the rock itself to be even and smooth, were laced with miniscule veins of gold and silver. They formed an inner circle and supported 3 floors of delicate balconies that protruded with carefully sculpted granite balustrades. High above, the ceiling curved upward into a sweeping, steep dome taller than any cathedral. At the very peak, a glass skylight was covered in a dusting of snow. Antoninus raised his muscular arms and gestured around the room. "Welcome to the Trials facility, Caius." His rich voice bounced around the chamber. Caius could only stare in awe.

Antoninus waited patiently, having been through this thirty times in the past week. The main chamber was certainly an incredible sight for one who had never seen it before. Marcus, on the other hand, looked ready to vomit seeing this place again.

58

"Follow me," Antoninus gestured with a wave to the left. Caius noticed that the circular main hall was lined with entrances to different tunnels that spread out like an anthill. *This place must be enormous!* "The Candidate bunks are through this door." Caius followed obediently, eager to see the rest of the building.

"I'm afraid that this is where we part ways, Caius. I've got to get to my own room near the other Advocates." Marcus extended a hand. They shook for a moment, before Marcus broke down grinning and grabbed Caius in a tight hug. "Good luck, boy. Stay alert. I'll see you early tomorrow," he whispered. With that, he walked into the shadows and disappeared down a different side hallway, followed by a train of baggage-laden servants. Caius and Antoninus were left standing in silence under the massive dome.

"This way," Antoninus said. He waved a hand at the narrow corridor branching off of the main room, and strutted off quickly. Above the entrance, an engraved sign read "HALL OF CANDIDATES."

The hallway was low and narrow, in contrast to the large open chamber. Rough wooden doors were spaced along the corridor every 20 meters or so. The walls were lined with marble busts, starkly white against the grey stone background and generally indistinguishable from each other unless one looked really closely at the exact shape of the noses. The display was interrupted every once and a while by the odd flickering torch that lit the hallway. Despite the chilling storm outside and the thick stone, it was surprisingly warm inside. "This is the Candidate wing of the facility," Antoninus explained with an open-palmed wave at the heads on pedestals, exactly like the many tour guides that Caius had seen around the Japanese Liberation Memorial in Fukuoka. Except Antoninus wasn't carrying a bright umbrella and waving it about. "The halls are lined with the statues of the many young men who have passed through the trials in this facility here and gone on to become Emperor." Peering closely at the labels, Caius did indeed recognize many of the names that he'd had to memorize in elementary school.

"This facility was built centuries ago," Antoninus continued. "Not all at once, of course. It started as a small cave in the mountains where a few Senators could meet in peace away from the politics and pressures of Rome. Isolated, private, and secure. The process of choosing the future emperor cannot be tainted by outside influences." Caius wondered how deep inside they were now. Secure, indeed. He rubbed a hand over the perfectly flat grey stone, wondering how many men had spent their entire lives smoothing out every single rough bit in this long hallway that only a handful of people would ever see. "Over the years, we expanded our facilities to accommodate the growing number of candidates, the increasing variety of tests, and of course, to expand the available comforts for candidates, advocates, Senators," he paused and gestured at himself with a smile "and for the support staff, of course."

Antoninus stopped and spun with a swirl of purple and gold. He gestured to the right and produced a key from one of the pockets inside his robes like a magician performing sleight of hand, inserted it into the lock, then swung the heavy door open with a creak. "Your room," Antoninus explained, and strolled inside. He tapped the small modern touchpad near the doorway, and the lights flicked on silently. "We do allow *some* modern comforts," Antoninus explained. The room was small, but richly decorated with handmade furnishings. On the wall hung a beautiful oil painting depicting a group of Chinese soldiers surrendering, with the Battle of Beijing in the background. Caius briefly wondered if whoever hung it here knew that *he* would be the one in the room. Was this supposed to be some type of intimidation, maybe?

"A servant will be by to wake you in the morning," Antoninus said. "I'm afraid that we don't allow any handheld electronic devices during the trials for secrecy purposes, even just to use as an alarm. No outside help allowed." He rapped a fist against the rock wall. "Not that it would matter, with this blocking any signal that you'd get."

"I don't have one," Caius responded. "I wasn't allowed to bring my belongings from the base."

Antoninus nodded. "None of the candidates are allowed to, but you'd be surprised at the number that try. We will see you tomorrow for the invocation, then." The door shut slowly, and Caius was alone with his thoughts. Opening the cupboard, he found a clean set of nightclothes, just his size. He changed and climbed into the bed. Exhaustion from the day's training, travel, and general excitement hit Caius like a brick wall, and he immediately slipped into a deep restful sleep.

CHAPTER 5

The creak of the door pulled Caius out of his sleep; Marcus flipped on the lights, flooding the room with brightness. Caius cringed and squeezed his eyes shut.

"Time for breakfast, Caius! Most important meal of the day!" Marcus was in a surprisingly good mood for so early in the morning. Caius rubbed the sleep out of his eyes and sat up. The wall clock read 7:21, but it seemed like the night had passed instantly.

"I brought you a gift," Marcus beamed, holding a brand new set of elegant formal robes. "I spoke to the tailors as soon as we got in last night and had him alter something. They worked through the night to have it ready." He held them out at arm's length, admiring the work. "These are the Emperor's favorite colors, you know." The robes were a rich cream color, with scarlet trim.

Caius rose and dressed. It did fit perfectly, but he still missed his familiar military uniform a bit. "Come, come!" Marcus enthused, practically pulling him out the door like an eager child. The hallway was much busier than it had been last night. Men and women walked to and fro with purpose wearing formal robes of their own. Many of them nodded to Marcus, but hardly even acknowledged Caius's existence. They each seemed to be heading to different rooms along the hall. *Other advocates,* Caius realized.

"You rest well, my boy?" Marcus asked, not bothering to slow down a bit. "Big day, you know. Big, big day."

"Slept fine," Caius muttered, still not entirely awake. He needed some coffee.

They reached the huge domed center room. Groups of people bustled back and forth between the hallways; the place was a hive of activity. Caius briefly wondered who all these people were; it didn't take *this* many people just to take care of a small group of candidates.

"Lots of spectators here," Marcus remarked, reading Caius's thoughts. He waved a finger at all the balconies, already full of observers looking down. "Sometimes, members of the Court are invited up by the Emperor, or by influential Senators, or anyone else with enough clout. They want to get the inside scoop on who the new Emperor will be, and see what he'll be like. Bunch of vultures…"

Together, they hurried out of the main chamber and through a broad set of doors. Inside, another cavernous chamber full of tables and chairs. Along the side, a set of counters held enormous platters of food from all over the Empire, as well as some exotic imports from the New World nations; tantalizing smells of roasting meats and something sweet filled the room. Caius's stomach grumbled like an earthquake; Marcus even turned around in surprise. "Let's eat, then!" he replied cheerfully.

They moved to the counters and grabbed plates, heaping them full of eggs, meats, bread, and fruit. Caius took a bit of everything. Probably too much, but his eyes and his stomach were working together and didn't know when to stop. An army of servants rushed back and forth, constantly refilling the platters of food with steaming portions. Caius could barely take his eyes off the meal as Marcus led the way to a table near the back.

"So, on the agenda for today," Marcus whispered as Caius tucked into his food, "You'll probably start off with a pretty comprehensive physical. Making sure that you'll be fit for the trials, making sure that you have no latent illnesses that would make you unfit for Emperor, etc." Caius could only nod, because his mouth was stuffed with papaya; he had never even seen one before this. Marcus looked around to make sure no one else around them was listening in. Caius followed his gaze, getting his first look at some of the other candidates. Or, at least, he assumed they were. Without exception, the women were beautiful and fit, and the men were all tall and muscular and handsome. Caius was suddenly conscious of his own height; somewhat tall by Asian standards, but a dwarf compared to some of these guys. One of them, with arms like tree branches and onyx-skinned (presumably from the African provinces), had to stoop slightly to even get through the rock doorway. But Caius was pretty confident in his physical abilities. He'd beaten the strongest men in his platoon at wrestling and sword fighting; how much harder could these guys be?

Another couple approached them. This Advocate walked with a cane and a noticeable limp. She had wispy grey hair and olive skin now wrinkled and weathered, but her eyes were bright and intelligent. Behind her, a rumbling mountain of pale skin: Tall, blond, blue-eyed, and clean shaven. Definitely from one of the more northern provinces, up in Scandinavia. Caius eyed them with a hint of suspicion, not certain why they'd be approaching him and Marcus when there were so many other empty seats around the room. But Marcus heard the gentle tap of the cane and turned with a slice of bacon still dangling from his mouth.

"Flavia!" he said heartily, throwing the bacon back to the plate and springing up in greeting. Marcus embraced the woman heartily, lifting her off of her frail feet. Luckily the

64

Candidate behind Flavia was already carrying both plates. Caius stood from the table, waiting for an introduction and not sure of what to do with his hands; the Nord candidate had pretty much the same expression, but luckily had the plates to hold. Marcus set the woman back down and engaged her in conversation.

"Where are my manners?" Marcus remembered. "This is my candidate, Caius Serica. Freshly arrived off the train just last night from Japan." Marcus gestured, and Caius gave an awkward nod, not sure what to do. "And this," he continued, "is Flavia Tuccius. She was *my* advocate, back when I was a candidate. Taught me everything I knew!"

Flavia reached out a hand; she was missing her pinky. Caius shook her hand back gently, not wanting to hurt her, but the old woman's grip was like iron and she pumped enthusiastically. "Pleased to meet you, boy! And this," she gestured behind her, "is Herennius Pacullan."

Herennius put down their plates and reached out a giant hand in greeting; his palm made Caius's hand look like a child's. His fingers were tough and calloused; *he must be an expert swordsman*, Caius thought to himself. "Pleasure!" the tall Nord said with a toothy smile. Caius did his best to not stare at the gap between his two front teeth. "How was your train ride here? From Japan? I've never been east of Constantinople, but I'd really love to someday." He wanted to know Caius's life story before they even sat down. Herennius just gushed energy and enthusiasm, and the mood was infectious.

Marcus gestured at the table and they all sat down together as Flavia and Marcus immediately launched into a conversation, catching up. Caius had to wait until Herennius took a big bite of food before he could ask a question. "What about you? Where are you from?"

65

"From Norway," he responded in between wolfing down cream cakes in single bites. "From a town just off the North Sea. You have probably never heard of it," he said with a wry smile. "Unless you eat a *lot* of fish." It seems like the Senate prefers to place candidates in small town families, except for Caius. "Probably not," Caius laughed, "I'd never even been to Europe before all of this."

"So weird to think of," Herennius responded. "That so many people in the Empire have never been to Europe. I mean, there are so many people here that it's almost inconceivable, yet there are what, almost a billion over in the East? You're from China, right?" Caius was conscious for the first time that none of the other candidates he had seen were Asian, but Herennius didn't seem to care one way or the other. "What part are you from?"

Caius told him all about Nanjing, growing up on the very outskirts of the Empire. Herennius was incredibly curious about Chinese culture and languages, and rattled off a long list of questions. Caius was happy to talk about his homeland. The conversation progressed to discussing their respective military experience; Herennius had studied the war in Japan extensively, and was quite interested in Caius's account of meeting with General Kaneshiro. The fate of Japan was apparently a hot topic of discussion around the Empire. Herennius was strongly of the opinion that the Emperor should just conquer the rest of the island chain in a pre-emptive attack. "Everyone knows another war is coming," the tall Nord opined. "Might as well get it over with while we've got the upper hand."

Herennius had been stationed across the world at the trading post of New Iberia, protecting the merchants and diplomats that had dealings with the tribes there. He had all sorts of stories about traveling across the New World prairies, meeting with tribal leaders. Herennius was particularly impressed by a group of tribes in the north who had formed a democratic government, and the parallels with Rome's own Senate. He was rambling on about his stay with them when Caius noticed Marcus, who had formerly been deep in conversation with Flavia and exuberantly waving his hands telling some story, fall silent mid-sentence. His jaw hung slightly agape and flecks of toast speckled his bushy beard. His eyes were fixed on another Advocate/Candidate couple who had just entered the room. Glancing around, Caius noticed that Marcus was not the only one who was surprised by their appearance.

Caius leaned forward over his empty plate; "Who is that?" he whispered.

Marcus didn't really respond; just gave a shocked "Ummm..." The pair nonchalantly sauntered to the food table and began heaping their plates like everyone else. They at least acted like they didn't know that everyone was staring.

Marcus managed to snap out of it and turned back to Caius, trying to hide his confusion. "His name is Andericus. He's another Candidate from my generation." His tone barely managed to mask his disdain as he scraped the crumbs away. Clearly there was some discord in their private wing of the Imperial Palace.

"So, why is everyone so shocked to see him?"

"He is... controversial in some circles," Flavia answered softly. Marcus nodded to her in thanks and agreement, clearly having trouble coming up with a nice way to say it.

There was a moment of silence around the table; the other groups around the hall buzzed, probably having the same conversation.

"Well, *why?*" Herennius asked impatiently, and probably a bit too loud. But he didn't seem to notice or care.

Marcus and Flavia looked at each other gravely, then turned back to the two candidates. Marcus leaned forward; Caius and Herennius met him in the middle. "The Emperor never reveals which former Candidate is next in line for the throne in case of death, because obviously that would give that person reason to plot against him. But of course there are always suspicions. The rumor mill in Rome works over time. In council, the Emperor always used to favor the choice that Andericus proposed. And in matters of state, that choice is most always war. In fact," Marcus said with a slight nod to Caius, "he's the reason that the simmering conflict in Japan has been getting more active. Why you'd begun to have those missions behind enemy lines instead of just playing defense."

"Always rash, that one," agreed Flavia.

"Anyway," Marcus continued. "The predominant theory around the Palace had been that Andericus would take the seat should anything ever happen, at least up until the new Candidate is ready."

"So, you guys are just political rivals?" said Herennius bluntly. Caius nodded in agreement, still unclear over what the big deal is; Marcus didn't seem like the type to get shaken up over a little jealousy.

"Rivals?" Marcus snorted, insulted. "Please. He just managed to convince the Emperor with his honeyed tongue, and I wasn't willing to stoop to his level, so maybe the Emperor didn't listen to me as often. But a little over a year ago, there was a large string of arrests. Prominent citizens, military leaders, and even a few Senators. They were accused and convicted of conspiring to overthrow the Emperor. It was well hidden, of course. Generals were supposedly fired for not adequately conducting the war against the Ming; the Senators resigned for health reasons or spending time with family or some such excuse... then they just slipped away into obscurity, never to be heard from again. Some died shortly after, though the cause wasn't really published."

"So, Andericus was arrested too?"

"No, no. He's too clever for that," Marcus continued, glancing in their direction as they searched for an open table with relatively few neighbors. "There was nothing really tying him to the plot. Just whispers and rumors, and the general assumption that he stood to benefit the most. Afterwards, the Emperor started ignoring Andericus's advice, and he was effectively sidelined. Even stopped coming to our meetings. Shortly after, we were all called to begin reviewing candidates for the heir selection and making our choices." Marcus and Flavia looked at each other significantly. "I guess we all just assumed that, with the accusations against him hanging over his head, he would be asked not to participate. What sane person would trust the selection of the next Emperor to a *traitor*?" He spat out the last word and glared in Andericus' general direction. Caius turned discreetly for a better look. The family resemblance was definitely apparent; he had the same prominent nose that Marcus had. His hair remained black, possibly dyed, and a shade darker skin. Caius tried to guess where he had been born: Spain, maybe? He

69

didn't have the paunchy belly that Marcus had gotten, though. He was in good shape, strong and fit.

Caius's gaze shifted to the Candidate sitting across from Andericus. She looked like she could have been her advocate's daughter: tall and slender, with tanned skin and dark hair tied tightly behind her in a ponytail. Her white teeth and wide smile glistened across the room as she listened intently to something Andericus was saying.

Caius turned back to the table. "You know anything about his Candidate?"

Marcus looked up again and studied the young lady across from Andericus. "Oh yes," he responded. "I remember this one's file. Her name is Althea... Postumius, I want to say? Hard to remember so many names when you're going through all the candidates. I thought about taking her on myself..." Caius looked at him, a bit wounded, "Before I saw the sample video file of her berating one of her superior officers while she was deployed. A lack of respect is a huge deal breaker for the Senate." Flavia nodded in agreement. "Oh yes," she said "that one is a gamble. Excellent schoolwork, good work at her apprenticeship, and a good military career as a sniper. On paper, seems like she would be a fine choice. But the Senators will sniff out her personality in an instant."

Marcus nodded in agreement. "I was wondering why her file got snapped up before I'd even finished taking a first look at the candidates. Not surprising that Andericus picked her, though. If he can train the girl enough to fool the tribunal, they've got a real shot. And of all the advocates, he's the one who needs an Emperor in his pocket the most right now," Marcus continued. "I'm almost certain that the Emperor has him watched from now on, looking for any sign of sedition."

The table fell silent again as Herennius and Caius absorbed that information, still not entirely sure what the Senators would be looking for in some of these tests. Were the other candidates around the room weighing Caius's odds too? Discussing what strategies he would need to win? Analyzing all of his weaknesses and flaws? They went back to scraping their plates and pushing around the leftovers, but the conversation had died out.

A trumpet echoed through the dining hall, interrupting the tinkling of silverware and the buzz of conversation. From the door, Quintus Aorius stood wearing full formal armor and holding a trumpet, looking like a warrior from Ancient Rome instead of the casual joker who'd picked them up from the train station last night. Behind him, two standard bearers filled the doorway with ceremonial flags: one banner, the eagle crest of the Emperor, red and gold on black. The other, the golden scroll of the Senate on vibrant purple, stamped with the letters "SPQR." Quintus blew the trumpet again, the dining room was dead silent.

He removed an actual paper scroll wrapped in purple and gold ribbon from his belt and opened it up. "The Candidates for Office of the Emperor of Rome are hereby called to order in the main audience chamber by the Senate Tribunal. By order of the Senate, any Citizen of royal blood who has been deemed worthy of the title shall present himself for the Trials. A recommendation for the full Senate chamber shall be rendered by the three Judges at the completion of the Senate Tribunal's course of tests." With a click of his boots and a gentle clang of armor, he stomped back out of the room, leaving the dining hall in silence. A wave of realization hit Caius: this was really happening. From the look on Herennius's face, he was getting that same mix of nervous excitement in the pit of his stomach as well. Whispers erupted from every corner and chairs around the room scraped in unison. The candidates marched back into the grand domed chamber at the entrance, where a stage had been erected. Rows of simple wooden benches had been set up in front of the stage for the Candidates.

Quintus moved to the podium, having disposed of his trumpet in the past minute but still in gleaming golden armor. He watched patiently as the candidates slowly filtered into the room, hesitating as each of them waited for the others to sit. Caius strode confidently to the front bench and sat, eyes forward. Herennius came and sat next to him, probably blocking the view of anyone but the tallest candidates behind him. Caius heard the shuffle of footsteps and the scraping of benches as others followed his lead; Marcus gave him an almost invisible nod and a smile from the shadows. Above, the privileged spectators leaned over the railing, pointing out the candidates and quietly talking amongst themselves. Quintus cleared his throat, and the room fell silent again, even the chattering spectators. He didn't need a trumpet this time.

Praetorian guards swung open the doors hiding an opening to the right of the stage, marked "SENATE HALL." From inside, three robed figures walked slowly from the hallway and up to the stage. Each wore the deep purple uniform of the Senate, and the high gold collar which marked their high rank. One struggled along on an intricately carved cane, and the others stepped slowly to keep pace. They mounted the stage and took seats on the three large chairs on the stage. The soldiers around the room snapped to attention and saluted, not daring to lower their arms until the robed figures shuffled onto the stage

72

Quintus waited until the judges sat, then looked down at his notecards on the podium. From his front row seat, Caius could see his hands quivering. One of the guards brought a copy of Lex Romani, the compiled judicial code of the Empire. Quintus placed his hand reverently on the cover.

"I, Quintus Aorius, Senate Sergeant At Arms, certify that this session of trials for the candidacy of the Emperor has been arranged to the best of my abilities without interference or corruption from any outside forces. Under penalty of death, I swear to uphold my duty to Rome and the Emperor in safeguarding this most critical function of the Senate. I will protect and serve the Tribunal and its candidates until I draw my last breath." He took his hand from the book of laws and saluted first to the red Imperial standard, then to the purple Senate flag. "I will now administer the Sacramentum to the three members of the Tribunal."

He turned to the Senators. The first, a fairly young woman with piercing, pale blue eyes, copper skin, and straight black hair, stood first and walked to the podium with a confident, almost royal bearing. She was elegant and beautiful. Caius had always thought of the Senators as a bunch of old prunes. There was an almost silent murmur from the spectators above, but none of the candidates made a sound.

"Senator Oventia," Quintus began, offering her the book of laws, "Do you swear a holy vow to uphold the duties of your office with wisdom and integrity? Do you pledge to make an impartial choice, free from corruption and outside influence?"

The Senator looked Quintus in the eyes, placed her hand on the book, and said "Yes, I do," in a thick Persian accent. Her dark eyes surveyed the crowd, flashing with excitement. She smiled and waved at the crowd, then turned back to her seat.

Quintus turned to the second seat, where a tanned, middle aged man waited with a patient smile. His head was noticeably balding, but he made no effort to cover it up or shave off the rest like most men his age. However, his beard, sideburns, and mustache were thick, curly, and brown. Caius had a vague notion that this had been fashionable a few decades ago. The Senator rose with a smile and gave a slight familiar nod as Quintus approached. The Senator was shorter than most of the men in the room; Caius felt a bit more comfortable.

"Senator Tullius," Quintus repeated, holding out the book, "Do you swear a holy vow to uphold the duties of your office with wisdom and integrity? Do you pledge to make an impartial choice, free from corruption and outside influence?"

"Yes, I do," Tullius answered. He was articulate and clear, without any hint of a regional dialect.

Quintus moved on to the third chair, where the older senator struggled to his feet, cane scraping inaudibly on the stage trying to find footing. Quintus stepped forward and offered him a hand up but the old man waved him away and stood on his own.

"Senator Vitellius," Quintus said after making sure the Senator was stable, "Do you swear a holy vow to uphold the duties of your office with wisdom and integrity? Do you pledge to make an impartial choice, free from corruption and outside influence?" The Senator reached a quivering hand toward the book of laws and placed it on the cover with just his fingertips.

"Yes, I do." Vitellius responded.

Quintus strode across the stage quickly, back to the podium. "Candidates, I present your tribunal of judges." The candidates and advocates clapped heartily, seemingly trying to upstage each other. Caius was reminded yet again that despite the trappings of formality, this was all part of the contest. Every little bit mattered. "And now, Senator Vitellius would like to share some words of encouragement with you on this most auspicious of occasions."

Quintus slipped silently off the stage as the crowd's attention turned to the Senator. He shambled over to the podium with the hem of his deep purple robes dragging on the ground. A praetorian hastily bounded up the stairs with a small stool and placed it in front of the podium so that Vitellius would be able to see the assembled Candidates. He managed to climb onto the stool with some assistance, appearing feebler with each step. He looked out over the crowd, pressing his glasses against his weathered nose. But when he spoke, it was like hearing a whip crack: he was smart, passionate, and incisive.

"This is the first day of the rest of your lives," he started, pointing at the rows of candidates. "Everything you knew before, everything you've learned, everything you've done… was simply working to get into this room. From here, one of you will become the Emperor. You will be tried and tested more than you ever thought possible: your strength, your intelligence, and your character. But in the end, each of you will play your part in the service of Rome, and the greatest among you will lead us for decades to come. Since the days of Caius the Rebuilder, the

Empire has survived because of the strength of its leadership. And the Senate's ability to approve the Emperor's heir has been a tradition almost for almost a thousand years. I, and my fellow senators," he gestured back at the two seated nearby, "undertake this role with the utmost gravity. Our predecessors were willing to fight a bloody revolution to win this power from the Emperor, and we don't intended to squander their sacrifice." Caius had always been a bit of a history buff and particularly enjoyed reading about the Second Uprising and the Senate's role in its resolution, but never thought about what it really meant until this moment.

"It is my great privilege and honor," Senator Vitellius continued as a guard handed him a scroll and a heavy golden stamp and another scroll made from real paper, "to initiate these proceedings. I now declare the three hundred and third trials for the candidacy of the Emperor open!" He thumped the gold handle down on the podium and looked back at the cheering crowd.

Through the applause, Caius heard a chair squeak; he turned just in time to see Althea rise up from behind another candidate, still clapping. She flashed a winning smile and casually brushed her ponytail over her shoulder. *Clever,* Caius thought. A standing ovation. If everyone followed her, Althea establishes herself as bold. A leader. If no one else follows, they look disrespectful in comparison. *Damn, I wish I'd thought of that,* Caius berated himself as he stood, just like all of the other candidates did, still clapping. The next few weeks would be one big game of chess, and Caius was already a move behind.

CHAPTER 6

The candidates were herded into a large, uncomfortable waiting room. The walls were bare stone, leading up to high, pointy arched ceilings; the only furnishings were rough wooden benches bolted to either side. At the north end, there was a gleaming metal door to an isolated room deep under the mountain. The doctor would take them one by one into her office, leaving the rest to wait. The thirty candidates circulated through the room, greeting each other, exchanging a few minutes of banter and then moving on. Plenty of hand shaking and useless small talk. Anything to avoid talking about the trials, or how they were supposed to be rivals, not friends. Unfortunately, they were still deep underground, so no one could even discuss the weather.

Caius and Herennius stuck together, meeting the other candidates and chit-chatting. Plenty of 'Oh, where are you from?' and 'Have a long trip here?' Almost every time Caius answered "Nanjing," he got a casually disinterested "Oh, interesting," in response. A few of them had been stationed in Southern China along the border with the Ming Empire remnants, but that was the limit of their experiences with his homeland. He'd never felt more foreign in his entire life.

Althea, however, had a different reaction from the others. Caius reached out a hand in greeting, and she looked at it like it was a poisonous snake.

"You're a candidate?" she asked, looking him up and down like she was wondering why he wasn't in servant robes. "I didn't know that the Trials were open to…" she trailed off a bit as she looked for the right word. Most people would be trying to find the most polite way to phrase things, but she seemed like she was trying to find the most hurtful. *"Mongols,"* she ended with finally. Despite Mongolia's status as tributaries of Rome, the word was used as a derogatory term for all Asians because of the Khans' refusal to settle into one spot and build what Romans considered a society.

Caius reddened and clenched his jaw. He took a deep breath and attempted to calm himself down. Hitting another candidate, particularly a woman, probably wouldn't make a good first impression for the Senators. It was just like his first few weeks at the Academy, where he was one of the few Asians in his class despite the fact that the school was in China. Most Chinese students couldn't afford the Imperial Academy's steep tuition. At least at school he'd been able to teach the bullies a lesson and leave them all with a few bruises. The racist remarks had stopped pretty quickly as soon as he'd loosened a few teeth.

A few other nearby candidates had heard the slur and turned to see who was responsible. Caius blushed even harder as they gained an audience.

"As I understand it, the Emperor represents all citizens, East and West," Caius responded coolly. "A worthy Candidate would understand that, though." He turned away from Althea and introduced himself pleasantly to another young woman, ignoring that bit of unpleasantness and her sneering reation.

Eventually, everyone had been introduced to everyone else, and they retreated back to the benches lining the walls to wait for their turn to go up. The low buzz of conversation in the room eventually died out until only Caius and Herennius were still talking, discussing a book that

78

they'd each read recently. Just two candidates had so far gone into the doctor's office; twenty eight left to go.

"Everyone is looking at us," Caius hissed, interrupting Herennius's passionate argument that the book had a more hidden subtext arguing for a worker's revolution. They both fell silent and looked around at the other Candidates, whose eyes quickly darted elsewhere. There was an intense quiet filling the room as every one of them sought some way to break the ice, but not wanting to make a misstep in the delicate game of competition. Apparently making new friends is significantly more difficult when you're all ruthlessly competing to rule the most powerful nation on Earth.

With a flash of inspiration, Caius raised a hand and flicked his wrist, the common gesture for summoning a servant. The door flew open, and a maroon-clad young man bolted into the room, hardly making a sound. *Well, that confirms that we're all on camera*, Caius thought. *Bet that the Senators are all watching this too.* "Would you please bring me a deck of cards?" The servant bowed quickly and left the room; almost simultaneously, a different servant brought the deck and scampered away. Candidates looked up from their feet on all sides, curiosity piqued.

"Anyone want to play?" Caius called out.

All of them had done a stint in the military somewhere, so they would all be familiar with many of the same games that every enlisted man would play during down time; seemed like that was really all they had to do around camp. A number of the candidates slowly stood from the benches, glancing around to see if anyone else was joining in and hesitant to be the first. Caius shuffled the cards with an elaborate flourish, showing off just a bit. Finally, another candidate emerged from the benches and sat down in front of Caius and Herennius. His name

was Florian, the dark-skinned Candidate that Caius had seen earlier stooping to enter the dining

hall. From Raphta, near the southern-most reach of the Empire in Africa, if Caius recalled

correctly. He smiled warmly at Caius, eager to break the awkward monotony of waiting.

"You know how to play Pharoah?" Caius asked, already dealing the cards. Florian and

Herennius nodded.

"We need a fourth," Caius announced to the rest of the room. Candidates seeped from

their hiding places along the wall like worms emerging from the ground in a rainstorm. Caius

pointed to Sera, a somewhat heavy candidate from Athens who had been the first candidate to

see the doctor, and had missed most of the impromptu meet-and-greet.

"We played this *all the time* back when I was stationed in the Punjab," Sera said as she

took a seat across from Caius. The other candidates gathered in a loose circle, peering over

shoulders and whispering amongst themselves. Caius noted, with just a hint of self-satisfaction,

that Althea had reluctantly joined the circle behind the rest of the candidates and checked out

Florian's cards.

Caius was crowned Pharaoh two games in a row. The other candidates were surprisingly

bad at bluffing. Or maybe they were just unable to read his Asian features as easily. Herennius

won next, then Sera. But the score didn't really matter; by the fourth match, the rest of the

candidates were taking sides, making bets, and swapping war stories. Caius let another candidate

take his place so that he could watch for a bit. Gideon, a candidate from Judea, even

congratulated Caius on thinking of asking for playing cards. Caius smiled and put an arm around

80

Gideon, not addressing the comment, but pointing to the seven in Florian's hand and placing a bet on the tall African candidate to be crowned Pharaoh within the next two turns. Gideon shook eagerly, pointing out Herennius' double nines. *How genuine is this?* Caius couldn't help but wonder. *Does he actually think it is a good idea, or does he just want to make it look like he's the type of person who recognizes good ideas and rewards initiative?* God, living like this could drive a person crazy, and the real trials hadn't even started.

The metal door opened with a clang. Laurentina, from Constantinople, emerged from the office and bounded across the waiting room with tight braids bouncing behind her, back to the card game.

"Caius Serica," called out the doctor's attendant and looking around the room. "Caius?"

He extricated himself from the circle; Herennius and Florian waved goodbye then went back to their hands.

The doctor's office was remarkably different from the rest of the compound. Instead of cool great stone, the room was covered in gleaming white tile. An exam table dominated the center of the room, surrounded by gleaming modern instruments of every kind. An enormous empty healing tank, tinted green, lurked eerily on the rear wall. The doctor herself stood at the counter, washing her hands in the steel sink. "Please, have a seat," the doctor remarked without looking up. She wore a clean white coat and the diamond-shaped insignia of the Imperial School of Medicine at the University in Constantinople. Her light brown hair was cropped close to her shoulders and curled up slightly against her neck. Caius hopped onto the examining table, swinging his knees a bit. The doctor dried his hands and picked up a light tablet computer.

81

"I'm Doctor Porcia," she said, extending a slender hand for Caius to shake. "Pleasure to meet you."

She looked back down at his medical history on her tablet. "Caius Serica... age 18... Born Nanjing, Jiangsu Province, 1979?" Caius nodded in response. The doctor's fingers flew across the screen, and the machines above stirred to life, scanning Caius with a slow whir and a bright red beam of light.

"Ok," the doctor said. "Any particular health issues that you've noticed or that I need to be aware of?"

"Well, I was wounded about a year ago," Caius responded. He pointed to a pale white patch of scar tissue on his leg, long since healed. "Just a piece of shrapnel. No residual problems."

The doctor pulled out a small pen sized item and pressed it against the leg. The tablet jumped to life in a stream of information: chemical signals, numbers, charts, etc. The doctor studied the information, resting her chin on her hand.

"Looks like this was treated pretty well at the time. No leftover scraps of metal, no permanent muscle damage... Any lingering pain?"

"No."

The doctor reached down to the tablet and made a note to store the information about Caius's leg. "Any prescription medications? Any drug use?"

"No, ma'am," Caius responded promptly.

The doctor looked him in the eyes. "No cameras or microphones in here, Caius. Doctor-patient confidentiality is still respected even during the Trials. The Senators would rather have you be honest with me and find out about bad habits some other way, rather than see you collapse in the middle of one of the trials. Tell me the truth: drug use?"

Caius again protested. Nothing. The doctor made a note on the tablet, apparently satisfied.

The rest of the appointment was pretty standard. The scanners above the operating table mapped out Caius's internal body parts, looking for any irregularities. A second scanner, with a pale green light, scanned his brain as he did a series of tests, looking for any unusual red flags. The doctor drew blood with a long syringe, then ushered Caius into a small restroom for a semen sample. "Got to make sure that you're ready to carry on the lineage," she explained with a bit of a grin.

Caius endured the poking and prodding, the questioning and the interrogation, and came through it with flying colors. "Clean bill of health," the doctor told him, taking off her gloves and checking off the last box on the tablet.

"So, we're all done?" The doctor nodded in response and gestured toward the door. "Best of luck in the trials," she said as Caius walked out the door.

Back in the waiting room, the rest of the candidates were still playing cards. Caius rejoined the crowd clustered around the players and took stock. Althea had managed to worm her way into the game, clutching her cards at her chest like there was a fortune at stake. Sera plucked

a card from her hand, then put it back and picked out another. She was either putting on a big

show for the sake of a bluff, or was completely stumped and really had no way to proceed; Caius

was fairly sure that it was the latter. Finally, Sera played her card: 4 of acorns. Almost

immediately, Althea slapped her 3 of acorns on top of the pile, so hard that she managed to

scatter a few of the cards. "YEAH!" she burst out, high fiving one of the other candidates who

had apparently been betting on her. Drusus, Caius recalled, from Egypt. "Err, very good hand,"

she said a bit more calmly, realizing that perhaps showmanship wasn't what the Senators were

watching for. "You played quite well, Sera." Her perfectly rehearsed tone sounded forthright and

sympathetic, but Althea couldn't quite hide the satisfied smirk that she got from winning.

Herennius let another candidate take his place in the game while Althea looked to hold

her title as Pharaoh. He nodded to Caius. "Nice move with the cards," he said. This time, Caius

wasn't suspicious of his motives; Herennius didn't seem to be the politicking type.

"Never underestimate a good icebreaker," Caius responded. "I can't count how many

times we've initiated a new man into our wing with a good trouncing at Pharoah."

Herennius bobbed his head in agreement. "And not a bad move with the Senators,

either." Caius had been dreading this moment all day: that first wedge between them. A stern

reminder that they were rivals, not friends.

"Yeah, I guess so." Caius didn't elaborate; he turned back to the game. Herennius didn't

push the topic.

They watched the ongoing game in silence. A groan erupted from half the circle and cheers from the other half as Althea scored another huge round. And again, Althea launched into her phony good sportsmanship routine. Her advocate must have really drilled into her that she needed to be more gracious. Sera wasn't buying it; he'd taken enough abuse. Through the crowd, he picked out Caius and motioned him forward. "You're back in, Caius." It wasn't a question; more of a challenge.

Caius stepped forward and took his seat again. A few of the candidates let out a short cheer, then the betting started for real. Althea shuffled the deck, eyes glinting but face emotionless. She dealt the hands, quick and deliberate. The crowd shuffled behind Caius, trying to see his hand; he did his best to block them out. Pharaoh required concentration. Althea watched his reaction carefully, looking for any tell. She placed her first card deliberately: ten of swords. Gideon and Florian played, practically forgotten by the rest of the group. Caius had gotten a pretty good set of cards, and hardly had to think about his next move.

After a few rounds, Althea was playing right into Caius's hand. Florian was almost out of the game, and Gideon was just barely holding on. The few candidates who hadn't placed their bets yet were starting to sway Caius's way. Caius played the four of crowns, expecting Althea to be forced to play another acorn… but as soon as he put down the card, he knew he'd made the wrong move. The smirk spread across Althea's narrow face like an unstoppable flood. A few of the other candidates behind began to point at her hand and whisper, gesturing wildly. Herennius and Sera groaned. *Shit.*

"Caius, that was a pretty great strategy!" she said, barely holding back the laughter in her voice and making a clear effort to be sportsmanlike "But I don't think it worked out this time." Caius could tell that Althea was just itching to rub it in his face. She reached for a card in her hand, still pretending to be deliberating what card she could possibly want to play. Then she tossed it casually into the pile: the one of swords. The single card that could beat Caius's play. Althea won that round, and everything just went downhill from there.

Caius lost hand after hand as Althea cornered him, flashing the same smarmy grin and cheesy politeness each time. Florian and Gideon were knocked out pretty swiftly. Caius was outmaneuvered at every turn, and Althea always seemed to have the right card at the right time. At long last, Caius was left with one remaining card and no other options. He conceded the game, and the candidates who had all bet on him let out one final groan. Althea was too busy slapping palms with her backers to take notice of Caius, who offered her a congratulatory handshake. She eventually looked back and noticed Caius waiting and gave his hand a quick jiggle with that same smug smile.

"Shall we play again?" Caius offered, shuffling with a flourish. The crowd of candidates fell silent again; only the flapping cards made a sound. Althea eyed him, one brow raised.

"No, I think not," she said finally, backing away a pace. "I think it's time for some others to have a chance to play instead." Althea clapped an arm on the back of Petillius, the pale candidate from Britannia who had been betting on her since the beginning. Petillius blushed, making his freckles stand out even more. Althea stood from the circle and retreated to a bench on the side, followed by Drusus; those two were becoming fast friends. With that, interest in the card game died out, and most of the candidates formed into groups around the room. But Caius's goal was accomplished: the shared experience had at least brought them together.

Candidates clustered around both Caius and Althea, still discussing the games, the trials, everything. The room buzzed with eager conversation. Plenty of "Good try though" and "You almost had her" handshakes and smiles. It became readily apparent that Caius was not the only one who was rubbed the wrong way by Althea's superior attitude and phony friendliness. Caius laughed it off.

Halfway through a conversation, he glanced up and caught Althea staring at him across the room. They locked eyes just for a moment. Caius nodded just the littlest bit and lowered his eyes. *Well played.* He wasn't referring to the game of cards. Althea rolled her eyes in response and smirked, turning back to her conversation with the other candidates. *Guess the sportsmanship act is pretty quickly forgotten as soon as she's confident that no one is watching.* Caius turned back to the candidates around him; Herennius had seen Althea's reaction too. "Can't win 'em all," he said with a half shrug and a grin. Caius laughed and jumped back into the conversation, unaware of Althea glaring at him covertly from across the room.

CHAPTER 7

Marcus paced nervously in front of the door.

"Settle down, Marcus. It's not like *you* are the one on trial."

Marcus waved his hand at him. "Hush, you! I'm concentrating." He continued storming back and forth down the hallway, waving his hand and muttering to himself, practicing various parts of his speech for the Tribunal. His footsteps echoed through the narrow corridor, a steady tapping that Caius found unsettling.

"Marcus, seriously. You're making me nervous here. Your speech is going to go fine. I have absolute faith in you to represent me; no one in the Empire could do better." To Caius's surprise, it worked. Marcus stopped his pacing and sat on the bench.

The hallway fell almost silent. Through the door, they could hear the vague droning of voices as another Advocate finished the presentation of his or her candidate. Marcus was fidgeting, plucking at his robes and high formal collar. Then drumming on his knees. Then tapping on the bench.

"Marcus, I *can* and *will* tie you up," Caius warned.

Marcus gave a *hrmph* of protest, but stopped twitching, for the most part.

The doors burst open with an ear-splitting clang that reverberated down the hallway. An older man, an advocate by the looks of him, burst out in a storm of pounding footsteps. He didn't even acknowledge Marcus and Caius waiting nearby; he was too busy swearing at no one in particular. His candidate scuttled out the door behind him. "Slow down, Pius!" As he passed, Caius briefly noted that his eyes were puffy and red from crying.

Marcus slowly heaved himself from the bench. "Well, looks like that went well…" he whispered to Caius.

Two Praetorian guards emerged from the dark room, followed by Quintus. His familiar friendly smile for Marcus was gone, replaced by an unflinchingly professional visage. He once again wore his flashy gilded armor. The two guards took positions next to the doors while Quintus approached.

"Marcus Geganius" Quintus announced with a crisp, almost threatening tone, "Are you prepared for your defense of this candidate, Caius Serica?"

Marcus looked down at his note cards one last time, then back at Quintus. "Yes, I am."

"Very well. Please follow me, both of you." His boots clicked as he turned sharply and re-entered the room. The guards stood at attention saluted as they crossed the threshold, then pulled the heavy metals door closed behind them with an echoing clang.

The room was long and narrow, lined by thick columns. In the center, a single, wooden chair waited under the center of a single bright beam of light. There were two simple wooden desks on either side, with nothing but a glass of water on the tabletop of each. The only other illumination in the room came from large fires lit behind three hooded figures who sat on a raised, curved dais at the far end of the room. The flames were probably fake; the room was bone-chillingly cold.

"Will the Candidate please be seated," called out the stern, forbidding voice of Senator Vitellius. Caius felt Marcus tense up at the very sound of his command.

Caius mustered his confidence and stepped forward. He and Marcus had practiced all of this on the train, though his role here would be relatively small. This was the traditional role of the Advocate, and Marcus had learned Caius's life backwards and forwards in preparation. His footsteps echoed through the silent room, and the chair squeaked against the stone floor as he sat.

"Very good. Who speaks for this Candidate?"

Marcus stepped forward, placing a hand shortly on Caius's shoulder as he brushed past. "I am Marcus Geganius, half-brother to the Emperor and Advocate for Caius Serica, candidate for the position of Emperor."

The room was silent for a moment; just long enough for Caius to wonder if something was wrong.

"And is there any who would speak against him?"

From the shadows between two columns, a hooded figure emerged wearing bright gold robes that made him look like a statue. "I shall serve as Inquisitor," he announced. The rich timbre of his voice was unmistakable: Antoninus, the caretaker of the facility who had greeted them the night they had arrived. Marcus had warned him that there would be someone filling this role but he didn't expect it to be someone that he would know or recognize. Marcus had even said that the role of Inquisitor is supposed to be anonymous, so that a vengeful future emperor couldn't punish whoever had taken on the role. Just like Marcus, the Inquisitor and his assistants had reviewed all the video evidence from Caius's life. Every moment possible caught on hidden camera to judge him. But the Inquisitor would be looking for moments of weakness and vice to speak against him and convince the Tribunal that he did *not* deserve to be Emperor.

"Very well," Vitellius responded, interrupting Caius's thoughts. "Caius Serica. The tribunal is gathered today to hear arguments from your Advocate and your Inquisitor. They will each present evidence from each of the five stages of your life to support their position, using video evidence that they feel best represents your character. Do you have anything to say on your behalf before we begin?"

"No, sir. I trust your fairness and impartiality in this matter." Caius and Marcus had practiced the response. It was a matter of strategy; apparently candidates with some darker moments in their past often took this opportunity to plead with the Tribunal to understand their circumstances. Marcus didn't think anything Caius had done needed this type of plea.

"Then we shall begin."

The robed figure of Antoninus strolled slowly to the front of the room. "Honored Senators: I am privileged to speak before you with the results of my research into the qualities of this candidate. Though he possesses good qualities, he has a serious flaw for the tribunal to consider. One which I believe disqualifies him as a serious candidate." A shiver went up Caius's spine. He wasn't perfect, but one quality that utterly disqualified him? The Inquisitor continued:

91

"The candidate, Caius Serica, is weak. He does not have the necessary force of will that a true Emperor requires to hold the reins of government."

From his pocket, he withdrew a small remote and clicked. An enormous monitor screen lowered from the ceiling on the left side of the room and hummed to life, bathing the room in light like a cinema. The faces of the Senators became visible, but Antoninus was wearing a dark mask that shrouded his features. Caius briefly glanced at Marcus, who tried to give a reassuring smile but just looked like he was ready to throw up.

"The first portion of a candidate's life is with his adopted birth family. Candidates are placed in wealthy homes around the empire, so that the child will be well taken care of. But more importantly, wealth and luxury are the first barriers to a potential candidate. They are seeds of weakness: laziness, cruelty, and indulgence. And thus, this age is one of the most important tests for determining the value of a candidate. And this brings us to the present Candidate. Caius was born in the city of Nanjing, 1979 and adopted by the Sericas, a prominent family who first earned their citizenship for their services to Rome during the Great War, before that portion of China even officially became part of the Empire."

The video screen showed an infant playing on a blanket; Caius recognized the bedroom from his childhood home. The beautifully carved wooden latticework windows, the soft blue wallpaper, the bed that had seemed so enormous back then, the dragon kite that protected him while he slept… the memories all came flooding back.

"Note the surroundings of the room," Antoninus pointed out. "What is missing? *Any* Roman influences! We see no depictions of the Emperor, no evidence of our Western religions,

92

no ancestral shrine…. Nothing to show any sort of acclimation to the ways of the Empire. The province of Nanjing had been a part of the empire for one hundred and eighty eight years at this point, and yet the population has refused to acclimate at all. You yourselves certainly know that it has taken an enormous amount of work to spread our language and culture, ensuring uniformity with the Empire."

The video skipped forward, showing Caius's mother bouncing him on her knee, singing in Mandarin. She wore a beautiful red silk dress that he remembered from his childhood. It jumped again, showing Caius at three or four with a picture book of Chinese myths and fairy tales.

"How well can this man lead us," Antoninus said, raising his voice, "If he was not raised as one of us, with our values and the qualities that our people respect? Do we know if he was raised to perpetuate the culture of the Chinese Emperor? How do we know that his parents were truly loyal to the Empire?"

Caius gripped the armrests of the chair, gritting his teeth. It was ridiculous. His family had been loyal to Rome ever since the Great War! His grandfather had been the one who organized the southern provinces against the Han! He had been the first Chinese citizen of the Empire! Marcus had warned him that this would happen. The Inquisitor would present conjectures and accusations, intended in part to rile him up. The Senators had already reviewed the tapes and decided to admit him to this round. The most important thing for Caius to do was to remain absolutely silent and calm. Marcus would argue on his behalf; any outbursts of his own would make him look weak and lacking self-control. But hearing his mother insulted… that was almost too much

"Next, I would like to discuss the attributes that Caius showed, even from childhood." The video flipped to a video of Caius in school, waving his hand at the teachers and stretching out of his chair.

"It became readily apparent that young Caius thrived on attention and approval from his parents, from his teachers, and from his peers. He wanted to please others, never working for himself. A great quality in many men, yes. But in the Emperor? No. It speaks of weakness. He will cave to the pressures of his advisors and competitors."

The video showed Caius sitting in his mother's lap, tracing words on the paper with his finger and reading the names out loud, then translating to Latin. Each time, he would look up to his mother for assurance that it was correct, and she would cheer and congratulate him.

"This attention-seeking behavior even led him to lie…"

The video flipped to Caius, telling his nanny that he had won a medal from the Emperor. How was *that* not proof of his loyalty to Rome, Caius wanted to shout. But he did his best to stay silent.

"It made him temperamental…"

The video showed Caius throwing a tantrum and screaming at the top of his lungs, with his father desperately trying to calm him. Who knows why? He was a child; that's what children do.

"And we have no evidence that this endless desire to be recognized has left him. The Emperor of Rome should be accomplished, but confident in his decisions without overt approval from others, and humble enough to work behind the scenes."

The Inquisitor finished his presentation. Caius was seething, but doing his best to stay calm and collected. His skin crawled as he felt the Senators scrutinizing him, waiting for any outburst or reaction to Antoninus's accusations. "An Emperor knows how to take criticism," he remembered Marcus reminding him in one of their practice sessions on the train. "The Inquisitor is going to do his best to rile you up."

Marcus stepped forward and bowed to the Senators.

"I am fortunate," Marcus started with a polite gesture at Antoninus, who had slipped back into the shadows, "That our Inquisitor was unable to come up with anything more troubling about Caius other than the fact that he was eager to learn to read." There was a short exclamation of laughter from a soft, feminine voice: Senator Oventia. Caius could just barely see Vitellius shoot her a look, and she quickly stifled it. Too late, though: Marcus's grin was unstoppable, like a hungry fisherman feeling a solid jerk on his line. Marcus had told Caius that the Senators were not supposed to show any reactions to the presentations either.

"For the first six years of his life, Caius was the model of what an imperial citizen should be. Yes, his family was Chinese, living in the former capital of that Empire. Yes, he learned the language spoken by 95% of the city's population. But the Roman Empire is an incredible blend of cultures and traditions that span the globe." Marcus tapped at the remote, and a video appeared of Caius in Nanjing's crowded marketplace materialized on the screen. It showed Caius running back and forth between merchants, helping his mother with the shopping. He bantered with the European merchants in fluent Latin, then bartered with the Chinese merchants just as easily, earning sweets from both groups. "When he becomes Emperor, Caius will be the bridge to fully integrate China into the Empire, a task that has so far failed even after nearly two centuries. Even in its earliest days, Rome learned to incorporate the best aspects of its neighbors to make it even stronger. This melting pot has allowed the Empire to thrive!" He pointed back at Caius. "And let us not forget that this was *by design.* The Senate Committee on Trials was the very group that established that Candidates should come from all over the Empire, to ensure that every group and province was represented. His ethnicity was specifically selected to ensure that the gene pool continues to diversify, making the Emperor himself a symbol of the united Empire."

The video flipped again to Caius in a classroom at one of Nanjing's private schools. His classmates were a hodgepodge of races and ethnicities from all over the Empire. Marcus again nodded at Antoninus, leaning on one of the thick columns. "By emphasizing the diverse atmosphere in which Caius was raised, the Inquisitor has only shown off one of his most amazing strengths. Caius will be able to relate to all citizens of the Empire, not just the citizens of Europe. And as the Empire continues to face foes in Japan and the Ming Emperor hiding in

Southern Asia, Caius's upbringing and knowledge of the people there will continue to serve him well. We will need the support of our people along the borders, which only Caius will be able to secure. This is an understanding that cannot be taught, so we are lucky to have a candidate who already possesses such skills."

"The Inquisitor's second argument seeks to portray Caius's natural intelligence and ability as the product of poor values and weakness." The video changed again, showing Caius slipping food to a classmate who obviously did not have as much. "Is this the face of a child desperate for attention? Who would charitably help another student and tell no one what he's done?" The video changed again, showing Caius reading with another student, doing their homework together. "Why would a student desperate for attention and recognition as the best help another classmate succeed? No, Senators. Caius is a student who received the level of attention that he deserved as a generally nice kid and a great student." He gestured back at Caius, who hoped that the Senators couldn't see him blushing in the dim light. This whole process was just humiliating.

"Instead," Marcus continued, "Let me tell you about the childhood that Caius had from my perspective. First, he is intelligent and inquisitive." The video shipped to show Caius and his parents on one of their summer visits to Putoushan Island, where they'd often fled the heat of the city. Watching the video brought back the smell of the sea and the feel of salt and sand caking his skin. In the video, he was picking shells out of the surf and running them back to his father, asking what kind of animal lived in that one.

"He is creative." The video changed to Caius playing the piano at age five, dexterous and talented. His parents had made an effort to teach him the arts early on, and he had particularly loved the piano. He still remembered his music teacher, an old widow who had moved all the way from Gaul and snuck him lemon-flavored candies when his mother wasn't watching. It had been years since he'd been able to play, and he missed the music.

"He is courageous." The video changed once more, showing Caius on a foggy wintery playground, standing between a crying child and another group of kids. The largest one stood with a fist raised against Caius. His name was Mengyao, Caius recalled. His family was an oddity in Nanjing: wealthy, but had not yet earned citizenship in the Empire and thus retained their native name. A bully, through and through. He'd picked on Caius for months, who had done his best to shrug it off. But when he punched Tiberus, Caius had intervened. *God, I haven't thought about them forever,* Caius realized. *I wonder where they are now.* "This scene in particular," Marcus continued, "is clear proof that Caius is *not* weak! Instead of bowing to peer pressure, he stood up to a much larger bully. And he will continue to do the same as Emperor of Rome." This hadn't been part of Marcus's original speech that he'd practiced in front of Caius, but he was clearly adapting it to refute the Inquisitor's arguments.

"And finally, he is kind." On the screen, the rain started. Little Caius, backpack swinging as he walked home from school, saw a homeless man huddled on a stoop. The small figure in a bright lime-green raincoat stopped midway through a puddle splash and stared. The street was deserted. Timid young Caius approached the homeless man and handed him a small plastic container of rice and vegetables, leftover from lunch. The homeless man took it, incredibly surprised. "Thank you," he managed to stutter in Mandarin. Caius only smiled in response then bounded home in an excited gallop, stopping only to jump into the deepest puddles.

Marcus paused the video just as the yellow raincoat was about to vanish into the mists. "Did that look like a child desperate for recognition, or was it simply a child who wanted to help others and was sometimes noticed by his peers and elders?" The image stayed on the screen as Marcus bowed to the Senators and retreated. Caius suppressed the urge to clap, and Marcus winked at him as he strolled past.

There was a brief lull as the Senators all conversed with each other. Caius strained to listen, but could only hear the low droning of their voices. Senator Tullius kept looking back at Caius, with a slightly cocked head as if trying to decipher some mystery. Marcus and Antoninus waited at their desks for the next round of presentations. Caius wished he could go tell Marcus how great he had done, but he knew he needed to stay seated.

Finally, the Senators turned back to the room. "You may continue," Vitellius ordered. "Inquisitor?"

Antoninus uncrossed his arms and emerged again into the center of the room.

"Thank you, Senator." His deep voice was strangely soothing, despite the fact that his presentation was designed to show all of the worst moments of Caius's life. "With your permission, I will continue to the Candidate's years at the Imperial Military Academy in Luoyang beginning at age 6."

He clicked at his remote again, showing a photo of the large, modern school campus built on a forested hill above the city. "The next phase in the life of a candidate is to be sent to a prestigious school for the finest education that the Empire has to offer. The Emperor must be intelligent and quickly able to grasp new ideas and concepts that could be of benefit to his citizens. The purpose of this is to weed out those candidates who are not the absolute best of the best, both in terms of sheer intelligence and work ethic. And does that include Caius? No. Once again, Caius showed that he was too weak to be an Emperor."

The video changed, showing Caius up late at night, cramming for a test the next day. His eyes were bloodshot and drooping as he pored over his hastily scrawled notes. The video must have been taken from a hidden camera inside his dormitory's desk lamp. "Is this the face of an Emperor? One who leaves his tasks for the last minute and has to stay up all night before a final? Is that who you want making important decisions of state?" A montage came onto the screen of Caius dozing off in various classes, his head slowly nodding down before jerking rapidly back up... then slowly nodding again. Of Caius falling asleep at his desk late at night. Of Caius talking to another student behind the teacher's back instead of paying attention. Of Caius doodling in his notebook, drawing pictures of airships instead of diagrams and equations. "Senators, what we have here is a textbook case of a procrastinator who has managed to get by solely on the natural talent and good genes that he shares with every other candidate. What we want in an Emperor is someone who is driven and motivated and decisive. Caius is none of those things."

The video changed again to show Caius at the school science fair, demonstrating some chemical reaction that burned bright green in a beaker. "And young Caius still continued his ever-present need to be recognized and please others, instead of charting his own course." The video switched to the awards ceremony, where Caius received second place. The video was shot from a camera somehow attached to the school Headmaster's lapel. Caius saw his own forced smile, trying to look gracious, but the video made it plainly clear that he had to bite his lip to hide the disappointment. He could feel his face burning, knowing that the Senators might be buying into this argument.

"The Emperor should stand above all," continued Antoninus, "not in line indistinguishable from the rest. And that is not what we have here."

Caius took slow breaths, remembering to always maintain his composure for the panel. But he was grinding his teeth down to stumps in an effort to not stand up and ask if any of *them* had ever been teenagers before.

"Let's put everything into context," Marcus started after bowing to the panel. "Caius was put into a school in an unfamiliar city, with nobody he knows. He was advanced *two* grade levels, to learn with boys much older and far more experienced. He constantly took on extra work and challenges, such as after-class clubs and sports. He was the consummate outsider, at every disadvantage. And yet, with all of those challenges, the worst that our dear Inquisitor could come up with is that the boy was occasionally *tired* in class?" He burst into a broad grin again. "Let's be honest: when I was a boy, I had a private tutor all to myself, just one-on-one. And yet I *still* fell asleep in front of him at least once a day."

Senator Oventia muffled her laughter once again. Caius thanked his lucky stars that he had Marcus as his Advocate. He'd met some of the other Advocates, and they were mostly dour and serious.

"I have reviewed the tapes of Caius's time at school just as thoroughly as the Inquisitor. I have looked for any instance of cheating, or negligence, or failure. I have found none. Caius was ever prepared for class, always intelligent and insightful, and usually alert." Marcus turned for only a moment and gave him a brief wink. For the first time in the past half hour, he realized how tense his muscles were; he was practically carving holes into the wooden arms of the chair with his fingers. He took deep breaths, just like Marcus had taught him, trying to calm himself without showing it too much.

Marcus was pacing back and forth to make his point. "Mathematics: marked 'Excellent.' Spelling and grammar: 'Excellent.' Rhetoric and Philosophy: 'Excellent.'" He held up his fingers and ticked off different subjects one by one. "In preparation for this, I went to the Luoyang Military Academy to speak with the professors who taught young Caius." Caius tensed up again; this was news to him. Marcus hadn't mentioned ever visiting his school. Marcus clicked on the remote and the screen flashed to life, showing his philosophy professor, a bit older and greyer.

"Oh, definitely I remember Caius. One of my star pupils, you know. I still keep some of his old essays around…" the old man shuffled through his desk in the video and pulled out a binder of loose papers. "I use them as examples for the new class. To show them really how things should be done. That boy was absolutely brilliant."

Marcus tapped the button again, and the video changed, showing Caius's chemistry teacher. He was surrounded by flasks and burners and all other sorts of equipment; Marcus had staged the video well to show his area of expertise. "Caius Serica," the teacher said, "There's a name I haven't heard in a while! Boy was a genius. I didn't even bother trying to teach him; he already knew it before he even got to the classroom. Eventually I just kind of took him on as an assistant and let him run around back, thinking up demonstrations to help his classmates get the gist of everything. Of course, he still had to do homework and take all of the same tests, but I really don't know why I bothered. I remember one time I was practically still explaining the instructions when he had already finished all of the answers. Gosh I miss that kid!"

Marcus gestured toward the Inquisitor. "Is this the same student that the Inquisitor was watching? Trying to cast him as lazy when in reality, he just wasn't challenged by any of his schoolwork? If anything, I would be thrilled to have an Emperor who was so smart that even the most challenging course at the Academy was a walk in the park for him."

Marcus flicked off the television screen and retreated back into shadows with a confident swagger. The nervous Marcus from the hallway who couldn't stop fidgeting was long gone, and thank god.

"Very well," called out Senator Vitellius. He motioned to the Senators to swivel their chairs around to discuss this latest round of arguments, but the Inquisitor stopped them. "With your permission, Senators, I have an additional argument to make concerning this phase of Caius's life," he called out in that rich, deep voice that seemed to fill the chilly room. Caius glanced back and forth, watching the reactions of the Senators. Marcus had said that it would be just one speech for each different part. Why was there another? Caius began to sweat, cold and clammy. This could only be something bad.

"Proceed, Inquisitor," Vitellius called out with an abundance of curiosity in his voice.

"Senators, I never argued that Caius was unintelligent, as the Advocate seems to frame things. I argued that Caius is *weak*. He does not have the iron will that the Emperor needs to have. I feel that an additional clip from his past represents this idea well. It is a moment that I'm sure the Candidate remembers well, and one that he'd rather not have you all know about."

He tapped the remote and the video flicked to life once again. It showed a barren schoolyard framed by skeletal trees. Only a few orange and brown leaves clung to the branches; the rest lay in great heaps around the pavement square. In one corner, a crowd of older boys in their bright red school uniforms were tossing a bookbag in soaring arcs overhead and laughing. In the center of the circle, a shorter, scrawny boy ran back and forth trying to catch it. Fannius Calvus was his name, Caius recalled, burning with shame as he remembered the moment. The video zoomed in as Fannius fell, tearing the pants of his uniform on the rough blacktop. He rose again, still grasping at the bag and crying out to his schoolmates. Finally, the bag flew into Caius's hands, who stood a head shorter than anyone else in the circle. Caius held the bag uncertainly, glancing back and forth around the circle and trying not to look the smaller crying boy in the eyes.

Everyone in the circle seemed to freeze, not knowing how Caius would react. Finally, the boy lunged at Caius, almost managing to lay a hand on the leather strap before Caius tossed it in the air. It sailed in a wide arc and landed directly in the hands of a towering brute, clearly the leader of the pack. The rest of the boys cheered and clapped, thrilled that Caius was joining in on their bullying. Fannius looked at him with betrayal in his eyes, tears streaming down his stained face. The video ended showing one of the boys clapping Caius on the back and them laughing together as Fannius simply sat down in the middle of the circle, giving up.

104

Caius shifted uncomfortably in his chair as he watched the video. The Inquisitor paced the room, first looking at Caius, then at the Senators. He spread his arms wide and said "I believe the video speaks for itself. The Emperor is the protector of the weak; he doesn't join in on such behavior. Caius did not have the strength to stand up to his peers because he does not have the will to do what is necessary. As I have shown before, he caves under pressure, and that is not what Emperors do." Antoninus slipped back into the darkness of his desk, and the room was completely silent. The video remained paused, showing Caius's laughter contrasting with Fannius's utter defeat. The room was silent and tense; he could feel the Senators casting their judgments.

Marcus stepped forward again, placing a firm hand on Caius's shoulder before beginning.

"Yes, it is so." He flipped the monitor, banishing Fannius's face from the screen to Caius's great relief. "A moment of weakness. You can see the shame clearly painted across the boy's face." Marcus swung a hand back at Caius, to his great surprise. Caius thought he'd been hiding his emotions well, but apparently not. Luckily Marcus knew how to use that to his advantage. "We must remember the context of the moment. Remember the adversity that Caius faced, trying to fit in with these pubescent boys, years his elder. You saw in the video how much smaller and younger he was. He was driven to bullying only by man's incessant desire to be treated as an equal. He found the quickest way to ingratiate himself, and though in hindsight it seems unfair, can we really blame him?"

Marcus flipped the screen back on and went to another video of Caius out on the school's athletic fields, training Fannius in sword fighting as the sun ducked beneath the trees. Fannius

105

asked to give up and go inside, but Caius pushed him onward, dueling with him until the stars began to twinkle.

"Caius made it up to him. He reached out to Fannius when none of the other students ever would. They became good friends. You can see here where Caius personally worked with the boy to improve his swordsmanship."

The video changed again, showing Caius tutoring Fannius in history. They were up late; the rest of the boys in the dormitory were snoozing in their bunks that lined the walls; only those two continued working.

"Lazy, eh?" Marcus interjected. "Caius probably needed to sleep at this point, but he stayed up late to help Fannius. He worked hard to make it up to his comrade."

Marcus turned, allowing this to sink in. Good work, tying those two points together. Marcus grinned at Caius as he continued.

On the video screen, Fannius appeared. Older, with a stubble of a beard and glasses that framed his still-boyish face. He'd certainly grown, and his chubbiness had completely evaporated with every additional centimeter. This time, the video started with Marcus speaking. "Do you remember that day? The one in the video?"

Fannius's lips tightened and his eyes narrowed slightly. "Yes," he answered without any elaboration.

"And you remember Caius participating," Marcus continued, goading him onward.

"Yes, I do." A trace of sadness flashed across Fannius's face.

"Anything you'd like to say to him about that moment?"

Fannius turned and faced the camera directly. "I know how hard it can be to be the only one left out. You were new, and young, short, and native, unlike the rest of us European imports... And I have to admit that I have done the same thing to younger, weaker students myself. I can't blame you for what you did; you just wanted to fit in. To be one of the guys. And for a while, I was still mad about it. But you made it up to me. You were a good friend, and I hope that everything is going well for you." He gave an almost nervous smile, and Marcus paused the video there.

Caius realized he'd been holding his breath for far too long. He tried to exhale slowly so that the Senators wouldn't notice. Marcus bowed silently and returned to the back of the room. This time, he didn't look at Caius as he walked back.

Antoninus rose from his chair once again. "It seems that the Advocate and I agree. Caius is certainly a nice person and a good friend. But that is not the issue here. The issue is the Candidate's strength of character, and I believe this incident proves it: he is weak. Making it up to this boy does nothing to undo the fact that he bowed to peer pressure and joined in the bullying in the first place. It just shows a guilty conscience." With a bow, the Inquisitor returned to the shadows.

The Senators leaned in close to each other, talking in hushed whispers. Senator Tullius was speaking loudly with his hands, waving back and forth. The firelight behind his profiled figure made him look furious; or maybe he actually was.

Crap, Caius thought to himself. *This was bad. But surely every candidate has at least one of those moments they're really not proud of?* He briefly twitched in the chair, wanting to turn around and see Marcus's reaction, but he stopped himself. He could practically hear Marcus's voice, and feel the sharp sting of the ruler: *"Don't show any signs of being nervous!"*

What was more concerning, though, was that maybe the Inquisitor had a point. Caius had never been that passionate firebrand or the ideologue who always had to have his way. He was flexible and accommodating. He worked with others, and tried to help whenever possible. That's just what good people did in China. *Was Rome so different? Was it a bad thing here to assist a friend?* The Inquisitor seemed to imply that, and Caius was starting to doubt his own qualifications. *Maybe the cultural barriers between us are insurmountable. Maybe I didn't have a chance from the beginning.*

After what seemed like years, the Senators rolled their chairs back into their respective places and faced forward. Tullius still didn't seem particularly pleased. Vitellius cleared his throat and readjusted some of the papers in front of him, then looked back up.

"Inquisitor, any additional arguments to present for this segment of the Candidate's life?"

Antoninus's resonant voice filled the room. "No, Senator."

"And you, Advocate? Any additional evidence to present of the boy's Character?"

108

"Hundreds of instances that I wish I could show you," Marcus answered cheerfully, "But I'm well aware of the time limits and have nothing further to present at the moment."

"Continue, then, Inquisitor."

Antoninus walked forward again; the dark mask covering his face made him a terrifying specter. Probably meant to intimidate the candidates who didn't know the man beneath the robes.

"As with all Candidates, Caius Serica was told that his parents had passed away in a car accident after he had spent 8 years at the Academy." Caius gritted his teeth again. Cruel bastards. But it was a necessary reminder for why he was here and why he desperately needed to win. It's easy to forget the stakes when you're just playing a game of cards with some friends.

"The Candidate was informed that the remainder of his parent's estate was needed to pay off the debts of the family and that funds were unavailable for him to continue his schooling at the Imperial Academy. As a result, Caius would have to leave at the end of the semester."

Caius clenched his fists and pretended to be looking at the screen; he focused intensely a small black blemish on one of the mighty stone columns nearby. He could feel the hot tears begin to well up, and was doing everything in his power to hold them back. The last candidate had cried too, and Caius had seen the look of pity in Marcus's eyes. *Emperors do not cry,* Marcus had warned him on the train.

He still vividly recalled the day the Headmaster had pulled him out of class to inform him of his parents' accident. *Well, to lie to him and say there was an accident,* Caius corrected himself now that he knew the truth. Caius hadn't really known how to react; he didn't cry, or lash out in anger, or anything like that. His teacher had offered to let him head back to the dormitories, but he only responded that he needed to prepare for finals just like the other students only later that night, as he walked back from the athletic fields, did he realize what it all meant. That his parents were gone. His home was gone. His life at the Academy was over. He'd have to strike out on his own; maybe find a job and save up enough to return to the school. And he broke down sobbing on the trail back up to the school, ducking into the woods so that no one could see him. He stayed out there, unable to face the friends that he'd soon have to leave behind, until the Headmaster organized the other cadets to come find him that night.

Luckily, Antoninus was not replaying those moments of his life; simply setting the stage.

"Caius left the academy in June of 1993 and set out into a life of the poor and wretched. The Senate designed this part of the trial to truly test the worth of the candidate. Many can succeed when given the bountiful resources of a wealthy upbringing, combined with the education at one of the Imperial Academies. But to persevere through poverty and torment is quite another matter; this segment of the trials is responsible for disqualifying the vast majority of candidates. And for good reason, because it is the most important. It teaches the candidates the lesson of humility, and they come to know the struggles that the poorest of the Empire's citizens face every day. When the successful Candidate becomes the Emperor, he will always remember to consider the effects of their choices on the poor."

The video screen turned on once again, showing Caius in an empty street. It looked like Weinan, though Caius had drifted through so many cities in the first few months of homelessness that it was impossible to be sure.

"Caius's acquaintances, both back in Nanjing and at the Academy, were discreetly warned that ties should be severed."

Not that I'd ever asked them for help, he thought to himself with a hint of pride. Though he had wondered why not one of them bothered to check up on him; this explained it.

"As planned, he was thrust into the world with nothing. And did he prove that he could make the hard choices? Did he show resolve and determination?"

The video changed to show Caius breaking into a home; it must have been caught on some security camera. He recognized it instantly; some vacation home of a wealthy Roman who loved the idea of spending the summers in the Far East but had never actually made it out there. But the home had been stocked with dried goods and canned food, and Caius helped himself.

"He stole," Antoninus announced, as if the video hadn't made it clear what he was doing.

The screen changed again, showing Caius in a narrow alleyway lined with neon street signs. Three grizzled men in their twenties circled him like a pack of wolves. Caius held up his fists, eyes darting between each of them. They launched themselves at him simultaneously as Caius lashed out with his fists.

"He fought," the Inquisitor continued.

The video changed once more, showing a smoke-filled room, full of boxes except for one circular table, where Caius sat with three older men playing cards. A game of Pharoah, funnily enough.

"He cheated," said Antinonus as they watched Caius slip a card up his ragged sleeves.

"Now, this behavior is to be expected," the Inquisitor said, looking briefly at Caius with the emotionless, blank mask. "From most people. But wouldn't we expect better from the Emperor? I, for one, would hope that the leader of the greatest Empire on the planet would at least not debase himself at multiple opportunities. He took the easy way out, instead of sticking true to his principles. That is not behavior worthy of the Emperor."

This part of the trial was fairly easy for Caius to shrug off; he relaxed and maintained his calm demeanor. None of them, except for Marcus, would know what this was like. The Senators had never been thrust out into the streets with nothing and been expected to make something of themselves. Caius had seen their biographies on the train ride in; each of them came from the wealthiest and most prominent families in the Empire; those were the only ones that the Senate could trust to perform this most important duty. How could they judge him for stealing food or defending his meager possessions?

The Inquisitor bowed gracefully, concluding his remarks.

"Advocate?" Vitellius called out.

Marcus once again stood from his desk and returned to the front of the podium.

"Honored Senators... this is an impossible standard to hold any man to, and you all know that. A future Emperor should be a man with many excellent qualities, but not a god. Caius, a fourteen year old boy who wanted nothing more than to return to school, was put into one of the most difficult positions imaginable: choosing between his duties as a good citizen of the Empire, or sleeping on the ground with an empty stomach."

The video changed again, showing Caius huddled against a brick wall in some unknown alley, cold and miserable.

"For every one moment that the Inquisitor shows of Caius forced to do such things, I can show you a hundred more where he resisted with honor."

The video changed again to show Caius waiting tables at a restaurant in Xian, deftly carrying trays loaded with steaming hot noodles swimming in sauce. The manager had always taken pity on him and allowed him to help himself to whatever food was left over from the night's meals. It tasted finer than any expensive banquet he'd ever had since.

"Caius worked hard, constantly. Any opportunity to earn an honest living, he jumped at the chance. And when he could, he was always generous with his bounty."

The video changed again to show Caius bringing back some of the scraps from the restaurant to other homeless men, clustered around a smoky fire under a railway overpass on the way into Xian. They'd been kind enough to take Caius in and give him what they could spare on his first night in the city, and he'd made an effort to pay them back whenever possible.

"Unlike many candidates, Caius was able to work his way up the ladder of industry. He took a chance after months and months of work, borrowed all of the money he possibly could, and went into business making components for the burgeoning field of aeronautics. He took the design of the crude engines that airplanes were currently using, and refined it to be more efficient and more powerful. Many of you Senators probably flew out here in a plane using his designs. Caius was intelligent enough to recognize the growing utility of these new devices, and bold enough to strike out on his own. He started with just a used tool chest and after more than a year, ended up with a company employing seventy one citizens."

The video shifted to a time lapse bird's-eye view of Caius's workshop floor, gleaming with metallic machinery and a busy blur of bustling workers. Brand new plane engines slowly rolled off the floor. Marcus paused the video and thrust a chubby finger at the screen.

"Note the light in Caius's office. How he is *always* there. He lived at that factory the entire time he was at the business, sleeping in a corner on a cot! *That* is the very picture of dedication! By the end of his two year period of homelessness, Caius was wealthier than ninety percent of the Empire's citizens. I have reviewed the files of every other candidate, and I can assure you that none of them thrived like Caius did. None of them pulled themselves out of the mud and started an entrepreneurial empire. Only Caius!" Marcus thumped a fist into the palm of his hand emphatically. Caius could tell that this was the section that Marcus had really been waiting for.

"Even after the Senate arranged for the purchase of Caius's company, it has continued to thrive as a state-owned businesses due to Caius's masterful engineering and business acumen." Marcus clicked the remote again and it showed an enormous workshop churning out gleaming steel parts. Hundreds of employees now were bustling back and forth like a swarm of ants, putting together the very same fighters that Caius had flown in Japan.

"Caius represents the hopes and dreams of the Empire. As a mere adolescent, he went from rags to riches in the space of only two years, proving that skilled, motivated workers can succeed in our society. As Emperor, he will be an example to the rest of the world."

Marcus bowed and retreated back into the darkness with an enormously pleased grin.

Caius watched as the Senators put their heads together to discuss. Senator Oventia looked at him sharply as if seeing him for the first time, with an impressed half-smile. Caius watched as her hand circled something on the paper in front of her and turned back to Senators Vitellius and Tullius. Caius struggled to keep his satisfaction hidden. Even before knowing that he was one of the Candidates, he'd harbored deep personal pride for how he'd started that business with next to nothing, hauling old engine parts kilometers back from the scrapyard using a decrepit gurney and rope and tinkering late into the night.

This discussion was far shorter than the others; after only a few moments, the Senators turned back toward Caius. Oventia looked particularly happy, Tullius looked like someone had hit him with a rotten egg, and Vitellius was an unreadable stone sphinx. The fires behind them spit and crackled, casting elongated shadows around the room.

"I think," Vitellius announced as he doodled something on his notepad, "that we will take a short break. The Candidate will remain in this room. Advocate and Inquisitor, you are free to leave if you would like."

With that, the Senators rose from their chairs and exited through some unseen passage to the right. Servants poured out of the same door, carrying armloads of wood and shining metal pitchers. They stoked the fires and replaced the glasses of water in front of the Senators' chairs, despite the fact that they seemed untouched. Antoninus also exited with a short curt bow to Marcus and Caius, fussing with his Inquisitor hood as he left; it must be damn uncomfortable in this hot room. Marcus brought Caius a glass of water; they had been left alone in the room. "Well?" Marcus asked. "Holding up OK?"

Caius glanced down at his hands, rubbed raw and red from squeezing the rough arms of the wooden chair.

"Got it," Marcus said, with a knowing look. "I sat in that same place, twenty six years ago. Hell, probably the same chair unless some other candidate broke it at some point. The Senate doesn't like to change anything unless they need to." He thumped Caius on the back, causing the chair to squeak. "You're doing fine. You haven't cried out yet or shouted at the Inquisitor, which means you're doing better than I did when I was the one being reviewed. So just keep your calm and let me do the talking."

Caius took the cup from Marcus and gulped it down; he hadn't noticed how thirsty he was until the water touched his lips.

"Do you think we are... doing well?"

Marcus laughed. "You know, I really have no way of knowing. I've only been through this once myself."

Caius looked back at his feet.

"But, I have been preparing for this for months," Marcus said. "Going through all of your videos, interviewing your friends and family and colleagues… far more than even other Advocates do. My worst fear before walking into this room is that the Inquisitor would get up there and just completely blindside me. He'd have found some video that I'd overlooked, showing you in some moment of cruelty or vice. And then the Senators would expect a response from me… and I'd have nothing."

The room was silent except for the popping and crackling logs on the fire. Caius had worried about that too.

"But it hasn't happened yet. He thought he had a surprise there with that moment of you bullying…" Caius felt the burning shame return to his cheeks, "If that was all he had, then we're going to be just fine."

Marcus grabbed the silver water pitcher from his desk and refilled the glass for Caius. This one he sipped, savoring the cool water running down his still-parched throat.

"The bullying…" Caius started, still dwelling on that moment. "Fannius really said that, right? You didn't coerce him or anything like that?"

Before Marcus could answer, the doors slid open again with an eerie flash of artificial light. The Senators stepped up to their stage in a whirlwind of purple robes and took their seats. The Inquisitor also emerged from the darkness to the left, light reflecting from his golden robes. The doors slammed shut behind them

"Inquisitor and Advocate, are you prepared to move on to your arguments for the next life phase?" Senator Vitellius's voice cut through the silence like thunder.

"Yes," Marcus and Antoninus answered in unison.

"Continue, then. Inquisitor?"

Antoninus stepped forward again.

"For the next phase of his life, a Candidate is placed into a prestigious apprenticeship for a year-long term in order to experience industry and business. This phase ensures that the future Emperor understands the needs of the employers throughout the empire and how best to stimulate growth. It also tests his work ethics and whether the Candidate can apply knowledge learned in the Academy."

The video turned on, showing Caius on his first day of work, trying to appear friendly and outgoing as he was introduced to his new coworkers.

"Caius's experience with his own business made the transition simple. After the purchase of his company, he was offered a position with the Emperor's own aerospace corporation, Samarkand Aeronautics, designing aircraft. As you all surely know," he gestured at the Senators, "this company has been responsible for building the third generation of planes for the Imperial Air Corps. After the Senate Committee applied considerable pressure, Caius was apprenticed to Licinius Pacilus, the division head.

The video changed to show Licinius meeting with Caius on the first day, presenting him with a quiz and clicking a timer. "You have one hour," they heard through the video. Caius remembered that vividly, feeling like he was going to vomit all over the page. Instead of easing him into the job, his new boss had presented him with a difficult exam on the very first day, and Caius was seriously expected to know ever answer. Naturally, he had failed miserably. But Licinius had at least been pleased that he had tried in the first place instead of giving up and quitting. Caius had interacted with plenty of brilliant people at the Academy, including professors, and never felt out of place. But talking to Licinius was like meeting with an alien from another planet; his thinking was just on another level of intelligence.

"And what kind of apprentice was Caius? How well did he do?"

Caius appeared on the screen, holding a piece of paper in his hands. Licinius wasn't shouting or angry; that's just not the person he was. But his disappointment was palpable even through the video. Something had gone wrong, and the video made it clear who should have caught it. Watching it over again caused Caius's stomach to roil with embarrassment all over again.

"The disappointment of Licinius is readily apparent here. Caius was supervising an important prototype's testing, and did not properly check the work of his subordinates. As a result, the prototype was destroyed, costing the company a significant fortune."

Caius's legs twitched without even thinking, and he had to quickly stop himself from leaping up and shouting. That just wasn't true. The cause of the crash had never been determined. Was the Inquisitor allowed to lie?

The video screen changed to show a fire in the middle of the arid desert plain around Samarkand. Thick black smoke billowed into the clear blue sky, and gleaming wreckage was scattered along a kilometer-long furrow of broken earth. Through the flames, one enormous wing jutted up, propeller still spinning wildly.

"Caius alone could have prevented this mistake if only he were better at managing his employees. Maybe it was again because of his willingness to please. Maybe he just didn't want to say 'No' to a friend. He is weak, Senators. How can we trust this man to be Emperor if he cannot even manage a small team of docile engineers? Will he be able to work closely with the Senate to pass important legislation? Can he oversee the operations of his many military commanders? What about the imperial bureaucracy that manages the affairs of the state? Or the state-owned businesses that lead the market and employ millions of workers? Or under his leadership, is this the fate of the Empire?" He pointed at the screen, still showing the video of the burning wreckage. Caius could see Tullius's head nodding. With that, the Inquisitor returned to his seat in the darkness.

Marcus again strolled to the front of the room. He clicked the remote, turning off the video of the crash. "Laughable," he said with emphasis, "That the Inquisitor would seek to have one setback define the entire term of Caius's apprenticeship." He turned on the monitor again, showing Caius hunched over his computer screen, perfecting diagrams while the others left for home. The video changed to Caius tinkering with engines and running simulations in the wind tunnel.

"With Caius working for Licinius, the department was able to roll out several improvements for the existing products, as well as an entirely new development: long-ranged bombers capable of flying hundreds of miles without stopping to refuel. Never has the Empire had such a capacity, and Caius's designs were essential for the recent successful bombing campaigns against the Chikogu prefectures in Japan." The video changed briefly to show the familiar landscape of Japan on a misty night, as seen from the perspective of a heavy droning bomber releasing its payload on a series of fortifications. Caius may have even been the one piloting the plane, depending on when the video was taken.

"The Inquisitor has shown you video of one test failure that occurred during Caius's term at Samarkand Aerospace. And do you know how many crashes they have had in the past year, after Caius joined the military?" He paused for effect, then clicked on the screen showing a montage of explosions in the mountains and fields around Samarkand. "Eleven," Marcus told them, gesturing at screen while they watched a test pilot eject from his plane moments before it smashed into a rocky outcropping. "But, why hear it from me? I have no expert knowledge of this field, do I? Let's hear from the man who really matters."

Licinius himself appeared on the screen across from Marcus; his intense black eyes and hawkish features were intimidating even through the screen. "Yes, I remember Caius Serica. One of the finest engineers I have had the pleasure of working with. Brutally intelligent, always hard working, just all around excellent. I hope to hire him back as soon as his military deployment stint is finished." Marcus had apparently not told him what this interview was for.

"There was a crash during his tenure here; do you remember that incident?"

Licinius leaned back in his recliner, lips pursed. Marcus held up a photo, presumably showing the crash. "Ah, yes," he answered finally. "A prototype he had been working on for a new four-turbine fighter, I believe. Shame that it crashed."

"And, were you disappointed by his work there?"

"No, no." Licinius answered without pausing. "When working with volatile fuels and uncertain principles, these incidents happen. The boy was really shaken up by all of it, though. I tried to encourage him. He has this way of thinking that is unique and rare. One setback shouldn't delude him into thinking that he went about solving the problem in the wrong way."

"How so?" said Marcus from off screen. "What do you mean that he has a different way of thinking?"

"He doesn't just follow what others have done." Licinius answered as if it should be obvious. "That's the problem with everyone coming out of the Academy: they see something working as is, and don't see any reason to change that. No thinking outside the box. It's why we're still using airships two centuries after they were so instrumental in the Great War. Scientists and engineers throughout the Empire were completely obsessed with making them lighter, or better armored, or faster, because that was just what we used. They improved on existing principles, instead of re-evaluating whether they were still good. The others completely ignored the potential of heavier-than-air flight. And it's the same with any other technology: if it isn't championed by some Imperial bureaucrat, then it's going to fall by the wayside, even if it's useful and valuable. Caius is different. He sees a problem and tries to solve it, regardless of what solution is already in place. And I need more men like that in my department."

122

"And in the Empire?"

Licinius gave his short bark of laughter. "If we had men like that running the Empire, we would have conquered the world by now."

With that, Marcus turned the screen back off. "I don't think I could have said it better myself." With a bow, he finished the presentation and returned to his desk.

As usual, the Senators turned to each other to discuss. Caius could see Senator Tullius pantomiming the explosion with his hands, not even bothering to try and hide the fact that he was arguing against Caius at every possible opportunity. This time, even normally stoic Vitellius seemed to be arguing in Caius's favor. Finally, Tullius simply crossed his arms and looked away, ending the debate.

"You may proceed with your final segment, Inquisitor." Vitellius said.

The Inquisitor bowed and took his place. He was quiet for a moment, and the video screen was off. Caius began to get nervous; this wasn't how things normally went. "Senators," Antoninus started, "After the end of the candidate's apprenticeship, the standard practice has been for the candidate to be drafted into the military. This instills values of discipline, leadership, and camaraderie. But more importantly, it is so that the Emperor understands what is at risk when he goes to war, and understands the needs of the men. He may not be so hasty to commit others to fight and die when he himself has been on the front lines before." He was pacing back and forth across the room. "Your honors... I have no presentation

123

to give for this section of the Candidate's life." He gave a short bow, barely bending his back at all, and retreated back to his alcove.

"*Nothing?*" Tullius called out. It was the first time that a Senator other than Vitellius had spoken, if one wasn't counting Oventia's unanticipated yelps of laughter. Caius could see that the other two Senators were similarly surprised. His heart leapt, and he was desperate to turn around and see Marcus's reaction. Against all odds, he managed to keep his calm and remain in his seat, staring unflinchingly ahead. The room was silent for a moment as the Senators waited for any response from the Inquisitor, but there was none.

"Well, then, Advocate. You may present your own arguments."

Marcus practically danced into the center of the room. He bowed with a flourish and flicked on the video screen, showing Caius leading a platoon up a mountain during training.

"Thank you, Senators. I was expecting to have some arguments to refute, so please excuse me if I am speaking more off the cuff. Caius's record in the military has been nothing short of exemplary. Zero official disciplinary marks on his record, and a long list of awards and achievements that would use up all of my time to list." As if on cue, the video on the screen changed again to show an award ceremony in which Caius was honored by General Lucullus, back at the base in Fukuoka. It had been a big service to celebrate Unification Day, commemorating the flight of the Ming Emperor from China and the subsequent annexation. Caius almost smiled at the memory before catching himself. *No emotion,* he remembered. On the screen, Lucullus was placing the red ribbon around Caius's neck. *Hard to believe that it's only been a few days since I last saw him as I drove out of the base with Kaneshiro,* Caius thought to himself. Seemed like a lifetime ago.

"But for the purposes of this trial, his most important achievement has been as a leader of men. He has been consistently recognized for his guidance and judgment, being assigned to missions that would normally never be entrusted to a man of his rank. Caius would be well on the path to General by now if it weren't for the strict orders that no Candidate should be promoted." Caius had wondered many times why he was consistently passed over for admission to the Officer's Corps. At least now he understood.

"He volunteered for multiple dangerous missions, going behind enemy lines repeatedly to scout enemy positions before raids." The video changed to show Caius in his cockpit; the video was practically looking up his nose. Behind him, the blurry background spun and swerved as he was clearly taking wild evasive measures. "His intelligence-gathering was essential to a number of successful missions that have kept our defensive edge against Japanese troops seeking to reclaim the Roman footholds on the archipelago."

Marcus clicked the remote again to a still image of Caius wearing his gleaming formal armor at the front of his brigade, saluting to his superior officer. There was a fierce look of pride and determination etched into his face; it was a powerful end to the presentation. "There are simply not enough good things I can say about Caius's military career, and apparently, no negative aspects for the Inquisitor to bring up. This experience has shown how prepared he is to lead the Empire, which cannot be said of any other candidate currently in the trials." Marcus bowed so deeply Caius was afraid that he'd hurt his back. But he stood with a smile and retreated back to his desk for the last time, barely containing his glee.

The Senators convened again at the table in front of the room; Tullius had the same sour expression on his face, but apparently had no arguments to make so he sat still as a statue. Oventia seemed particularly impressed; even old Vitellius was nodding enthusiastically. The discussion ended, and they returned to their normal seats.

Vitellius stood and held his arms open. "Gentlemen, your presentations in this matter have been enlightening. We Senators have been given valuable information to judge the faults and strengths of the Candidate, and we shall take your words into consideration when assigning our scores for this round. Before we conclude, are there any additional points to present, either for or against the Candidate?"

"No," Marcus called out immediately. Antoninus replied with a booming "No," shortly after.

"Then I declare this session finished. Caius Serica, you may now rise and exit the chamber with your advocate. Guards?" From the very back of the room, the Praetorians sprang to life and pushed open the heavy doors, flooding the room with light. Marcus was practically skipping as they exited, but Caius felt completely drained. He did his best to hold his head high and walk out. As he crossed the threshold, he turned to see Antoninus, still wearing the thick mask of the Inquisitor, watching him leave. At the far end of the room, Tullius remained seated with a frustrated scowl.

As soon as the doors slammed shut behind them, Marcus gripped Caius in a bear hug, heaving him into the air. "Brilliant, boy! You did great."

Caius couldn't help but smile a bit. "You weren't so bad yourself, old man." It wasn't a lie; Caius had not expected Marcus to have been so thorough, digging through every moment of his past and even tracking down old acquaintances.

"I thought I was going to explode when the Inquisitor said he had no arguments! God, we got 'em good." Marcus kept chattering a thousand miles a minute, giving a play-by-play of all of his best moments with child-like delight. Caius, on the other hand, was silent. His thoughts were still dwelling on the Inquisitor's arguments. Maybe he wasn't cut out to be Emperor. The word "weak" that Antoninus kept repeating echoed through his mind. And it looked like Senator Tullius had been convinced of it.

"Come on, Marcus. I'm starving." They headed back toward the dining hall.

CHAPTER 8

A chilly wind cascaded down the side of the mountain, though the weather was sunny and clear. Caius and Marcus walked along one of the many steep paths that ascended the rocky peaks surrounding the trial grounds. Even from this distance, Caius could see some of the doorways and windows peeking out from the mountainside. He wondered which Candidate was currently trapped in there, watching his or her entire life history scrutinized by strangers. The interview trial had continued for the past three days, and the last candidate should be finishing up right about now.

When they were a sufficient distance away from any hidden microphones and prying eyes throughout the facility, Marcus hopped into the air and shouted with happiness. "A 26!!"

They had awoken this morning to find a public scoreboard posted in the main hall, showing the rank of all of the candidates so far based on the first trial. Caius had scored a twenty six, the fourth-highest. His new friend Herennius had gotten a 29. Caius's heart had sank when he saw that, if only slightly. Great that his friend had done so well in the personal history phase, but at the same time, he was still a competitor. Even before seeing the score, his presence constantly reminded Caius that only one of them could become Emperor.

"And… how did the others react?"

Marcus's face split into a wide grin. Right after the scores were announced, he'd had an early breakfast with a bunch of the other advocates while Caius stayed in and studied a bit more. "That's the good news. Most of them looked like they'd just been thrown into that lake." He

128

pointed down at an ice-covered pond filling a cleft between two ridges. "Utter shock. And a fair amount of anger, too. Naturally they tried to hide it, but they're all terrible at hiding things from me.

"And Andericus?" Caius asked, having noted that the rude Althea had somehow managed to get a score of twenty seven. Clearly the scores had been based on how the candidate acted, not the content of the video; Caius had a hard time picturing her being a nice person before she learned that her character would matter. Caius had to admit that Althea must be an excellent actress.

"Andericus was thrilled, naturally. And I can't really blame him. He took a big risk in picking her as his candidate, and it looks like it paid off. So you're behind both Herennius and Althea, but not by much."

Caius nodded and climbed up a particularly large, rocky ridge, still slick with ice. "Then what do we do?"

"Well, for Althea it's obvious. For Herennius... it's a bit more difficult. I hate to have to tell you this," Marcus grimaced, "but you need to differentiate yourself from Herennius. You need to show the Senators why you're better than him. By any means." His intent was pretty clear.

"I don't want to undercut him, though." Caius searched for a reason that would satisfy Marcus, stalling by taking a breather from their hike. "Wouldn't that make me look bad in front of the Senators? It will seem like I know that he's better and so I'm targeting him instead of winning based on my own merit."

Marcus took a seat on a nearby rock, huffing and puffing from the climb. He didn't answer Caius for a moment; just looked down into the valley below, crisscrossed by snow-covered farms and sheltered patches of forest that the empire was trying to re-introduce in the area. "I suppose you're right," Marcus said finally. "Undercutting Herennius would make him even more of a front runner, which would cause the Senators to focus on him even more. And really you can make up those three points very quickly. But if you just happen to be in a position where you *could* make him look bad..." Marcus trailed off, but he didn't really need to finish.

"I'll think about it," Caius responded finally.

Marcus nodded, satisfied that at least Caius was cognizant of what needed to be done; this had been a constant battle between them on the train, and Caius's experience so far was proving Marcus more and more right by the day. They sat together on the rocky outcropping and listened to the wind, watching wisps of snow twirl through the air.

From inside his jacket, Marcus withdrew his shiny pocket watch.

"We'd better get back down there," Marcus said. "The athletic trials begin in 45 minutes, and you've got to get changed." Caius pulled himself up and offered a hand to Marcus, who was struggling to get back on his feet. They hiked down the mountain and back inside the training facility to get ready.

The candidates emerged from the narrow hallway to find a large, grassy field on an outcropping overlooking the valley below. It had recently been cleared of snow, heaped near the sidelines into large piles that reflected bright flashes of sun. The grass had a dull grey tinge to the normally bright green color, and it crunched underfoot.

Above the field, on rows of stone benches carved into the side of the mountain, the advocates all sat in the front row. Caius saw Marcus sitting next to Flavia just as he walked out next to Herennius. He also spotted Andericus, wrapped in a heavy coat and sitting with some of the other advocates that Caius didn't know. Behind them sat the spectators: the aristocracy and privileged few who were considered trustworthy enough to have knowledge of the trials. Servants had arranged large, portable heaters to blast shimmering waves of heat over the benches to keep them warm, so most of the spectators wore only robes or light jackets. At the very front, right next to the field, was a stone platform with three plush chairs for the Senators.

The group of candidates slowly trickled onto the field from the tunnel. Each candidate had been outfitted with shorts, athletic shoes, and a bright jersey in either yellow or red, as well as a correspondingly colored plastic helmet. They stood shivering in the grass, clustered into groups. The thirty of them had only been assembled for a few days, but most of them seemed to have found at least one or two other candidates that they felt comfortable with. Caius stood with Herennius and talked with Florian, the tall African candidate who'd played Pharaoh with them. Closer to the benches, he noticed Althea standing with Drusus, the Egyptian who had taken to following her around like a loyal dog; they both glared at Herennius when they noticed him. Obviously they knew that he was the current leader of the pack, and they didn't seem to share Caius's reservations about taking him down a peg.

131

"Gather round the center of the field, please," boomed the voice of Quintus, from some hidden set of loudspeakers. The spectators all sat up straight and got their binoculars out, ready for the action. Quintus emerged from the tunnel again in his bright gold formal armor, to announce the trials. The Senators made their way out of the tunnel behind him at a snail's pace as Vitellius struggled up the icy steps, waving off servants who attempted to help. The Senators crossed the field and took their assigned seats while the candidates gathered loosely around Quintus, who stood directly on top of a white chalk line drawn across the center of the field.

"Candidates," he said with a nod to the group standing before him, "Advocates, spectators, and Senators: welcome to the Second Trial. This will be our first athletic competition. The leader of the Empire requires many attributes, such as intelligence and honesty. But the Emperor should also be a strong, fit example of strength for the citizens. And not just physical strength: *moral* strength. The Emperor should value teamwork, good sportsmanship, strategy, and courage. He or she serves as the model citizen for all others to emulate, and that includes maintaining health and skill. So today, you candidates will be playing a little game that will effectively test these attributes. There are many popular sports throughout the empire that our candidates have no doubt experienced many, many times and with varying levels of prowess. So, in order to level the playing field, we have chosen something a little different today. We wanted a new challenge that will test how well you can adapt to a new situation, with new rules and unfamiliar skills."

He clapped his hands, and a stream of servants poured out of the tunnel, carrying armloads of athletic equipment. Two teams reached each end and set up large nets, while others carried bundles of sticks with some sort of basket attached to the top. One last servant walked straight to Quintus and handed him a small grey rubber ball; Quintus tossed it into the air with a casual flick of his wrist. Out of the corner of his eye, Caius noted that Herennius had a broad grin on his face, instead of the mix of curiosity and confusion that the rest of the Candidates had.

Caius leaned over and whispered: "What is this?"

Herennius just smiled. "They'll explain it." Servants were making their way through the crowd, handing one of the sticks to each Candidate. "But trust me: it's so much fun!"

"This game is known as 'Teewaraathon,' and comes to us from our new friends of the Haudenosaunee tribes in the New World." Quintus announced. "I personally learned it from the Mohawk ambassador in Rome, and it's been one of my favorite sports ever since."

That's why Herennius is so pleased, Caius realized. *He was stationed near that tribe in the New World. He's probably the only one here who has actually played this already.*

"The many tribes in the region have been playing Teewaraathon for centuries. Only those who have attained the ranks of warrior in the tribe are permitted to participate, and a victory brings honor to their native tribe. And it is also used as a way to alleviate tension between the groups, instead of resorting to war. Given the importance of this game to the Haudenosaunee, the Senate Tribunal decided this would be the perfect opportunity for you candidates to prove your worth."

The Senators, spectators, and advocates all clapped at that. The candidates turned and looked at each other furtively, gauging the reactions of their peers.

133

"The game is fairly simple." Quintus motioned toward the nets at each end of the field. "The goal is to get this ball…" he held it up in his hands so that every candidate could see, "into that net." Quintus took one of the sticks from the closest servant and dropped the little ball into the basket at the top, then he spun quickly and whipped it across the field at blinding speed, right into the large net at the end. The crowd broke out into applause, as did Herennius. The candidates were too busy studying the sticks and figuring out the mechanics of how it works. "The game is one hour long, divided into four fifteen minute quarters. The team with the most points at the end wins. However, please note that while winning will certainly reflect well on you, what really matters is how you perform *individually*. The Senators will be watching each candidate closely to determine who best reflects the values and image that the Emperor must project. So, a successful candidate could still be on the losing team, and vice versa."

Candidates looked at each other with suspicion. The most popular sports in the Empire were ones like sword fighting or wrestling or boxing; sports that didn't require reliance on a whole group of people to do their jobs.

"One of you will be playing as the goalkeeper, who stands in front of the net and attempts to block any shot from the opposing team. This candidate will be allowed pads to be placed over the chest and shoulders, as well as a broader stick. There is also a buffer zone around the goal where no other player may enter. The rest of you will be working together as a unit to move the ball down the field using only throws and catches with your sticks. The quarter starts with a faceoff: each team lines up around this circle," he gestured to the chalk circle in the center of the field, "and sends one member forward to fight for the ball. Under normal circumstances, the team is divided up into sections for offense, defense, or both. However, we have suspended those

134

rules for this match; you all may play as a team wherever you see fit. If you wish to leave members back as defense or offense, you can. But you do not have to." Quintus hefted the stick and swishing it through the air. "Keep in mind that this is an aggressive, fast-paced, physical game. You may not hold another player, nor lash out or stab at each other with the sticks, but you may use your body to hit the other players if that person has the ball in their net or if they are nearby a loose ball. I will be watching the gameplay and looking for any violations of these rules, which would not reflect well on a candidate." He gestured to the watching Senators in case his warning was not clear.

The candidates looked around, seeing each other in a new light and sizing one another up. Caius turned and looked up at Herennius, who was significantly taller, and twice as bulky; one hit from him and Caius would probably be thrown off the field. And Florian was even bigger.

"So, you've played this before?" Caius asked under his breath.

"Oh yes. It's an important tradition with the nations of the New World. Or at least the Northern part where I was stationed. They would often come play exhibition matches at the embassy, and the military company there put together a team so that we could play against them. It's quite fun!"

Great, Caius thought. If Herennius hadn't locked down the front runner status yet, this would certainly do it.

"For the female candidates," Quintus continued "we understand that many of you are significantly smaller than your male compatriots, which will be a disadvantage in this game.

Because of this, the Senate has offered to allow any female candidate to not participate this round, and it will not reflect negatively on your character. Instead, you can accept a score of 7.5 for this test, which is simply half of the points available in this round; a 7.5 is completely average."

The candidates looked around at each other; the female candidates all seemed to be looking around for any other woman who was going to throw in the towel. But no one volunteered, and the crowd was silent. They had all been through military training with men and served side by side for up to a year. Women had been part of the army since the Great War with China. This game couldn't be harder than what they'd been through in basic training, could it? And even if the Senators said it would not affect the outcome, they all knew that it would matter, at least subconsciously. None of them wanted to be seen as a quitter.

"Very well. You will have thirty minutes to prepare your strategies and to get used to the equipment," Quintus announced. One by one, the candidates were called forward and divided into teams of 15. Luckily, Caius was sent to the Red team, same as Herennius.

"Finally, we need one team member to volunteer as captain," said Quintus. He didn't say it, but every candidate had the same thought: if the team fails, the captain will take the blame. But, the captain could also get credit for a victory. Immediately, a tall, pale candidate with dark black curls stepped forward for the reds. Caius tried to remember anything about him: his name was Spurius, but they hadn't had much of a chance to talk yet. Across the field, he noticed Althea volunteer as captain for the yellows. *Just perfect,* Caius thought. At least it was a bit of extra motivation to win.

"All right. The game will begin in half an hour." Quintus blew a whistle, and the candidates gathered into two huddles on opposite sides of the field. Servants streamed out of the tunnel carrying large platters of food and pitchers of refreshments for the spectators and Senators.

Herennius drilled the Red Team on using the sticks, and Caius was just managing to get a hand on the passing and catching when Quintus whistled again and gathered the teams around him. Althea stepped forward for the Yellow team, and Herennius pushed Caius forward for the reds "You're small and fast," he told Caius. Quintus placed the small rubber ball on the center line, and the rest of the team fanned out across the field, looking at each other for cues as to where to go.

The whistle blew, and Althea whipped her stick forward before Caius could barely even react. She pulled the ball into her net and took off down the field, followed shortly by Caius. Red and yellow jerseys darted back and forth across the field, and the spectators roared, not sure who they should be cheering for. Althea made it a quarter of the way down the field before another candidate plowed into her like a moving truck, sending her skidding across the still frozen grass and sending the ball flying. There was a communal shout as every candidate in the area scrambled after it, churning through the frozen turf. Caius was buried under 10 other heavy, squirming bodies, all trying to show off their enthusiasm and athleticism for the Senators.

Somehow, a member of the yellow team managed to crawl back out of the pile with the ball in the net of his stick and dashed toward the goal net. Three red-clad candidates converged on him like wolves. Caius couldn't really tell who they were; wearing the helmets made them all

137

practically indistinguishable. The Senators must have been scoring based on the numbers on the shirts. "PASS IT," Caius heard Althea shouting from somewhere behind him, but the guy with the ball either didn't hear or didn't care. He tried to weave between the three interceptors, but he didn't make it; one of the plowed into him and threw him across the field boundary. Quintus blew the whistle and handed the ball to Spurius to start the play over.

From the sidelines, Spurius chucked the ball to Caius, who was miraculously able to pull it out of the air. He looked into his net with shock, hardly comprehending that he'd managed to catch it. But the herd of thundering yellow jerseys coming down the field after him snapped him out of it pretty quickly, and he turned and ran. Just as they were about to catch up to him, he saw that Herennius had managed to evade his defender. Caius tossed the ball clumsily, but Herennius caught it regardless and took off down field. But Althea slammed into Caius anyway, knocking the wind out of him and throwing him to the ground.

"Oh, sorry there, Caius!" Althea said, dripping in phony sympathy. "Good throw, though! For a man of your size, you're really getting the hang of this!" Through the face mask of his helmet, Caius could see Althea's sarcastic sneer as she reached out a hand. "Here, let me help you up!" Caius glared back at her and heaved himself back to his feet without Althea's help but still having difficulty breathing. Althea patted Caius on the back, glancing out of the corners of her eyes to make sure the Senators were taking notice, then took off after the ball. Caius gritted his teeth, wrapped his fingers around the stick, and ran down the field. Behind the goal, Herennius was weaving between yellow players, looking for any red teammates in place to score. His eyes locked onto Caius approaching, and he whipped the ball over the defenders' heads, right into Caius's net. Althea was right on his heels, charging like a bull. Caius planted his feet as

138

Althea slammed into him again, this time successfully standing his ground and sending Althea reeling. Just at that moment, a narrow path between Caius and the goal opened up, and Caius launched the ball at top speed straight into the net. Red scored!

Herennius galloped across the field and clapped him heartily on the back. "Amazing shot! I couldn't have done it better myself!" Other candidates from both teams offered up their congratulations as well, but more muted and tame. In the back of everyone's mind, it wasn't a match between red and yellow, but against each individual. They were all trying to keep their eyes off of the Senators, no doubt noting who had scored the goal. From the bleachers, they could hear the spectators all roaring; Marcus's throaty cheers boomed across the field, clearly distinguishable from the others. Quintus blew the whistle, signaling the goal and starting the game again. A yellow player snagged the ball and ran downfield at breakneck pace; every other candidate took off shouting behind him.

The dirt and grass underfoot was beginning to turn to mud as the icy layer of frost began to melt under the bright sun and constant trampling. After about half an hour of dozens of rounds running back and forth, both teams were starting to fade. Caius continued to push himself to the limit, but his legs were turning into lead underneath him. Althea was still dashing back and forth with an incredible amount of energy; she'd already scored, and the smirk on her face had only grown. Only Herennius was any match for her, pivoting and dodging expertly despite his massive size.

A member of the yellow team managed to get ahold of the ball and made her way downfield; she made it a few yards before Drusus, Althea's friend, knocked her to the ground and picked up the ball. He, in turn, was bowled over by another yellow team member. The ball flew back and forth each time.

"No one is passing," Herennius said from behind Caius. He had explained how essential it was to the game, but no one on the red team had listened, and apparently the yellows hadn't learned either.

"Because someone else gets the glory of scoring if you pass of the ball," Caius observed.

"And they all just keep going after the ball…" Herennius realized. "Well this is just perfect!"

The ball was stolen yet again; a yellow candidate charged toward them, head bowed down like a battering ram. Herennius easily sidestepped him and slammed his hip into the other candidate, sending him sprawling. Herennius had barely even moved upon impact. Caius reached down and scooped the ball into his net. "Remember: passing!"

They trudged toward the opposite goal; their competitors eyed them, trying to gauge which one to go after. The yellow team decided on Caius and charged forward; Red team members followed, hoping to scoop up the ball after Caius had been run over. But just when they reached him, Caius arced the ball overhead to Herennius. The charge collapsed as they decided they didn't want to expend the energy tackling him anymore. Caius ran past them as everyone changed targets and moved toward Herennius. But just as he was going to be tackled, he tossed the ball back to Caius. The duo moved like this back and forth down the field as the yellow team wore themselves out even more changing targets. Althea was shouting orders to defend them, but no one really listened to her. As they reached the yellow goal, Caius had the ball and dashed around behind the net only to find a wall of yellow players. He glanced to Herennius, but apparently someone had finally heard Althea, because he was defended too. At the last second, Caius launched the ball to Gideon, who had been left wide open right in front of the goal. Gideon looked more shocked than anyone else, but caught the ball expertly. Valeria, a slender brunette candidate from Armenia, was guarding yellow's goal; she suddenly realized what was happening and tried to dive back into the opening, but it was too late. Gideon launched the ball into the net and scored another one for Red.

The crowd roared, and he heard Marcus yelling "That was the best assist I've ever seen!!" Herennius ran over to Gideon and wrapped him in an enormous bear hug, lifting him straight off the ground. Caius wasn't far behind. Most members of the yellow team were clapping politely, but Althea was stomping down the field. Caius snuck a furtive look at the Senator's table and noticed them all scribbling furiously. Quintus blew the whistle, signaling that the second quarter had finished.

"There will be a twenty minute break," Quintus announced. Teams of candidates trudged to opposite ends of the field, panting and exhausted. Herennius went to the front of the group without even considering whether he should. Spurius, who had volunteered as captain, looked for a moment as if he might say something, but then sat down quietly.

"Did you guys see that last play?" Herennius said, gesturing to Caius and Gideon. "We've been running around out there like headless chickens for the past half hour because nobody is willing to pass the ball. Well, that's not what this game is all about. This isn't

141

wrestling: you can't do it all by yourselves. But you saw what happened when we worked together! They didn't even know what hit 'em!" A few members of the team looked down at their feet, realizing that they were the problem. "So, here's what we need to do. First, defense: you pick a guy, and you stick with him. They're going to be trying to pass the ball now, so you need to get in there and block it. And we need some people to hang back as defense."

There was a painful silence in the locker room.

"Look," Caius said, jumping up next to Herennius. He saw his chance to impress the Senators, or at least keep up with Herennius. "We're all in the same boat: you want to look good. We get it; we're all being judged. But you know what looks worse? Losing the game. If we get back out there, and the yellow team is all organized, who are the Senators going to be noticing? Whose strategy are they going to appreciate? We will *all* look better if only some of us are willing to stay out of the limelight for part of the game. And, there are two quarters left, so we can just trade off in the middle, ensuring that everyone on the team gets an equal amount of action."

There was an uneasy silence as the candidates all gauged everyone else's reaction. "I can live with that," Gideon said finally. There was a low chorus of agreement. Herennius gave Caius a slight nod of approval.

Across the field, they saw Quintus stand from his seat and return to the center of the field.

142

The red team helped each other up and ran across the muddy field, newly energized and ready to go. The yellow team followed shortly, trying to match the enthusiasm of their opponents. The spectators cheered, ready for their entertainment to begin again.

The yellow team had no clue what hit them. Red scored three goals in the next quarter, passing the ball back and forth like circus performers. The yellow team was melting down, yelling at each other and scrambling across the field. Herennius was the star of the show, passing to every team member, scoring one of the key goals, and the Senators could absolutely not take their eyes off of him.

As they celebrated the third goal, Caius watched Althea rip off her helmet and hurl it to the ground in anger. Andericus stood on the bleacher sidelines and wavered, clearly wanting to shout at his Candidate to keep the temper in check. But if he said it out loud, it would only draw attention to Althea's fit of rage; she kicked at the grass, sending beads of sweat shaking off of her long black hair. Mud and clumps of grass went flying into the sidelines. *God, I hope the Senators saw that,* Caius thought. *So much for her phony good sportsmanship.*

Finally, she picked up her helmet off the ground and hustled after her teammates, catching up to a tall candidate that Caius barely recognized. Marius was his name, maybe? Althea pulled the other Candidate in close and seemed to whisper in his ear. Her face was intense, severe, and wrathful. Marius nodded resolutely and glared down the field. *Wonder what that was about,* Caius thought. Althea pulled on her helmet again and strapped it into place as the ball came into play.

The yellow team charged forward, screaming like barbarians with Althea leading the

pack. The red team members wavered for a moment, but Caius drew them forward, passing the

ball and sprinting to the next open section of the field. It was more intense than any of the

bombing missions Caius had been on in Japan. The yellow team seems to have finally gotten

their act together and were aggressively defending everyone; particularly Herennius. Caius was

only briefly aware of the crowd on the side of the field, roaring and cheering for one team or

another, betting and laughing amongst themselves.

Halfway down the field, Gideon had the ball, but he was cornered by Drusus. He

swiveled back and forth searching for anyone to pass the ball to. Caius pushed away his defender

and sprinted forward, trying to get open. Gideon saw what he was doing and braced himself to

break out and make the pass.

There was a loud *CRACK* from behind Caius that echoed off the sides of the mountains.

He heard Quintus's whistle shrieking over and over as he skidded to a halt in a muddy splash.

The spectators had all fallen entirely silent, and the advocates and Senators were standing in their

seats for a better view. Behind him, a shifting red and yellow blob had massed near the goal net.

Caius and Gideon pushed their way forward as Quintus waved a hand at servants. On the ground,

Herennius clutched his leg and rolled through the grass, grimacing in pain and clenching his

broad jaw. His uniform was covered in mud, but darker blood began to seep through the fabric as

Caius watched. Marius, the one Althea had whispered to, clutched the lower half of his shattered

stick that ended in jagged splinters; the other half with the net on the end lay in the grass under

Herennius. Marius looked around defensively, lowering the stick to his side as though nobody

would notice that he was carrying it.

Doctor Porcia rushed from the tunnel out of the facility, trailed by two servants lugging cases of equipment. Caius cleared the crowd away from Herennius and knelt down to help while Doctor Porcia pulled out a pair of scissors and cut away the pants over Herennius's shin. His leg was gushing blood, and a jagged spit of white bone stuck through the skin.

"Definitely serious," the doctor muttered to herself. "I need to take him back to the medic's office. He'll probably need surgery." Herennius moaned in pain as four servants unfolded a stretcher and placed him carefully on the canvas. "Don't worry," she told all of the candidates, "He will be perfectly fine." Herennius was carried off the field with the doctor by his side, leaving the rest of the candidates clustered around the bloody puddle of mud where he'd fallen.

Quintus walked to the Senator's table and conferred with them briefly, then returned to the candidates. "Marius, please return to your room," he said shortly. None of the other candidates said anything, or even looked at him as he backed out of the crowd, throwing the other broken half of his stick to the ground. "The rest of you, get back to the game," Quintus said.

Althea gave a sickening, satisfied smirk and enthusiastically said "Yes sir!" She flipped the ball into her net and called to her teammates as the game picked up again.

CHAPTER 9

Marcus sawed through a meaty hunk of sizzling ham in the cafeteria. "A fourteen!" he said enthusiastically. "Excellent work, boy!"

He wasn't even bothering to control his tone; other advocates and candidates nearby were listening in. They were already aware of the score if they had checked the latest results, but it was still uncomfortable. "Quiet, Marcus!" Caius reminded him.

"Yes, yes," Marcus said, glancing around. "Sorry about that. But still, bravo! That almost moves you to the front of the pack with Herennius!" His friend had been penalized for missing the rest of the game, despite breaking his leg. He'd only been given a score of eleven, leaving the two of them tied. Althea, however, had scored just enough to remain in second. Apparently the senators had missed her role in the 'accident.'

"Shouldn't we, be keeping that quiet? Look what happened to Herennius when he was ahead of the pack."

Marcus rubbed his chubby fingers through his wild mane of hair. "You're probably right. They'll all see the score, but we best downplay it if possible. There's really no need to paint a target on your back for absolutely no reason." Caius nodded in agreement. Marcus took another bite of his breakfast, unable to stop smiling.

"It was Althea," Caius said finally. Marcus looked at him quizzically. "She was furious that they were losing, and she came up and said something to Marius, and then Marius attacked Herennius. It was all Althea."

"Are you sure?" Marcus said.

"Absolutely."

"Did you hear her say anything?"

"Well, no…" Caius admitted

Marcus took another bite of his breakfast and leaned back in his chair and looked around the cafeteria. Althea and Andericus hadn't come in yet. "There isn't much that can be done about it, then. Marius and his Advocate are already gone; left sometime in the night."

"And can we report her or something?" Caius asked.

Marcus tilted his head in thought, then frowned. "We don't have any evidence. There weren't any microphones on the field, so there's no way of knowing what Althea said. We'd only really be able to prove that they talked before the incident, which isn't enough. And then it looks like we're afraid; like we are trying to get Althea disqualified because we don't think we can beat her. The Senators would see that as cowardly."

Caius sighed and plunged a spoon into his oatmeal. Marcus had pretty much nailed it. Althea was a snake, but she covered her tracks.

Halfway through breakfast, Herennius hobbled in wearing a gleaming metal cast over his leg. He gave a wan smile as he loaded his plate with apple oatcakes and joined Marcus and Caius. Flavia wasn't far behind.

"How's the leg?" Caius asked.

Herennius looked down at the metal shell clamped around his shin and gave it a pat. "Ah, it's not that bad. Doctor Porcia got the bone back in place and set it in the pressure cast. It was a particularly bad break, so it will take about a week to heal fully. But Senator Vitellius came by personally and told me that there won't be any more physical trials until I am healed, so I'm not out of the game yet."

"Good," Caius said, wondering if he really meant it. Would have been an easy way out if they weren't competing against each other anymore. "Glad to hear it."

Herennius nodded and dug into his breakfast; Caius wasn't too hungry anymore.

"How'd the rest of the game go?" Herennius asked through a mouth full of cream, oats, and apples.

Caius was just getting through the highlights of the last quarter, telling Herennius how he had scored the last goal with a brilliant dodge, when Quintus entered the cafeteria, flanked again by Praetorian Guards.

"Candidates and Advocates, please gather in the central hall as soon as you are able. The programmers need some advanced notice in order to set up your simulations." With that cryptic message, Quintus retreated back into the entry hall, leaving everyone chewing in silence. Marcus, Caius and Herennius finished their meals in a rush and headed to the next trial.

They entered the large domed chamber to the sight of thirty humming computers and bright monitors arranged in a circle, lining the edge of the domed portion of the room. Above each desk was a second enormous monitor, set to the level of the balconies that ringed the room, so that the spectators would be able to see what was happening on the screen. Many of the other candidates were already there; some milling around the computers, others conversing with men carrying tablet computers and typing rapidly. As they entered the room, a pair of programmers approached both Caius and Herennius and whisked them into different corners where they could talk.

"Ennius," the programmer introduced himself, shaking Caius's hand.

"Caius," he answered. "So, what is this all about?"

"They're having you run a military simulation," Ennius explained. Caius broke out into a broad grin; back at the Academy, these war games had been a favorite activity of all of the students. He'd spent hours in the computer lab facing off against his friends in all sorts of different settings and challenges.

The programmer tilted the tablet so that Caius could see. "The scenario is a hypothetical war against the Mapuche Empire. Your goal today is conquest of the fortified city of Ollantaytambo, in the New World. It lies in the mountain range on the southern continent, at an elevation of 2800 meters." In his hand, the tablet played a video showing steep rocky cliffs and a

149

large metropolis with terraced farms and stone buildings carved right into the mountainside. Not too different from the underground complex they were currently in.

"You have your choice of military units," Ennius said, flicking a tab on the tablet and handing it to Caius. The brilliant display showed pictures of soldiers and equipment: armored cars, legions of soldiers, snipers, tanks… everything they would ever need for an invasion. "You need to study the city and the geography and determine the best way to get in. There is a maximum of 100,000 units available, but extra points will be awarded for using fewer troops. And the enemy forces will be automatically set by the AI to a proportional level. So you just need to let me know how many units you will be using and what equipment you would need, and I'll go ahead and program it in."

Caius studied the city and the surrounding terrain closely. There was only one entrance winding through the valley toward the city; an easy target for enemy artillery and entrenched defenders. Depending on the sophistication of the simulation, the AI could even block off the road or bury the invaders in a landslide. A frontward assault would be suicidal.

"And everyone will be doing the same simulation, right?"

"Yes," Ennius answered. "And your moves will be displayed on the screens above your station, so that the Senators and spectators and advocates can watch you progress."

Caius continued studying the map. "And air power?" He'd been working with planes for years, and knew their capabilities pretty well. The Inca city was too steep for an airstrip for fighters, and seemed woefully underprepared with anti-aircraft weapons. They'd be pretty powerless to defend against bombing.

Ennius tapped another tab, showing the selection of planes and airships available. Caius knew the models well, having designed or worked on most of the engines with his company and in his apprenticeship. He surveyed the selection, plotting his strategy.

"Ennius," he asked. "I know that many pilots use a particular piece of equipment in case of engine failure called a 'Parachute.' Do you have this in your inventory?"

Ennius went through pages and pages of specialized equipment that had been designated for inclusion. Flamethrowers... night vision goggles... finally, he was able to find it.

"Excellent!" Caius said, inputting his orders into the tablet. Ennius gave him a confused look, but shrugged and did what he was supposed to.

As they were finishing their conversation, Quintus made his way onto the raised platform at the center of the computers. Caius looked up from the tablet and noticed that the balconies were suddenly full of spectators; he'd been so busy inputting his orders that he hadn't even noticed the room filling up.

"Today's trial is a test of strategy," Quintus announced. The screens above the computers jumped to life. "The Emperor is of course the head of the military and should be well versed in the art of war and conquest. As each candidate has spent time in the military, they should all be familiar with standard operations and protocol. The candidates have been tasked with planning a military assault of the Mapuche capital, known as Ollantaytambo. This heavily fortified city, located deep in the mountains of the New World, is only approachable by one road."

The screens showed a swooping aerial view of the road up the valley, blocked by multiple gates and scores of troops in their mottled green uniforms. Caius was particularly impressed by the detail in the simulated environment; the programmers must have worked on this for ages.

"There are four primary targets for the candidates to seize," Quintus continued. The video screens switched to an overhead view of the city, which looked odd and didn't quite convey the steep hills and winding streets. "First, the main entrance into the city needs to be controlled." The gatehouse of the inner wall turned bright red, standing out from the other grey buildings. "Second, the communications hub of the city, which allows the Mapuche king to communicate with troops throughout the west coast of the continent, needs to be neutralized." That building lit up too. "Third, the military headquarters, which will contain vital intelligence as well as their highest ranked leaders, ought to be seized." An entire block of the city lit up on the map. "Fourth, the palace itself should be taken, and the King with it." The top of the mountain turned red. Each of the four targets stood out like beacons as the map zoomed out to show the entire valley.

"The candidates have all selected the size of their deployment and the specific equipment that their men will use. They will be issuing orders from their computer here," he gestured at the banks of screens and keyboards below, "and will be judged on the effectiveness of their strategy in terms of their protection of their men and how well they accomplish the objectives. With that said, let the trial begin!"

Herennius limped back over to Caius to wish him luck before heading over to his assigned spot. Caius found his own computer and looked up to the balcony, trying to spot Marcus's mane of grey hair, but no luck. It didn't affect the outcome, but Caius was a bit disappointed anyway; it was comforting to have Marcus watching. He sat at the computer, running his fingers over the keyboard in anticipation. When he looked up, Althea was standing over him with that trademark look of haughty disdain.

"Hello, Caius," she said as she slid into the closest seat.

"Althea," Caius answered, just as icy and cold as Althea had been to him.

There was a tense silence between them as the other candidates chattered amongst each other and the spectators were served drinks. "Looks like Herennius is walking again," Althea remarked finally. "So glad to see he is making a full recovery. I was really worried about him!" Hopefully, if the Senators were somehow recording this, they would detect the sarcasm. Althea always managed to control her tone, but the sneer curling her lips always made her intentions abundantly clear.

Caius gritted his teeth and kept his hands on the keyboard to prevent him from punching Althea. "Yes, the doctor here is excellent. I'm just glad that it didn't affect his chances in the Trials; he'll be able to compete fully. And he's been doing so well already!" Althea's eyes flashed; she apparently hadn't known that Herennius was still in the mix, and seeing Herennius

153

ahead of her was worse than any insult Caius could have come up with. She must have thought there were more athletic trials, and she was so pleased to have taken out the other frontrunner.

"Of course," Althea forced herself to say. "So glad that he's still a contender!"

The monitors in front of them flashed to life, interrupting the tense conversation. A tutorial flashed over the screen, showing them how to deploy and control units; it was fairly intuitive and Caius clicked through quickly. The city was spread out before him, ready for the taking.

"All right, Candidates: begin your invasions!"

The candidates all jumped to life with furious clicking and typing. The spectators above were watching the monitors and pointing out various strategies and methods, taking bets only seconds into the simulation.

Caius deployed his artillery first, shelling the few anti-aircraft positions that had been set up. He was glad that the simulation was at least a somewhat accurate depiction of what the city was really like. The Mapuche didn't exactly have the technology to develop very good anti-aircraft capabilities, and they certainly weren't in any financial position to buy sophisticated equipment from any of the more civilized nations. The AA guns were taken out fairly quickly, and Caius set the artillery to simply select its own targets.

Next, he began to deploy armored troops to the gates of the valley. As expected, the Mapuche army rushed from the city and took up defensive positions along the outer wall. Caius looked over at Althea, who was hunched over her keyboard pounding in orders with a look of

154

fierce determination. He noticed that the spectators on the balcony to the right were pointing down at her, fascinated. She must have been doing something different. Most other candidates had probably started out the same way Caius did.

But Caius's real plan was about to go into effect. He deployed three massive airships that floated over the mountains like bloated whales and poured gunfire into the city below, tearing apart the few defenses within the inner wall. The AI kept most of the military at the main outer gate, still thinking that the armored units Caius had placed there were the bigger threat. With a single keystroke, waves of bombers began to soar over the city. Caius had always had a fascination with airpower, ever since the Empire had first constructed an airfield outside of Nanjing when he was six. His father used to take him to a park just near the runway, and he'd spend the entire afternoon just waiting for one of them to take off. Back then, planes were rickety wood-and-canvas deathtraps, manned only by the bravest pilots. The technology had grown so much more sophisticated, in part thanks to Caius's work.

The bombers targeted the steep walkways leading up to the main gate of the city. The beautifully rendered simulation showed stone crumbling as the mountainside slid away under the force of the explosions. The AI began to pull troops back from the main gate, suspecting that something was wrong, but the collapse of that main road had essentially cut the city off from reinforcements, and the Mapuche soldiers were trapped outside. It was time for Caius's master stroke.

A second wave of planes soared over the simulated mountain peaks and dropped their payload. This time, it was not bombs or bullets or fire, but men. Caius had outfitted all of his soldiers with the parachutes normally only worn by pilots. They descended on the city in a white cloud, falling thicker than rain. Almost all of his troops managed to make it into the city unharmed and quickly began to organize into units. He sent in a second wave of men, dropping straight into the city. The AI units between the outer gate and the inner walls scurried back and forth, searching for some way up the mountain; the city's natural defenses had been turned against the Mapuche.

From above, spectators began to notice Caius's strategy. He distinctly heard one of them pull aside a man in a military uniform and ask what those big white blankets were; presumably referring to the parachutes. As they were only ever used by pilots (and only in emergencies), many people had never even seen one. A crowd began to cluster on the balcony over Caius.

The first to fall was the main gate. The airships overhead poured covering fire down onto the Mapuche troops, who had nowhere to hide. A third wave of planes came soaring overhead and dropped more troops, filling the sky above the city with floating patches of white. Caius zoomed in on the gate and noted some of the computer players surrendering. He very briefly noted how impressive the AI was for this simulation; it was even able to take morale into account! It wasn't a factor he had considered when planning his aerial assault, but it was certainly working in his favor.

Once his troops secured the gate, a green light went on above his screen. The spectators on the balcony broke out into applause and scrambled to change their bets. Caius couldn't focus on that now; he had to concentrate on the simulation. He tasked one of the airships to hover over the gate and keep spraying bullets onto the Mapuche troops trying to climb up the mountainside.

156

Caius sent another wave of bombers into the city to soften up the Communications

facility, but found that it was relatively undefended. His troops were able to take it with hardly

any loss of life. Another green light on top of his monitor jumped to life. He was vaguely aware

of the spectators above him jostling around the balcony, trying to get a better look at his screen.

They had almost entirely stopped paying attention to the other candidates, none of whom had any

green lights yet. From the corner of his eye, he caught Althea glancing over, looking equal parts

nervous and angry.

From the Palace at the very apex of the city, a heavily armed Mapuche company emerged

and made their way down the mountain to the rest of the city. Caius had expected that at least

some of their forces would be held in reserve in the palace. There was intense street-to-street

fighting as the AI took up positions around the military headquarters and in bunkers carved into

the mountainside that were impervious to aerial assault. They even managed to shoot so many

holes through the one of the airship envelopes that it was forced to crash land in the city center.

Caius ordered another bombing run to destroy some of the buildings that had been fortified, and

ordered his men to target the mountain wall with their explosives. Just like with the main road

into the city, the brittle rock cracked and crumbled, blocking the bunkers or collapsing them

altogether. Caius's men stormed the military complex, taking pretty severe casualties but in the

end victorious. As the third green light appeared, a tiny Imperial flag was raised over the

building on his screen, and Caius made a mental note to find the programmers who had made the

simulation and offer them his congratulations for the level of detail. The spectators were going

wild, spilling their drinks over the balcony and fighting each other for a better view.

From the corner of his eye, Caius could see the other candidates glancing around nervously and sweating. They thumped on their keyboards and clicked furiously, thinking that Caius had used a similar strategy and was just doing so much better. They couldn't tell what was happening on his screen, just that he had already acquired three of the four objectives. Althea was doing her best to glance over Caius's shoulder, but she was too far away. Not that it would have done her any good; she'd already picked her equipment and likely hadn't requested thousands of parachutes. So instead, she resorted to swearing under her breath and clenching the edge of the desk until her knuckles turned white.

Caius's simulated soldiers began the slow climb up the mountain to the palace, encountering heavy resistance from fortified positions along the way. Caius set one of the airships to circle the mountain level with the elevation of the path and provide cover for the soldiers traveling upwards. Down in the valley, the Mapuche AI units had realized that the city was almost taken and had turned their own guns on the city. Caius ordered another bombing run to take out those cannons on the valley floor, even though destroying the capital wouldn't really affect the outcome of the trial. If this were real life, Caius would have ordered his troops to preserve the city as much as possible. Having grown up in Nanjing, he'd heard all about the devastation that the Great War had caused in his homeland, and would have wanted to avoid that at all cost.

Finally, his troops made it up the mountain and approached the palace grounds. The airship hovered over the intricately detailed gardens as the men rushed through the trees and up the grand stairs. The simulation began to play a small cinematic of the Mapuche king marching down the steps flanked by Caius's legionnaires, and the final green light at the top of his screen

158

turned on. The spectators roared and laughed and toasted. "And before the appetizers were even served!" he heard one of them shout distinctly. Next to him, Althea slammed a hand down on the desk and looked up from her computer, eyes narrow at Caius.

"You must have cheated!" she hissed. Caius only smiled and stood up from his chair as his simulated men continued their victory celebrations on the palace steps.

Quintus came into the room and ushered Caius out into the hall. Spectators held up their drinks toasting him as he walked away.

In the hallway, Marcus was waiting with the biggest smile that Caius had ever seen. He wrapped Caius in a bear hug, lifting him into the air. "That was AMAZING!" he shouted. "Brilliant!" He set Caius back down and looked him in the eye. "Remember when I told you that I picked you because you had an indescribable quality that would make you a winner? THAT is what I'm talking about!" He shook his head, laughing. "They told us this would take most of the morning, and you managed to do it in under an hour." Marcus thumped him on the back so hard it almost knocked him to the ground.

Caius was blushing pretty heavily, and really had no response. Marcus continued to praise his performance, giving a play-by-play to no one in particular of what Caius had just done. Quintus brought them back to the waiting room where each advocate was watching his own Candidate's performance on hand-held devices. As soon as they entered the room, Andericus stood up and stormed up to Quintus.

"I demand that you check his performance again," Andericus said. "He must have cheated somehow."

Quintus only smiled and shook his head.

"There was no cheating. I supervised everything myself. Caius selected standard equipment used in the military and used it in a non-standard way. That's the simplest way to describe it. Any other candidate had the option of using these parachutes, and all of them seem to have opted for more traditional tactics." The other advocates were looking up; none of them looked particularly pleased with Caius's success, but none were as angry as Andericus.

Marcus stood behind Quintus watching the argument with an expression of pure, boyhood glee. "He did it fair and square, Andericus. Quit being a sore loser and go back to watching Althea struggle to even get in the gates."

Andericus looked away from Quintus with fire burning in his eyes. He thrust out a thin bony finger at Marcus. "You helped him somehow! You planned this ahead of time."

Marcus laughed and spread his arms. "I was in the room with you the whole time! And I don't know the first thing about computers. You know that probably better than most people here, having seen how much time I spend in the library back home. How could I possibly have helped him?"

Andericus continued thrusting his finger in Marcus's face. "I don't know," he answered finally. "But there's something wrong about this. And Quintus, you need to investigate."

Quintus shook his head slowly. "Andericus, there's nothing to be done. There was no cheating."

Andericus gave all three of them an angry look, huffed loudly, and then returned to one of the plush seats in the waiting room clutching his monitor that showed Althea's progress. The rest of the advocates turned back to their own monitors, now that the scene had ended.

"How did you come up with that?" Marcus asked.

"Just something that's been rattling around my brain for a while," Caius said. "I decided to take a risk. When I was working for Samarkand we had a test pilot bail out of his plane and use one of these, and he landed on the roof of some office building in the city. It made me think how useless the city defenses were if he could just drop in from above. I talked to Licinius about it and we ran a bunch of simulations like this, showing that we could easily drop in right over a city with concentrated air drops from bombers. He mentioned it to someone in the military, but as soon as they heard 'jumping out of planes,' they flat out rejected it without even hearing if it would work and told us to go back to building engines."

"The military can be like that," Marcus agreed. "Unless you have someone whispering in the Emperor's ear to give it a shot, new ideas go nowhere fast. But with your success today, I'm pretty sure you'll see this implemented, regardless of whether you're the one that the Senate picks."

Caius glanced around the room. Each advocate was glued to their own handheld device, watching their candidate struggle up the mountain.

"Is there any way we could watch the rest of them?" he whispered to Marcus.

"Sure…" he said slowly, looking around and noticing the other advocates like he'd forgotten they were even there. "Let me ask Quintus."

Five minutes later, they were on their way to the spectators' balcony, surrounded by a complement of guards. Caius could hardly believe he was in the same building; instead of barren stone walls, the floors were covered by plush carpets and rich wood paneling. Servants manned the corridors, holding drinks and food for anyone that happened to pass by unexpectedly; they thrust their platters out like robots as Caius passed. Quintus led Marcus and Caius past ballrooms and banquet halls; it looked more like an expensive hotel than the sparse interior of a mountain.

Surprised servants opened up a set of white wooden doors with intricate carvings, revealing the crowd of spectators on the balcony. The vast majority of the crowd was busy watching the rest of the Candidates, but one young woman turned back casually to see who had entered. "It's him!" she said, tugging on the ornate, gold-patterned sleeve of the man next to her. He turned around with an expression of annoyance, but quickly spotted Caius, whose Asian features made him fairly recognizable in this heavily European crowd. The spectators quickly surrounded Caius and Marcus but the guards held them back. "That was amazing," one of them shouted to him. "Fantastic job!" said another. Most of the other voices were lost in the clamor of the entire group trying to talk at once.

"You know the rules," Quintus called out to them. "No unapproved contact with the Candidates! Everyone back!" The crowd grumbled and retreated reluctantly back to the balcony to watch the rest of the candidates, still keeping one eye on Caius.

"To prevent corruption," Marcus explained with a whisper. "They don't want the spectators bribing you or something."

Caius made his way to the railing, followed by Marcus and two of the guards. Three candidates had two of their green lights lit up, including Herennius and Althea; Caius couldn't see who the third was. A few others had captured the gates to the city but were still facing intense fighting through the steep winding streets. Herennius seemed to be making good use of airpower to take out enemy positions and was using small teams of highly trained troops; Althea, on the other hand, seemed to be simply leveling the city with artillery as she made her way from target to target. Some of the other candidates were still struggling through the valley and hadn't even made their way close to the city.

Servants came by with silver platters of snacks and drinks; he grabbed a glass of juice off the platter. Marcus had warned him to stay away from alcohol during the trials, even if others were having some. Caius noticed some of the spectators still staring at him; some with admiration, some with anger. Apparently he'd ruined quite a few bets. He nodded to them, unsure how to act.

Luckily, a green light went on back down in the center of the room, taking everyone's attention back to the match. Althea had taken the military headquarters. Caius watched the animation on the big screen of the flag raising again, this time against a backdrop of rubble and smoke instead of the lush green valley. The spectators clapped and cheered in excitement as the Mapuche troops in the palace poured out to defend the last position. Caius looked over the railing to see Althea hunched over her computer, face practically pressed up against the monitor.

Even from this distance, Caius could see her muscles tensed and the sweat dripping from her brow.

Three more candidates breached the main gates, leading to their first light. Another one took the communications building, tying their score with Herennius at 2. Caius glanced over to his friend's screen to see his men bogged down in front of the military headquarters by fire from the cliffside, which wasn't vulnerable to air power. Caius wished he could go down and offer him some advice, but remembered that it was competition. Reinforcing that, Marcus leaned in and whispered: "None of them are even close to matching you. This definitely sews up the front-runner status. You're going to be a big hit at the party tonight."

"The party?" Caius asked.

"Oh…" Marcus said. "No, I didn't say that…" he trailed off.

Luckily, Herennius captured the third objective right then, so Caius forgot their conversation for the moment. Yet again he watched the Imperial eagle flag fly over the headquarters. He took a quick look at Althea, who was having a lot of difficulty mounting the final hill. The Mapuche had managed to destroy the main road, and her forces had been so destructive that they were unable to find suitable materials to replace it. Herennius still had a chance!

The spectators were back to betting as Herennius's troops charged up the hill toward the palace. Green lights were going on all around the room as more candidates made it into the city but all eyes were on the battle for second place. Althea's troops were beginning to scale the

164

mountainside, but she seemed to be out of bombing runs, or at least wasn't using them. Herennius, on the other hand, was pounding the mountaintop fortress in wave after wave of flights, and his troops were quickly catching up to where Althea's men were all pinned down. Herennius looked calm and relaxed and in charge as he commanded his men forward up the mountain. Althea, on the other hand, was practically panicking, clicking wildly and pounding on the keyboard like an ape. *Please be Herennius, Please be Herennius,* Caius was whispering under his breath, even knowing that Marcus would probably prefer to have Herennius lose this one, just to make sure that Caius's lead was certain.

Althea had a lucky break, and she broke through the enemy defenses. The spectators around the balcony began to cheer as simulated soldiers poured into the mountaintop palace and marched the Mapuche king out onto the lawn. The fourth light on top of her monitor blinked green, and she pushed herself away from the desk and let out an audible cheer. She walked out of the main room, where Andericus was presumably waiting in the hallway with Quintus.

Herennius finished only a few moments later, but the drama was gone and he only got a short round of applause. Caius clapped loudly, as did Marcus, but the spectators had gone back to their betting, predicting which candidate would come in fourth. Herennius limped over to the door, with his metal cast making a solid *thunk* sound with each step. Quintus ushered him inside.

The remaining candidates tried to conceal their downtrodden expressions as they vied for fourth place. A cascade of green lights now appeared as more and more objectives were taken. The crowd on the balcony began to lose interest and the servants rushed in carrying steaming plates of lunch. Only Caius continued to watch as the other candidates struggled against the computer.

Herennius and Althea entered the balcony, escorted by Quintus. The line of guards dividing the area tensed up, but the spectators had gotten the picture and were distracted by their lunches; none of them even tried to talk to the two candidates. Andericus and Flavia followed their candidates in. Caius offered a hand to Althea.

"Good work out there," he said. Althea looked at him with disdain before realizing how many spectators were watching, so she forced a smile across her face and took Caius's hand. She squeezed sharply, trying to make Caius look weak.

"Thanks," she answered. "You did well too." She leaned in close and whispered into Caius's ear: "For a cheater, at least."

Caius just smiled smugly. If Althea couldn't accept that she'd lost fair and square, then so be it. Herennius approached with a friendly smile and grabbed Caius by the shoulder with his enormous, meaty hand.

"How in the *hell* did you beat that so fast?" he asked with a tone of astonishment, not accusation. "I wasn't even inside the city by the time you had already won!" Caius just laughed and patted Herennius on the back; he didn't seem to have a mean bone in his body, which was the most refreshing attitude ever given the cutthroat climate among the rest of the candidates. Caius explained his strategy while Althea did her best to look like she wasn't listening intently to the details. More and more candidates were finishing up the challenge, and most of the green

166

lights were on for those still fighting. Practically all of them came by to congratulate him and find out how he'd beaten it, so he ended up having to tell the story over and over. Marcus hovered nearby like a proud parent preening in front of the other advocates. Humility wasn't exactly his strong suit.

After at least an hour had passed, the last candidate finished the trial and conquered the Mapuche palace. Despite her victory, her face was a mix of shame and disappointment as she saw every one of her peers above her on the balcony watching.

Quintus emerged from the doorway and walked to the center of the room.

"Candidates, well done. Each of you has completed the trial successfully and demonstrated your ingenuity and strategy. We appreciate your enthusiasm, and as a reward for a job well done, the Senate has a special treat planned for you all. Please take the afternoon off to rest, relax, confer with your Advocates, etc. This is your free time. This evening, however, we will see you at 20:00 sharp in the central hall for a little surprise. Please wear your formal robes." There was a murmur of excited confusion as the candidates left the hall, wondering what they could be planning.

Caius returned to his room, intending to rest a bit, but was surprised to find a visitor: Antoninus was waiting for him.

CHAPTER 10

"Hello Caius," he said in his rich, booming voice. It gave Caius flashbacks to his presentation as Inquisitor, and he suppressed a flash of rage. *It was his job,* he reminded himself. *Antoninus did that for all the candidates, and he's supposed to try and show you in the worst light possible. He didn't mean it.*

"H...hello," Caius stuttered, failing miserably to act casual and nonchalant.

Antoninus smiled warmly regardless, either not noticing or just ignoring Caius's behavior. He strode into the room to shake Caius's hand. "I hear that you really blew them all away this afternoon at the strategy simulation."

Caius nodded and gave a brief recap, to which Antoninus politely listened. Both of them knew that they were just beating around the bush before getting to the real point.

"I was asked to bring you downstairs," Antoninus said finally. "One of the Senators requested a personal meeting with you."

Caius's heart thumped against his ribs like an angry prisoner, and he felt his cheeks burning. *Had they believed Andericus and Althea? Did they think he had cheated somehow? Could he prove that he hadn't? Where was Marcus?* The faster his mind raced, the slower time around him seemed to go. His entire body started sweating at once.

Antoninus must have seen the panic in his eyes, because he gripped Caius by the shoulder with one firm hand. "No need to worry; the Senator just wants to talk to you and congratulate you on your success. They sometimes do this with Candidates when they feel like getting to know them better will help with the decision making."

Caius's breathing slowly went back to normal and he managed to look normally again. "Good," he managed to utter. "All right, let's go then." He tried to smile, but probably looked more like a dental patient getting his gums examined.

Antoninus strode quickly out of the room on his long legs, and Caius had to hustle to keep up. A few other people in the hall gave Caius an unusual look as he was escorted away. They headed further down the hall of candidates, to a staircase that Caius had never been up. Antoninus led him through winding walls and narrow passages until they reached a large columned atrium, filled with lush green trees growing under artificial lights.

"This is part of the staff area," Antoninus informed him. "Generally off limits to the Candidates, so don't tell anyone I let you in here." He winked, and Caius forced a laugh in response. He led them down a long hallway that seemed to come to a dead end.

Antoninus pushed a button that was hidden in a rocky crevice, and the smooth rock wall in front of them slid open with a gentle *whoosh*. Inside, the elevator looked like it was from a completely different world: the floor was rich, velvety red carpet and the walls were paneled with vibrant chestnut wood with distinctive knots and grains, all under soft lights. Caius stepped in and the doors closed. The motors whirred gently as it lurched downward, deeper into the mountain. After an eternity, the elevator bell chimed gently and the doors slid open again.

The elevator opened into a grand atrium. The cold stone walls of the rest of the facility were gone, replaced by smooth plaster walls painted a warm red and supported by dark wooden beams from some exotic jungle. A dozen lamps hanging from the ceiling cast a soft glow around the room. Plush red carpet underneath was patterned with the Emperor's insignia in bright gold thread. On either side of the room, wooden staircases spiraled upwards to other floors. Like most grand theaters, Caius assumed that there would be elegant box seats up there. And in the center of the Atrium, there was a large arched doorway blocked by red curtains.

Antoninus led him through the curtains and into a massive theater, bigger even than the airplane hangars that Caius was used to. There were enough seats for every candidate, Advocate, and spectator in the entire facility. The walls stretched at least four stories up, punctuated by small, private balconies; Caius suspected that one of them, seemingly made entirely of gold and with a large eagle emblazoned on the front, was reserved for the Emperor. The ceiling at the very top was covered in a beautiful painting depicting Carus the Rebuilder's crossing the Rhine river to complete the conquest of Germania. The whole room looked like something that would be found in the wealthiest part of Rome, not buried under a mountain in the middle of nowhere.

Antoninus gestured to down the aisle towards a row in the middle of the room where a single lone figure sat waiting, facing the stage. Caius took a few steps down the aisle, and Antoninus retreated to the elevator. "Thank you for joining me, Caius," a voice called. It took Caius a moment to place the Persian accent of Senator Oventia. "This room used to be used for a public speaking trial for candidates," she said, gesturing around at the massive theater and the large stage at the front, "in addition to entertainment for guests. Don't worry, though: we've decided not to put you through that this time." She craned her neck to look at the painting above.

170

It must have taken an artist's lifetime to complete. "It's a shame we won't have a chance to use this most beautiful room." She took a deep breath, inhaling the atmosphere. "Please, come have a seat." She turned and gave Caius a beaming smile then nodded to the velvet cushion next to her.

Caius did as he was told, and they sat in silence for just a second. "I have a surprise for you," Senator Oventia said with an enigmatic, barely contained smile. "Of all the candidates, *you alone* will really be able appreciate this."

She clapped her hands, and a troop of costumed figures rushed out onto stage and began setting up scenery and props. A tall man stepped to the front of the stage and took a bow; he was clearly of European descent but wore a wig of straight back hair and makeup to make him appear Asian. "Honored Senator Oventia," he called, his voice booming through the massive room, "I have the honor of presenting our latest opera for you! The Silent Dragon: the story of Magnus Serica."

The Senator was watching Caius from the corner of her eye, waiting for some reaction. But Caius didn't know how he was supposed to react. A play about his grandfather? And more importantly, what was she trying to test? If Marcus had drilled one thing into him on the train ride from Japan, it was that every single second with the judges mattered. He couldn't let his guard down for even a moment.

On stage, the play began. Orchestral music swelled from hidden speakers, opening on a scene of the Great War between China and Rome. Actors in emerald green Chinese military uniforms were huddled in a trench with their weapons. One figure, presumably Caius's grandfather, broke out into song about the tragedy of the war and how many lives had been lost

171

fighting against the unstoppable Roman juggernaut. That certainly wasn't accurate; his grandfather was never on the front lines.

"I'm on the Arts and Information Commission in the Senate, you know," Oventia said. "I commissioned this play about your grandfather almost a year ago, before I even knew that you would be a candidate. Quite serendipitous, don't you think? Almost like destiny."

Caius nodded, noting how pleased with herself Senator Oventia seemed.

"Your grandfather was a man of great character," she continued. "He effectively shortened the Great War by *years* when he pledged allegiance to the Empire and brought the southern provinces into the fold. There has been some... difficulty along the border with the Ming, and we thought that this," she gestured up at the play, where the actor playing Caius's grandfather was still singing, "might serve as a gentle reminder of how joining Rome was the best decision your grandfather could have made."

On stage, the soldiers who had been huddled together in the trench were now dead from a mortar strike. Reminding the south what would happen if they *didn't* support Rome seemed to also be an important part of this opera. Caius didn't mention that, though; he just stayed silent. *Only speak when spoken to,* he heard Marcus reminding him.

"Do you have any thoughts on the performance so far, Caius? It would be useful to have a native's opinion."

Caius felt a brief flash of anger at the term *native*, but tried not to let it show. "I'm honored that you would create a play about my family," he answered. That should be a safe response. "May I ask... will it be performed in Latin, or in Mandarin?"

172

"Latin, of course." Oventia seemed a bit confused by the question. *Why wouldn't it be Latin?* Caius could practically hear her thinking.

"If I might offer a suggestion," he said, "I would offer performances in both Mandarin and Cantonese. Those who are most likely to support the rebels in the South are exactly the types who wouldn't learn Latin in the first place."

Oventia narrowed her eyes, thinking about his suggestion, then nodded. She didn't want to admit how much sense that made (and worse, that she hadn't thought of it), so she just didn't respond. Instead, they both went back to watching the play. Magnus Serica's song on the battlefront had wrapped up, and now he was consulting with the Emperor's generals, who were ordering him to continue sending his men to their deaths in battle for no other reason than their own refusal to face facts.

"How are you finding the trials so far?" she asked after a few moments. "What do you think?"

Caius's mind was racing, trying to figure out where this was going. What the angle was. Was she looking for some sign of weakness or giving up? His mind reached back to Marcus's training for the interview phase: stay confident, but honest.

"I'm doing my best," Caius said finally. "Of course it is difficult, but it would not really be effective if any of us could pass the trials easily."

She turned her gaze from the stage, looked Caius in the eyes, and smiled. "You don't need to keep your guard up like that right now. Just relax and let's have a chat."

Caius took a deep breath. "It's hard," he said honestly. "I've been put through a lot in my life. Well," he chuckled slightly, "I guess you know that. You've seen the videos from the Inquisitor." She nodded in agreement, and Caius remembered how she was the only one to laugh at Marcus's jokes during that test. "And even though I knew what this was all about and what kinds of tests I'd be put through… I guess it just never really sank in. I didn't understand how hard it would be to be directly competing against everyone else. I mean, the rest of the candidates are all really great," his mind flashed to Althea's sneer, "well for the most part. And yet we're fighting each other tooth and nail in this contest while pretending that we're all friends."

She nodded. "Yes, that's the part that the candidates never expect, from what Vitellius says." Caius waited for her to elaborate; maybe some way to make it better. But she just looked back at the stage.

"Caius, you did a fantastic job this morning with the strategy trial. Really, really amazing," she said. "You should have seen us in the other room; everyone had to go back and watch the videos of the other candidates later. We were all glued to your screen, just like all the spectators."

"Thank you," Caius said. He still wasn't really sure where this was going.

"And not just that one trial," she told him. She had an honest and enthusiastic voice tone that made Caius feel at ease. On stage, the actors continued their play even though neither of the audience members really seemed to be paying much attention. "You've handled everything we've thrown at you so far, and excelled at it. And that's really the point of these Trials. We

174

want to find that person who can succeed at *any* situation. From what I've heard about this process in the past, it normally it takes a few tests to really get an idea of who's making it to the front of the pack. But I really feel like that's not the case; you made it pretty clear from the beginning."

"I'm really flattered," Caius said, "But I don't know if..."

"Just wait," she interrupted him. "I know that you're modest, and it is definitely one of your best qualities. We don't want an emperor who is going to let the power go to his head. But at the same time, you don't really need to prove it to me anymore. I'd really just appreciate a more honest discussion with you." She smiled pleasantly, clearly very adept at soothing people and getting her point across. "Caius, I have been in the Senate for 17 years now. I have fought tooth and nail every single day. My own version of these Trials, I suppose. Against other Senators, against the Emperor, against other competitors who want my seat... just constant fighting. And I am sick and tired of it."

She leaned back against the plush velvet chair and drew lazy circles on the armrest with one finger. Caius remained silent.

"So I want out of the Senate, and I think you're the man to help me. I think I would be much more generous with my points for you if you would consider appointing me as your Minister of Finance when you become Emperor."

Minister of Finance? The most important cabinet minister, responsible for taxation, the central bank, and oversight of the state-owned corporations. A huge responsibility… with a lot of influence to sell.

"And I'd be more than willing to help talk some sense into my two colleagues, Tullius and Vitellus," Oventia continued, trying to sweeten the deal. "Tullius is a particularly hard nut to crack; he seems to have something against your candidacy on principle. I'd heard that he and your advocate have had some past disagreements, and maybe he is just determined to make sure that Marcus doesn't wield any influence. Or maybe it's just something about you that he doesn't like." She shrugged nonchalantly as if she *hadn't* just told Caius that he was already doomed to lose this competition because of something he had absolutely no control over. "And Vitellius? He's got his heart in the right place, but maybe a little too much, if you know what I mean? He refuses to pick a favorite or pay particularly close attention to any one candidate yet. Thinks he should give all of them equal attention, whereas we both already know that there are only a few gems. So you can't count on Vitellius being in your corner either." She looked him straight in the eye. "Caius, you are going to have a very difficult time in this, unless you work with me. I know all of Tullius's pressure points, and Vitellius will listen to my judgment. You could lock this competition up *right now*. Between your performance thus far and my assistance… no one else would stand a chance."

"Senator…" he started, not exactly sure what to do and just trying to stall for time. *Gotta be some kind of trick*, thought the part of his mind that had listened to Kaneshiro about not trusting anyone. *This is just another trial and if I say yes to her offer, then they'll say that I'm corrupt and I'll be disqualified. The minute I agree to this, Quintus is going to walk through that door and arrest me. It's so obvious!*

What if it's not, the other part of his brain asked. The part that sounded disturbingly close to Marcus's voice. He wished he could talk to Marcus right now and get his opinion; he would know what to do. *This whole ordeal could end now, and you could be with your mother and father again in a matter of days. You could be the new Emperor!*

"I understand it's a lot to take in," Oventia began again. "But I came to you specifically with this offer because I truly believe that you're going to win it. You're the best man for the job. And I know we can both make sure that that is how it goes."

"Senator Oventia, I don't think that I would be allowed to make such a promise…" *Obviously,* Caius thought to himself. It sounded stupid to say, but he had to at least hear her response.

"The Emperor makes his own rules," she replied simply with that disarming smile.

His mind was still locked in a desperate struggle, having difficulty focusing on her exact words. The play in the background was completely forgotten. *Has to be a trap. No way that she would promise this. It's just another Trial to weed out anyone corrupt enough to accept the offer.*

On stage, Caius's grandfather began another song. He'd made the decision to swear allegiance to Rome and pledge his armies to fight the Ming Emperor instead. In a rich baritone voice, the actor was explaining how hard choices aren't so hard to make when you follow the

177

honorable path. And after what seemed like years of internal struggle, he listened to his grandfather's advice.

"Senator, I'm sure that you are well qualified for the Finance Ministry position," he told her. "And after I complete the trials, I will be more than happy to review your candidacy. But at this time, I am not in a position to promise any ministry title to any person."

A maddening silence filled the room despite the opera on stage. Caius could barely hear what they were saying; he was just waiting for Oventia to say something.

"Caius, I don't think you understand," she finally said with a smile on her face but murder in her eyes. "You can't prevail here without my help. And this is a one-time offer." With that last sentence, her sweet, disarming tone turned into a dangerous hiss.

Caius opened his mouth to answer, and his tongue wasn't ready to cooperate. His mouth was completely dry. "I know, Senator." *This had really better be fake.*

She gave him a hard look, not showing any emotion. "Very well," she said curtly. "If that is how you feel, so be it." *Is she just acting upset about this? Is this part of the trial, designed to see if I would change my mind after seeing her reaction?*

The silence returned. Caius's other voice urged him to yell out 'Just kidding!' and take the deal, but he managed to resist. The velvet chair squeaked slightly as she lifted herself off the cushion and turned to face him.

"I wish you luck in the remaining trials then." Her tone made it clear that all the luck in the world wouldn't help him. "I trust that you will keep this conversation between us?"

Caius didn't respond right away, and her tone grew cold and icy. "And I need not remind you that there was no recording of this conversation, meaning it would simply be your word against mine. And the word of a candidate means little against the word of a Senator." *Why is she saying this? If it's a trial, does this mean the second part is to test whether I report her to someone or not? Or does this mean that it really wasn't a trial? Should I try to accept the offer now?* His chest rose and fell with his quick short breaths, and his heart was pounding in his chest.

"All right," he managed to get out.

"You know the way out, then." She nodded curtly and left the room with a long sweep of her dress as she walked up the aisle.

Caius exhaled, trying to breathe normally. He felt like someone had dropped a heavy weight right on his chest. He sat back and tried to watch the play, even though the actors seemed to have stopped caring now that their patron had left the room.

The elevator dinged, and Antoninus entered the room once again. He saw Caius's pained expression and cocked his head inquisitively. *Did he know what Oventia had offered him?*

"I have orders to bring you back to the Hall of Candidates," he said simply. Caius only nodded in response and lifted himself off of the chair. His stomach felt like it was full of lead.

God, what was I thinking? I made the wrong choice! She really was offering me a deal. Why didn't I take it??

Antoninus led him back up the aisle, into the elevator, and through the resident quarters; Caius barely paid any attention to where they went, and they just walked in silence. The same scene replayed over and over again in his mind. *You idiot! You should have agreed!*

They finally arrived at the simple wooden door of his room. Antoninus bowed and left without another word. Caius stumbled inside and flicked on the lights, hardly noticing where he was going. The mattress squeaked as he flopped down helplessly, then again as he rolled over and hit the button to summon a servant. After only a moment, the door creaked open and a small, pale girl in red robes bowed before him.

"Please find Marcus Geganius, one of the Advocates. Tell him that Caius needs to speak with him urgently." She nodded and scuttled away down the hall.

An undetermined amount of time passed while Caius replayed the scenario again and again, alternating between that and imagining all the ways it could have gone if only he had said yes. His daydreaming was interrupted by a gentle knock on the door, and Marcus's bushy grey hair poked in around the side. "You needed something?"

Caius heaved himself upright with a sigh and told Marcus what had happened. How Antoninus was waiting for him and had spirited him down to the theater under the mountain. He repeated everything that Oventia had told him, and what she had offered. Marcus stroked his beard thoughtfully throughout the story, pausing only to ask some questions at various parts.

"You should have come and talked to me before going with Antoninus," he remarked after Caius had finished telling him the whole story.

"Thanks, Marcus. That's a big help now that it's already happened." Marcus grinned back at him sheepishly. "It's driving me crazy, though! Was this another test?"

Marcus leaned back in the cozy chair and stared up at the ceiling.

"All I can really tell you is based on my own experiences. They don't tell us advocates what the tests are going to be, so we just have to kind of guess. But when I was a candidate, I never went through anything like that. No offer to exchange favors, or anything."

Caius's heart sank, and he saw any hope of becoming Emperor slipping through his fingers. Oventia would certainly never vote for him now after rejecting her offer and knowing that she was willing to sell her vote.

"But on the other hand," Marcus continued, "This sounds like exactly the type of thing that they would do. Ministers taking bribes and exchanging favors and things like that have been rampant over the past few years. Almost everyone at the head of one of the state-owned corporations bought their way into those positions." Caius thought back to his time at Samarkand Aeronautics and realized that he had never actually seen the CEO despite a year of working in one of the most important divisions of the company. "Of course the Senators want to make sure that the Emperor is incorruptible, and now is when Candidates are at their most vulnerable. It makes perfect sense to test you all out by offering the one thing you need most right now."

A glimmer of hope! Caius sat up on the bed as Marcus continued.

"I've heard many things about Oventia over the years. Stubborn, strong-willed, cunning... but never corrupt. Which, believe me, is a rarity among powerful Senators. Most of them are willing to sell their souls to get a better rank on their favorite committee. I suspect that her uncrackable nature is one of the main reason she was even assigned to judge the Trials in the first place."

Caius's heart was almost beating normally again. *It was a trial. She was lying to you the whole time. That room was probably full of cameras and microphones, just like every other room around here. And you passed with flying colors!*

"You did the right thing," Marcus finally concluded. "I don't believe that Oventia would do something like this unless she was directed to. At least, I hope not."

CHAPTER 11

Caius stood in front of the mirror as the servant silently adjusted his robes for him, trying to brush his straight black hair into the wavy pattern that was currently in vogue with Rome and failing miserably. It hung flat over his scalp like tasteless curtains. At least the robes were nice: a sky blue with detailed golden trim and tiny dragons stitched onto the collar and sleeves. "To highlight your heritage," Marcus had said. Despite China having been part of the Empire for over two hundred years, Asian citizens were a rare sight in most of the large cities of Europe. And even more unusual to see an aristocrat of Chinese descent in the West; some of the spectators had probably never even interacted with someone from Asia. Marcus had said that all of the guests would be fighting for the chance to talk to him about his home province.

There was a gentle knock on the wooden door, and Marcus poked his head inside. The normally wild mane of hair had been neatly combed down to a more manageable level; Caius didn't even want to guess how many servants and broken combs that had taken.

"Looking sharp!" he told Caius enthusiastically, practically dancing into the room. "Good job, fellow," he told the servant, who only bowed shortly and went back to work; they were trained not to be particularly talkative.

"You're certainly in a good mood," Caius remarked, still fussing with the belt of his tunic.

"God, yes!" Marcus said, checking his own robes in the mirror over Caius's shoulder. "My normal social calendar is devastatingly empty, considering the fact that I'm always locked

183

in the Palace! The Emperor's siblings are not supposed to let anyone know their real identities.

Only a select few vetted people with knowledge of the trial process know what happens to

candidates after the trials are over. Some Senators, Ministers of State, etc. Servants, of course,

but they aren't very good for socialization: bred for stupidity and docility, and drugged to the

point of blissful ignorance. They can barely string a coherent sentence together. After years and

years with just the other candidates, we just get bored of having a lot of the same conversations

over and over again..."

He grinned sheepishly, realizing that he was rambling.

"So anyways, yes. I am excited to get out there and have a chance to speak to some

normal folks again."

"Every one of the spectators gets to know?"

"Oh, heavens no! Some of these people have no clearance whatsoever. Mistresses of

Senators, rich people who practically bought their ticket up here... there'll be all sorts of people

out there who can't know who I am. The Praetorians even gave me a cover story..."

He rummaged through his inner breast pocket and pulled out a thin leather wallet, and

showed Caius his new state ID; occupation listed as "Venture Capitalist" and residency listed as

Lamu, the southernmost city in the Empire and gateway for most of the trade with the African

Federation nations.

"No way anyone is going to believe this," Caius laughed. "You? In Lamu?"

Marcus smirked and tucked it back in his breast pocket. "I know."

"You're not even the least bit tan," Caius said. "Even if you were a European who moved there, you'd be crispy and brown by now!"

"I didn't pick the story," Marcus protested. "I'll just have to hope that people don't think about it too hard. That's pretty standard for most of Rome's high society." He smirked at Caius in the mirror, and they both laughed. One last adjustment to their outfits, and they headed out the door.

Other pairs of Candidates and Advocates were slowly meandering down the hall. At the end, the arch leading to the Hall of Candidates had been blocked off by a fine mesh screen. One by one, Quintus was taking candidates into the grand domed entryway and announcing them to the crowd to the sound of polite clapping. In the background, Caius heard the delicate sounds of a Chinese mandolin that reminded him of home.

Althea and Andericus strolled up behind them, wearing matching robes of navy blue with black trim, going for a formal look. Althea was genuinely smiling for once as they talked, and for just a brief second, Caius got the impression that she might be friendly and sweet. Then she spotted him, and the scowl returned to her face, and he remembered exactly what she was really like.

They greeted each other with the icy politeness that Caius had come to expect from Althea when she assumed someone was watching. All of the same words and tones that you'd expect from someone being warm and friendly, but accompanied by a half-hidden sneer and hostile body language. But that was nothing compared to the look exchanged between Marcus and Andericus. Marcus reached out a hand to shake, and Andericus looked at it like he was holding a poisonous snake. He sniffed with disdain and then barely tapped Marcus's palm before pulling away a moment later. There was a tense silence as they sized each other up.

"Where did you learn that trick with those parachutes, boy?" Andericus asked. That was about as close as Caius was going to get to a compliment on his strategy.

Marcus smiled broadly and answered first: "So, realized he didn't cheat, did you? Finally decided to quit making excuses?"

Caius hadn't thought it possible for Andericus to look even angrier, but apparently he had been wrong.

"It was unclear from the instructions that such equipment could be used for soldiers, and the rules should have been clarified," Andericus answered, not quite getting to Marcus's question. Althea nodded in agreement. "If it had only been explained better, I might have done the same."

Marcus snorted in laughter; Caius managed to restrain himself a bit more. "Well, in the future it would probably be better for us all to ask for explanations of unclear rules." Neither of them had a retort to that, so Althea simply turned her back toward Marcus and Caius and began conversing with her Advocate in low tones.

The awkwardness was broken as the line moved up; the candidate ahead of Caius marched out of the hallway and into the hall. Caius heard the footsteps going up a short flight of

186

wooden stairs, then heard Quintus call out the Candidate's name, followed by muted applause from the gathered spectators. Caius felt his cheeks burning already.

"Just relax. You're going to be a huge hit," Marcus told him. "Everyone's talking about your stunt at the strategy trial." Caius took a deep breath and closed his eyes, shaking his hands and bouncing on the balls of his feet to get rid of the tingling energy coursing through his veins.

Quintus opened the narrow door and gave a slight smile as he saw Caius. "Here's the star of the show! They've all been asking about you."

"Good evening, Quintus," Caius said politely.

"You boys ready?" They both nodded. "Good. When you head up on stage, just bow to the crowd and then circle around to find your table. We've arranged all of the seating to ensure that each candidate gets equal treatment. The candidates should all be seated before any of the guests sit down. Got it?" Caius nodded again, and Quintus spun around and marched out. The door swung open, and a brilliant spotlight blinded Caius straight away. He squinted involuntarily, but was suddenly conscious of his already slanted eyes and tried to open them wide despite the glare. He took slow, deliberate steps up the stairs, paranoid that he might slip and fall in front of everyone. The room was strangely silent except for the footprints of their boots, and a slight jingle coming from Quintus's armor as he walked.

In the center of the stage, Quintus stood in a beam of light and gestured at the pair to his right. His golden breastplate reflected little patches of light across the room.

"I present Advocate Marcus Geganius of Lamu…" Caius clenched his teeth and tried not to smile as he remembered the ridiculous cover story that someone had cooked up for Marcus, "and his Candidate, Caius Serica of Nanjing." Marcus and Caius took a bow, and the audience broke into applause. Not the gentle patter of finger tapping as the audience took a break from their conversation, but the swelling roar of enthusiasm. There were even a few stray whistles and shouts; the other candidates certainly hadn't gotten this reception. He felt his cheeks burning red and hoped that the audience couldn't notice under the lights.

Marcus stepped off the stage, and Caius followed. The crowd thronged forward in a moving wall of silks and other brightly colored fabrics, all trying to speak to Caius at once. "One at a time," Marcus was telling them, pushing through the crowd toward the table that had been designated for them. Caius was overwhelmed by the sound of so many people speaking at the same time, but he tried to smile and wave to as many as he could.

On stage, he was briefly aware of Quintus leading Althea and Andericus up to the front. They paused awkwardly, waiting for the crowd to notice that another Candidate had been brought up. Quintus started to announce their names, but stopped and started over louder when he couldn't grab the audience's attention the first time. It didn't really work the second time either; Althea bowed low and gave an elaborate sweep of her hand, but was only met with a slight smattering of applause. Half of the room was still on their tip-toes, trying to get a glimpse of which table Caius was at. Althea's lips were smiling, but her teeth were clenched tight and she couldn't cover up the rage in her eyes at being overlooked. Andericus didn't even bother trying to look pleasant as they stomped off the stage and pushed their way through the spectators to their table.

The crowd slowly dissipated and went back to their earlier conversations after Marcus assured them all that they'd each have their chance to talk to him later in the evening. They found their assigned table, marked with a tiny, detailed nameplate indicating where they should sit. Spectators peered over their shoulders and circled the table like sharks, seeing who else was sitting there. Caius saw the hurried whispers and covert handshakes of a makeshift black market as his tablemates were tempted to exchange their nameplates for all manner of favors. Marcus watched it all go down with a grin, ribbing Caius each time he suspected another offer being made.

Quintus paraded the rest of the Candidates into the grand entry chamber and introduced them one by one. Caius clapped politely for each of them. But he stood and cheered heartily for Herennius, who had to thunk across the stage in his metal cast with its tiny flashing white lights. His blue eyes were accentuated by the sky-blue tone of his outfit. He flashed Caius a thumbs up as he found his way to his table, which was surprisingly difficult. Caius had forgotten how *large* the room was: the enormous dome was at least a hundred meters high, and tables for the crowd of two hundred or so spectators fit easily inside along with the thirty Advocates and thirty Candidates. *29*, Caius corrected himself. *Marius is gone.*

On stage, Quintus finished introducing the last candidate. Gideon was smiling nervously and waved at the crowd instead of bowing. Quintus stayed in his spotlight and watched them head off the stage, clapping politely until he and his advocate made their way to their seats.

"Well then!" he announced cheerfully. "Welcome all to this little gathering of the most prestigious citizens of the empire! We hope that you all have so far enjoyed your view of the

189

trials. You are a privileged few who are allowed to even know of this procedure. But tonight shall be a particularly special treat: you all shall be given the honor of dining with and socializing with your future emperor, whichever one of the Candidates he may be." Caius noted a few eyes swivel back toward his table. "So please take this evening to get to know them; your future may depend on it!" Qutinus gave a short chuckle, but no one else laughed. "Well! Please take your seats, and dinner will be served momentarily." With that, Quintus himself bowed, and the spotlight shut off with a snap and the soft mandolin music returned.

Around the room, the crowd began to disperse as patrons found their particular markers. The winners of the bidding war who had been hovering like vultures over the round table pulled out their chairs and took a seat; most of them did their best to not see too impatient. Marcus nodded to some of them that he already recognized.

"My great pleasure to make your acquaintance!" said the woman on Caius's right, jumping into a conversation before anyone else could get a chance. She had creamy pale skin and curly red hair pulled back in a long ponytail that draped down the back of her dress. Her chin was thrust up and her bosom out in a desperate attempt to show off the gaudy jewels dangling above her breasts. "I was positively *astounded* at your performance the other day out there on the field, playing that native game from the New World. Aren't those tribes there just fascinating? Anyways, I resolved to keep an eye on you throughout the trials, and lo and behold, you amazed us all again with your work today on the strategy simulation!"

"Thank you," Caius said, not exactly sure how to respond.

"I'm Capurnia, by the way," she told him, extending a slender hand for him to kiss, sparkling with rings of multi-colored precious gems.

"However did you come up with that brilliant plan?" interrupted a man across the table who wore so much makeup that Caius couldn't even be sure what his real features looked like. This was much easier to answer. He told the table all about his past experiences and his love of all things related to flight. He mentioned that he'd started his own company building engines, and had had an internship working for Samarkand Aeronautics. They *oohed* at that, either very impressed by its prestigious credentials, or just wanting to flatter Caius. He told them all about the test pilots and how they sometimes had to bail out of the planes in an emergency. Capurnia had never even heard of these parachutes before today. A grizzled old man who introduced himself as Admiral Titus Rufus launched into a long and probably made-up (or at least drastically embellished) story about a time when he'd had to abandon ship off the coast of Formosa during the last war against the Ming Emperor. Caius nodded along politely, relieved to let someone else do the speaking for once.

The first course was served just as the Admiral was describing his courageous last stand, firing away at a Ming cruiser while the waves lapped against his heels. This man apparently had enough clout that the other guests were afraid to interrupt him. But as soon as he was done speaking, there was a mad scramble around the table to see who could control the conversation. A man to his left wearing expensive otter furs imported from the New World managed to grab control first by shouting his introduction over everyone else's. His name was Publius Naso, head of the Lower Rhine Steel Company. A powerful industrial player, he assured Caius, who was inclined to believe him based solely on his presence at the secretive trials.

"What are your thoughts on the Servant Occupation Laws?" he asked Caius, practically

spitting out the name. His position on them was made abundantly clear before Caius even knew

what they were.

"I'm afraid I don't know very much about them," Caius responded, hoping that the

conversation might switch to something he did know about. His other dining companions were

clearly of the same mind, but Publius managed to shout them down once again, so loud that

guests at other tables were turning to see what all the commotion was about.

"Of course you know! The laws that restrict the servant class to certain occupations:

waiters, chauffeurs, maids, etc. Asinine, if you ask me! Why, they are fit for all sorts of other

menial tasks and yet the Senate refuses to even consider expanding the set of jobs that they can

be used for!"

"Let me guess," Caius responded: "Mining, smelting, that sort of thing?"

"Naturally!" Publius said with a smile, not quite catching the hint of disdain in Caius's

voice. "Labor costs are by far the biggest expense when producing our steel, even when hiring

non-citizens! And there are so few of those left in Germania that we're reduced to importing

laborers from the lesser developed provinces like China." Caius felt a flash of anger, but

maintained his smile. Marcus had warned him that the Senate would be watching for any signs

that the candidates couldn't fit in with high society. "It's prohibitive!"

"But isn't working in your plant hard, dangerous work, even for normal workers?

Servants aren't particularly clever or independent, and the drugs wouldn't make them very good

192

steelworkers, would they? They can't take care of themselves, and we have an obligation to them to keep them out of harm's way. I think we should absolutely keep these laws in place."

Publius gaped like a hooked fish; clearly not a man used to being told he was wrong. Caius briefly wondered if this would have any impact on the trials, but imagined that defending a policy that the Senate clearly wanted in place would only be a net positive. And standing up for his values might matter a bit, too. Just as Publius was taking a deep breath, preparing to belt out a response, another guest stole the conversation away from him, moving on to nature conservancy out in the horn of Africa. Caius stifled a giggle as he mentioned that his own Advocate was from that region of the Empire. At his side, Marcus blushed and kicked at Caius under the table. Luckily none of the guests had any questions about Lamu.

The conversation carried on this way throughout dinner, with each of his companions trying to monopolize the conversation and steering it to their own topics of choice. Over soup, they discussed diplomatic relations with some of the southern African nations, and the growing trade in cocoa beans from the New World; Publius Naso noted sourly that many cocoa farms were staffed with servant laborers. Capurnia, on the other hand, raved about mixing the cocoa with milk and sugar. With salad, the Admiral wanted to talk all about starting colonies in the Pacific islands before Japan and the Ming could get to them. When the fish was served, Capurnia wanted to know all about the fashion trends in China and what the next big thing would be. Apparently everything Chinese was all the rage at the moment in Rome, and she really loved his current ensemble. "I wish I could make my eyes look like that," she exclaimed, staring obsessively at Caius's features. By the time the entrée came around, Caius had learned all about

193

the financial problems that the Imperial Railroad Authority was currently suffering, the latest automobile racing scores, and the many hijinks of Capurnia's cats.

The dinner was of course delicious; this was the cream of Roman society, the wealthiest of the wealthiest citizens and those with the Emperor's ear. They were used to the finest foods and most expensive wines, whereas up until a few days ago, Caius had been eating military barracks gruel. The meal was 9 different courses of meats and vegetables gathered from across the entire empire as well as a number of those exciting foods from the New World; Caius particularly enjoyed trying tomatoes. Caius was awkward throughout the entire conversation, chiming in when he could but otherwise picking at his food. Marcus, however, was the picture of perfect social grace and civility, charming everyone at the table.

Across the room, he could see other candidates in the same predicament, trying to manage the small talk of Roman high society. They'd all been through the same phases of the trials, including living in the streets. Dealing with the wealthiest members of society over the finest steaks doesn't really have the same allure when you've fought for scraps against addicts and vagrants. Herennius had a glint of despair in his eyes, but a happy smile was plastered on his face and he really was doing his best to pay attention to the spectators at his table. An old man in bright yellow robes seemed to be droning on and on about something. Behind him, Caius noted Althea telling a story with a fake smile and animated hand gestures; the guests at her table were laughing heartily.

Back at his table, dessert was being served. Publius was still giving Caius dirty looks and hadn't mentioned his desire for slave laborers since that first conversation. The other members of

194

the table, however, were having a fine time getting to know Caius. The CEO of the state-owned electronics company was grilling Caius on the details of airplane avionics systems, while Capurnia looked like she might jump on that man and stuff her napkin down his throat at any minute. The only thing holding her back was the succulent chocolate cake in front of her.

As the servants were clearing the last dishes, Senator Vitellius walked slowly to the center of the stage. The room fell silent.

"Well, ladies and gentlemen, I hope that you have had a chance to get to know at least one of our candidates this evening." Caius's table clapped loudly, except for Publius. Other spectators applauded as well, though not as enthusiastic. "And I hope you all have enjoyed the meal. But now we're going to break out of our groups and allow you all to just mingle." Servants filled the room from every side, and folded up the tables with amazing speed and efficiency.

Immediately a mob formed around Caius. All the spectators who had impatiently shoveled down their meals in anticipation now had their chance. They crowded around him in a blur of handshaking for the men and hand kissing for the women. Questions flew at him from all sides on any number of topics, so overwhelming that he couldn't answer any of them.

Caius managed to snag a passing servant and take a glass of water from the silver tray. He sipped slowly, giving him time to single out which question he wanted to answer. Through the crowd, he could see other candidates eyeing him with a tinge of jealousy. They were chatting with other spectators, but nowhere near the excited crowd that Caius was handling. Patiently and pleasantly, Caius worked the crowd. He shook hands and made small talk. He explained his feat at the strategy trials at least a dozen times, and repeated the inspiration for it at least two dozen

195

times. He answered questions on his home province and what he thought of the Western Empire so far. Upon learning that he hadn't seen much of it yet, dozens of them invited him to stay at their homes in various cities. Apparently these were the spectators who didn't have a high enough clearance to know what happened to losing candidates.

Caius's throat was parched from talking so much. He tried to peer over the crowd to spot a servant, but his short statute made it difficult. "Could you please ask a servant to bring me a drink?" he said to Marcus, who had been by his side throughout the process. Marcus nodded and disappeared into the sea of multi-colored robes.

A tall glass was pressed into his hand less than a minute later and he sipped at the cool liquid thankfully; some type of sweet juice from the New World that he didn't recognize. The attention from the spectators was non-stop. The topic had now turned to the war against Japan, and what Caius had been doing in Fukuoka. He told them all about his missions over Tokyo, but didn't mention his most recent patrol where he spotted the Ming ship. That little tidbit might still be confidential.

Caius started to feel a bit dizzy; too much excitement for one night. "I'm going to sit down," he told the crowd, gesturing to the chairs around the room. They followed like an obedient herd of cattle.

Marcus returned ten minutes later holding a glass of apple juice and motioned to the cup already in Caius's hand. "Where'd you get that one?"

"A servant handed it to me," Caius explained, looking back down at the glass. "I thought you'd sent him."

Marcus shrugged and sipped at the apple juice himself. He too had decided not to have any alcohol at the party. It wasn't worth risking any possible embarrassment. They could drink wine any other day of their lives.

"It wasn't a servant," chimed in an elderly lady in the crowd just as they were about to forget about the issue altogether. "Well, at least he wasn't wearing servant robes," she continued.

One of the Praetorians pushed his way through the crowd. They'd been lurking on the outside, waiting for any potential issue but not interfering in the proceedings.

"Only servants are allowed to handle the food and refreshments," he announced emphatically. His voice was stern and commanding, even though it was muffled by the mask. "Who gave this candidate the drink?" His hand drifted to the holster at his side. Caius thought about interfering. *They wouldn't shoot an old lady in the middle of a crowd,* he told himself. She hadn't done anything. But part of him wasn't so sure; he'd heard worse stories about the Praetorians.

"I… didn't get a good look…" she said, practically trembling at the prospect of talking to the intimidating guard. "It was someone in blue robes, though. That's how I noticed it. The servants never wear blue!" She shrank back trying to hide among the other spectators, roughly a third of whom were wearing some shade of blue.

"Man or woman?" the guard said, advancing toward her as though he were about to lash out. "Tall, short? What hair color?"

"I… I don't know!" she sobbed, clearly regretting that she'd ever spoken up.

"Stay here," he warned her. "We'll need to speak with you more." The guard turned back to Caius and snatched the glass from his hand. He sniffed it for a moment, then pulled a thin white instrument from one of his robe's interior pockets. He dipped it into the drink, stirred it into a whirlwind, then waited silently. The rest of the crowed remained frozen like statutes, both terrified to leave in case it made them look suspicious but also insatiably curious about what was happening.

Only Caius moved. His legs were wobbly and uncertain. His mouth felt like it was full of cotton and his throat tightened up.

"Marcus, can you get me a chair? I need…" his sentence was cut off as blood rushed to his head and his vision blacked out for a moment. He swooned to one side, and Marcus had to place a hand on his shoulder to steady him. There was a soft gasp from the crowd. The rest of the candidates and advocates from around the room had been drawn by the unusual scene, and all eyes were on Caius now.

The Praetorian's instrument beeped, and a red light flashed at the top. "Call the doctor," he announced swiftly. Perfect timing, too: Caius's knees buckled and he dropped to the floor. The smooth stone felt so refreshing against his warm skin. The room spun around him, and Caius was dimly aware of the spectators all backing away as though half a meter's distance would protect them from accusations of involvement.

"Caius, you were poisoned," Marcus was saying into his ear. "I need you to try to vomit, right now. You need to get whatever is left out of your stomach." Caius could feel his heart pounding in his ears. He tried to stand again, but his legs weren't responding very well, and he just ended up toppling over again. Marcus's hands gripped his shoulders and pulled him back up, and Caius managed to get on his hands and knees. He could distantly feel Marcus opening his mouth. The bright robes of the spectators all ran together into a rainbow blur as his vision faded. Marcus's fingers wormed their way into Caius's throat, and he felt his dinner coming back up. There was a reflexive cry of disgust from the spectators, as vomit splattered on the flagstones. His stomach heaved again and again as he tried to remain conscious.

I hope that the Senators don't mark me down for this, Caius thought just before passing out.

CHAPTER 12

Doctor Porcia shone a bright light directly into Caius's eyes, testing his pupil dilation. "It was a close call," she remarked. "You're lucky that we detected it in time. The initial symptoms of dizziness, thirst, and muscle weakness are all similar to alcohol. Whoever did this was probably expecting you to have been drinking, and didn't think you'd know what was going on in time. Very clever." She sounded like she almost admired the murderer.

"He's ok, though? No lasting side effects or anything like that?" Marcus had been wringing his hands for the past twenty four hours as Caius recovered in the medical office.

"Everything looks fine," she said. "It was a quick-acting poison, and it ran its course fairly swiftly. And, you got most of it out immediately." Caius blushed a bit at the memory of vomiting in front of every spectator and candidate. Even with good reason, it wasn't really a stellar first impression on Rome's high society for someone who wants to be their ruler.

She checked her chart again to make sure everything had been examined. "Well, Caius: you're all healthy. You can go back to the trials now. They delayed yesterday's test for you, and I'm sure Quintus is eager to get back on track."

Caius and Marcus thanked the doctor and slipped into the hall. Caius was still a bit unsteady on his feet, but got the hang of it as they went.

"Have they made any progress on catching whoever did this?" Caius asked. He'd been fading in and out of consciousness for the past day and hadn't been able to keep track of the investigation. He briefly remembered speaking with the Praetorians during one of the more lucid phases, but really had nothing to add. His attention had been entirely devoted to the spectators and hadn't taken any notice of who had passed him the cup. Why would anyone pay much attention to a servant?

"Not much," Marcus admitted. "Lady Amarada was unable to recall any more details. It didn't help that the Praetorians scared the wits out of her; she's already on her way back to Rome." Caius didn't have a hard time believing that.

"They do have a theory though," Marcus continued. Caius cocked his head, waiting for his advocate to continue. "They're saying that it was another candidate. That's who has the motive for it. And that an advocate is the only one who knew about the trials long enough in advance to procure the poison and then smuggle it in."

"Althea," Caius said immediately. She'd been threatening him since day one, and she'd already gotten someone to break Herennius's leg. And according to Marcus, Andericus didn't exactly have a stellar reputation for honesty and fair play. It all fit.

"We don't know that," Marcus cautioned. "She was wearing blue, but there really is no evidence. And the Praetorians are still looking into it. They'll find out who it was."

After a short pit stop at Caius's room to change, they met up with Herennius and Flavia for breakfast. Both of them were genuinely relieved to see that Caius was OK, and just as curious about who had poisoned him. Other candidates came into the cafeteria and stopped by to share their condolences, but Caius looked at each of them in a new light. One of them wanted him dead. Even if his gut told him it was Althea, he could never be sure.

They were all still discussing the assassination attempt over breakfast when Althea stomped into the dining hall. She took one look around and zeroed in on Caius at his regular table. She scowled, and Caius was briefly concerned that the failed attempt might not have been enough. Maybe she would try to kill him right here. Instead, she just swaggered over to the buffet table and heaped her plate. Andericus was conspicuously absent, so Althea threw her tray down at an empty table and ate alone.

Caius and Herennius finished breakfast early and meandered toward the main hall. The servants were still setting up everything necessary for the next trial, so the whole area was cordoned off by a row of guards gripping their rifles. Quintus was very serious about preventing any more interference with the Trials. Between their uniformed shoulders, dotted with Praetorian patches, Caius could see a number of large desks arranged in a wide circle that traced the perimeter of the dome far above. The balconies overlooking the hall, normally full of spectators eager for the next trial, were completely empty this morning. They weren't taking any more chances. On each of the columns that supported the high rooftop, signs had been posted asking Advocates to head back to their quarters. There would be no observation today. *Strange,* Caius thought. *What is it about this test that they don't want anyone to see? Was it something to do with the poisoning?*

Herennius and Caius chatted casually as they waited for Quintus to announce the start. Herennius was doing all the talking as usual, telling Caius all about his favorite Scandinavian specialties and how when he was Emperor, they would be serving pickled fish at every state banquet. Caius retorted that he'd had rather be poisoned again, and they both had a good laugh. Even the mention of some of those foods made Caius want to vomit up his breakfast, but Chinese cuisine probably sounded just as bad to the citizens of the Western half of the Empire.

Other candidates began to slowly filter into the room, attempting to peek over the line of guards in the most discreet fashion possible. A few of them joined Caius and Herennius. The group was just about to get big enough to begin another card game when Quintus strode through the doorway from the Senator's Hall. He was unaccompanied by any of the judges, though they were surely watching from somewhere.

The circle of guards formed ranks and retreated as Quintus mounted the stage at the front of the room. "Everyone please find your assigned desk," he called out, gesturing to the positions around the room. There didn't seem to be enough for all twenty nine candidates. Yet, everyone seemed to be able to find the seat marked with the correct name. Caius took a closer look, and realized that four other candidates had gone missing, just like Marius. Glancing to the scoreboard that dominated the wall next to the Hall of Candidates, he noticed that the some of the lowest-ranked names had simply been wiped away, erased from existence. The pool had been winnowed down to only twenty five remaining contenders. Caius took a quick headcount to determine who was missing. Most of them had been doing poorly, but the dismissal of Petillius had been a complete surprise. He'd done very well during the strategy trial, coming in sixth.

"Where'd Petillius go?"

Herennius laughed. "He had had a bit too much to drink at the party and had somehow made a fool of himself after you got poisoned. The last anyone had seen of him was his Advocate escorting him back to his room. When Drusus went over there to check on him after the party ended, the room was already cleared out."

Caius shook his head. Marcus had drilled it into him that every moment was a trial; apparently Petillius's Advocate hadn't done as well. Or maybe that was just the reason they were giving. Maybe the Praetorians had determined that Petillius was the real murderer.

Caius sank down into the comfortable office chair; Althea had been seated once again at the desk next to Caius, where she sat grimacing. *God, what is she planning now?* Caius thought. *Not much she can do during a test, though.* That was at least a comforting thought. The poisoning attempt had been pretty bold, but there was no way that she was stupid enough to attempt something with at least twenty guards within twenty meters. But Althea didn't say anything to him. She just sat down at her desk and stared down.

Caius surveyed the items before him. There wasn't much to see; two pencils, and two overturned paper booklets. "Please do not open your booklets yet," Quintus called out just as Caius reached out for one of them. He noticed that they had been sealed with a paper sticker.

"Today," he continued, "Begins the test for intelligence and education. Though each of you has succeeded as a pupil of one of the Empire's prestigious academies, this is not enough. The leader of the Empire must have a mind like a steel trap, retaining all information that could potentially be helpful. You will be required to make decisions on every single aspect of life for your citizens, and there is absolutely no way of knowing what knowledge will be needed. You will of course have advisors, but a thorough background will be necessary to understand their advice. Because of this, the Senate considers this one of the most important aspects of the Trials, and this phase will be very, very thorough." Caius thought back to Marcus's description of the previous generation of candidates and how the tests had focused instead on physical trials.

Quintus checked his pocket watch, then went back to his speech.

"Starting in four minutes, you will have four hours to complete this first booklet of questions, at which point we will break for lunch. The categories have all been randomly selected, meaning each of you will be taking a different test right now. As a result, there is no point in trying to cheat off of your neighbor. To select your answer, completely fill in the bubble…" They had all been through these same standardized tests by now, so the instructions weren't really necessary.

Quintus finished early, leaving the candidates to squirm nervously while the seconds ticked by. The audience hall was filled with the faint rustling of candidates fidgeting and trying to get more comfortable.

"All right…." Quintus said, drawing out the last syllable as he watched the seconds tick away, "START!"

Everyone reached for their booklets simultaneously, and the tearing of paper echoed from every side. Caius flipped to the first page of the booklet, titled "LOGIC." *Interesting,* he thought, *not a subject I'd had in school.* He had been expecting math and physics and history, not something more esoteric. No matter.

A store owner has six pieces of merchandise to display in an empty case with three shelves. Three of the items are red jackets: F, G, and H. Three of them are blue pants: K, L, and M. The three shelves of the display case are labelled 1 to 3 from top to bottom. Any of the shelves can remain empty. The merchant's placement of items must conform to the following conditions:

> K and M cannot be on the same shelf
>
> F must be on the shelf immediately above the shelf that L is on.
>
> No single shelf can hold all three pieces of red merchandise
>
> L cannot be on Shelf 2

God, Caius thought, *I almost fell asleep reading that. Maybe it was an effect of the poison.* He had to go back through and read it a second time just to make sure he'd gotten it all.

If G and H are on Shelf 2, which of the following must be true?

1. L is on Shelf 1

2. M is on Shelf 2

3. K is on Shelf 3

4. G and K are on the same shelf

5. F and L are on the same shelf

Caius stared at the page, running through the different options in his mind. *Must be true,* he reminded himself. Key word being "Must."

"L could be on shelf 3..." he whispered softly, "So it isn't A..." *God, this is maddening!* Recalling facts and figures from his education was always easy for Caius, but this test was completely different. He struggled his way through the question, and decided to just skip this one and come back to it.

If no blue items are on Shelf 3, which pair of items must be on the same shelf?

1. F and G

2. M and H

3. M and G

4. L and J

5. G and H

Are they all going to be like this?? His mind was wrapped in a thick, impenetrable fog as he tried to read through the questions. He took a moment and flipped ahead: more and more of the same. Four hours' worth. The eggs and sausages that he'd had for breakfast suddenly weren't settling well in his stomach. Caius read over the question again, trying to make sense of it.

Finally, he drew out a tiny diagram in the margins and reasoned that G and H would have to be together.

He was suddenly aware of the clock counting down at the front of the room. This was taking forever, and he had an entire booklet to do. Would it be enough? If he didn't finish, would he get them all wrong??

A flash of movement in the corner of his eye caught his attention. Althea was turning the page of her booklet, already done with the first sheet of questions. Caius had only answered one so far! Althea was tracing the words of the next question with the tip of her pencil. She tapped the page, searching for an answer. Caius should have gone back to his own test. Time was slipping away, and these ridiculous logic questions weren't getting any easier. But there was just something that kept his attention riveted on his neighbor.

Althea slipped her forefinger and thumb into her sleeve and unraveled a long, thin roll of paper from under her watch band. Caius turned his head, trying to get a better view. There was some kind of writing on it that he couldn't quite make out, but Althea certainly knew what it was. She tucked the paper back into her robes and then scribbled into the answer booklet, far longer than she needed to just fill in one bubble. Turning back to her test booklet, she flipped the page and pretended to study the question again before rolling out the paper and then copying all the answers down.

That bastard is cheating! Caius should have been focusing on his own exam, but it was taking all of his willpower not to stand up and throw Althea out of her chair and rip out that cheat sheet for everyone to see. He kept watching as Althea copied every single answer from that sheet in her sleeve, then just pretended to read the questions for a while to look like she was really doing the work. *I hope the Senators are watching all of this on camera. I want to see the Praetorians storm in here, drag her out the door and chuck her into the snow.*

Caius thought about the best way to handle this as he struggled through the quagmire of logic puzzles before him. He had to tell the Senators. It would be easy to prove; they would just need to have the Praetorians march her up on stage and pull down the sleeve of her robe in front of everyone. No way to hide it as long as they caught her unawares. Caius was getting excited just thinking of the prospect of his rival being publicly humiliated and disqualified from the competition like that. With a renewed sense of purpose, Caius threw himself back into answering the questions as best he could.

It was hard to pay attention to the test. The questions themselves seemed designed to make it hard to focus, forcing Caius to have to constantly go back and forth between the facts and the question itself. And Caius was having a hard time not watching Althea constantly cheating with that little slip of paper in her sleeve. As the hours ticked by, Caius got more and more excited about the prospect of being able to report him to the Senators. Even if he completely failed this current test, it would be entirely worth it just to see Althea leave.

Quintus strode on stage and announced that time was up. There was a simultaneous clatter of pencils and a joint sigh of relief as each candidate put in their last answers. Caius had to guess blindly on the last dozen or so, but he could not be happier that it was over. Finally!

Across the room, he saw Marcus and Flavia enter from the Advocate's Hall, and just couldn't help it as a big grin spread across his face. He tried to rein it in as best he could while the other candidates were around.

Marcus approached, probably about to ask how the test had gone. "I need to talk to you," Caius interrupted before his advocate could get out the first word. "Alone."

Marcus furrowed his brow with concern, but nodded and led the way back toward Caius's quarters. Caius was practically skipping down the hall behind him. Flavia and Herennius watched the pair go, probably wondering what that was all about.

"She was cheating!" Caius shouted the second the door shut behind him. "Althea! She was cheating. She had the answers to the test already. I don't know how, but they were all written on a little roll inside of her sleeve and she kept looking at it every time that she turned the page. I don't think she saw me watching…"

"Slow down," Marcus warned. Caius realized that he hadn't really been breathing, just blurting out his sentences as fast as possible. He took a deep breath and repeated his story with details of what he had seen Althea doing.

Marcus leaned back in the chair, soaking it all in.

"Well?" Caius demanded, "Are we going to go bust her? Let's tell the Senators what she did and get her out of here!"

The advocate took a moment to think, weighing the idea. His lethargy was driving Caius crazy!

"You're right," Marcus finally relented. "If they catch her coming back into the test with all of the answers hidden under her sleeve, then they will have absolutely no choice but to expel her from the Trials. She certainly has it out for you now, so we have nothing to lose."

He stood from the chair and strode out the door without another word. They made their way down the hall to the test grounds, where Quintus was overseeing the distribution of more test booklets. The Praetorians blocked their path, under orders to prevent any candidates in. "Quintus," Marcus called out over their shoulders, catching his attention.

"Hello Marcus. Everything all right? You know the Candidates are supposed to be in the cafeteria having lunch."

"We need to speak with Senator Vitellius," Marcus said. "It's very urgent. We need to see him immediately."

Quintus was an unreadable sphinx. He stared down Marcus like an old timey gladiator meeting his opponent.

"Is this related to the assassination attempt? That information should go to me." Marcus shook his head no. "Very well," Quintus said at last. "I'll send one of the guards to fetch him." He turned to his men to pick one of them out, but Marcus stopped him.

"It would be better if we met with him alone, somewhere else. It is a matter of the utmost sensitivity, and I know that he would prefer that the matter remain just between us."

Quintus studied Marcus again, then turned back to his men. "Appius," he barked, and one of the Praetorians turned and saluted, "Please go find Senator Vitellius in the observation room and ask him to meet us at his office." The soldier nodded and ran off down the Senators' hallway, armor clanging noisily. They waited impatiently until the guard returned, huffing and puffing, informing them that the Senator would meet them there. "Follow me," Quintus said, marching off briskly.

Quintus brought the pair down the Senator's Hall, which Caius had not visited yet. It was as luxurious and beautiful as the quarters for the spectators, yet this section was more stately and sophisticated. Busts of famous Senators lined the hallway, and at the very end, a full sized statue that even Caius recognized: Senator Hortensius, who had ended the Succession Wars and started the Trials in the first place. At last, they arrived at a stout wooden door, and Quintus knocked briefly. From inside, Vitellius's voice invited them in.

Caius's first thought was that they had forgotten to furnish this room. It was at least 5 times bigger than his own small bedroom, but the space was largely wasted. All the room contained was a simple wooden desk with two plain wooden chairs in front of it. No rugs, tapestries, paintings, statues, or busts: the room was spartan and undecorated. There didn't even seem to be any computers or projectors or monitors, which he'd expect to find in the office of one of the most powerful men in the Empire. The cold from the stone floor seemed to seep through Caius's shoes as they crossed the vast, echoing chamber to where Vitellius waited.

"Take a seat," he told them, gesturing to the two spindly wooden chairs in front of the desk. "What is so urgent that we needed to speak right now?"

Caius looked at Marcus, unsure who should be the one to explain. Marcus nodded back at him.

"Senator Vitellius, during the most recent trial, I witnessed another Candidate cheating. She somehow had all of the answers to the test already, and wrote them all on a little slip of paper that she was hiding underneath the band of her watch. She unrolled it multiple times during the test and wrote the answers down, not even bothering to do the questions."

Vitellius's wooden chair creaked a bit as the Senator leaned back, considering Caius's words. "This is a severe accusation," he said. "Severe enough to remove this Candidate from the Trials, if true."

"I know, sir." Caius responded.

"Who was the Candidate?"

Caius swallowed, hard. A lump had appeared in his throat somehow.

"It was Althea, sir. She was sitting right next to me."

Vitellius gave a sort of half smile and looked at Marcus this time, thrusting Caius out of the conversation and onto the sidelines.

"Marcus, we know what.... *troubles* your candidate has had with this Althea. The two do not get along; that much is plain. And, if I am remembering correctly, your candidate was accused of cheating by that same person the other day during the strategy session. This kind of retaliatory behavior just looks petty."

Caius had to clench the arms of the chair to stop himself from interrupting the Senator. Thank god for Marcus's training.

"With all due respect, Senator," Marcus started, darting a reassuring look to Caius, "That is simply not the case here. Caius would have no issue with facing off against Althea in a fair competition. But if someone is feeding that girl the answers to the tests, then that is not fair at all, is it? Caius would not make up such a story."

The Senator sighed. "We just do not have time to engage in some outlandish investigation of a candidate based solely on the word of another. And in particular when those two have a history of meaningless accusations like this. Maybe Caius is still suffering from the effects of the poison and needs some more rest. Is that the case, candidate?"

This was not going as expected. Instead of seeing Althea shown the door, it appeared to be more likely that he had just given Vitellius the impression that he was a petty liar, or at best drug-addled.

"No, Sir," Caius answered. "I feel perfectly fine, and I know what I saw. It would be a relatively simple matter to prove. If she cheated on the first test, it is likely that she would attempt to do the same for the afternoon session. Simply send a Praetorian to bring her here, and to make sure that she keeps his wrists out and visible the whole time. Don't give her an opportunity to get rid of the evidence. Bring her here to the office, and check."

The office was silent. Vitellius contemplated Caius with just a hint of smoldering anger. This was really not going well.

"All right," he said at last. He pulled his tablet up from a drawer under the desk and scribbled a note; Caius heard the "Whoosh" sound effect as the message was sent. "I've let Quintus know what the situation is, and asked him to dispatch a guard to bring Althea here. We will get to the bottom of things."

The office was deathly silent while they waited for Althea to arrive. Neither Marcus nor Caius dared move, and Vitellius went back to work, seemingly annoyed at this unwelcome interruption. Caius was afraid to even breathe.

After what felt like hours, the door opened. Althea marched in, arms held in front of her like a blind woman trying to feel her way to her destination. She had a look of confusion on her face that turned to suspicion as soon as she saw Caius and Marcus waiting in the office.

She was followed shortly through the doorway by Quintus, looking annoyed, and Andericus, who was ready to tear someone's head off.

"Althea," Vitellius said, "You have been accused of cheating in the most recent trial. Caius here has informed us that you had a roll of paper in your sleeve which had all of the answers written ahead of time. How do you respond to these accusations?"

"This is a complete outrage," Andericus burst out before Althea could even answer. "Caius is the one who cheated during the strategy simulation. And yet Quintus here was unwilling to even hear our complaint. He just brushed us off, all the while laughing with his chum Marcus. It's bias, I tell you! You should…"

Vitellius silenced him with a raised hand. "I just want to hear from Althea. It's a simple question."

If nothing else, Althea was a good actress. She put on her most innocent face and smiled sweetly. "Absolutely false," she told the Senator. "I don't have any idea what he is talking about, and I would certainly never cheat in one of the Trials."

Vitellius looked her over, judging her honesty. He nodded to Quintus, who stepped forward and pulled up Althea's sleeves, and searched inside the cuffs. Nothing. Quintus even took off Althea's watch and checked there. Empty. No rolled up paper with the answers.

Caius stirred in his seat, getting ready to protest. Althea must have hidden it right after the trial, or something like that! But Marcus put a hand on his arm and shook his head slightly, almost imperceptibly. *It's over,* his expression said. Continuing to fight it would just anger Vitellius even more.

"As you gentlemen can see, there is nothing in her sleeves. Is there anything else?"

"No, Sir," Caius responded quietly, eyes glued to the tips of his boots. "Nothing more."

"Very good. Quintus, please escort these two candidates back to the main hall, so that they can have some lunch before the trials resume. I myself have to return to the observation room."

Althea bowed deeply to the Senator. "Thank you for your wisdom and fairness, Sir," she said as Quintus ushered her out of the room. Really laying it on thick.

Quintus brought them back out into the hallway, followed by the pair of advocates.

"Quintus," Althea said with the same saccharine sweet tone that she'd used on the Senator, "Could you please give Caius and I a moment alone to talk?"

She's going to try to kill me again, Caius thought immediately. Quintus seemed to have the same idea, and was getting ready to say no to her request.

"It's all right, Quintus," Caius said, sizing Althea up. "I'll be fine. I just have to make sure not to accept any food or drink from her." Marcus chuckled at the joke, but Quintus didn't even crack a smile.

"All right," Quintus relented. "You can talk down the hall. Don't go out of sight."

Althea led him as far as they could go until the hallway curved away deeper into the mountain. Each of them leaned against opposing walls and waited for the other to speak. Finally, Althea huffed and spoke up.

"You're getting desperate, Caius. Accusing me of cheating?"

She must be delusional. "How am *I* getting desperate? I'm ahead of you!"

"You're desperate enough to bring this wild accusation to Vitellius," she retorted with a grin. Caius clenched his jaw and resisted the urge to punch her.

217

"Caius, why are you here?" she continued.

Caius cocked his head and gave half of a laugh. "Because you said you needed to talk to me about something..."

"No," Althea responded, with the same sour expression that she usually wore. "I mean here in this facility. At the trials."

Caius waited for her to elaborate a little more, but there was nothing else.

"Because I want to be Emperor," he said simply. Wouldn't that be the case for all thirty of them?

Althea rolled her eyes and paced back and forth down the hall casting a flickering shadow. "Don't be stupid," she said dismissively without even noticing how rude and condescending she was. "I mean, why do you want to be Emperor? What's in it for you?"

Caius was quiet for a moment. "I want to see my family again, after 12 years of separation. I want to help the people of Rome and do something good. And I *don't* want to be cooped up in some hidden wing of the Palace, isolated from the rest of society and only useful when the Emperor decides to call for my opinion on something." His mind flashed back to Marcus's sad expression back on the train when he'd been describing the life of the losing candidate. *Like a servant, but without the drugs to take the edge off,* he'd said.

Althea nodded, at least satisfied with this answer. "I've seen you go through these trials for the past week, and you're honestly just not cut out for it."

"Oh, and you are?" Caius responded.

"Yes," Althea replied with a hiss. "YES! The Senate will never admit to it, but they are looking for something completely different than what they claim. They **say** that they want this romanticized idea of an Emperor who should be some unrealistic paragon of virtue and morality. They claim they want someone who is nice and sweet and friendly. Like you." She said the last few words with a sneer and a mocking tone. "That's not what politics in the Empire is like. Hell, even one week in the trials should have shown you that by now. It's a dirty, messy, all-out brawl that leaves the losers broken and bleeding and dead in the gutter."

"Like Herennius and his leg?" Caius reminded her. "Or me being poisoned?"

"Metaphorically, I meant," said Althea, not bothering to deny her role in either attack. Even smiling a bit. "But come on. If you're already sick of having competitors at your throat after one week of trials, how will you feel after a year as the Emperor? Foreign enemies seeking to steal your territories, political rivals in the Senate seeking to steal your power, competing businessmen trying to drive the state-owned corporations into the ground.... you'll be besieged on all sides! Your entire life will be nothing but stress and worry until you keel over and have a heart attack. Assuming you're not assassinated, of course." She said the last bit with a smile, and Caius just knew that she had had something to do with him being poisoned.

Althea was really getting into her speech now. She was gesturing wildly and speaking passionately. "And those are just the external concerns. But what about the responsibility you'll bear?"

Caius's heart beat just a bit faster. This whole process had been such a shock and a rush that he hadn't even given much thought to what it would be like to really be Emperor. He'd of course fantasized about the opulent palaces and all of the material perks, but not the burden of actually ruling. But he maintained his composure in front of Althea.

"Think of everyone depending on you," she continued. "Businesses that you can make or break with one stroke of the pen. Each one employing dozens, or hundreds, or even thousands of citizens! Each one trying to just make a living, and you could wipe out their entire livelihoods with just one mistake or relying on some bad advice from one corrupt official." He immediately thought back to Oventia's offer and realized he would never trust anyone like that as one of his ministers.

Sweat started to accumulate on Caius's palms, and he rubbed them unconsciously across his robes, trying to wipe it off.

"And those are just financial decisions! What about regulating safety, or health care? So many lives, all depending on you to make the right choice. How many orphans did you know when you were forced to live on the streets, Caius?" Althea had of course been through the same phase in her own life, so she knew at least some of the hardships that Caius had gone through. "How many of your fellow vagrants came from broken homes? Would you really want responsibility for doing that to a whole new generation of children while you sit easily in your palace and hand out your edicts?"

Caius tried to stammer an answer, but Althea wasn't done yet.

"And let's not forget the military, Caius. We were both out on the front lines just a few weeks ago, but you don't *really* know what it was like. You're a pilot; you get to just fly over the battlefield and drop your bombs like a kid killing little insignificant insects. You've never experienced the real horrors of war. *I* was stationed in a sweltering jungle in some Burmese swamp, staring over the border at the Ming guards in their own towers. Everyone clutching their guns just waiting for someone to go crazy and start shooting, then gunfire would just ripple down the line like dominoes until both countries were at war. We both know it's coming, Caius. The Ming will never forget what happened. When you're emperor, are you going to be ready for that? Will you be willing to send thousands and thousands of your countrymen into those jungles again to die? Could you keep that up for years? *Decades* of seeing those bodies marched down through the center of Rome covered in the red Imperial flag? Do you really have the stomach for that?"

Caius looked down at his feet as a triumphant grin spread over Althea's face. *Could he live like that?* He'd even felt a pang of guilt when the soldiers died in his little simulated invasion of the Mapuche capital earlier this afternoon. Was he heartless enough to do it knowing that it would be real men fighting and dying instead of pixels? Did he really have what it would take to be Emperor?

Althea leaned in close. "*I* can do it, Caius. You know that. You know that we're different. I'm cold and calculating, whereas you're friendly and nice. The Senators pretend to want the latter, but we both know that the best emperors are made of hardened steel, not cotton. You'd let the rest of Rome walk all over you, where I would do what needs to be done. I would be willing to stand up to all of those who would challenge me. I'd be the Emperor that Rome deserves." A vein in her forehead was throbbing from the passion and fervor of her little tirade. She truly believed what she was saying.

"I have an offer for you, Caius. You will have exactly what you want, without any of the nasty parts of being the Emperor. I'll appoint you as the head of one of the state-owned businesses. An easy one, where you won't have to do much work." Caius pictured himself as the head of Samarkand Aeronautics, where he could pursue whatever projects he wanted. "You'll have a *very* generous salary. More than you'd ever need. You'll live a life of luxury and happiness. And you can be reunited with your family, and any of your friends from the Academy. I don't really mind; I wouldn't see you as a threat. You'd have all the perks of being the Emperor without the stress. All I ask is that you drop out of the competition now. I can do the rest, and once I win, I'll make sure that you are taken care of."

"And why would I have any reason to believe that you'd honor that deal?"

Althea looked at him, feigning insult. "I'm hurt, Caius!" She broke out into an authentic, eye-crinkling grin, clearly amused at her own joke. It wasn't the teethy show that she often put on for the Senators. "The real question is, what reason do I have to not honor it? It really means nothing to me. I'm going to have to pick new heads for the companies anyway and I'd rather have somebody that I at least know will be competent. And I think we both know that the risk of me welching on the deal is significantly less than the risk that you'll lose the Trials. That you'll lose, and you'll be forced to live in the palace's private prison, cut off from the rest of society for the rest of your life."

It wasn't a bad offer. She'd pretty much nailed everything that Caius wanted and everything that Caius feared. And despite everything that he'd seen so far, he honestly believed that Althea would honor the deal once the trials were over. *If* she became Emperor, that is.

"What I think," Caius replied slowly, "Is that you're scared. You're probably dreading going back to the trials right now because you'll be watched from now on, and you won't be able to cheat anymore. You're going to wake up tomorrow morning and see the scoreboard, and your name will still be under mine." He took a deep breath, savoring the opportunity to knock Althea down a peg. "And you're not just scared of today's results. You're scared because you slowly see the lead slipping out of your grasp, inch by inch. Every day, new scores come in and Herennius and I get just one more step ahead of you. So, this offer of yours is just a last-ditch, pathetic attempt to save your own candidacy that is currently circling the drain."

He hadn't made up his mind on the offer until just this moment, but it just felt so right. He went with his heart.

"If you'd approached me with that deal on the first morning we met, I probably would have said yes. Because I'm scared shitless that I'm going to lose the trials and never see my family, or anyone else, ever again. And I'm absolutely just as scared that I am going to win, and I'll be Emperor. And I'll have to deal with all of those same problems that you already mentioned. But you know what? Those fears *pale* in comparison to how afraid I am that a power-hungry, manipulative person like *you* could become the leader of the Empire. So no. Absolutely no. I'm not just in this to become Emperor; I'm in it to make sure that you *don't* become Emperor."

A glowing feeling of warmth and happiness sent excited jitters like lightning dancing from spine to fingertips. It felt so good to let out his true feelings for once after constantly having to hide his emotions through the trials. He bowed sarcastically to Althea, who still hadn't moved. Her face was contorted in a mix of anger, confusion, and disbelief.

"I'm going to go have some lunch now." Caius told her with an amazing display of calmness. "Best of luck to you in the coming trials."

CHAPTER 13

Caius rolled out of bed with a groan and managed to drag himself over to the closet. He tried to pick a matching outfit, but his brain was completely fried; it was hard enough to even get his eyes to focus.

For the past week, the Trials had focused solely on testing knowledge. Economics, mathematics, philosophy, history, grammar and language... everything the candidates had ever studied. They were cramming 8 years of final exams into a one week period. Every time Caius closed his eyes, little multiple choice bubbles swam through the darkness. Interviews, presentations, and quizzes had filled up each of the past seven days, and Caius just couldn't take any more.

Marcus was waiting patiently in the chair next to him, wearing a slightly bemused grin as he watched his Candidate struggle through the morning routine. Caius dreaded this part the most because it ended with heading to the main hall and seeing the scoreboard. Yesterday had been a 5, his lowest score yet. Meanwhile Herennius had been consistently scoring 10s on every single exam, overtaking Caius's hard-earned lead. Even Althea had been "excelling" at the tests; she took a particular pleasure in showing her latest scores to Caius every morning. Naturally, she had been cheating, and Caius knew that, but no one believed it. And ever since Caius had rejected her offer, Althea had had a particular vendetta against Caius and took any opportunity possible to insult him. It had become a daily ritual to try and shovel down his breakfast before Althea spotted him and ran over to discuss her latest 10 on the scoreboard.

"I just don't know what I'm doing wrong," Caius said, biting back the frustration and anger on the tip of his tongue. "I have been a model student my entire life; not a single bad mark. And now I'm coming in average? I honestly don't get it."

Marcus nodded, not quite sure what to say. "You just have to keep pushing. If it makes you feel any better, a lot of the other candidates are having a hard time too."

"Not Althea," Caius responded with a grimace.

"Well we *know* why she isn't struggling. We just need to push through. Do our best and focus on the rest of the trials."

Caius let out a sigh and fussed with his collar. He *had* been focusing.

They marched off to breakfast, barely speaking. Flavia and Herennius were already sitting in their regular spots, eating steaming bowels of oatmeal with cream and fruit. Caius grunted in greeting as he tossed his tray onto the table and plopped down onto an open chair.

"Morning!" Herennius said in between bites, always chipper. "How'd you sleep?" Caius could only grunt in response; it was probably pretty clear anyway.

"Food and sleep," Herennius said as he shoveled another spoonful of oatmeal into his mouth. "Those are really the secrets to this. It's not about how much you've learned in school, it's all about how well your brain is working."

Caius nodded and dug into his own food, holding up the first spoonful to Herennius to show him that he was following his advice. "There you go!" his blond friend replied with a laugh and a spoonful of his own. Despite his sour mood, Caius couldn't help but smile just a bit too.

After breakfast, the four of them walked back to the main atrium, expecting to see the same twenty desks that had been there for the past week. Twenty, not twenty five: the group had been narrowed down even further midway through the week of exams.

But today the desks were gone. Some of the other remaining candidates were milling about the base of the massive columns, wondering what to do with themselves. Caius could hardly hold a shout of joy or some other celebratory outburst. *No more stupid tests!* Marcus thumped him heartily on the back, definitely sharing the same sentiment. Around the enormous, bright expanse of the room many of the other Candidates wore the same look of relief.

"What do you think the next trial is going to be?" Herennius whispered to Caius, who only shrugged.

"Maybe another physical trial?" Marcus suggested. "There's only been one so far, and we had *five* back when I was a candidate." Herennius patted his leg, which had recently been declared fit by the doctor and removed from the cast. It may have looked fine on the x-ray, but was it good enough to compete with?

Flavia shook her head. "That was only because Senator Apurnia back in your year had some obsession with having a strong, fit emperor. She didn't care so much about intelligence."

"Clearly..." Marcus said. Caius wasn't sure if he was complimenting himself or insulting the Emperor. "Probably why they've had so many knowledge tests this round; trying to make sure they don't make the same mistake twice." Looks like the latter; maybe both.

More and more candidates arrived from the cafeteria; looks like almost everyone was already present. Althea's face, with her usual sour expression, poked out of the crowd. They locked eyes for just a second across the room. Her eyes brightened and she flashed the same smile that Caius had seen every morning this week. She pointed at the scoreboard across the room; Caius didn't need to check to know that she had gotten another 10. His teeth clenched and he balled his fists involuntarily. Luckily Althea was too far to slug in the face. At least this would be the last day he had to deal with this gloating.

"Just ignore her," Herennius said, also glaring at Althea. "She's just being an ass; she's bitter that you didn't give up."

Right on time, Quintus and his small troop of masked Praetorians marched into the center of the room and unfurled another scroll. The edges of his mouth tipped up into a slight smile as he read the orders.

"Candidates, today we will begin a new trial that will truly test your limits. It will bring out the best in each of you and display resourcefulness, teamwork, and independence." A look of comprehension dawned across Marcus's face, and his eyes lit up. He didn't want to interrupt Quintus, but he clapped his hand firmly on Caius's shoulder. "We will be escorting you all far out into the wilderness, beyond the reach of all civilization. Either survive on your own and make it back to the facility, or you can team up and work together to make it back faster."

228

A few of the candidates were nodding their heads, clearly confident that their military training had been sufficient in this field. Some of them had been rangers, or snipers, who received extensive training on what to do in such a scenario. As a pilot, Caius's survival instructions had been limited to "get out before it explodes or crashes."

"The trucks are out in front of the building waiting to take you to the starting point. Please proceed through the main entry hall!" Quintus gestured toward the high arched hallway where Caius had entered the facility that very first night. It felt like ages ago that he'd arrived in that howling snowstorm and walked through those enormous metal doors.

Quintus and the Praetorians led the way; a trickling stream of candidates and advocates followed, hurriedly discussing the test in low tones.

"We did this in my round," Flavia whispered to Caius and Herennius. She had been a candidate in the generation before Marcus and the current Emperor. "They led us up the mountain on horseback and gathered us at the top. Then they made us pick supplies, and had us hike back down. It was too far to do in a day, so you'd probably have to spend at least one night out there. It may seem like it's big from here, but this facility is really hard to spot. From afar, it just looks like every other mountain. They key is going to be finding the little town down in the valley. From there you'll be able to get up pretty easily, I think." Other nearby candidates were getting similar advice.

The metal doors in front of Quintus groaned open, flooding the hallway with soft light that bounced off of the guards' armor. Caius had to shield his eyes for a moment while they adjusted. Large trucks, probably the same ones that had conveyed Marcus and Caius up to the

229

mountaintop that first night, idled in front. The weather was cloudy and grey and gloomy. In the background, Caius could see that the valley was filled with heavy clouds, so thick that the mountains on the opposite side were invisible. It was like a big bowl of grey soup.

"Ok, Candidates. Load up; four to a vehicle." Quintus gestured to the five waiting trucks. "But before you get in: because the challenge is to find your way back, we can't exactly let you see the route there." He held up a handful of large black face masks with the eyes covered. "You all need to have one of these put on by the guards. You *cannot* do it yourself! Advocates, please come help your candidate into the truck once the masks have been applied." One of the Praetorians approached holding the masks and slipped it over Caius's face. The bright sun was suddenly erased; he opened and closed his eyes, with absolutely no difference. The mask blocked the light perfectly. He felt Marcus's hands guide him toward one of the vehicles.

Caius and Herennius climbed into the lead truck, followed by two more candidates. They exchanged greetings, and Caius recognized the deep, smooth voice of Florian and the higher, more nasal voice of Gideon. Florian cried out in pain, having hit his head on the top of the truck cab. They made small talk complaining about the quizzes and put on their safety harnesses while they waited for the convoy to get going.

The truck shifted into gear with a rumble and shuddered to life. The candidates all fell silent as they took off. The seats bounced and vibrated as the trucks navigated the same steep road that Caius had gone up his first night; Herennius practically crushed him as they went around the steep mountain turns, and potholes in the road sent them all flying into the ceiling with a crash.

Caius's ears popped as they reached the valley floor. The sound of the rough unpaved road disappeared as they made it back to the main roadway. Caius was trying to tell which direction they were heading, but the driver seemed to be taking a lot of unnecessary and confusing turns back and forth.

The Candidates tried making small talk on the way, but it petered out after a few minutes. Each of them was more focused on trying to remember every scrap of wilderness survival training they'd had. Some of the others had been stationed in Europe and knew the native plants if they had to scrounge for food. It would be totally alien to Caius, compared to what he knew from China and Japan.

After at least an hour's drive, the trucks turned into a gravely road, causing little bits of rock to plink endlessly against the metal undercarriage. The truck bounced and jostled, sending them regularly flying off their seats. Caius could feel his body pressed against the seat by the gravity as they started going uphill again. His stomach churned with car sickness as they went back and forth on a switchback trail up the mountain. From the noises coming from Herennius next to him, Caius wasn't the only one suffering through the ride.

"Can we open a window and get some fresh air in here?" Caius asked, trying to silence the quaver in his voice. The guard said nothing in response, but they were all hit suddenly with an icy blast of wind that swirled through the car. Caius shivered immediately in his robes, feeling wet snowflakes hit his skin. "Never mind!" he yelled over the howl; the truck must be going pretty fast. The driver chuckled and must have closed the window, because the chilling gust of air stopped immediately. "Damn," Herennius said. "Just like home!" This got a short laugh from the other candidates, but then they all fell silent again.

Caius frantically ran through any tidbit of wilderness training he'd had. Back at the Academy, they'd had a survival course as part of their fitness class, but it had never really focused on cold-weather survival. He knew how to make a fire, but it would be difficult to find dry wood if it was really snowing out. A shelter probably wouldn't be too bad; there was plenty of wood and foliage around, but making it wind-resistant would be difficult. Finding his way back would probably be the most daunting part. Maybe climb up one of these mountains and try to spot the valley? But summiting these peaks would be no easy task, and certainly time consuming. And who's to say that he would even be able to see the right valley? Maybe there were a dozen similar areas in the region, and he'd spend all day walking to the wrong one.

Caius's heart thumped a little harder as he continued thinking of all the difficulties he'd have getting back. Maybe it would be snowing so hard that there'd be no visibility. Maybe the Senators had some other trick up their sleeves that would make things even harder. He stopped and took a deep breath, trying not to make it too obvious to the others that he was starting to panic. *Just relax and take things one step at a time,* he told himself.

The truck continued to speed wildly around curves, going ever upwards. It seemed like they'd been climbing the slopes for hours. Caius half expected that they'd all find themselves at the very top of a mountain and be expected to make their way down off a cliff. The sound of the gravel hitting the side of the car had stopped, replaced by the sounds of tires spinning through mud and slush. There may have not even been a road anymore.

After an eternity of traveling, the truck came to a stop. The driver's side door creaked open, followed by the sound of feet landing in snow, and then slammed shut again. The candidates inside all waited for something to happen. Hopefully they had arrived, and it wasn't just a piss break for the driver.

The door next to Caius opened unexpectedly; he would have tumbled out into the mud had it not been for his harness. "Careful, son," Quintus said with a laugh. "You can all take off your masks and get out of the truck." They pulled them off and blinked their eyes, adjusting to the light. Caius hopped off his seat and into a patch of powdery snow. They were in the middle of a non-descript field framed by tall, snow-laden pine trees. Nearby, five more trucks had arrived and were unloading the rest of the candidates, as well as the Senators and guards. At the far end of the meadow, a rustic wooden lodge was perched just against the tree line, puffing white smoke out its stone chimney. More fluffy white flakes were slowly drifting down around them, and Caius suddenly realized how ill-equipped he was in his formal robes. He'd freeze to death before he could even get his bearings!

Quintus must have read his mind. From the back of the truck, he produced 4 pre-warmed coats and sets of waterproof trousers, made of some synthetic fabric. Caius threw the clothes on over his robes and felt like he'd just sat down next to a roaring fire.

"Head over to the stage, Candidates," Quintus told them. For the first time, Caius noticed the large wooden platform only a few yards away. A wall behind it was shrouded in a big red curtain. The candidates trudged through the snow that was already up to their ankles and falling fast. Servants meandered through the crowd of candidates and guards, serving steaming cups of cider and bearing large platters of sandwiches for lunch.

The Senators made their way onto the stage, assisted by Quintus and the Praetorians. Senator Oventia could not have looked more miserable; she was from Persia after all, and probably not used to such extreme temperatures. Her eyes briefly locked with Caius's, and he turned away hurriedly. She had not acknowledged his presence in any way since their last meeting in the comfortable lounge at the top of the facility when she had tried to sell her vote for a position in his government. Or, at least pretended to.

Vitellius, however, was happier than ever. There was a spring in his normally frail step, and his broad smile made him look ten years younger. "Candidates," he said, "This trial is one of my favorites. This is more a test of character than a test of anything particularly useful for ruling. Once you become emperor, you'll have no need to go out into the woods and forage for yourself, and you'll probably never be lost again. But what this test does prove is your ability to think on your feet, to adapt to new situations, to keep your calm, and so many other valuable character attributes. And it's a lot more fun than sitting inside taking hours-long tests, isn't it?"
This statement got an audible cheer from almost all of the remaining candidates, with the exception of Althea. She was sulking near the back of the crowd with the expression of a cat who had been dropped into a bathtub and finally managed to claw its way out. She clearly was not a fan of the wet and cold, and would rather be inside taking more tests so that she could rub the scores in Caius's face the next morning.

"But, we are not dropping you all out in the woods unprepared," Vitellius continued. "Which brings us to the very first phase of this trial: resource management."

Behind him, Quintus whipped the red curtain away, revealing dozens of little cubby holes full of all kinds of things. Caius couldn't tell exactly what they were.

"First, you will all be able to keep the winter clothes that have been provided for you. Additionally, we will give each of you two self-propelled flares. If you feel that you are unable to continue the trial, simply light the flare and the Praetorians will come find you. However, using the flare does mean that you forfeit any points in this part of the competition. Third, some of you will perhaps encounter locals. There are a number of farms and other small villages scattered through the area. We have spoken with the residents and told them that a military training exercise is taking place, and they should not give aid to any of you, under any circumstances. Attempting to get directions or material aid from anyone not affiliated with this competition will result in immediate disqualification." His eyes hardened with that warning.

"Now, on to the rest of the equipment!" He gestured behind him, grinning like a traveling salesman. "I have here forty objects, all of which will be of great assistance to you in your journey back to the Trials facility. Here is our current inventory: six lighters and kindling packets, six all-purpose knives, two flashlights, two sets of night-vision goggles..." he gestured at each item in its cubby hole as he spoke, "Four books on which local plants are edible, two sets of binoculars, three water bottles with funnels to capture melted snow..." he adjusted his glasses as he went down the list, "three tents, four warm blankets, and five lengths of good rope." He ran a finger down the list, wiping flakes of snow off of the laminated paper and double-checking that he had made sure to name everything and gotten the numbers right. The candidates who could do math quickly realized that that those numbers only added up to thirty seven.

"Additionally, we have three special items: the first two are *halves* of a map back to the facility, each of which counts as *one* item. If you wish to take the map, you must use one turn to get the first half of the map, then use the second turn to get the second part. You do not get to pick which half of the map you get; it will be chosen at random." There was a momentary pause while the candidates all considered the implications of those rules. This meant that if one candidate selected the map, another candidate could take the other half, rendering it practically useless. The half of the map that led away from the mountain would be somewhat beneficial, but you wouldn't even be guaranteed to get it. It would be a complete waste. On the other hand, a complete map back to the facility would make things a whole lot easier.

"The second special item," Vitellius's smile grew even wider, "is additional points." He let it sink in for a moment; the importance did not need to be said. Even one point could make a huge difference. "You may forgo one item in exchange for *ten* extra points in the Trials, to be added immediately to your score. However, you *only* receive the points if you come in first. Otherwise, you get no extra credit despite having chosen that item. Only *one* candidate may choose this item." He looked around, eyebrows raised, to see whether he'd piqued their interest.

"Now, each candidate will be allowed to pick *one* item during their turn. The order has been established by a random drawing. Whoever picks first during the first round will pick last during the second round, and vice versa. Once every candidate has received their items, you will leave here in staggered order, fifteen minutes apart; this is to ensure that one candidate cannot simply follow another back to the facility. Second, Candidates may not attack or otherwise hinder other candidates. This trial is to be conducted with honor, and the winner should win on his own merits." Althea smirked; that was clearly how she intended to win. "And finally, you may not trade or steal items from any other candidate. If you are stuck with items that are of no use to you, then too bad." The candidates stood silently, taking the rules into account and plotting their strategies in their minds.

"And, last but not least," Vitellius continued, clearly enjoying stringing the candidates along with each additional twist thrown into the game, "this is *not* an individual exercise. I told you that this trial would test your teamwork. If you wish, you and as many other candidates as you'd like may pool your resources and get just as many points crossing the finish line together as you would alone. Points will be allocated based on the size of the team; a win by one single player will be worth twenty points; a win by two, twenty five points. It is all organized on this chart here." He gestured behind him to where a graph appeared on a video screen, showing a sloping curve of diminishing returns. "The only drawback is that if you choose a team now, you may not abandon your team later. You must cross the finish line together. And, if you are a member of the team with the extra points, then those points will be equally distributed to all teammates. So, a team of five would each get two extra points."

The candidates all looked at each other, minds racing to figure out what the best strategy would be. A big group could pool items and knowledge, working together to get home quickly. And the biggest group would be most likely to get the map and the extra points, while still being able to use the other items. But it would take longer to gather food, build a shelter, and all of those other daily activities. Not to mention that they might not all agree on where to go or how to

237

proceed. A smaller group or one individual would travel faster and have an easier time making decisions, which compensates for being worth less points.

"I'll give you all a moment to discuss the proposition and form your groups."

For a brief second, the only sound among the twenty remaining candidates was the hushed whisper of falling snow. They turned and sized each other up, wondering who would be most useful out there and (more importantly) who was down in the points. Teammates would get the same amount, so there was no reason to help someone who didn't need it. Gideon and Florian paired off first, followed by Livia, one of the candidates from Gaul. The rest of the candidates clumped together in huddled groups, quietly negotiating teams. It became a silent struggle to get the best teammates while excluding those who would only be a drag on the group.

Caius moved forward as if to join in on the talks, but was met with daggered glances warning him to stay away. He'd been seen as the leader of the pack for too long, and the spectacle at the party had solidified that image. He noticed Althea getting the same treatment; apparently showing off her test scores for the past week was not the best strategy. By his side, Herennius too, was left waiting and alone. He looked incredibly conflicted, almost to the point of physical pain. Caius could practically hear the gears turning in his head as he worked out different scenarios and possibilities.

"You want to team up?" Caius asked slowly, unsure if he even meant it himself. If they did well, it would be enough points for him to at least beat Althea. Marcus would probably yell at him for this; he'd been telling Caius repeatedly that it didn't matter if they were friends. Telling him that he needed to find some way to pull away from Herennius and get a better score.

"Coming in second means nothing in this competition," Marcus's voice said, echoing through his mind. And yet here he was, tying their fates together. If Caius did well, so would Herennius. No way for him to take the lead. His mind ran through excuse after excuse, telling himself that he needed Herennius's survival skills, and items, and anything else he could think of. And at least they could try to knock Althea down a few pegs, which would be helpful.

"Caius," Herennius whispered slowly, not answering the initial question, "Can I trust you?"

What a weird question, Caius thought instantly. *He's worried I'm going to leave him stranded or something? The Senators said that if we team up, we have to cross the finish together.* "Of course," he answered without really even stopping to think about it. He and Herennius had become pretty good friends over the past two weeks despite the competition, and even if Caius lost, he couldn't imagine that disappearing.

"I mean it," Herennius said, glancing furtively at the other candidates. Particularly at Althea, who was meandering around the other groups, looking for anyone who might let her join. She had to know that no one would let her in, so why bother? Caius smirked a little, glad to see that she was finally getting her comeuppance for being such an ass. "I need to know that we're in this together no matter what."

"Absolutely," Caius answered. "We can win this."

Herennius eyed Caius with an unfamiliar expression of suspicion that made Caius particularly uncomfortable. *Does he think I am trying to sabotage him in some way? He's probably at least realized that it is in my best interests for him to do poorly...* Finally, Herennius nodded in agreement, and a look of relief washed over his face. "We'll make a good team," he said with a weak smile.

"All settled, then?" Vitellius said on stage after it seemed that all of the candidates had finished negotiating their teams. "Please stand with your team and spread out so we can see who is with whom, please!" The candidates shuffled through the snow; Caius and Herennius stayed standing next to each other as they had been. On stage, Quintus was making notes on his tablet of which candidates were working together. Caius noted with glee that Althea was all on her own, and looking particularly furious about it, probably because it would net her the least amount of points. She stood on the very edge of the clearing, arms crossed and arms set in a pout. In the center of the clearing, eight of the remaining candidates, including Gideon and Florian, had all grouped together. Caius noted that they were the ones that he estimated to be the lowest-ranked; they were all making one last desperate grab to stay in the game. There were two other candidates choosing to go it alone along with Althea, two more groups of two, and one group of three.

"Excellent!" Vitellius said from the stage, happy to see that Candidates were taking different approaches. "Excellent. Now, let's all gather around and pick your equipment."

The candidates trudged toward the stage through the snow, which was still falling and even heavier than before.

"First up, Candidate..." the ancient senator squinted close at the tablet to see the name. "Florian Rutlius!" Florian stepped forward quickly, so tall that he was almost on eye level with

240

the Senator despite the raised stage. "I'm honored, Senator. I would like to take the map," he said without hesitation. One of the praetorians lifted one of the laminated papers from its cubby then moved toward Florian but Quintus stepped in and intercepted it first. "Not till after the other section of the map is chosen," he reminded the guard.

The Senator called out Spurius next, who had headed Caius's team during the Teewaraathon game where Herennius had broken his leg. He had made the choice to go it alone, and picked the knife. A guard handed it to him, and he flipped it expertly into the air with a practiced twirl.

Vitellius nodded approvingly then glanced back down to his list. Caius thought he saw a hint of a smirk as the aged Senator looked back up at the crowd looking for the next Candidate.

"Althea Postumius!" he called out clearly, and Althea shoved her way through the front row to stand in front of the stage, doing her best to hide the anger that seemed to have been building up all day.

"The map," she said, without any of the polite pomp that Florian and Spurius had added. Vitellius gave her a hard look, perhaps in reprimand for her disrespect, but nodded to the guards to fetch the item. There was a collective gasp from Florian's group, who had used their very first selection for half of the map. Why the hell would anyone bother choosing the second half now, except to spite them?

Herennius and Caius shared a confused, silent glance. Althea was going alone; she would need the survival gear more than anyone, and she only got to have two items! Why would she

241

even want the map, knowing that she couldn't have the second half? Was it really worth it to sabotage the other candidates that she was already beating? Or maybe she was just gambling on the chance that she would get the first half of the map, which would at least give her a head start making his way back? Whatever the motivations, it was a surprising choice. The large group of candidates were all glaring at Althea's back as both she and Florian received their respective halves of the map; Caius half expected them to jump on her and beat her to a pulp. She turned away from the stage, pretending to study her new map with a sickening grin on her face. She'd definitely picked it to screw over the others.

Vitellius moved on to the next candidate: "Herennius Pacullan!" Next to Caius, Herennius stepped to the front and greeted the Senator. The duo hadn't really talked about what survival gear they would grab, but Caius trusted Herennius to know what they needed.

"I would like the extra points, please."

Caius's jaw dropped along with the eight candidates in the group next to him. *The points?* The thought of selecting those hadn't even crossed Caius's mind; why would Herennius take a gamble like that? And as for the others: Caius didn't think that they could be any more furious once Althea took the map, but he hadn't considered what would happen if someone else took the extra points. Florian's muscles were visibly bulging even under the layers of warm clothing, and his fists were clenched tight like holding his fingers down was the only thing preventing him from strangling Herennius. The others looked just as upset, not even trying to hide their rage from the Senators.

242

Even the Senators were surprised; Tullius leaned over and whispered something into Oventia's ear, and Oventia nodded, smiled, and shrugged. Probably saying "No idea why he'd pick that." Vitellius gave an amused smile, clearly enjoying the drama of his little game. "Quintus, please add the points to the tally for these two candidates." Quintus nodded and typed something into his tablet. With a bow, Herennius retreated back to the line, avoiding the hateful gazes of the other candidates… and the confused, suspicious scrutiny from Caius.

Vitellius continued down the order, naming candidate after candidate to pick various pieces of gear for the long hike back. Caius and Herennius ended up with a flashlight, a knife, and a length of rope. There was an uncomfortable silence when the last item was chosen. The different groups stepped back from each other; Florian was still shifting his withering glare from Althea to Herennius and back.

"Excellent choices, Candidates!" Vitellius told them, either ignorant of or just plain ignoring the air of tension and hatred between all of them at the moment. "Now, on with the show. Groups will depart in order of size in fifteen minute intervals; you will be timed between now and your arrival back at the Trial facility, ending at the moment you touch the main door." He gestured to the large group of eight candidates. "You gentlemen will be going first; the rest of us will be heading back to the lodge to wait. Quintus, wait out here to make sure the departures go smoothly." He turned and hobbled off the podium, leaning on his ornate wooden cane. "Best of luck to you all!" The other Senators followed closely behind, with Oventia making a big show of shivering in the cold. The guards ushered the other candidates toward the cabin while the group of eight prepared to depart.

Inside, the cabin looked like it hadn't had visitors in a decade. Someone had apparently come by long enough to make a fire, leaving a trail of footsteps through the dust. Once inside, Caius turned to Herennius to talk about the challenge and the items, but before he could even utter a word, Senator Tullius entered and addressed the group. "No talking!" he warned them. "No advantage over the other candidates who are already out there." The Senator then pulled his coat closer around his neck and stomped off to stake out a spot next to the fire.

After forty five minutes of torture, the door creaked open, letting in a cold gust of wind and a blast of snowflakes. Quintus stomped back inside, shook off the snow from his head and shoulders, and pointed to Caius and Herennius.

"Your turn," he told them.

CHAPTER 14

Quintus followed them outside and shepherded them into the center of the meadow, where the snow was flattened and trampled by the candidates who had already gone; even a bit of grass managed to poke its way through.

"Ok, boys," Quintus said, looking at his stopwatch, "It is exactly 13:28 right now; you will depart from this spot at 13:30, which is when your time begins. You heard the rules from Senator Vitellius; do either of you have any questions before you leave?"
They both shook their heads in unison, ready to get started.

"All right, then. Best of luck to you both." He eyed the ticking pocket watch carefully, mouth open and at the ready. "Aaaand... go!"

Herennius took charge immediately. "This way," he pointed, gesturing across the field. The snow was falling faster than ever in large, sticky clumps that stuck in Caius's hair. The snow was no obstacle; Herennius was an unstoppable plow clearing his way through the half-meter high layer of powder. Soon they reached the tree line, where the thick green boughs were weighed down by accumulating clumps of white. The ground began to slope downward slightly, and grey boulders and cliffs poked out of the blanket of snow. Herennius barely even noticed, sliding down hills and jumping over cliffs in his race down the mountain. Caius did his best to keep up, but his legs were half the size of the tall Nord's.

"Hey, slow down!" he yelled to his friend over the sound of the blowing wind and snow crunching underneath their boots. Herennius stopped suddenly and turned back, looking at Caius like he'd only just remembered that he was there. He spun around, gazing up at the trees. Maybe looking for something?

"Are we going to talk about the points?" Caius asked. "What the hell were you thinking? You should have just let Florian's group get them! There are so many Candidates in that group that it would be less than one point per person! It wouldn't do anything! Now we're out here with less gear and with nothing to show for it."

A bemused smile spread across Herennius's broad, pale face. He didn't interrupt Caius's rant.

"We really could have used some of the other equipment there. What about that book of edible plants? We need food to make it through this race! Those extra points won't mean anything if we don't have enough strength to climb up that mountain! God, and you should have at least discussed it with me first. We're a team here; it wasn't just your decision to make!"

His rant ended, and the only sound around them was the soft, wet whisper of the continued snowfall.

"Done?" Herennius said, still smiling. Caius nodded, still catching his breath from the hike and from his little outburst.

"Good," Herennius responded. "Remember what I said to you before we started? Before we agreed to become a team?"

"Yeah…" Caius said, remembering his friend's little episode of insecurity. "You asked if you could trust me. Which you know you can; I want to win this just as much as you. And if I don't win the whole thing, then I'd at least rather have you as Emperor instead of that asshole Althea."

"And you still mean it?" he asked.

"Of course," Caius repeated. Herennius glanced around again, then back at Caius, sizing him up.

"All right then."

From inside his robe's breast pocket, he pulled up a folded-up patch of paper. He looked back at Caius, waiting for some reaction, but Caius didn't recognize what it was. Slowly, Herennius opened up the paper, revealing squiggly lines, rough circles, and patches of green and grey. A map.

"Where did you get this?" Caius whispered, unable to take his eyes off of it. There were two markings on the map, showing the location of the field that they'd just vacated, and another showing the location of the Trial facility, their eventual target. Roads and towns were marked in deep purple, and an alternate path was drawn in red, navigating around mountain peaks and over river crossings. Most of the roads appeared to go so far out of the way that it would be faster to just trek straight across as the crow flies. The others would probably not realize this and try following the roads back.

"Where did you get this?" Caius repeated, his voice a mix of amazement and apprehension. *This isn't good,* he thought. *This must be stolen or something. Oh god, we're cheating. We're going to get disqualified just like Marius. And after I reported Althea for cheating, too. All of this work and stress, and we'll just disappear, never to be seen again. Probably dead or in prison for the rest of our lives or something.*

"My advocate," Herennius answered simply. "I don't know exactly how *he* got it, but he came to my room before breakfast and told me that a friend of his had just happened to leave this lying around and had also mentioned what the trial would be."

"*Flavia* gave this to you?" Caius had a hard time believing that. He didn't seem like the type who would cheat.

"Yes," Herennius said defensively, flattening the paper. "He said that the Senate expects players to bend the rules a little bit. That it happens all the time."

Caius had no other response; he was too busy staring awestruck at the map. The other part of his brain had realized what was happening. *We'll win, easily. Neither Althea nor Florian's whole group has the entire thing; they'll only be able to navigate half of it, at best. This is the biggest leg-up we could ever get. No wonder that Herennius picked the extra points! We don't even need survival gear, we'll be back so fast!*

"Are you sure this isn't a test?" Caius hadn't told Herennius about Oventia's offer, and had to bite back his tongue. "They're probably watching right now to see if we'll use it, then they'll swoop in and throw us in prison."

Herennius's eyes flickered with panic just for a second. He probably hadn't considered that possibility. But it made sense: how else could he get this map?

"It's not a trap, Caius. Just trust me on this. The only way this works is with trust."

A war was waging through Caius's mind as he raced to consider all the options, weighing evidence and probability.

"Caius," Herennius asked, interrupting his internal argument, "Can I still count on you? We're a team now. You heard the rules, too: if we don't make it back together, neither of us get the points. I need you to follow me, using this map, or we both lose this game and that puts Althea squarely in first place with an insurmountable lead"

"This is cheating," Caius burst out in response. "We shouldn't be doing this!" *How was Herennius even considering this?*

"Don't be so sanctimonious, Caius. Do you really think that this is the first time a candidate has received some extra help? From what Flavia has told me, that's the only reason that the current Emperor is on the throne in the first place. She says cheating is more of a time-honored tradition during the trials. You know the stakes, and I *thought* that you'd take any advantage you could get." Herennius's eyed narrowed suspiciously. For the first time in the few weeks they had known each other, his broad smile was replaced by a thin line, and his eyes were hard and cold, the color of steel.

"Caius, you said that I could trust you *no matter what*. I need you with me on this. No one is ever going to find out about this if we just stick together."

He moved one step closer, crunching through the snow. Caius stood his ground, still contemplating his options.

"This is a *gift*, Caius! Don't you want to beat Althea? We both know that you are a few points down after all of these tests…"

"She was cheating! You know that!" Caius interrupted. "Just like we would be, if we use this map."

"And what happened when you brought this up with the Senators, *hmmm*?" Herennius had found his weakness. "Did they care?" Caius would have blushed if the cold had not already brought out the color in his cheeks. He could clearly picture Vitellius's dismissive expression and almost bored tone; he'd barely even registered Caius's complaint before sending them away. Why would this be any different? "Did you ever stop to consider the fact that maybe the Senators want us candidates to cheat? That it shows resourcefulness? An Emperor has no rules, so why should we? Maybe playing by the rules is just failing one of their tests."

Caius had no response to that; it wasn't something he had considered.

"Would you rather live in the palace answering to Althea for the rest of your life? Obeying her orders and being sent back into hiding whenever you weren't useful? Because you know as well as I do that she would do *anything* to win this competition, and we need to have the same mindset. We could knock her out of the game right now and have the rest of the trials settle things between us!" Herennius took another step forward, and Caius briefly noticed that his gloved hand was curled into a fist. Behind his normally smiling eyes, Caius could see flashes of fury that had never been there before.

"I need an answer..." Herennius said, trailing off at the end. The implication was becoming increasingly clear: he would be using the map regardless of what Caius decided.

"All right," Caius said finally, picking up the other end of the map and pulling it taut to study it a bit closer. "But only because I want to be lounging in front of that door with a drink in my hand when Althea comes struggling up the mountain. I want to see the look of defeat in her eyes." He was afraid his voice would quaver as he gave the answer, but he managed to hide it and forced a grin.

The smile returned to Herennius's face like Caius had just flipped a switch. The fire in his eyes was extinguished in a second, replaced with the same laughing glint he always had.

"Good," he answered finally. "Good. Then this race is ours." He gestured down at the map, pointing to the red line. "I already traced out the best route, so that we keep a fairly consistent elevation and don't have to be constantly hiking up and down mountains. Should get us back to the Trial Facility in under forty-four hours, even taking into account time for sleeping, foraging, and all that."

Caius nodded, tracing the red line with his finger.

"When did you draw this out?"

Herennius shrugged, looking off into the trees. "Just last night," he answered, "Wanted to make sure that I didn't waste any time today."

Caius looked back down at the map.

"Come on," Herennius said. "The snow is getting a bit heavier. We should really get going." He folded the map back up and slipped it inside his robe.

They marched in silence together for almost an hour. Herennius was like a horse; he could just walk and walk forever and he never seemed to even get out of breath. Even following the trail that his companion carved through the snow, Caius was panting the entire time, spouting out little puffs of steam with every gasp. They scrambled over fallen branches and navigated ledges until they finally reached the edge of the cliff. The earth simply dropped away before them, sloping downward toward the valley floor below, dotted with small farms. Herennius pulled out the map again and compared locations.

"Ok, we're here…" he muttered, pointing out a spot right along the golden line drawn through his map. He turned to the south, matching the shimmering, perfectly blue lake at the end of the valley with the blue spot under his finger. "We're on the right track," he said. "There are a series of cliffs here that lead almost all the way to the valley floor. And this is the fastest way down." He unspooled the rope, tied it around a nearby tree, and sprang lightly over the side of the cliff.

Caius leaned over the edge, watching his friend rappel carefully more than ten meters down. Being a pilot, Caius never really had a hard time with heights, but sliding down an icy cliff is different than being safely strapped into the cockpit of a well-engineered plane. Herennius reached the bottom and looked up at Caius, flashing him a thumbs up. Caius turned back to grab the rope and make his way down, and came face to face with Spurius. Caius only had time to think: *Why is he here?* Then Spurius smiled cheerily, placed two hands right on Caius's chest, and pushed as hard as he could.

Caius felt a brief moment of weightlessness as he went flying over the edge. His stomach leaped into his throat, and he locked eyed with Spurius, who didn't even seem the slightest bit remorseful. Caius flailed helplessly, boots brushing against the sheer rock wall. Time seemed to stand still. Then he landed in a snowbank with a crash.

"Give me the map, Herennius," Spurius shouted from above. "I took care of Caius, and I'll kill you too." He waved his knife through the air menacingly.

Herennius was staring at Caius laying in a white crater. There had been enough powder to safely break the fall, but Spurius apparently didn't know that. Caius, still recovering from the impact, was more than happy to play dead for a while. *Two murder attempts in a week. Probably a new record for someone who isn't even Emperor yet.*

"What map?" Herennius responded.

"Don't bullshit me," Spurius shouted down. "I've been listening to you guys talk for a while now. I heard everything you said about the map. No wonder you took the extra points. Pretty clever. Makes me wish that my advocate was as resourceful."

Caius had never seen Herennius look so furious. "You're making a big mistake, Spurius," the tall Nord called out.

The other candidate laughed heartily. "Yeah, I'm sure I'll be really regretting this when I cross the finish line first while you're still dragging Caius's body through the snow about a kilometer from here. Gotta finish together, right? Have fun with that."

"Spurius, I'm warning you," Herennius said. His voice was calm, but Caius could detect the seething rage behind it. Like a dam ready to burst.

"Just drop the map," Spurius said. Caius was faking death, so he wasn't able to look up, but he could tell that the other candidate's confidence was clearly shaken by Herennius's tone.

Caius heard the rustling of paper from where Herennius was standing. He opened his eyelids just the slightest bit to see Herennius stooping down and depositing the map in the snow. "Fine, Spurius. Here."

"I'm not stupid, Herennius. Climb down the cliff behind you, please. I'd rather not have to fight you for it." He twirled his knife through the air. "But I will if I have to."

Herennius glanced back at Caius's 'body,' and Caius nodded just a tiny bit to confirm that he was ready. They didn't need to discuss; the plan was clear to both of them.

"All right," Herennius answered. "You're going to regret this, though. Soon." Caius watched him clamber over the cliff edge and disappear.

"Yes, I'm sure I will regret it when I'm winning the competition. And best of all: what are you going to do about it? Complain to the Senate? Tell them that you were *cheating*, and somehow think that *I* will be the one disqualified? It's perfect, really. The only way for you to stay in the game is to let me win." He finished his monologue with a dramatic leap down the cliff using the rope still tied up above. It took him just a few seconds to descend.

Spurius knelt down and picked up the piece of paper that Herennius had dropped.

"I'll follow you, Spurius," Herennius shouted from below. "You think I'm just going to let you get away with my map?" *Good job, Herennius,* Caius thought. *Keep him talking.* Caius moved silently into a crouching position behind him, ready to spring into action. "Hell, even if you manage to make it back to the facility, you think I'm just going to let this go? You'll be dead before the week is out. I'm a resourceful man, I swear to you."

"You might try," Spurius answered. Caius crept closer, trying to find solid footing so that he could pounce before his foe was even aware that he was still alive. At least he was so wrapped up in the map that he wasn't looking around. "I have faith in the Praetorians. Marius broke your leg and was promptly dragged off to some secret prison. I don't think you'll risk it just for revenge."

"They'll want to know what happened to Caius, too," Herennius said. "And I'll tell them what you did. Hell, I could light the flare right now and summon them before you can even get away."

"And they'll find me with the map, won't they? They'll find ou...."

255

Caius didn't let Spurius finish his sentence. He launched himself forward, straight into Spurius's midsection. There was an "oomph" as Caius knocked the air out of Spurius's lungs. His arms windmilled about wildly, still clutching the map tightly. Then he flew over the cliff and landed right in front of Herennius. Sweet justice.

Caius scrambled to the edge of the cliff and watched his partner pounce like a vicious beast. Herennius was clearly muscular and strong, but Caius had never really see his friend put that strength to use before now. Each fist plowing into Spurius's face sent a spatter of crimson blood squirting into the nearby white snow. Even at the top of the cliff, Caius could hear bones cracking under the force of Herennius's blows. Caius descended the cliff face as fast as possible to the sound of Spurius's moans and cries.

Herennius paused for a moment and stood, breathing heavily and holding his fists out as if still trying to decide if he was done beating on Spurius. Sunlight glinted from the blood coating his knuckles.

"I think that's enough," Caius said, surveying the damage. Herennius turned, chest heaving. The rage was still burning in his eyes, and Caius was afraid for just a minute that Herennius would come after him too. Without considering Caius's words, he turned back to Spurius and lifted him up like a limp ragdoll. Caius could barely recognize Spurius's face anymore; it looked more like a raw steak straight off the butcher's block. What remained of Spurius's lips twitched, trying to say something. Probably begging for his life. Herennius did not wait to hear what it was: he took aim and threw the rival candidate over the cliff edge. Unlike the

256

ten meter fall that Caius had survived, this one was at least fifty meters down, and onto solid rock.

Caius didn't know what to say. They both stood on the edge, listening to the wind whistle through the craggy canyon. Spurius's body clearly visible below, limbs askew at crazy unnatural angles. Caius would not have been surprised if the beating alone was enough to kill him, but this fall certainly was.

"You killed him… with your own bare hands…" Caius had been in battle before, but never one so visceral. As a pilot, he would be far away before his bombs even fell. To take a life with your own fists… Caius was just in shock. Herennius barely seemed to notice.

"I had to," Herennius answered. He reached down and rubbed snow on his fists, leaving big pink stains. It didn't help wash off the blood as much as he'd hoped.

Caius didn't respond. He could have just beaten Spurius and left him there. Hell, the cold probably would have killed him anyway. If not, dehydration would have eventually finished the job. Maybe even bears; the Empire had been reintroducing them into this area.

"I had to," Herennius repeated, more emphatically this time. "He *pushed you off a cliff,* Caius. He had absolutely no remorse about ending your life just for the map. He needed to be taken care of. He would have set off his flare, gotten rescued, and told the Senators about the map. We both would have been disqualified, and that murderer would have been hailed as a hero."

Two good points, Caius thought. He had never been fond of people trying to murder him, and regardless of his feelings about the map, he wasn't eager to be disqualified from the Trials.

"You're right, Herennius," Caius answered. "I wasn't accusing, just a bit surprised." He laughed, but it covered a note of fear. He never wanted to see that look of rage in his friend's eyes ever again.

They both stayed at the cliff edge, staring down at Spurius's body. Still no movement, and the carrion birds had taken notice. Only twenty minutes ago, Caius probably would have named Spurius as a friend. They weren't *too* close, but he'd at least always been friendly with Caius, and they'd made a good team during the teewaraathon game. How could he just turn like that? With that despicable sneer as he pushed Caius over the cliff? Caius remembered that same look on Marius's face and wondered if Althea had played a role in convincing Spurius to do this. He briefly wondered if Spurius had been behind the poisoning too.

"Should we light a flare or something? So that they can come recover the body?"

Herennius looked down at his victim sprawled across the jagged rocks. Even at this distance, they could make out the streams of blood trickling into the white snow. "No need for that. It will just raise questions if they know that we were up here when he died. We'd need a story to explain why Spurius came after us."

Caius agreed, thankful that he had teamed up with Herennius. He was always a step ahead.

"I can't look at him anymore," Caius told his friend. "Let's keep going." They made their way down the next set of rocky outcroppings; this time, Caius made sure to check for any other rogue candidates behind him.

After an hour of dangerous scrambling over uncertain, snow-covered terrain, the duo made it safely to a more gently sloping incline leading down to the valley floor. The snow was lighter here, barely up to Caius's ankles. A few remaining flakes drifted through the air like lost travelers who had missed their train.

Caius kept picturing Spurius's corpse at the bottom of that rocky valley. "I still don't feel right about this, Herennius." Caius couldn't hold his thoughts in any longer.

"I did what needed to be done, Caius. If he'd lived, then we'd all be disqualified. Maybe in prison. Who knows? Flavia told me that cheating is common in the Trials, but she never said what happens to those who get caught. Do you really want to find out?"

"No," Caius admitted. It was hard to argue against Herennius's point. It was the only rational outcome for both of them. But to kill over this map? It didn't sit right.

"What if the Senators find out what you did?"

"They won't," Herennius answered confidently. "Spurius tried to make his way down a particularly icy cliff. He was in a rush. Accidents happen."

"And what about the map? There's a risk that they'll find out about that, and they'll connect the dots. They'll see footprints. They'll know that Spurius came after us."

"What risk? There is no risk! The snow will cover the footprints. No one else has noticed that I have the map yet, and I'm going to get rid of it as soon as we're able to see the mountain with the trial facility. I'll tear it into a hundred pieces and bury it; no one is ever going to find it. The only way they would ever know about it is if you tell them." He ended the sentence slowly and deliberately, enunciating each syllable of the last four words. Caius couldn't see his face from behind, but he could imagine the accusing stare.

"I already told you that I'm not going to tell anyone," Caius said. In the back of his mind, he wasn't sure anymore. There was a nagging voice trying to break free, shouting about how wrong this whole situation was and that this would get them both disqualified. *I really need to talk to Marcus about this,* Caius thought. *He'll know what to do.*

"You can't even tell Marcus about this," Herennius continued, reading his thoughts. "You know the advocates all talk, and Marcus is the biggest gossip around. If you tell him, it is going to get out sooner or later and then we will both get disqualified."

"He's not going to tell anyone," Caius responded, tacitly admitting that he was planning to tell his Advocate about everything.

"Caius," Herennius started with a sigh, "You're a great guy, you know that? You have honor and honesty and all those other things that they're looking for. But I'm starting to think that Althea was right about you. What she said when she made you her offer? About how an Emperor needs to be bold, and ruthless, and cunning, and all that other stuff? It's true, you know. These trials are just the beginning. People are going to be coming after you for the rest of your life. Spurius *threw you off a cliff.* If you feel guilty about him getting what he deserves, then I

260

don't know if you're ready to be the Emperor. And as for the map... if you can't even accept this *gift*, then I don't know what to tell you. I mean, I didn't have to bring you along, did I? I could have gone solo. Hell, I could have still gotten the extra points and just made it back with a knife alone. But I took you on as my teammate because I like you and I wanted to be able to trust you with this, so that we can both get the points. And I want us to be in this together up until the end, just the two of us. And if you keep bringing up this map, then that's going to be a problem."

"You say all that like it's a bad thing. The trials are to show who can thrive even with honor, and you all are acting like the point is to try and skirt the rules as much as possible and get away with anything you can."

Herennius snorted audibly. "That's just life. Everyone is trying to get ahead, and often times it is at someone else's expense. You didn't learn that when you were kicked out of school? That's where human nature really comes out: when you're in the dirt fighting for scraps. I don't know what China is like, but being homeless in Scandinavia is brutal. You can be killed just for your spot close to a fire. In the end, everyone is out for themselves, and things like honor are just luxuries that we can indulge in when there's nothing significant at stake."

There was silence between them.

"Did you ever have to kill anyone, Caius?" Herennius's tone was hushed and somehow distant. "Not from kilometers up in the safety of your cockpit. I mean in person. With your own hands."

"No," Caius answerered. Spurius would be the first person he'd ever even seen killed in cold blood like that.

"I did," Herennius answered. He sounded almost proud. "You know, my very first night out of the Academy, I was robbed. Just some fuck with a knife. He was probably half my size, and his weapon wasn't anything special either. I could have snapped his neck before he ever managed to stab at me, but I didn't. Back then, I was like you still. I thought it would be immoral to kill this man. I didn't know what I needed to do to survive. So I let him take my money and all of my possessions. I'd been wealthy for so long that I didn't value what I had."

Caius thought back to his own first night, when he'd stayed under and overpass with the other homeless of Xian, and they'd shared their stew with him. These Westerners did not understand the idea of a community and taking care of each other.

"It got worse and worse for me," Herennius continued. "After about 5 months, I was sleeping on the street one night. It was snowing, and I'd climbed into a dumpster for warmth. I'd made it about as cozy as you can make a trash bin, so some other guy decided that he wanted it as his own. And he had a gun, so he thought that gave him the right to make the rules." Herennius sounded angry as he recalled the incident. "I don't even know what happened. One minute, he was waving it around acting like he was the Emperor himself, and I just snapped. The gun went skittering through the alley, and I punched that guy in the face until you couldn't even recognize him anymore. And you know what? After that, no one tried to touch me. No one threw me out of my dumpster or took my food or anything like that. That's when I realized how the world really worked." He looked back at Caius as they hiked through a snowbank. "You can't let

262

the rules hold you back and just hope that everything works out, Caius. You need to fight for what you want, tooth and nail if need be. And others will see that, and you'll get the respect you deserve. I guess you're just not ready for that yet."

Caius stomped through the snow as they neared a small farmhouse, thinking about what Herennius had said and remembering his own experiences in Xian. He'd only been able to survive because the other vagrants there took care of him at first, like an adopted son. They'd been his new family. That was how he'd been able to go on and found his company. He'd only made it through because he had the support of others. He trusted them. *Maybe things are just different in the West,* he thought to himself. *And I need to adapt.*

They both fell silent, walking side by side but not daring to look at the other.

The sun was low now, still barely managing to shine through the thick grey clouds. The icy wind whipping down the valley blew straight into Caius's face, numbing his lips and making his eyes water. Herennius hardly seemed to notice, continuing forward at a breakneck pace. They reached a tiny homestead. Enormous, lumbering pieces of automated farm equipment were busy clearing snow and treating the soil so that it would be ready for the earliest possible planting. Nearby, a farmhouse chimney puffed smoke that mingled with the low clouds. Bright, warm light shone through the windows, and the scent of the fire drifted over them. Even the smell made Caius feel just a little bit warmer. They skirted the edge of the property, careful to avoid breaking Vitellius's 'no contact' rule.

Caius's stomach grumbled and moaned; the sandwiches up at the starting point seemed like forever ago. The confrontation with Spurius had flooded him with adrenaline, and when it left, he felt like an empty husk. But Herennius showed no signs of slowing down. "We should take a break soon and find some food," Caius volunteered.

Herennius stopped suddenly in his path and turned back, like he'd forgotten that he had a companion. And it didn't look like he was happy about that. He was silent for a moment as he contemplated whether or not eating was really that necessary.

"Fine," he relented at last. "Let's make this quick. And keep heading in the right direction." The woods nearby yielded a few edible plants and mushrooms, and soon enough they made it to the river running through the center of the valley. The banks were clogged with chunks of ice that bobbed restlessly in the rapid current, and snow-covered rocks stuck out of the water like soapy bubbles. Beneath the surface, silvery fish flickered in and out of still pools that formed near congealed ice. Herennius wrenched a slender branch off of a nearby tree with a silence-shattering crack, causing clumps of snow to break free and rain down from the higher limbs. With the knife, he quickly whittled the end of the stick down to a sharpened spear, impaled a leaf growing near the river bank, and stuck the tip into the water. His arm was like a statute, remaining perfectly still even as the rushing current washed against the stick. Fish came cautiously closer and nibbled at the leaf, ready to dart away at any second. Just when they had been lured to safety, Herennius struck like lightning and lifted the wriggling victim into the air.

"Whoa," Caius managed to utter. "Good reflexes."

Herennius laughed and slid the still-writhing fish into the snow, then added another bit of bait to his spear. "An old trick that I learned from one of the Hodenosaunee while I was in the New World. Some of the braves used to invite the trading post security guards out when they

264

went hunting. They were really amazing: brilliant, athletic, charismatic… I'm telling you, we should stop worrying about the Ming stuck in their jungles and start worrying about what happens when the New World natives start using modern technology. That's the real threat to the Empire."

Caius managed to find some dry wood and built a fire, then cleaned the first fish while Herennius worked on catching a second. They chatted more about the New World natives and their primitive ways of doing even normal tasks like fishing. The earlier incident was practically forgotten, and they were back to being friends. Dinner was devoured in a second, only slowing to pick out the bones from the fish.

Herennius rose to his feet and began to kick snow onto the fire. Caius knew it had to be done, but dragging himself upright was the hardest thing he'd done all day. His legs just refused to stand; they wanted to sit and enjoy the warmth a little more. Herennius pulled out the map again and used the flashlight to check their progress along his red-lined route. Caius had to suppress the urge to bring up the topic again. They'd been out here for hours using it; the deed was done. And he suspected that Herennius would just throw him in the river and go off on his own if they had that conversation one more time. He wouldn't be the first candidate to die for this piece of paper.

The sun had fallen below the mountain peaks by now, leaving only orange streaks through the sky. But at least the clouds had moved on as well, and with them, the snowstorm. The night air was crisp and cold and clean, rejuvenating and energizing. Overhead, they heard the droning buzz of a plane; Caius recognized the sound of the engine as one of his own designs.

Private planes were an expensive and strictly-regulated rarity, and the military would have no reason to be patrolling the peaceful heart of the Empire, so it was certainly the Senators, checking in on them. Caius noticed Herennius holding his hand protectively over the pocket where he was keeping the map. It was a small victory for Caius, but at least Herennius was conscious of the fact that he shouldn't be cheating.

Other than that short flyover, they didn't encounter a soul. The bright full moon rose, filling the valley with light, but the stars were still dimmed by the clouds overhead. The only sound in the forest was the gentle crunch of snow under their boots, and the occasional crack as a branch collapsed under the weight of settling ice. Caius and Herennius marched through the night at a grueling, unrelenting pace. They scrambled up steep hills, causing Herennius to belt out traditional folk music from Scandinavia; he said the singing helped his breathing. They descended sheer cliffs, always in danger of crumbling rock and slippery ice.

As the sun rose, the only thing that kept Caius's feet moving was the regular, constant pattern of walking. They had stopped briefly for a two-hour break, but sleeping the full night would slow them down far too much. The other groups could be pushing through all night and possibly catch up. Herennius was pretty confident with the map, but not enough to be able to sleep peacefully.

Morning brought a second wind to the pair, and they were treated to a spectacular dawn view of the sun-drenched mountains, covered entirely in a blanket of white. Somehow, it made the climb up the ridge just the littlest bit easier. By the time they reached the summit and could see over to the next valley over, it was almost mid-day. The sun's warmth filled the valley, so intense that Caius had to take off the heavy winter jacket that the Quintus had given him. Unlike yesterday's wintery mix, today's weather was perfect and clear. According to Herennius's map, this was it: the Trial Facility was carved into one of the mountains across the way. Studying the landscape more closely, Caius could pick out the freshly plowed railroad tracks snaking along the course of the river and into the little town where he'd arrived only a few weeks ago. He was able to spot the tiny sliver of a bridge over the river that they'd crossed that night, which must eventually lead to the tunnel up the mountain.

They took a breather on an enormous rock overlooking the valley, snacking on some of the food they'd managed to forage along the way. Herennius was buoyant and energetic despite the lack of sleep, talking about how amazed everyone would be that they had made it back so early. *Except Flavia, and the friend who had given her the map.*

The end of the race became a giddy, headlong rush fueled by adrenaline and sleep deprivation. There were no signs of the other competitors in the valley, and both Caius and Herennius were fairly certain in their victory. After a quick march, they arrived at the banks of the river in the valley and carefully navigated across a series of steep rocks. Once they were safely on the other side, Herennius reached into his pocket and withdrew the folded up map. He tore it into small pieces, then tossed them one by one into the river. They were quickly grabbed by the rapid, churning current and washed downstream to safely disintegrate. It should have made Caius feel better to have that accursed thing out of his sight, but it didn't help. It just made the pit of worry and foreboding sink even deeper into his stomach. He briefly wondered whether anyone had found Spurius's body yet.

Herennius, on the other hand, was positively thrilled. With the evidence gone, they had gotten away with everything and still won the race. He was practically skipping through the woods and singing along with the few birds that had remained for winter. Caius had never seen him in such a good mood.

They found a narrow footpath traversing the cliff side; it looked like it had been carved by a series of waterfalls during the summers, but now was dry and rocky. Caius could feel the sleepy haze in his mind dragging him down, but the finish line was so close that he was able to fight back, stopping occasionally to dunk his head in a snowbank to snap back to wakefulness. There were a few tense moments where seemingly sound footholds collapsed under his weight; dangers that he would have spotted if he was more alert.

Somehow, the pair made it to the top, taking a victory breather on top of the precipice. The wind whistled through his ears as he looked down on the rest of the valley. One thin trail of smoke drifted up from the forest, near where they had come through. It wasn't from the tiny village further south, and he couldn't recall seeing any cabins or farmhouses in that neighborhood. Perhaps one of the other candidates, hot on their heels?

"Come on," he told Herennius. "Let's just get this done."

In less than half an hour, they found the steep, winding road that Caius had gone up that very first night they had arrived; he still remembered the sickening feeling of those sharp turns and the driver swerving around just to make Marcus more uncomfortable.

They struggled up another hill, huffing and puffing with exertion; they were practically running at this point. Caius felt like his legs would fall off, but he didn't care. He would drag himself over the finish line on his elbows, and then promptly fall asleep. Finally, they reached the top of that hill. Like a miraculous desert mirage, they finally saw it: the massive stone doorway leading into the mountain. It looked deceptively close, due to its tremendous size; Caius had forgotten just how big it really was.

Herennius took off in a mad dash, expending the very last of his energy. Caius followed closely behind. There was no reason to run; no chance that any of the other competitors would suddenly sprint ahead and steal their spot. It had become a matter of pride; the need to be first. When the next batch of candidates would be sent out into the woods, the Senator leading them would say "And you'll never do as well as Caius and Herennius." The adrenaline was overpowering and intoxicating; his extremities felt numb and his breathing was ragged and shallow. But he didn't care anymore. Just one hundred meters! His own feet below him threatened to stumble and trip him; the soles had gone completely numb. *Don't you dare,* he silently threatened them. Face-planting in front of the Senators was not what he needed right now.

Fifty meters. Herennius's blond hair bobbed in front of him, bouncing slightly with every step. His companion looked back briefly, just to make sure that Caius was ready to cross the finish line with him. They only got points if they were together. The grin on his face was infectious, and Caius felt his own confidence growing.

Twenty meters! The Senators stood with Quintus and a herd of Advocates in front of the doorways, under the dual banners of the Emperor and the Senate. Behind them, a stand of bleachers had been erected on the driveway where the trucks had been parked; the stands were full of spectators. They were all clapping and cheering as Herennius and Caius painfully dashed closer and closer.

Ten meters! Faces became recognizable. Caius could see the enormous smile hiding under Marcus's bushy beard, and Flavia looked like she was so happy it might bring on a heart attack. Caius recognized some of his own more ardent supporters in the crowd, who had been cheering exclusively for him ever since the strategy simulation trial. But what really made the whole race worth running was Antoninus's sour expression, barely managing to hide a ferocious scowl as he pretended to clap like the others.

The finish line was marked by a thick red ribbon. It was all Caius could focus on for that last bit of the race. Herennius made it there first, breaking through it and falling to his knees almost immediately, breathing heavily. Caius just managed to stumble over the line before rolling over onto his back and sprawling out in front of everyone and puffing clouds of steam into the cold air. Congratulatory cheers and applause washed over him, a wave of noise after two days of near silence in the forest. It felt good just to be around people again.

Herennius and Caius struggled to their feet as the Senators stepped forward to greet them.

"Very impressive, gentlemen," said Vitellius. "We were not expecting you for hours; the poor servants had to work overtime to get the bleachers up in time for your arrival."

Caius and Herennius could only nod; they were still too weak to speak.

"I suppose it goes without saying," the Senator continued, "But you boys are first to cross the line, and have won the maximum number of points." Quintus leaned over and showed the Senator the screen of his tablet, which apparently had the statistics available. "Victory as a two-man group nets you twenty-five points, and in addition, you selected the extra points in lieu of some survival gear, bringing your total to thirty for each of you for this competition. Wow!" He shook both of their hands enthusiastically, with an iron grip for a man of his age. He gave Caius a peculiar smile, as if something had surprised him about the score.

Senators Oventia and Tullius congratulated the duo next, both formal and relatively cold, as expected. It was a sobering moment after the warm reception from Vitellius; a reminder that regardless of how well he did, he may still lose for no good reason. He would just have to beat the other Candidates so resoundingly that there was no question of his right to become Emperor. Herennius's score above his was not something he wanted to think about now.

Finally, they were done. After all of this standing still, Caius's legs felt rubbery and ready to just collapse under him. The next visitor they had was the doctor, who recommended a bit of rest, a good solid meal and a nice warm drink. She had also bandaged Herennius's battered knuckles, but luckily didn't ask any questions about how it had happened; some scrapes and bruises were to be expected. Herennius and Caius were escorted back to their rooms, followed by a trail of red-robed servants carrying platters of food, probably enough to feed ten men. Caius saw it as more of a personal challenge. Marcus pulled one aside and whispered something into his ear; the servant nodded in agreement and returned quickly with steaming mugs for both of the

Candidates. It wasn't coffee that he had been expecting; it was that chocolate drink from the New World. Caius took a sip and practically melted into his chair as warmth spread through his belly; nothing had ever tasted so good. Or maybe it was just that the only thing he had eaten over the past 36 hours was parts of a scrawny fish and some cold mushrooms. He took a few bites and another gulp of chocolate, savoring the comfortable chair and wondering if this was how luxurious life would be as the Emperor…

Marcus shook him awake after an indeterminable amount of time. The meal had long since gone cold.

"Sorry to disturb you," he said, "But Althea is just about to arrive. I thought you might want to be there." He smiled knowingly as Caius leaped out of bed like a coiled spring. Seeing Althea's reaction as she crawled across the finish line only to see Caius waiting was all that had gotten him through this race. Caius thought about taking the opportunity to tell Marcus about Spurius, but held back. Now wasn't the time to do it, and he still wasn't sure that he wanted to tell his Advocate what had happened. It was too late to change anything, right?

Caius pulled on his robes and a heavy cloak, in case it was cold outside. Together, they took off at a brisk clip down the hall, once again lit by the overhead lamps that simulated a roaring ball of fire. It must be night out already; Caius often lost track of time here under the mountain.

Outside, servants had erected large spotlights to illuminate the finish line. Down the road, Caius could see Althea sauntering confidently toward the finish line. She obviously wasn't close enough to make out who was already standing there. Behind Caius, Herennius also emerged

272

from inside the facility; the two friends traded looks of glee. Definitely worth standing out in the cold for. The spectators in the facility were not of the same opinion; barely a third of them had come out for Althea's arrival. The rows of benches that had been set up for them were sparse. The few who did come out were huddled into tiny groups talking amongst themselves instead of cheering like when Caius and Herennius had won. The spectators really only cared about seeing who came in first.

Althea realized something was wrong as she approached. Her walk changed, turning into a hurried shuffle as she mounted that final hill. Caius savored every second of it.

At long last, Althea was close enough to make out the figures standing next to the Senators in front of the door. There was no mistaking Herennius's massive frame. Caius watched as her face fell, switching instantly from cocky assurance to simmering fury in a second. She came to a dead stop, only steps from the finish line. Under her forced smile, Caius could tell that Althea was clenching her teeth. She finally managed to shuffle across the finish line. The Senators stepped forward to congratulate her, but inform her that she had only come in second.

"Welcome, Althea!" Vitellius said, conjuring the same level of enthusiasm that he'd had when Caius and Herennius had crossed the finish line. "We've been expecting your arrival for some time now." That almost seemed like a bit of a jab, at least to Caius. "Unfortunately, you have arrived second, behind two of your peers." He gestured to Caius and Herennius behind him; they each smiled broadly at Althea, who just scowled back. Althea shook the Senators' hands stoically, then Caius and Herennius stepped forward.

"Better luck next time," Caius said, unable to contain his smirk.

273

CHAPTER 15

Marcus was just finishing up practicing his speech. After three weeks of continuous trials, the Senate had so graciously decided to give them the morning free to unwind and relax a bit. For Caius, at least, it had not helped him relax at all. The fact that the Senators wanted them all to be rested only worried him more. But at least it gave him some time to listen to Marcus rehearse his closing arguments.

"Over the past three weeks, Caius has demonstrated time and time again all of the attributes that we should aspire to have in our leader. In particular, he has showed exceptional honesty, integrity, and sportsmanship." This was a deliberate reference to the 'offer' from Oventia and reporting Althea to the Senators. Marcus was still convinced that it had been one of those secret trials meant to weed out Candidates, but Caius was not so sure. Caius wasn't a big fan of the sportsmanship line, either. Marcus still didn't know what had happened to Spurius. The Praetorians had found the body after he didn't show up at the finish line. Caius had been a nervous wreck ever since, but nobody had questioned him or Herennius about it.

"He has treated his fellow candidates with kindness, and still excelled in every respect. I would particularly note his brilliance in the strategy simulation; I have recently learned that members of the War Council have already asked to review the simulation and hope to adopt his tactics with the parachutes for future use. He has changed the course of the Empire before even being selected as its leader!" Marcus was particularly proud of that point; he'd only just learned that little factoid yesterday. Caius had to admit, it was a very good reminder of how well he had done

275

that day, and the Senators wanted to keep that in mind during the final review. They hadn't officially announced that the end was near; hell, the trials could go on for weeks as far as Caius knew. But with only eight remaining candidates, everyone recognized that there was little time left.

"He has met every challenge thrown at him, showing fierce determination while still maintaining an upbeat, cheerful attitude. I have been truly honored to serve as his mentor during this entire process, and I find myself amazed at how his performance has exceeded my expectations. My only regret is that I do not have the words to describe how much he deserves the title of Emperor."

He left off there. "Well... what did you think?"

Caius nodded and grinned. "Hard to not like it when you're saying all of these good things about me!" Marcus laughed.

"But, on a more serious note, do you really think that we should emphasize my honesty and integrity so much?" He had not told Marcus about the map that he and Herennius had used during the wilderness survival challenge, either. A part of him kept nagging: what if the Senate knew about it somehow? What if Marcus got up there, talked all about how honest and great Caius was... and then the first thing they ask is "then why did he use that map to cheat?" Marcus would be absolutely blindsided, and it would completely sink any chance he had at winning.

"Of course!" Marcus responded. "You turned down Oventia's offer, *and* you turned in Althea for cheating. Even if we couldn't prove it to Vitellius, I think he knew it. He understands that Althea is a snake and that you were doing the right thing."

Caius nodded. "I guess you know best." He felt like he was going to throw up.

"Other than that, how is the speech? Really?"

"It's great, Marcus." Caius forced a smile. "I really can't thank you enough for everything that you have done for me. You've been an amazing advocate."

Marcus didn't really respond, but gave a crooked smile and sort of hugged Caius around the shoulders, lips quivering. He didn't need to say anything. Instead, he looked away, checking his pocket watch.

"Oh! Quintus said it would start at two; we had better get going." The perfect excuse as Marcus tried to cover up his watery eyes. Caius laughed and pulled Marcus in for a real, back-thumping squeeze. Marcus couldn't help but laugh too. Together, they headed out the door.

The eight remaining candidates and their advocates all met in the central hall, echoingly empty. The spectators had all been sent home once the pool of candidates had been reduced to fifteen; Marcus said that the Senators were worried that they would be able to influence the process and get their favorites picked.

Caius greeted most of his companions warmly. They had grown close through the trials, despite the competitive and sometimes brutal aspect of it. Most of them had been able to put that

277

aside and come together as friends outside of the game. Herennius, of course, would be a lifelong companion regardless of how things turned out; he and Caius were practically inseparable despite the fact that Herennius had taken the lead. As the number of candidates dwindled, his spot at the top of the board seemed almost insurmountable. Florian and Gideon were still contenders, and did not begrudge Caius's and Herennius's success (at least, not openly). Caius was not particularly close to two other remaining candidates, Valeria and Apona, but they were friendly and courteous. Valeria's high score during the public speaking trial had been enough to compensate for her poor performance in the survival trial. The remaining two, however…

Drusus, currently ranked last, had been Althea's lapdog from the very first day. The only thing that had kept him in the game was his suspiciously high scores on the tests. Caius was ninety-five percent certain that Althea had been feeding him answers just to keep him in the competition. The only remaining five percent of doubt was because Althea was so competitive and selfish that it was hard to picture her helping anyone else. Those two stood apart from the other six candidates, whispering to themselves while the others chatted. Caius did not even bother to greet them; they'd just sneer back.

After only a few minutes, Quintus emerged. He was dressed in his impeccably polished formal armor, just as he did for every Trial. His boots clicked against the smooth stone, echoing through the silent room.

"Well, Candidates," he started with a smile, nodding to the winnowed-down group, "You all have truly been through a lot. We know that this process has been physically exhausting, mentally strenuous, and emotionally draining. And you all have handled it extremely well, just as we expected. Enduring the stress of this process is one of the Trials itself. You've had to endure freezing cold and starvation while lost in the wilderness…" Caius fidgeted uncomfortably, "to academic challenges like the exams, to social challenges like interacting with the spectators and working as a team. The eight of you who remain are those who have best exemplified the qualities that the Senate is looking for in a future leader." He clapped, and the guards around the room followed his lead. There were only so many of them, though, and the echoing applause felt fake and forced. And their masked faces remained in a permanently intimidating scowl.

"Today, however, you get to take a break. It is your Advocate's turn to speak on your behalf one again. This is the true essence of the Advocate's role, going back hundreds of years to when the Trials consisted solely of an interview and the Advocate's argument. It is a time-honored role, and one which the Senators still value very highly. So, with that, if you will all follow me to the observation room, the speeches are about to begin."

Quintus's boots clicked as he turned sharply and marched down the Hall of Senators. He led the group of Candidates through the twisting, maze-like hallways that made up one of the oldest parts of the facility, past Vitellius's office where Caius had accused Althea of cheating on the written tests. Even the memory of it filled him with seething anger, especially because Althea had *clearly* cheated. But that was in the past. Nothing to be done about it now.

The group of candidates marched briskly to the very end of the hall and up a staircase to the left that seemed to get progressively narrower. Except for the shining steel rail bolted to the side, the worn stone tunnel looked a thousand years old, and the flat steps had been worn down into a curve by centuries of foot travel.

Quintus grabbed the doorknob and waited with an excited smile on his face, building the tension. He swung it open, revealing a beautiful, palatial room. At the far end, a fire roared in a masterfully carved stone fireplace. Darkened windows lined the entire right-hand side, and cozy-looking overstuffed leather armchairs and footrests were positioned to look through them. The wall on the other side of the room alternated between tables of food and drink, and waiting servants standing like statutes in expensive-looking uniforms.

"Damn," Florian muttered under his breath. Caius was too busy soaking in the details to comment. Quintus led the way into the room as the candidates followed slowly behind him like children not sure if they were allowed to touch anything. The Trial facility had not been uncomfortable, but the small dark rooms and cafeteria food were only a slight step up from the air force barracks that Caius had left behind back in Japan. This room was on a whole different level.

Everyone was still crowding the doorway nervously, waiting for the other shoe to drop.

"Go ahead!" Quintus encouraged them, "This is all for you! Eat, drink, make yourselves comfortable!"

There was a stampede over to the food tables. Caius heaped his plate with strange looking delicacies that he had never even seen before. For the past eighteen years of his life his diet had consisted mainly of rice, and Caius was ready to make up for lost time.

The candidates settled into the comfortable chairs with their food and drink in hand. Caius was pleased to note that the chairs were heated and gave massages. Servants paced back and forth behind them, eager to replace or clean away any dishes.

"Candidates," Quintus said loudly from the front of the room. Most of them were so busy enjoying the luxury that they seemed to have forgotten that he was still in the room. "Welcome to your new life. Win or lose, you will be treated to every possible extravagance. The finest clothes, food, living accommodations, travel... whatever you want. Your resources will be practically limitless. However, with these comforts comes a burden. For seven of you, that burden will be secrecy. The intimate details of the Trial process cannot be made public, nor can candidates be released into the world, free to rally men around their own banner against the Empire. You will be forever bound to the imperial palace by a leash."

He turned and gestured back at the enormous set of windows behind him. "For one of you, however, you will have a different burden: the weight of the crown. Every decision you make will linger in your mind, wondering what could have been if you only had done something different. And even worse, you must make decisions with only the information you have, which will never be the complete picture. Your advisors will lie to you. Your enemies will deceive you. Your simulations will not account for every factor. No matter what you do, it will never be enough."

The windows behind Quintus lit up, revealing the columned room where Marcus and Antoninus had presented their video evidence of his life and argued for and against his value. It was so dark that day that he hadn't been able to see the windows lining the wall.

In the room, Senators Tullius, Vitellius, and Oventia waited in their same chairs on the raised platform at the far end of the room. Fires again roared in the hearths behind them, but the overhead lights were on. Caius could see the scroll insignia of the Senate in the prominent seal that marked the fronts of their desks.

"For your last test," Quintus said, "You will be watching the final oral arguments of your Advocates. They will make a case for your candidacy, and the Senators will question them about the weaknesses that have been observed in your character. The Senate will then score the presentation. You can earn up to twenty points if they are impressed with your candidate's performance. But if not, then they are able to *take away* up to twenty points from your current score. You will have to make a choice: you can choose to accept your score and have it added to your current total. Or, you can reject the score and stay at your current level."

The candidates all looked at each other. Sounded easy enough; if they were observing, they would know how things went. Quintus knew that, though:

"*However...*" he seemed to take pleasure in this part, "the catch is that you only get to *see* the presentations. You do not get to *listen* to what your advocate says, or what questions the Senate asks, or how your advocate answers. You must use the information available to you to make your choice, just like one of you will have to do when you are the leader of the Empire."

A hushed silence filled the room. Even the dim-witted servants sensed the issue and tried to retreat further against the back wall.

"You're free to discuss it with your peers, of course. Once you are the emperor, you will have your fellow candidates by your side at a moment's notice to ask for advice. But, like your more formal advisors, remember that they also have an agenda in your decision. Particularly today. It is up to you to determine whether their advice is genuine, or only given to further their own ends."

He paused, like he had something else to say but couldn't think of it. "Good luck, then," he said simply. With that, he turned and left the room.

"I knew it was too good to be true," Caius said. The rest of the candidates chuckled, excluding Althea of course.

"Even when they've finished testing us," Herennius said, "They still had to throw in some little lesson, didn't they?"

The other candidates chimed in, griping about the trials in general and everything they had been put through over the past few weeks. No one bothered to mention that they all thought it would be worth it if it meant becoming Emperor.

The conversation was brought to an abrupt end as a man entered the room below: Messalina, Valeria's advocate. She bowed to the Senators and stepped into the center of the room, launching into her speech. Valeria stood from her seat and pressed against the glass, soaking in every detail. Quintus was absolutely right; the room was utterly soundproof, and no one could hear a word of Messalina's speech. After a few minutes, she bowed again and stood waiting. Tullius shuffled papers on his desk and waved his hand as he spoke, though no one could tell what the question was. Messalina looked nervous as she answered, and Valeria started pacing. It was over shortly; Messalina bowed one last time and left the room.

The other candidates were completely silent as they waited for Valeria's reaction.

"Well," she finally asked, wringing her hands. "What do you think?"

No one responded, lest they look like they were trying to somehow manipulate her into deciding one way or another. The silence lasted for far too long.

"I would accept it," Caius finally answered. She looked deep into his eyes, trying to gauge his honesty. "Look at it this way," he explained bluntly. "You're second-to-last in the rankings right now. What do you have to lose by taking that shot? Either you stay where you are and lose out easily to one of the higher ranked candidates," Herennius looked around, a bit self-conscious and wary that he would be called out, "Or you gamble and try to stay in the running."

She studied him for a moment before responding, then smiled. "You're right. Thank you, Caius." It may have undercut his chances only slightly, but he would have felt guilty had he not said anything. He was getting increasingly good at ignoring Marcus's voice in the back of his mind telling him to try and sabotage the other candidates. Valeria was hardly a threat, anyway. Caius was far enough ahead that even in the worst possible scenario for him and best for her, they would be roughly tied.

Herennius shot him a look of skepticism, but didn't say anything. Florian's advocate was entering the room and all attention turned back to the windows. Florian remained surprisingly casual, munching on some shrimp and reclining in the chair.

284

"Stressing out now won't really help me," he explained. "And this shrimp is too good to pass up." He smiled and placed yet another empty tail onto his waste plate, where a servant was standing by to dutifully clean it off.

His advocate seemed to be doing a good job, pacing back and forth with a slight limp and gesturing emphatically with his hands. The Senators seemed skeptical, and took turns asking questions. Florian was doing his best to remain relaxed, but his knuckles were wrapped around the edge of the couch. Finally, his advocate bowed and left the room.

"I'll take the points," he said without bothering to ask the other candidates for their opinions. "Nothing to lose!" He bit another shrimp and smiled.

Althea's advocate Andericus entered the room, looking smug and bored. Caius had thought that he would at least try to be pleasant for the final argument, but apparently not. Who knows, maybe that is the kind of thing that works in the Senate? Instead of standing like the rest of the Advocates, Andericus remained seated; Caius was surprised that he didn't put his feet up on the desk. The speech seemed surprisingly short, and even the Senators were shocked. Each question was met with a terse response, so short that some of them may have just been one word.

"Is he trying to sabotage his own candidate or something?" Herennius whispered.

"If Althea were my candidate, that's what I'd do," Caius whispered back. They laughed together while Althea shot them angry looks from down the room. Finally, the Senators just kind of gave up and Andericus left without a bow. Althea remained silent; she apparently didn't want to hear opinions from the other candidates. Fair enough.

Caius forgot all about Althea's reaction as soon as Marcus stepped into the room next. He had managed to comb down his bushy mane, looking almost presentable. He took a bow for the Senators and launched into his speech, gesturing emphatically. Caius remembered most of the lines and was able to keep pace with Marcus giving the speech. Everything looked to be going well even without the note cards. The speech finished, and Caius clapped softly to himself, which made Herennius laugh a bit.

The Senators began their questions. Senator Tullius launched into it first, narrowing his eyes and pointing his finger in the air. His question went on for far longer than most normal questions do; even normally-confident Marcus looked a little intimidated. But he recovered quickly and seemed to come up with a good answer. He'd hardly finished before Oventia launched into a similar tirade. Marcus was getting battered relentlessly. *Well,* Caius thought, *I guess that settles it. I'll be rejecting the score.* Completely unfair that Tullius and Oventia were already biased against him; they hadn't been able to take him out of the contest with their trials, so they were just taking it out on Marcus.

He managed to survive the barrage of questioning, and bowed his way out of the room.

"Well, what do you all think?" Caius asked the rest of the candidates, unsure if he actually wanted to hear their answers. Althea and Drusus only sniggered, pleased that the Senators had been so rough in their questioning. The rest of the group stayed silent.

"Marcus seemed to handle the questioning well," Herennius said finally. "And the Senators seemed impressed too." He didn't state the conclusion, but it was clear that he thought Caius should take the points. *Or did he?* Their scores were close enough now that maybe he was just trying to knock Caius out of the competition once and for all. Sure, they had become friends but that didn't mean they weren't competitors. Maybe Herennius was just counting on Caius to value his opinion because they were friends.

"The Senators looked angry," Florian said. "Oventia did not seem particularly pleased by the end. I wouldn't risk it." *Maybe he was only saying that because he thinks he can catch up.* Caius struggled to remember just how many points Florian had. *Or maybe he wants me to follow Herennius's advice and thinks that he can trick me with contradictory advice.* There were layers and layers of manipulation and psychology going on here.

Caius was still deciding when Flavia came into the room to argue for Herennius. She tottered around the room on her cane while giving her speech, then stood in front of the desk while casually answering questions. Herennius was lucky to have an advocate who had been through this entire process twice before, as both candidate and advocate. She looked calm and casual, as though he were just having an afternoon conversation instead of an interrogation that would decide the fate of the Empire.

"I'll take the points," Herennius announced as soon as his advocate finished. No deliberation whatsoever.

Caius, however, was still making up his mind. He barely paid attention to Drusus's and Apona's advocates or how the Senate reacted to them. He was only dimly aware of the buzz of conversation while the others discussed whether it was a good idea to accept the points. Caius knew they would: just like Valeria and Florian, they had nothing to lose in choosing to take the risk. The decision was only crucial for Althea, Herennius, and Caius because they had the leads to lose. And Althea and Herennius had already decided to accept, which made the pressure on Caius even more acute.

The chance that *both* of them had done poorly was too small, Caius reasoned. In order to keep up, he had to take the chance and accept the points. There was no way around it.

"Well?" Quintus asked from the back of the room. Caius had been so lost in thought that he had not even noticed his return. "How did you all enjoy the closing arguments?"

The candidates were all silent. The fine food and drink were not worth the stress. Probably not a good sign, considering the fact that Caius was competing to do this full time.

Quintus nodded understandingly. "Very well, then. Have you all made up your minds? Once you tell me your decisions, I shall go receive your scores from the Senators for this test and input the numbers along with the rest. This evening, the Senators will deliberate the results and decide on which Candidate they shall put forward for full Senate confirmation. Expect the announcement sometime tomorrow."

Caius's stomach roiled just at the thought of it. There was no way he would be able to sleep tonight. From the looks on everyone else's faces, most of them felt similarly.

"You are all free to continue enjoying this room, and you have the rest of the day free. When a decision has been made, a servant will be sent for you, so just don't wander too far. Got it?"

He looked around; the candidates all gave a slight nod.

"Great! Is everyone ready, then?" One by one, the candidates formally announced their decisions. Unsurprisingly, six of his peers had chosen to accept whatever the Senate gave them; only Althea and Caius had not yet answered.

"Althea, do you accept the score that the Senate determines?"

"Absolutely," she answered confidently. Far too self-assured given how brusque and casual her Advocate had been in there. Something was wrong.

Quintus turned to Caius last. "And Caius, what do you decide?"

The other candidates were all looking at him curiously. Althea sneered as usual; she clearly thought that Marcus had done poorly, and Caius's couldn't win either way. Herennius looked on, trying to hide the glimmer of hope in his eyes that Caius would make the wrong decision.

"I also accept the points," Caius announced.

"Very well," Quintus said with finality. "Next time we see each other, one of you will be the new heir!"

With that, he vanished out the door. Caius felt like he was going to throw up.

CHAPTER 16

He met Herennius, Flavia, and Marcus in the usual spot outside the cafeteria to get breakfast. The halls were eerily silent; Caius did not see a single other person. Even the guards who normally stood outside the doors were gone. "Quintus has them all up watching the Senate deliberations," Marcus explained. "Has to make sure that no candidate does anything to interfere. Each one of the Senators has a troop of guards with them at all times."

Inside, the long table was full of steaming breakfast dishes as normal. But every single table and chair was empty; none of the other Candidates were up yet. Their words carried across the room, but there was no need to try and keep quiet.

By the time Caius finished his meal, he was starting to get unnerved. At least one of the other six should be down by now, right? He poked at his eggs, stalling for time and just waiting for anyone else to show up. But they never did.

Marcus brought him to the greenhouse, down on the lowest level of the Trial Facility. "It'll calm you down," he said. He brought some tablets for entertainment; there was no internet connection, but they still had access to hundreds of books that Marcus had downloaded. Additionally, he'd had the foresight to ask the servants to come set up two comfortable lounge chairs next to the pond.

It helped, kind of. Caius enjoyed getting some fresh air, basking in the artificial sunlight, and listening to the bubbling flow of the water. Every once in a while, a fish would breach the surface to gobble up some fallen leaf or insect. It reminded Caius of the koi pond that his parents had had in their backyard when he was a child. He used to sit and watch the flickering yellow, orange and white fish for hours.

Marcus and Caius lounged in their chairs, waiting for news. Caius had picked a cheesy, mindless action novel about a Roman sailor who becomes marooned in the New World and falls in love with a Native princess. The protagonist had to fend off bears and primitive, spear-wielding tribes in order to make it back to the New Ostia colony. Caius managed to just turn off his mind and enjoy the story. It wasn't particularly regal of him; these types of books were popular with the lower classes who would never be able to afford a ticket over to the New World anyway and had to live vicariously through these books and movies.

Just when he had managed to relax enough to possibly think about taking a mid-day nap, his sensitive ears picked up the gentle pitter-patter of feet coming down the hall. The tablet fell out of his hands as a breathless servant came around the corner holding an envelope. Marcus and Caius leapt out of their chairs at the same time, but Caius beat him over to the servant and grabbed the envelope.

Caius Serica, please join the Senate Tribunal members and your fellow Candidates in the Inquisitorial Chamber as soon as you are able. We regret that Advocates will not be invited to this ceremony.

Marcus looked a bit crestfallen, but covered it up well. "Finally!" he exclaimed. "We'd better get you upstairs and put on your formal robes and armor. This is the big one! You could walk out of that room as the next Emperor!"

Caius could tell that he was forcing the enthusiasm, but hugged his advocate nonetheless. They both knew that at this point, it was a bit of a long shot. Marcus had told him all about the pointed questions during the final arguments, and how Senator Oventia had outright said that she doubted Caius's resolve and ability to effectively manage Roman politics. Marcus had tried to reassure Caius that it was just posturing, but it made sense: she didn't want an Emperor who knew that she had tried to buy her way into the cabinet.

The duo hurried upstairs and put on the heavy armor. Caius turned in the mirror, making sure that everything was all cinched up in the right places. The gold-plated exterior bounced soft yellow light onto the walls, and the stout sword by his sight clinked annoyingly with every movement.

Marcus walked him into the atrium where they had sat that first day of the trials, waiting for Marcus to give his presentation.. He had been so nervous that day, and Caius had been able to reassure him. Now, the roles were reversed. Caius's palms were practically dripping onto the smooth stone floor, soaking the robes underneath his armor. It suddenly felt ten times heavier, making it difficult to breathe.

"Just relax," Marcus said. "There is nothing that can be done now, so there is no need to worry. You did your absolute best, and that's all you can do. Win or lose, you have definitely proven your worth. We both know that you deserve it the most, and that is what matters. Go in there with your head held high, and walk out of there with the crown."

The pep talk did help a bit. Even if he lost, he was at least reassured that he truly liked most of the other Candidates who would be in the palace with him, and he would get to know everyone from Marcus's generation as well. It wouldn't be so bad.

Caius closed his eyes in front of the door and took one final, long, deep breath. *Everything is OK,* he told himself. *If it's not you, it will be Herennius, and he will treat the other Candidates well.* At his very core, he knew that Vitellius saw through the façade of courtesy and sportsmanship that Althea tried to put on during every trial. The senators *knew* that she had cheated on those tests. They had to have known.

The two guards on either side of the door nodded at him as he approached. They each grasped one of the heavy handles and pulled it open. Caius turned, caught one last glimpse of Marcus, and waved goodbye. It was too far to tell, but he thought he saw a tear drip down his advocate's cheek.

Senator Oventia greeted him curtly at the door. "Thank you for coming, Candidate." She gestured inside, where Caius could briefly see the silhouettes of the other Senators against the roaring fireplaces. The rest of the room was too dark to make out who else was there.

"Marcus," she called out. He perked up like a dog who had heard his master call. "Please return to your room; we will send someone to fetch you as soon as we are finished here." She turned to the two guards at the door. "You two, please report back to Quintus at the central hall. We require absolute secrecy for this announcement, and I'm afraid that even Praetorians do not have clearance." They nodded and marched down the hall, boots clicking against the stone. She flashed a brief, formal smile at Caius before returning to her chair.

293

As he came closer, Caius was able to pick out two figures standing in the center of the room. Herennius's massive frame was practically unmistakable, and his blond hair seemed to reflect the firelight. He did not turn to greet Caius as he approached; his face was solemn and serious like etched stone. Caius briefly noted how enormous his formal armor was; they probably had to make it especially for him.

Next to Herennius was... Althea. Great. Her dark hair blended with the shadows. Normally, it was done up tightly in a bun or a pony tail, but today it fell elegantly on her shoulders and cascaded over the plates of her armor. She looked surprisingly good when she wasn't trying to be snide and intimidating. But as Caius took his spot in line, she glanced at him with that same familiar look of disdain, and his hatred came rushing back into his mind.

Caius had been worried that he had taken too much time putting on his armor, but it appeared not. The other five candidates were still not there. He breathed a soft sigh of relief.

The room was completely silent. Oventia took her place behind her desk, illuminated eerily in the firelight. Senator Tullius looked utterly bored despite the important nature of the moment; his bald head was resting in his hand as he leaned on his desk. Senator Vitellius, however, was sitting up straight and at attention, eager to get started.

"Thank you for coming, Candidates." He shuffled the papers on his desk as he read the speech. "The three of you have been deemed the best of the best." Caius quickly realized what that meant: the other five were gone. "As is tradition, two of you will have the great honor of welcoming the third as the next Emperor of Rome. This show of allegiance dates back hundreds of years, in which the winning candidate received pledges of fealty from the others before returning to the capital. We continue to honor our rich history today with the same ceremony."

Vitellius nodded to Tullius to continue the speech.

"You are all so accomplished and deserving," the Senator said in a dull monotone voice that made him sound more like a phone operator than the man crowning the next heir. "This crop of candidates has truly been better than any the Empire has ever seen before." It was so cliché that Tullius could have copied this straight out of 'Consolation Prize Speeches 101.' Caius had to stop himself from rolling his eyes, lest the Senators see. Not like it would matter; they had already made their choice. "Each of you has shown so much promise and talent during these trials; we truly wish that all three of you could be chosen. Unfortunately, as you know, there can only be one." Tullis nodded to Oventia to continue.

Come on, stop dragging it out like this, Caius thought, gritting his teeth.

"After careful and cautious deliberation," she said, "A candidate has been chosen. This decision was reached impartially, based on the scores of that Candidate during the trials and based on the Tribunal's judgment of that person's character and values." Caius's heart beat a little faster. He may have been behind Althea and Herennius in points, but Oventia was saying that points weren't the be-all and end-all. They were looking at other factors; he still had a chance! "So, without further ado," she continued, "Senator Vitellius?"

295

The older Senator unfolded the paper in front of him dramatically. Caius was about to scream if they didn't hurry up and read it! He could feel Herennius tense up next to him, and heard his breathing stop in anticipation.

"The winner is…" Vitellius paused and adjusted his glasses… "Althea Postumius!" He looked back at the row of candidates. "Althea, please step forward."

Caius blinked. *That's it, then. My life is over. Well, not quite: Althea is going to enjoy making it a living hell for me for the next few decades while I live as a prisoner in the palace.*

Althea practically danced forward, shooting a smug grin to Caius and Herennius. She wasn't even trying to hide her attitude now that she'd won. Caius hardly even noticed; it was too late to get angry. Or to even care at all. He had just gone numb.

Next to him, he felt Herennius exhale. He'd still been holding his breath after the announcement, waiting for the other shoe to drop. One quick look over, and Caius could tell that he was as, if not more, upset about this decision. *What could the Senate be thinking? Althea would be an absolute disaster. How had they been fooled like this?*

"This candidate has shown extraordinary perseverance and tenacity in the face of overwhelming odds. Her determined and aggressive attitude has shown that she truly has the capacity to go head to head with Rome's toughest politicians and emerge victorious."

Herennius was right, Caius realized. *Back on the hike, where he said that the Senators were encouraging cheating, he was right. It was just a test to see who could sink the lowest. Because apparently that's what you need to govern Rome: no morals or scruples.*

296

"She particularly excelled in the academic trials, showing a quick mind and resourcefulness that will serve her well in the coming years."

How can Vitellius live with himself? He knows that that is a lie and that she stole all the answers ahead of time.

"Althea, please turn and face your fellow candidates."

Firelight bounced off of her armor as she swiveled away from the senators, sending her loose hair twirling. Her eyes sparkled and her smile stretched joyfully across her entire face.

"Candidates," Vitellius said, "let me be the first to have the pleasure of introducing the next Emperor of Rome, Althea Postumius! You should now pay your respects."

Neither Caius nor Herennius moved. How could they pay their respects when they did not respect Althea at all? There was a terse silence in the room. Althea looked at the both, head tilted slightly to the side and a slanted smile that said "I told you so."

Finally, Caius moved forward. His legs were on autopilot as he walked over to Althea and extended a hand. She grasped it with her own and shook heartily; Caius let his own hand dangle like a limp fish.

"Althea," he started, "I know that we do not necessarily see eye to eye on many things, and we have drastically different approaches. But please know that I will be available to you whenever you require counsel, and in any other way that I might serve the Empire." He hadn't pre-rehearsed that concession, but it sounded pretty darn good. Even Tullius, normally sour and negative, nodded approvingly.

"Thank you, Caius. If I ever have need of you, I appreciate knowing that you will be there." She might as well say "Enjoy your years trapped in the palace alone, because I will never ask for your help."

Caius retreated back to the line where Herennius still stood. There was another terse silence.

"Herennius, please come pay homage to the next Emperor," Vitellius said, his tone bordering on threatening. Marcus had told him that the trials had become more civilized in recent years, but Caius had no doubt that Herennius would be thrown in some hidden prison if he wasn't willing to step forward and shake Althea's hand. Caius quietly elbowed his friend forward, which must have somehow snapped him out of his daze.

Herennius lumbered forward slowly like he had completely forgotten how to walk. He had always been so confident that losing had apparently just ripped the rug out from under him and he had no idea how to act. Althea was savoring the moment; seeing Herennius so dumbfounded was only encouraging her to be even more condescending. She thrust out her hand for him to shake and beckoned for him to come closer like calling to a trained pet.

"Herennius, is everything all right?" Senator Vitellius asked. Oventia half stood, leaning over her desk for a closer look at what was happening.

"Fine, Senator," Herennius said serenely, like he was sleep walking.

He took a final step forward and grabbed Althea's fingers tightly. "Congratulations," Caius heard him say. Althea thanked him, followed by a snide laugh. Herennius released her hand and turned back to Caius, looking like he was about to cry. Then, in one swift motion, he ripped his ceremonial sword out of its decorated scabbard and turned back to Althea. Before anyone knew what was happening, the sharp steel blade sank straight through her armor with a sickening squeal of tearing metal. There was a liquidy squelching sound like putting on boots that had been left out in the rain.

Herennius took a small step back to survey the damage, leaving the sword planted in Althea's chest. Thick red blood dribbled out of the hole in her armor and ran down the golden metal, outlining the decorative patterns that had been stamped into it. Herennius reached back toward her, grabbed the hilt in one massive hand, and slid his sword from the wound, spattering gore in a trail across the floor. Althea looked down at the hole in her chest and gasped. Then she collapsed on the floor in a puddle of blood.

CHAPTER 17

There was a moment of absolute silence. The only sounds in the room were the crackling fires behind the Senators, and Althea's shallow, gurgling sobs and moans. Then, everyone erupted into a flurry of activity.

The Senators all stood at the same time and started shouting simultaneously. Tullius was shouting for the guards; Vitellius was shouting orders at Herennius as if he was still convinced that Herennius would actually listen. Senator Oventia was shouting "You fucking idiot," over and over again. Caius cried out too: "Herennius, what are you doing?!" He ran to check on Althea, but Herennius stood over the body and swung his sword protectively. Caius retreated and drew his own sword with a *swish*, beginning to slowly circle around Herennius. The big Nord stood silently in the center of the room, still clutching his blade and looking like he hadn't quite planned what was next.

"QUIET," Herennius roared, loud enough to be heard over the din of everyone else trying to talk at once. Senators Tullius and Vitellius stopped talking, but Oventia continued to berate him:

"I can't believe how thick you are!" she shouted, pounding her fist on the desk. "God, I knew something like this would happen. I knew it!"

Herennius retreated a bit so that he could keep an eye on Caius and still talk to Oventia. "What do you mean?"

"You fucking idiot," she repeated, ignoring the question. "It was another test, you dumb cow! Why do you think there are three of you here? Althea *was a plant.*" She paused for a moment to let that sink in. Herennius looked back down at the girl lying face down on the stone in an ever-growing pool of blood.

"A plant?" he mumbled.

"Yes," Vitellius volunteered, though not happy that Oventia had revealed that fact, even now. Even with Althea dying in the center of the room, Vitellius had still been focused on seeing how the test would play out. "She was an actress that I hired to pretend to be one of the candidates. She has been following my orders the entire time." He gave Caius a pointed, almost apologetic look: "I trained her ahead of time and gave her all of the answers to the test scores to make it believable that she was remaining in the competition despite her demeanor. She needed to remain on top to motivate the actual candidates."

Ah, Caius thought. Everything fell into place. How the Senators had conveniently overlooked everything she did. How she had sabotaged the other candidates and tried to get them to sabotage themselves, like Marius breaking Herennius's leg, or when she approached Caius and tried to persuade him to just quit. He looked at her broken body on the ground and felt a wave of guilt wash over him for how he had treated her. Although maybe that was just a sign of how good of an actress she was.

"She was *trying* to provoke you!" Oventia interrupted, shouting furiously. "The whole fucking point of this whole ceremony was to see how you would act once you lost! To see if you could be gracious and all that crap once you 'knew' that you'd have to live under her rule! It was

301

just another trial; this whole time she has been trying to get you to hate her. And you fucking fell for it!"

Herennius was confused. And angry. "Well why didn't you warn me??" he asked Oventia.

This made the Senator stop talking immediately, and the room was once again absolutely silent.

"I didn't know," she finally answered. "Vitellius kept this secret even from me and Tullius. We only found out this morning, and I was being watched by guards ever since. I had no way to communicate this to you."

"How did you not know?!" Herennius shouted back.

"Vitellius kept it from us!" Oventia repeated. "Even hired children to fake videos of her for the review trial. He was *trying* to deceive us too!"

"What does this mean, girl?" Senator Vitellius asked, voice as hard as steel. He spoke to her like a young servant who had been caught in the bed of a citizen, instead of like a prominent Senator. Even Herennius seemed a bit intimidated by the old man's harsh gaze. "Why would *you* warn him? What. Does. He. Mean. By. That?" he punctuated each word with a stamp of his cane against the stone.

"God damn it, Herennius," she said.

It was Caius's turn to volunteer some information. "Because Herennius accepted the offer that I rejected, didn't he?"

Oventia looked at him as if remembering for the first time that he was there.

"That's right," she said. "I offered it to you first. You turned me down, so I went with my second choice. He was wise enough to accept, and played the part perfectly." She turned to look at him with fire in her eyes. "Until *now*, that is."

"WHAT OFFER?" Vitellius roared. He seemed to have forgotten that he was old and frail; his fist thumped into the desk and Caius could have sworn he heard the wood crack.

"She brought me down to the theater, and told me that she would help me through the trials if I agreed to appoint her my Finance Minister once I became Emperor."

"And you rejected it?" Tullius said incredulously. He'd been in the Senate so long that he'd forgotten what it was like to be around someone who would turn down a bribe.

"Yes," Caius said. "I assumed that it was a test; just another trial. That it had been planned by the Senate to test our honesty, and that anyone who accepted the offer would be disqualified. I even talked to my advocate about it and he said that Oventia was known for not being corrupt."

Tullius nodded, looking more sympathetic than Caius had ever seen him. "Yes," he said, "She did have that reputation." He looked at her with disappointment.

"She said that she could help persuade you and Senator Vitellius," Caius continued. "To vote for me in the final decision. And she said that she could help me with the trials along the way. Like..."

It all dawned on him at once. How Herennius had done so well on the written exams; he had had the scores too, just like Althea. And how he had been so confident in accepting the points from the final trial… he knew that Oventia would be giving him as much as possible. And, of course, the map. He hadn't gotten it from his advocate. He'd gotten it from Oventia. She had told him what the trial was, and how best to get back. *How could I have missed this?* He berated himself. He'd let his friendship with Herennius block his common sense.

"You just caught on, didn't you?" Herennius said. "Yes, that's how I got the map."

"Map?" Senator Vitellius asked just as Senator Oventia cried out: "You showed *him*?"

"Herennius had a map," Caius explained to Vitellius and Tullius. "During the survival skills trial. We were on a team together," he reminded them, "And as soon as we got out of sight, he took it out of his jacket and showed it to me." Vitellius did not respond in any way; he just looked down at his papers with a slight frown of disappointment. Caius felt a twinge of guilt surface that he'd tried to shove down ever since that day.

"You IDIOT!" Oventia screamed. "You could have ruined everything, just so you could show off to your little friend?"

"I had to!" Herennius shouted, repositioning his blade as Caius tried to slowly move around behind him. "I needed a teammate for the extra points to catch up to Althea. Had I *known* that Althea was just a plant then it would have made everything a lot easier!"

Caius circled, lowering the tip of his blade just a bit. Maybe if he kept Herennius talking, he'd drop his guard. "Did Flavia know?"

"*Ha*," Herennius snorted sarcastically. "Of course not. That was the first thing Senator Oventia told me after I accepted. Don't tell anyone, not even your advocate. Flavia would have spilled the beans in a second. Probably to Marcus, who would have gone straight to Vitellius, or Quintus. The servants would come by with whatever Oventia was going to pass along for that day's trial, before we would all meet up for breakfast. Flavia never had a clue." Herennius paused and even looked a bit remorseful for a second. "I felt a little bad about it when she told me how proud she was that I was doing even better than she'd ever expected."

"You feel bad about *that*," Caius said, "And not about *her?*" He pointed his sword at Althea's inert body in the center of the room. "Or *Spurius?*" A look of recognition dawned on Senator Vitellius's face as he caught the meaning of that and realized that Herennius had killed his fellow candidate.

Herennius looked back at Althea like he'd already forgotten. "Both of those were necessary," he responded. "I came here with one goal: becoming Emperor. So did you. In hindsight I wish I acted differently in this case, but how was I supposed to know? I saw my chance slipping away, and I saw the easiest way to grab hold and not let go. You probably would have done the same if you'd thought about it."

305

"And if it was me?" Caius asked. "If Vitellius had announced my name, how would you have acted? Would I be the one over there with a hole through my chest?" Herennius didn't respond; his expression said it all, though.

"Oh, don't act like you're better than me, Caius." Herennius's eyes narrowed mockingly as he spoke. "We're not different at all. The only reason you rejected Oventia's offer is because you thought it was another test. If you had realized that she was serious, you would have taken it in a heartbeat, wouldn't you?"

Caius didn't respond, partially because he had no response to that. It was true.

"Exactly," Herennius continued. "You just wish that you'd recognized the truth. You're jealous you didn't think of it. You were perfectly happy to win that survival competition using the map that Oventia gave me, weren't you?"

"No!" Caius responded, "I didn't want to cheat, and you threatened me!"

"And when Spurius died, you agreed that it needed to be done. You were willing to kill so that you could cover up our use of the map, weren't you."

Caius tried to protest, but Herennius continued.

"I didn't hear any protests when we were watching Althea cross the finish line, either. And you certainly didn't end up going to Vitellius with it, did you?"

"That's enough," Oventia said. "This has gone on far too long. Herennius, you know what needs to be done." Without even taking enough time to draw a breath, she lunged at

Vitellius. A sliver of flashing steel appeared in her hand from somewhere beneath her robes. The next moment, they were both on the floor and Vitellius's walking stick went flying. Caius's view was blocked, but he heard the scuffles and cries. After a moment, Oventia stood back up, alone. She wiped the knife on her sleeve and eyed Tullius, who had gone scrambling for a weapon and come up with a large iron fire poker. He hadn't even tried to help Vitellius. "Stay away from me!" he shouted, swinging it back and forth to point at both Oventia and Herennius.

Herennius apparently did not know what needed to be done; he had simply stood by and watched while Oventia murdered Vitellius.

"Herennius, *how thick are you?*" She looked like she was really regretting her choices at the moment. "Kill Caius and then help me with Tullius. We'll just tell the Praetorians that Caius here attacked Althea and the Senators." For a woman who was utterly relying on Herennius to do her dirty work, including killing a Senator, she wasn't being particularly respectful to her minion.

"You don't want to do this," Caius told Herennius as the tall blond Nord advanced. Caius stiffened his stance as they each meandered through the room, trying to get the edge on the other. And Caius would really need that edge. Herennius was *enormous*. Probably a quarter of a meter taller, and with a far longer reach. Not to mention the fact that the tall Nord was muscle-bound and incredibly strong; one good swing would probably tear through Caius's decorative armor like flimsy paper. Caius had seen Spurius crumble under his fists, and didn't even want to think about what Herennius could do with a blade in his hands.

"I *do* want to," Herennius said. "I've gotten to know you fairly well over the past few weeks, wouldn't you say? And if there is one thing I have learned, it's that there is no way you will keep this quiet." He was slowly pacing closer as Caius retreated until his back was rubbing against the rock wall. Caius could only wait as his former friend approached. His constantly friendly smile now looked demented and evil with a bloody sword in front of him.

"Herennius!" Oventia shouted suddenly. In the background, Caius saw Tullius trying to make a break for it across the room. Herennius turned and dashed toward the door to cut him off. "Don't let him out!" Oventia was shouting. "He'll get the guards!"

Tullius was cut off, and retreated back behind his desk brandishing the fire poker like he actually stood a chance against an attack. Herennius had forgotten all about Caius and was slowly closing in on Tullius.

"I'll kill Senator Oventia," Caius shouted to him, moving closer to the other Senator's desk. Herennius stopped in his tracks, sword still pointed at Tullius. "You take one more step," Caius continued, "And I'll kill Oventia. That little knife isn't going to stop me. And if she is dead, then there will be no Senator that can vouch for you. This will all be for nothing, and we'll probably both go to prison."

Herennius was considering it. Oventia's eyes danced wildly between Caius's sword and Herennius's expression. "Do what he says," Oventia told Herennius. Of course she would say that.

They had reached an impasse. If Herennius came across the room after Caius, Tullius would escape through the unguarded door. If Herennius attacked Tullius, Caius would kill Oventia, leaving Herennius with no one to lie on his behalf. The four remaining occupants of the room were frozen in place, each waiting for one of the others to make a move.

"The guards are going to come in soon and see what happened," Caius warned. "It's not too late, Herennius. You can put an end to this right now."

Tullius nodded. "We can get you full clemency," he promised. "As far as I am concerned, it was Oventia who killed Althea. I'm sure Caius would see it the same way."

"Don't listen to them," Oventia said, eyes darting back and forth, still clutching her knife. "You'll be rotting in prison for the rest of your life. Just give me some time to think."

The silence returned. Only the fires crackled. Looking closely, Caius thought he could see Althea's chest gently rising and falling. Or was it just a trick of the light? Regardless, she needed medical help. There was no way to check until Herennius was disarmed. And every second brought her closer to death.

"Fight me," Caius challenged.

Herennius openly laughed. "So Tullius can escape? Sure." He didn't take his eyes of the Senator, hunkered down in the corner with his firepoker.

"It's either that, or we wait here until Quintus comes back. It won't be too long from now."

Herennius didn't respond, but Oventia started pacing, never taking her eyes off of Caius.

"Caius," the Senator said suddenly, "This isn't necessary. Your friend Herennius is about to be the most powerful man in the Empire, and I'll be his most important advisor. If you just go along with the story, then we can end this here and now."

Caius laughed. "You'll kill me as soon as you get the chance."

"We can set up a safeguard," she promised. "A dead man's switch. If we kill you, then the truth comes out and we're all ruined."

Caius didn't respond.

"There's nothing left for you anyway," she pleaded. "Tullius knows all about the map now." She turned to her former colleague. "Don't you? You know that Caius cheated, just like Herennius. You've always been a stickler, right Numerius?" Caius almost didn't recognize Tullius's first name. The Senator glared back at her, waving the fire poker, but didn't respond. "Caius is disqualified, just like Herennius. No matter what you say now, you're going to throw both of them in prison if you make it out of here alive, and go with one of the other Candidates."

"That's not true," Tullius said, eyes darting to Caius for the first time in a while. "That's not true!"

"Yes it is," she sneered. "He's probably going to prison regardless of how this turns out, isn't he?"

She turned back to Caius. "You see? Your only option is to just cooperate with us. You know Herennius. You know he's a good person." Caius laughed audibly at that part. "He'll honor his word."

There was a long pause. Tullius was looking increasingly panicked.

"He has no honor," Caius responded finally, turning back to Herennius. Even in the firelight, Caius could tell that his face was turning bright red.

"Prove me wrong," Caius taunted. "If you have any honor left then let's finish this here and now. And once you're dead, everyone will know that you were corrupt."

"He's just trying to provoke you!" Oventia shouted, just as Herennius lunged across the room, teeth bared. Caius parried and blocked, but Herennius's blows rained down like lightning. The firelight made him look like some mythical demon as he hacked away at Caius. Oventia was shouting something, but the sounds of clashing metal and grunting with exertion were too loud. Caius forgot about everything around him. Herennius left himself open, and Caius dodged to the side and landed a kick squarely on his opponent's knee. The same one that Marius had broken during the Tewaarathon game. Caius hoped that maybe there was some small unhealed part left, but Herennius barely even flinched. There was hardly time to duck as his enemy's short sword whistled through the air where Caius's head had been only moments before. Herennius may have had the strength and the reach, but sword fighting was largely dependent on speed.

Caius ducked to the side and managed to retreat away from the door. Herennius followed closely, swinging the sword through the air like he was trying to swat at a fly. One good hit

311

would gut Caius like a fish; the formal armor was made to look nice in victory parades, not to actually use in combat. Herennius snorted like a mad bull as he closed in; light bounced off of his whirling sword, matched in speed only by Caius's defense.

"It's not going to work," Caius panted in between loud clashes. "Even if you win, the Senate is still going to want to know what happened." Each word was punctuated by clanging steel and gasping breaths. "They'll want to know how two Senators and two candidates ended up dead." Herennius charged forward like a bull, forcing Caius to dance out of the way, closer to Oventia's desk. "You think you'll be home free after you kill me and Tullius?"

"SHUT UP!" Herennius roared, slashing wildly at Caius. He was getting nervous, and that made him reckless. "We'll just blame it on you, or on Althea!" Caius scampered to the side, and Herennius's sword scraped against the rock wall with a loud grating whine. Caius deftly twisted his wrist and slide the blade an unprotected opening in Herennius's side. The cut was rewarded with a hint of blood and a bellow of pain.

"Marcus knows," Caius continued taunting him. "He knows all about Oventia's offer. And Quintus knows that Althea wasn't a real candidate. And neither of them will believe that I went on a killing spree. They'll put the pieces together."

Herennius's wound hadn't slowed him down. If anything, it only made him angrier. He lunged at Caius again and managed to slice across his arm, just where the shoulder plates ended. Caius winced and ground his teeth together, dodging the follow-up blow and retreating further across the room. They were both bleeding now, and getting more and more tired by the second.

Herennius advanced, still confident in his abilities. Caius continued to block his attacks, but his arm was going numb from the constant vibrations of the swords clashing. He couldn't last much longer.

Caius dropped his defenses, just long enough for Herennius to notice. With a sneer that was remarkably reminiscent of Althea's standard look, Caius's opponent lunged forward sending the already bloody tip of his sword through the armor over Caius's shoulder. The thin metal squealed and crumpled beneath the weight of the blow, and Caius felt fiery pain spread throughout his whole chest. That was followed by the wet, warm sensation of blood seeping into his robes. Every breath was like being stabbed all over again.

"NOW, TULLIUS!" Caius screamed as loud as he could. Blood spewed out of his mouth onto Herennius's golden armor. At the same time, he gripped Herennius's wrist and held him down. With his other arm, Caius drove his own sword between the gaps in the metal plates guarding Herennius's thick, muscular legs.

Across the room, Tullius got the message and bolted for the door. Oventia scrambled after him but couldn't make it over the desks in time. Herennius roared and twisted, but Caius held on with all his might. The blood oozing out of his shoulder was beginning to make him woozy, whereas Herennius seemed to only draw strength from having a sword shoved through his thigh.

It was long enough, though. Caius heard the metal doors groan open, and Oventia's scream of frustration.

Herennius seemed to go limp for just a moment as he realized what had happened. His enormous, meaty fingers relaxed slightly around Caius's throat. Over Herennius's shoulder, Caius saw Oventia give up the chase and collapse in the middle of the room, sobbing and pounding her fist on the rough stone. Herennius rolled off of Caius and fell against one of the thick columns, panting. He wrenched the sword from his thigh like it was a splinter and tossed it across the room where it clattered into the shadows.

"Well," Caius coughed. "I guess that's it." His vision was starting to swim.

Herennius just laughed, resigned to his fate. "I did everything right. I was almost there, and there was just this one stupid test and now it's just slipping away…"

"Could have been different," Caius gasped. His pulse was pounding in his chest and the blood was starting to pool around him.

"Yeah…" Herennius trailed off.

The doors screeched open again. Caius's sight faded, but he could dimly see guards flooding into the room. Tullius led the charge, and two of the praetorians dragged Oventia to her feet and clapped cuffs on her arms. She was still sobbing as they dragged her from the room. Tullius, still holding his fire poker, pointed to the corner where Caius and Herennius were collapsed. The last thing he saw was guards rushing over, weapons drawn. His eyes drooped close. In the back of his mind, he heard Kaneshiro's voice, whispering into his ear weeks ago in the Fukuoka train station: "Don't trust them." Then everything faded to black.

CHAPTER 18

Monitors nearby beeped and whirred constantly, tracking all of Caius's vital signs. His body was immersed in the healing tank as his lung tissue regenerated; a faint, irregular stream of bubbles rose through the amber liquid around him. Doctor Porcia stood by at all times, watching for any sign of regular motion in case the sedation wore off early.

Caius slowly drifted back into consciousness. At first, everything was just a blur of light with a few fuzzy, dark shapes. "Stay calm, Caius," one of the shapes told him. "Don't try to move." He was dimly aware of other moving shadows in the room. Everything went black again.

The next time he awoke, it stuck. Doctor Porcia was waiting with a smile and a shot of something. "Good to see you back with us," she said as she plunged the needle into Caius's arm. "It was touch and go there for a while. When the guards brought you in, your right lung had collapsed, and there was severe blood loss. They reached you in the nick of time. We had to keep you on the ventilator in the tank for a while." She gestured over to the now-drained tube across the room. "You should be able to breathe now, but don't exert yourself." Caius tried to nod, but there was a brace around his neck. He looked around with what limited motion he had, recognizing the familiar gray stone of the Trial Facility. The arched ceiling of the room was covered by strange, dangling metal instruments that Caius eventually recognized as the medical office. That checkup from the first day of the trials seemed like it had been years ago. There would be no Pharaoh game outside to return to.

"You have some visitors," Doctor Porcia said casually as she finished up her tests. "They've been waiting a while to speak with you." She turned to the doorway; Caius tried to look too, but couldn't turn his neck. He could only see a bushy mane of greying hair just on the periphery of his vision. A moment later, Marcus's smiling face was peering over him. Behind him, Caius could just see the very top of Quintus's bald head, and hear the clanking of his uniform.

"Finally," Marcus said with mock indignation. "I've been trying to get you out of bed for days. What's the holdup?"

"Good to see you too, Marcus," Caius said. "How long have I been out?"

Quintus reached over and adjusted the bed, allowing Caius to sit up and have an actual conversation. The doctor's office came into view under the bright artificial light streaming through the fake windows. They were still deep under the mountain, but the windows were set to adjust brightness depending on the actual time of day.

"For about a week now." Quintus responded. "They had to keep you under for your lung to heal."

Marcus was back to wearing the same faded white robes that he'd worn on the train ride over; fashion was not his forte. But he looked comfortable and happy, instead of constantly nervous about the next trial. Even Quintus's martial bearing had relaxed a little now that his duties were done.

They're over, Caius remembered. *We're done with the trials.* And this realization brought back all of the other memories of that day.

"What's happening now? Did Vitellius and Althea make it? I could have sworn that I saw her breathing…"

"She lived," Marcus reassured him. "Herennius severed the spinal column, and a few of the organs were, well, let's say rearranged. Luckily, he was too distracted to check and see if he had finished the job." He nodded to Caius. "But the doctor was able to put everything back together as best he could with the facilities here. She was sent back down to Rome, to be treated by the Emperor's own surgeon. He has back problems, you know, so he keeps one on staff. Well no, I guess you wouldn't know." He was rambling at this point, as he tended to do when he got too excited. "But the point is that yes, Althea is alive."

Caius nodded as best he could. Which wasn't very much. "You didn't mention Vitellius."

Quintus frowned. His face said it all. "Vitellius was not so lucky. Oventia slit his throat; he died within a minute. There was nothing that could be done. She probably suspected that Herennius would react the way she did, and deliberately sent the guards away."

Caius had no response to that. The image of Oventia leaping across the desk and brandishing that knife played over and over in his mind.

"Vitellius was a great man," Marcus said, trying to reassure Caius. "And a good Senator. I mean, the idea of planting a candidate is honestly brilliant! I never saw it coming. And Vitellius picked the perfect actress, really. She was bugging me and I wasn't even part of the competition!

318

And Andericus! No wonder he didn't go to prison; he made a deal with the Senate to act as their agent within the group of advocates. I mean…"

"Marcus, you're rambling again," Quintus interrupted. It put a smile on Caius's face, if only for a moment.

"Right," Marcus replied. "Sorry."

They all fell silent. The only sound in the room was the beeping of the monitors attached to Caius's chest. This next subject was difficult.

"And Herennius? What happens to him now?"

Marcus and Quintus exchanged looks.

"Happen*ed*," Quintus said finally. "Justice moves much swifter for certain enemies of the Empire. The Praetorians took him into custody and he was down to Rome by afternoon. The Emperor himself sat in judgment after hearing what happened, and the trial was over by midnight. Even *I* don't know where he is now; I work for the Senate, and the Praetorians are their own branch."

"But he's alive?" Caius asked.

Quintus shrugged as if he didn't really care. "Probably." His tone became hard and heartless. "He deserves whatever he gets. The Praetorians didn't maintain their position as defenders of the Emperor for two thousand years by being merciful to their enemies. They're not going to kill him; they're going to take it slow." Quintus's bloodthirsty expression made it clear that he'd rather be doing it himself.

"Sorry," Marcus said. "He's still a bit upset about what happened. He was responsible for the safety of the candidates and for combatting corruption. He's taken the whole thing a bit personally."

Caius tried to nod again. "We were all fooled," he told Quintus. "And we should have come to you as soon as Oventia made her offer.'

Quintus nodded stiffly. "Yes, you should have." Marcus laughed heartily; Caius chuckled a bit, but it hurt his chest.

They were interrupted by another arrival: Senator Tullius. He looked like he had aged ten years since the trials first began.

"May I speak with Caius alone?" he asked. Marcus bowed and retreated out the door. "I promise not to hurt him," the Senator said with a smile to Quintus, who was still lingering near the exit. Quintus closed the door behind him on his way out.

Tullius looked at his hands, not quite sure how to begin.

"First, I want to thank you for your service. I know what it takes to stand up to a friend." Caius sensed that there was a story there, but didn't push it. "And I know that you sacrificed yourself to stall him and get me out of there. And I really appreciate that." Caius sensed the "but" coming soon.

"We need to talk about this map that Herennius mentioned." A shiver went down Caius's spine, and he saw his chance slipping away from him. Maybe Oventia was right. Maybe he should have taken her offer.

Senator Tullius seemed reluctant to even bring it up. Maybe even guilty. "It is a serious issue. Corruption is a constant problem for the Senate, especially given the habits of your predecessor. The vast majority will want to make a big show about preventing corruption even as half of them stick their hands under the table for their take. It will certainly be a question during your confirmation hearings, and if you answer honestly, no one will vote for you; we'll have to do the Trials all over again. And if you lie, then I have a duty to bring it up." Caius stayed silent. "I need you to tell me *exactly* what happened between you and Herennius on that hike."

Caius recounted the story as best he could remember. Tullius was encouraged by the fact that Herennius had implicitly threatened him. "You really had no choice," he remarked gleefully, scribbling at his notepad. "And you never actively sought out any favors…" he bit the end of his pen as he thought. "And there are multiple instances of you rejecting offers from Senator Oventia… yes, we can definitely work with this. We'll have to publicize what happened in the final trial, but that was probably going to come out anyway, given the inquest into Senator Vitellius's death."

He adjusted his reading glasses and looked up at Caius. "After careful consideration, Caius, I have decided to nominate you for the Senate's ratification." For the first time since the Trials began, his dour face broke out into a broad, welcoming smile.

"That's it?" Caius asked. "I cheated in the trials! Even if Herennius made me, I still had a big advantage over all of the other candidates. And you don't even care?" This whole time, Caius had been dreading the reaction from the Senators, and now Tullius was *looking* for ways to excuse his behavior?

Tullius gave him a hard look. "You really want to do the Trials all over again?"

"No," Caius said immediately. Three attempts on his life was enough to last a while.

"Well what's the problem, then?" Tullius replied. "The whole purpose of the rules is to prevent someone corrupt from getting into office, right? Not only did you resist when Herennius cheated, but you also turned down Oventia's offer! She was willing to hand you her vote, and you would have easily won votes from me and from Vitellius. And you still resisted! Do you really think that this isn't enough proof that you're incorruptible? If I punish you for cheating somehow, then that's all the Senate will see in the full report, and they'll probably disqualify you no matter how much I argue in your favor."

"I just… don't feel right about it," Caius said. Hard to pinpoint exactly what was weighing on his conscience. He just didn't feel like he deserved the honor.

"Everyone will have things that they regret in their history, Caius. You will have fewer dark spots than anyone I know, but no one is 100% unblemished."

I wanted to be, Caius thought to himself. Maybe it was an unrealistic goal; sometimes the Emperor had to make hard choices and sacrifice. That's what everyone has been saying throughout the Trials. Becoming Emperor is no different.

322

"So am I going to have to do this all over again?" Tullius asked with clear exasperation. Because clearly he was the one who had endured the most hardship due to the Trials.

There was a pause. "No," Caius finally answered. *I just can't let it happen again*, he told himself. *No more shortcuts or taking the easy way out.*

"Good." Tullius smiled and shook his hand. "Believe me, Caius, you are by far the best candidate even with this map issue. Before I knew Herennius was corrupt, I *still* voted for you."

"I thought you hated me," Caius said, more confused than happy.

Tullius snorted. "My personal feelings are not a factor at work here, Caius. If I am known for anything, it would be my professionalism." His smile turned sheepish. "And besides. I don't dislike you. Just that ass of an advocate you were assigned to." He nodded toward the door, where Marcus was probably waiting outside. "But I can forgive you for associating with the likes of him." Caius smiled back. Marcus could come off as a bit pompous sometimes. "There is just one last hurdle before you can officially become the heir to the throne. Shouldn't be a big challenge."

Caius tensed up again. How many "last hurdles" were there going to be in this charade?

Tullius walked to the door and leaned his head outside. Then he stepped back and held it open.

A man entered, tall and stately. He wore fine silk robes, fastened at the neck with a glistening silver eagle. His hair was wavy, brown, and perfectly manicured into place like a

323

statue. He strode through the doorway without even glancing at the Senator holding it open like a common servant. His presence filled the room, and he knew it. His hazel eyes settled on Caius, and a charming smile lit up his face.

Caius recognized him immediately. From all of the TV broadcasts. From the posters plastered around the base back in Japan. From the portrait hanging next to the barracks door. From the coins that every citizen used. *Emperor Clodius XII.*

He strode to Caius's bedside in one swift, confident motion and extended a hand. "Very nice to meet you at last," he said. He spoke to Caius like he was an equal, and not a worm beneath his feet. *We are equals*, Caius suddenly realized. *I'm going to be Emperor too.* "You of course know who I am." It wasn't a question.

"Yes, sir," Caius answered.

The Emperor smiled. "No need for that, son. 'Decimus' will be fine." He turned back to Tullius. "And this is the one you picked?"

Tullius grinned like a proud father. "Yes, Emperor Clodius. This is your new heir and future Emperor, Caius Serica."